Betrayed by Her Guardian Angel

a 151,000 word novel
based on actual events

By

Stacie Spielman

ISBN: 1-4033-4374-8 (e-book)
ISBN: 1-4033-4375-6 (Softcover)

Library of Congress Control Number: 2002108028

This book is printed on acid free paper.

Printed in the United States of America
Bloomington, IN

1stBooks — rev. 11/14/02

Acknowledgement

To my dear friend Cliff,
who set in motion the chain of events
that led to my writing this book

Stacie Spielman

Author's Note

Betrayed by Her guardian angel is based on actual events. Names of characters and spirit guides have been changed, as have some locations and physical descriptions. Certain time frames and scenes have been combined and/or compressed to enhance the flow of the story.

Dedication

For Katy, Chet, and Kevin
(Not their real names, but they know who they are.)

Without Katy's encouragement, this book would not have been written. Without Chet's support, it *could* not have been written. Without Kevin, there would have been no book to write.

Special thanks, also, to Amy.

Prologue: 1966

"I need a show of hands. How many in this lecture hall believe in Superman? How many of you believe a man actually exists who can fly without the aid of an airplane, leap tall buildings in a single bound, and has x-ray vision that can see through brick walls?"

A titter of laughter rippled through the lecture hall at the University of California.

The professor's bald head gleamed pink above the fringe of shoulder-length gray hair. "I don't see any hands," he said. "I saw Mr. Frasier's *arm* twitch, though, and for a minute he had me worried." Another titter filtered through the hall. "Let me ask you this," the professor went on. "How many of you learned students of Folklore and Mythology think Superman is the product of a vivid imagination? A fictional hero who offers hope to the downtrodden in the world of fantasy?"

Seventy-five hands rose into the air.

"Mr. Wilson," Professor Wilkerson said, singling out a lanky redhead in the center row. "Your hand is up. Why don't you believe Superman is real?"

"Because he's a comic book character," the student said with a smirk.

"And what if he weren't a comic book character? What if I stood here at this podium and presented the adventures of Superman as historical events from the turn of the century? Then would you believe them?"

"No," the redhead scoffed. "Everyone knows a man can't fly or jump over buildings. And the human eye isn't capable of x-ray vision."

Students throughout the lecture hall nodded in agreement.

"Alright," Wilkerson said thoughtfully. "So you don't believe the *eye* has super-human powers. What about the skin? Are human skin and clothing capable of withstanding a raging fire without any outward sign of singeing, blistering or charring?"

"Of course not," the redhead said. "That idea's ridiculous."

"Is it?" the professor challenged. "How many in this classroom are Christians? How many of you believe in the Bible?"

Thirty-two hands went up, including Eve Tarlton's.

"Miss Tarlton," the professor said with a smug smile. "Are you acquainted with the Old Testament characters Shadrach, Meshach, and Abednego?"

"Yes," Eve said uneasily. Eve was a slender girl with blue eyes and brown hair. Her face bore an expression of innocence, bordering on naiveté.

"What do you know about them?" the professor queried.

The story had been one of Eve's favorites as a child. In vacation Bible School, she'd been chosen to place the felt characters on the flannel board while the teacher, Miss Jessup, read the story to the class. The character labeled 'Abednego' had been stained with chocolate fingerprints, but he'd been dressed in dark clothing so the stains hadn't shown. "They were three men who were faithful to the real God and refused to worship an idol," Eve said. "So the king had them thrown into a fiery furnace."

The professor's pale eyes gleamed, as he wrung his pudgy hands in anticipation of his next challenge. "Am I to understand that this so-called *real* God allowed his followers to be thrown into a furnace?"

Eve hated when Professor Wilkerson called on her—especially at times like this, when he was being sarcastic. "I guess God figured He could protect them," she said in a small voice. "Just like Daniel in the lion's den."

When she saw the gleam in Wilkerson's eyes, Eve knew she'd made a mistake. *Damn,* she thought. *Now I've given him more ammunition.*

Picking up on the ill-advised reference to the lions' den, Wilkerson began to pace. "Ah yes, *Daniel,*" he scoffed. "Another of God's faithful servants. Only this one He allowed to be thrown to the lions! Tell me, Miss Tarlton. Were these lions tame? Or would you classify them as ferocious?"

"They were ferocious," Eve replied. "The king used them for executions."

"For executions," Wilkerson repeated. "Yet if memory serves me correctly, according to the Bible, not a hair on Daniel's head was harmed." Here, the professor stopped mid-stride and paused for effect before driving his point home: "I'm afraid I find that a little hard to believe, considering that *other* Christians thrown to the lions were devoured. Where was the real God *then,* Miss Tarlton—*if* He *exists*? Or does this real God play favorites?"

An uneasy stirring was heard in the room.

"Our time is up for today," Wilkerson said brusquely. "Your assignment for next week is to read your Bible. If you don't have a Bible, get one from the library. I want you to read the book of Daniel, the book of Jonah, and the book of Luke. Then I want you to think about what you've read. Forget what you were told in Sunday School. Think about it with an objective mind. When you come to class next week, I want all of you who claim to be Christians to tell me whether you still believe..."

1979 twelve years later:

Chapter 1

Drained of emotion, Eve closed her burning eyes and willed herself to breathe. When she'd married Tom, she'd meant what she said when she repeated the words, "Till death us do part." Neither of them was on the verge of death, so how had it come to this?

Eve sometimes wondered how she would have survived these last three and a half years if it weren't for her young son, Kevin. With Tom growing ever more distant, Kevin had become the focal point of her life.

The roar of a neighbor's lawnmower drowned out all thought in Eve's mind except how to comfort her son. "You'll still see your daddy three times a week, Sweetheart. He just won't be living in the same house with us. You and Mommy will be moving to a new house."

Kevin's lower lip was trembling, and his blue eyes were swollen. "But I don't want to move to a new house," he said tearfully. "I don't want you and Daddy to get a revorce."

The small boy's use of the word "revorce" brought a faint smile to Eve's lips in spite of her pain. "I know, Sweetheart. But sometimes—" The lump in her throat caused her to pause. "Sometimes bad things happen, and there's nothing we can do about it. We have to accept them—whether we like them or not." Eve realized this response was inadequate. But she had no better explanation to offer.

"Will I still get to keep my toys?"

The pathos in the question tore at Eve's heart. "Of course you'll still have your toys, Sweetheart. You can take the toys you have now to our new house, and we'll get you some new ones to keep at Daddy's."

At thirty-two, Eve's total identity was tied up in her role as wife, mom, and homemaker. It had never occurred to her that her blue eyes and velvet skin were features other women her age would die for. Her slender figure, too, set her apart. Yet she had no idea she was attractive to men in general. Tom no longer found her attractive. Why should any other man? Now she was going to be on her own: on her own and alone, except for Kevin.

Eve had told Tom he could buy out her half of the house. She couldn't stay here with the memories it contained. But where could she and Kevin move, and how would she support them? She'd been out of the workforce so long that she had

1

no idea where she could find a decent job. Leaving Kevin with a sitter was out of the question if there were any way to avoid it. Child support would definitely help, but beyond that she'd need at least a thousand a month to make ends meet... Suddenly the answer came to her. She would find a house in a neighborhood near a school, and take out a daycare license. That would fell two pigeons with one stone. Kevin would have built-in playmates, and he and Eve would have an income. The solution wasn't ideal, but it would have to do until Eve could come up with a better plan.

That afternoon while Kevin was napping, Eve dabbed the tears from her cheeks and flopped onto the nubby-textured sofa. Unable to shake the depression that had engulfed her, she reached for the magazine on the birch coffee table. A large title in gold letters caught her eye: "Get In Touch With Your Guardian Angel."

A tearful scan of the three-page article revealed that this author not only believed guardian angels could be contacted; she actually believed there could be two-way communication. "Ask for a sign," the article said. "Make it simple: a sound, a shadow on the wall.... You don't have to tell anyone else what you're doing. Choose a time when you're totally alone..."

"Right," Eve groaned. "I'm just sure my guardian angel is going to cast a shadow on the wall or speak my name if I ask him to." She didn't believe for a minute that anything of the sort was going to happen. Still, she laid the magazine aside and spoke to the air in the direction of the ceiling. "If I have a guardian angel and he's here in this room, please give me a sign. Move the curtain. Speak my name. Make a shadow on the wall. Do *something* to let me know you're here."

For five minutes, Eve alternated between watching the drapes and staring at the wall. The article hadn't said how long to wait. It seemed to Eve if there was going to be a response, that response should have been instantaneous. When the curtain finally stirred and a cloud passed in front of the sun, she attributed it to a breeze that had blown in through the open window. That was too iffy. She needed a better sign than that. "Tell you what," she whispered. "I need to find a house where I can have a home daycare so I can stay home to raise my son. I'm going to make a list of everything I need or want in a house. If you find it for me, I'll know you exist."

It was disappointing that no guardian angel had responded. But it would probably have blown Eve's mind if one had. Dismissing the idea with a shake of her head, she went to the dining nook and took a pen and paper from the drawer in the oak telephone stand. Guardian angel or no, making a list would be helpful for when she was ready to call a realtor. While she was at it, she might as well be specific:

"Number 1: Good daycare location, close to school or preschool." This was a must. "2: Three bedrooms and two baths." She could do with two bedrooms if need be, but three would be much better. "3: Two-car garage, fully sheet rocked." She could use this to put her car away at night, and for the kids to play in on rainy days. "4: Plenty of storage space. 5: Fenced play yard. 6: Fireplace." She had always had a fireplace when she was growing up, but had never had one as an adult. It would make the house seem so much more homey. "7: Swimming Pool." This was a luxury she could definitely do without. But while she was dreaming, why not go all the way? "Eight: HBO T.V." She had never had HBO. She knew she could sign up for it at any time. But hey, this was her wish list. She would like to find a house where HBO had already been installed. "9: Price must be seventy-five thousand or less." She couldn't go a penny over.

After writing the list and reading it aloud on the remote possibility her guardian angel was listening, Eve tucked it away in a bedroom drawer for safekeeping. Of the nine house qualities she'd listed, she figured she'd be doing well if she found a house with five.

Three weeks after making her list, Eve called Barb Frasier, a realtor friend, and made an appointment to go house hunting. While they were on the phone, Eve read Barb the main items on her list.

"I do have one house that came on the market about three weeks ago," Barb said. "It might be what you're looking for. It needs a little fixing up. But it has potential."

While waiting for the realtor to pick her up, Eve took her list from the bedroom drawer and put it in her purse.

The yellow and brown house in question was a mile and a half from Tom's. The brown paint on the garage door was peeling, and the front grass was half dead. But Scotch taped to the front window was a sign that said "Daycare."

"The backyard backs up to a schoolyard," Barb said, signaling to turn in at the driveway. Smiling to herself, Eve took out the list and checked off item 1.

"If you like the house, you might be able to take over with the daycare kids who are already staying here." Eve could tell from the tone of the realtor's voice that she, herself, didn't care much for the house. But that was neither here nor there. *Barb* wasn't the one who'd be living here.

As she stepped out of the car, Eve glanced up at the HBO antenna on the roof. A quick scan of her list located the antenna just above Swimming Pool. *Check off number 8.*

The blonde realtor opened the driver's side door, casting a doubtful glance at the old cars in the next-door neighbor's driveway.

Stepping out on the passenger side, Eve dismissed the cars with a wave of her hand. It was true that the cars were an eyesore, but an eyesore would be a small price to pay if she could have her home daycare, and wouldn't have to put Kevin in someone else's care.

The scent of incense greeted Eve's nostrils when the realtor unlocked and opened the door, instantly plugging her sinuses. She wondered if the people who lived here were into meditation.

The small kitchen was old and somewhat dingy. But a coat of paint and some bright colored curtains would take care of that. She would have to re-grout the brown counter tiles. The existing HBO hook-up and Swimming Pool had been frivolous wishes on her list. But a good daycare location with three bedrooms and two baths had been a must. The three bedrooms and two baths in this house needed a fresh coat of paint, but the carpet and drapes were in good shape. The stone fireplace in the living room was a nice touch. *Thank you, Guardian Angel.* And the two-car garage was fully sheet-rocked, with floor to ceiling storage shelves. Eve took stock of her list and counted the check marks: six out of nine. So far so good...

The fact that the house was currently being used for daycare meant there must be a fenced play yard out back. When they came in from the garage and Barb pulled the living room drapes, the view through the glass patio doors made Eve gape. To the right, as she'd expected, was a fenced play yard. To the left of the yard, beyond the patio, was a full-sized pool! Eve's heart was in her throat when she asked her next question: "What's the price?" She had told her guardian angel she couldn't go over seventy-five thousand. She was almost afraid to hear the answer.

"After tax and closing costs, the price comes to seventy-five thousand."

Nine for nine! It was perfect! Why was *Barb* looking so *uneasy*?

"There's just something about this house that gives me the willies," Barb said. "Maybe it's just the incense. But I'm sure if we looked around a little longer we could find something else that would still be good for daycare."

"But it fits everything I had on my list," Eve cried. "Right down to the HBO on the roof!"

"You can sign up for HBO wherever you live," Barb argued.

But Eve was adamant. She wasn't about to look a gift horse in the mouth. With a little bit of fertilizer and a fresh coat of paint, the house would be just fine.

Later, after Eve had presented an offer, she allowed herself to acknowledge the probability that her guardian angel had acted on her request. "Thanks, if you did this," she said, tongue in cheek. "If I'd known you were going to take my list so literally, I would have said I wanted the yard to be landscaped, and the house to be in perfect condition."

Chapter 2

It was Christmas Eve, and if Eve did say so herself, the house was looking pretty darned good. Within a week of getting her license, her daycare quota had been filled. With Tom's help, she'd gotten the front and side lawns in shape, and the garage door scraped and painted. Despite recurrent bouts of depression, painting the bedrooms and re-grouting the kitchen tiles had proven to be excellent therapy. All that remained to be done was to paint the two small bathrooms.

In an effort to capture some semblance of Christmas spirit, Eve and the daycare kids had strung popcorn and brightly colored wooden beads to add to the tree's old-fashioned ornaments. Eve had been working on Christmas projects since Halloween. All the projects were finished except for the final spray on the hydro cal Indian chief she'd painted for her friend Pam.

"What do you think, Kevin? How do you like Kochise?"

"Is that his name? I thought you said it was Ger-moni-mo."

"I guess we could name him whatever we like," Eve said, reaching down to ruffle her son's blonde hair. "Do you think Pam will like him?"

"If she doesn't want him, you can put him in *my* room," Kevin said with an impish grin. Kevin was a cute little boy with blue eyes like his mom's, and light hair the color hers had been as a child. Sometimes it was hard for Eve to believe he was only three-and-a-half years old.

The last of the daycare kids had gone home early today. Before their parents arrived, Eve had closed the drapes to darken the living room and built a cozy fire in the grate. Sitting on the floor in a semi-circle around the tree, she and the kids had sung Christmas songs and she'd read them the story of the Littlest Angel.

Despite the fact there was somewhat of a pall hovering over their Christmas this year, Eve was doing her best to make it a happy holiday time for her son. "How about if I read you The Christmas story from your Bible storybook before you go to bed?"

Eve's own Agnosticism, dating back to college, had not prevented her from teaching her son the tenets of Christianity and buying a book of Bible stories for his collection. If she was on the wrong path herself, she didn't want to risk leading her son astray.

"How 'bout that one *and* the one about the fiery furnace?" It seemed ironic to Eve that Kevin's favorite Bible story—other than the story of Jesus' birth—was the one over which Eve had been called on the carpet her junior year in college. Until that day, Eve had been secure in her Christian beliefs. She'd gone to Sunday School every Sunday as a child, and to vacation Bible School during summer vacations.

Along with her strong Christian beliefs, she'd grown up with a fascination for psychic phenomena. To her mind, the two had been mutually exclusive. Her interest in the psychic realm had not interfered with her Christian beliefs—even when her high school Geometry teacher had introduced her to a Ouija Board. Thinking back now, Eve shook her head with a wry smile. That had been a real trip when the planchette had started moving and she'd known *she* wasn't the one pushing it! She never would have tried the Ouija Board if it hadn't been for Margot.

The youngest member of the faculty, Margot Richardson had been fresh out of college the year Eve had signed up for her class at Graysville High. Living in a furnished garage apartment, Margot had been friendless in the small valley town until she'd met Eve.

During study hall, Margot had told Eve about the Ouija board she'd purchased, and asked if Eve had ever used one. Convinced that Ouija Boards drew their messages from the subconscious, Eve had said she'd never had the chance to use one, but would be interested in trying it. That was all Margot had needed to hear.

After school, the young teacher had brought the board to Eve's house. Nervous at the thought of having both her teacher and a Ouija board in the house while her mom was at work, Eve had invited Margot in and closed the drapes so no one who might approach the house would see what they were doing. Together, they'd sat on the living room floor with the board on the beige carpet between them.

"How do we do this?" Margot had asked in a hushed voice. "Do we use both hands, or just one?"

"The pointer doesn't look big enough for four hands," Eve had replied, "so I guess we'd better each use just one."

Together, they'd each placed the fingertips of one hand lightly on the plastic planchette. For thirty seconds or more, nothing had happened. Then the planchette had begun to move, and Eve's heart had done a flip-flop. Convinced that Margot was unconsciously pushing the pointer, it had never occurred to Eve that a spirit could be involved.

Later, when Margot left the board with her, Eve had taken it to her room and tried it out by herself. It had freaked her out when the planchette began to move for her alone. Since she had known she wasn't pushing it, the fact that the plastic pointer was moving had been proof to her that her subconscious was responsible. Eventually, Eve had had filed the experience in the back of her mind and forgotten all about it. Odd that it would come to mind now.

Thoughts of the Ouija Board led by stream of consciousness to memories of automatic writing: Eve's first year in college, she had read a Psychology book that described automatic writing as a method of getting in touch with one's subconscious. The book had described in detail how to do it. Eve had felt like a fool—sitting at the table alone in the darkness, holding a pen poised above a blank sheet of paper. Her heart had nearly jumped out of her chest when she'd felt the pen drawn to the paper like an iron bar drawn to a magnet. Holding her breath, she had concentrated on *not* controlling the movement of the pen, and read the words as they'd appeared on the paper...

When she'd transferred to the University in her junior year and signed up for the class in Folklore and Mythology, the professor had blown her mind with his attacks on the Bible. She'd gone the distance that school year from a solid Christian background to her current status as an Agnostic.

In 1967, she'd met Tom. When, after seven years of marriage, Eve had been unable to get pregnant, her sister Cheryl had suggested she go for a psychic reading. Eve didn't know what she'd expected at the reading: maybe a black-haired woman with red lips and a floral robe. At the very least, dim lights and a crystal ball. Instead, a middle-aged brunette in black slacks and a casual top had taken her into a pleasantly furnished room and asked her to take a seat at what looked like a card table. Seated across from Eve, she had taken Eve's right hand in hers and closed her eyes for a long moment before she'd begun to speak.

"I see a house surrounded by flowers—roses, and a bay window. In the back of this house, or maybe in the garage, there's some sort of problem: a weakness that needs to be shored up. Is this making any sense?"

The house with the bay window and a yard surrounded by rosebushes couldn't have been more accurate. But Eve had had no idea what the woman was talking about with regard to a "weakness" in the house or garage.

"Why are you here?" the psychic had asked bluntly.

Careful not to reveal too many details, Eve had said she wanted to know what the future held with regard to children.

"Ah yes," the psychic had said. "I see that you and your husband have both been stressed over this for a very long time, perhaps not for the same reason. I also see that you've had a miscarriage."

To Eve's knowledge, she'd never been pregnant *or* had a miscarriage.

"The pregnancy wasn't far along," the psychic had told her. "Your period was late, and unusually heavy. You didn't realize you were having a miscarriage." She'd gone on to say that Eve would be pregnant again within the year—perhaps with twins—twin boys. One would have curly hair. The other's hair would be straight.

When Eve had gotten home from the reading, Tom had told her a building inspector had stopped by while she was gone. It seemed the rear addition to the garage had been built without a permit. The inspector had said the structure was weak and a beam needed to be added for structural support. *If the psychic had been right about the house, maybe she was right about Eve's having twin boys!*

Eve had given birth to Kevin thirteen months later. To bring in additional income, she'd agreed to take care of a neighbor's child. Jason had been the same age as Kevin, with curly blonde hair as opposed to Kevin's straight. Everywhere Eve had taken them together, people had asked if they were twins.

7

It had been while Eve was pregnant with Kevin that Tom had gone on a business trip and Eve had received a visitor in her bedroom. The visitor had come in the dark of night—a beautiful woman with flowing blonde hair. Sitting up in bed, Eve had gaped at the apparition. "Who—*What* are you?" she'd rasped.

Surrounded by a bright light that seemed to glow from within, the woman had told Eve in a voice as soft as rosebuds not to be afraid. But how could Eve not have been afraid? The woman had been suspended in mid-air! "I'm not here to hurt you," the woman had said softly. "We've been trying to contact you."

"I don't know who's been trying to contact me," Eve had croaked, "but whoever it is, I don't want to know about it. Go away! Get out of my house!"

The apparition had stayed until Eve had *shrieked* at her to get out, and then she had vaporized without a trace. The rest of that night and for the remainder of the week that Tom was gone, Eve had slept with the bedroom light on and chanted in her mind each night until she'd slept: "No visitors tonight…No visitors tonight…Please dear God, no visitors tonight…" It was odd that, even as an Agnostic, she turned to God in times of stress.

Eve had never told Tom about her experience. She'd managed to forget it until tonight. Why had these memories come flooding back now? First the memory of the Ouija Board, then the automatic writing, then the psychic reading, now the woman who'd looked like an angel…

After snuggling Kevin on her lap and reading the bedtime stories, Eve carried her sleepy son to his room and tucked him in. Bending to kiss his cheek, she whispered in his ear. "Sleep tight, Punkin. Tomorrow when you wake up, it'll be Christmas."

"I don't think I'm gonna be able to sleep," Kevin said with a monstrous yawn. "Do you think Santa will bring me that tricycle I asked for?"

Eve really didn't approve of the Santa Claus tradition. She'd never actually told her son Santa was real, but she'd never told him the bearded elf was a fantasy either. "I guess that's something you'll find out in the morning. Night night, Sweetheart. Tomorrow's going to be a very big day."

Christmas without Tom: Eve hoped she could pull it off without falling apart.

Back in the kitchen, Eve applied the final coat of spray to the statue and allowed it to dry to the touch before carrying the colorful chieftain to the master bedroom. When she'd seen the hydro cal statue at the ceramics store, she'd envisioned it as it would look in Pam's apartment with its earth tones and western décor. Pam had been with her when she'd found it, and had commented that the chief was very sexy. Eve had gone back to the ceramics store and bought the statue that very day after taking Pam home.

The finished statue was striking. One might even call it *regal*. Leaving the chief on her dresser, Eve cleared a space in her closet. With no clothing above him and nothing within two feet on the floor, the statue could finish drying during the night without danger of anything touching it.

Before taking out the last of the presents to be wrapped, Eve checked on Kevin to make sure he was asleep. She had put the wrapped presents under the tree, and was in the process of cleaning up the kitchen when she heard the loud crash from the back of the house.

Alarmed, Eve rushed to her son's room, but Kevin was in his bed sleeping soundly. Thinking that a picture must have fallen off the wall, Eve proceeded to the guestroom and turned on the light. The wall pictures were straight, still anchored beneath the corners by masking tape. The same was true in the master bedroom across the hall.

Eve knew the crash had come from inside the house. It had been too loud to have come from outside. An eerie feeling of unease crept over her. She knew the *statue* couldn't have fallen over. The closet floor was level, and there hadn't been an earthquake or sonic boom. There'd been nothing that could have fallen on or against it. Cautiously, she crossed to the closet and slid open the mirrored door. What she saw caused her heart to leap to her throat. The painted chief lay on the carpet, smashed to smithereens.

Tiny hairs prickled at the base of Eve's scalp. Hugging her trembling arms to her chest, she stared down at the broken statue. From the living room came the strains of the Halleluiah Chorus.

Muscles tensed, Eve peeled off her jeans and forest green turtleneck, and slipped into a blue nylon gown. Her skin crawled with the uneasy sense she was being watched. She knew she was being ridiculous. There was no one in the house but her and her son. She was certain there was a logical explanation for what had happened to the statue. It was just a matter of finding it.

With this thought in mind, Eve checked on Kevin one final time, then reluctantly went to bed. The clock on the nightstand hummed, and glowed a bright fluorescent green. The tree outside her bedroom window swayed gracefully in the breeze. And from the street outside the guestroom, she could hear the faint sound of a neighbor wishing someone a Merry Christmas: perfectly natural sights and sounds. So why did she feel so anxious?

By three in the morning, despite the fact her eyes were closed, Eve was still wide awake. Clutching the blue comforter under her chin, she tried to ignore the nagging feeling that someone or some *thing* was watching.

There's one way to find out, she chided herself. *All you have to do is open your eyes.* When after five minutes the feeling had grown stronger, Eve forced her eyelids apart. What she saw caused her to sit up and gasp. Two people—a tall dark-haired man, and a shorter woman of approximately Eve's height, were standing in the bedroom doorway, lit by filtered moonlight beaming in through the curtained window. The tall man was thin, with dark eyes and a moustache. The woman had straight dark hair to her elbows, and was dressed in jeans and a white long-sleeved shirt that hung over her wide hips. When Eve blinked, the apparition vanished.

Heart racing, Eve swung her legs over the side of the bed and raced to Kevin's room to make certain he was alright. In the moonlight from the window, she could see that he was smiling softly in his sleep. She wondered what he was dreaming about: probably Christmas morning. Bending to kiss his cheek, Eve whispered against his skin, "Sleep tight, precious one. Mommy's here. There's nothing to be afraid of." She wondered who she was trying to convince: Kevin? Or herself?

9

Chapter 3

Christmas morning, Kevin was awake at dawn. Bounding out of bed to charge into the living room, he shouted for Eve. "Wake up, Mom! It's Christmas!"

"Don't open anything till I get there!" Eve called back, throwing her covers aside. She felt as if she'd just gone to sleep. The fact was she *had* just an hour ago.

Eve had put a large bow on the red tricycle and hidden it in the hall closet. Now, as she arrived in the living room clutching her nylon robe to her breast, her heart melted at the disappointed expression on Kevin's face. "What's wrong, Sweetheart?"

"Santa didn't bring me a tricycle," Kevin mumbled. "He promised he would. But he didn't do it."

"Maybe he knew I'd already bought you one," Eve said with a loving smile. She hadn't planned to give him the trike till all his other gifts had been opened. But what was the point in waiting? When she saw the look of joy on her son's face, she forgot last night's visitors and the broken Indian chief in the bedroom.

Breakfast this morning was Cheerios and canned peaches. Kevin couldn't wait to go out in the play yard and try out his new trike and the tow truck his grandma had sent him. "Pam and the boys will be here at ten," Eve reminded him. "And you'll be having another Christmas this afternoon at your dad's."

She hoped Kevin wouldn't get spoiled, having two Christmases instead of one. Pam and her boys had been doing this for years, and it didn't appear to have spoiled *them.* Maybe Eve was worrying over nothing.

With the Indian chief broken, Eve had nothing else to give Pam when she arrived. Much as she hated to do it, she would just have to explain to her friend what had happened—No, if Eve told her, Pam would think the house was haunted, and pull her boys out of daycare. Eve would have to lie and say there'd been a sonic boom, and the statue had toppled over. She would make Pam a gift certificate promising another statue, and go back to the ceramic store tomorrow...

A week after Christmas, Eve was no closer to solving the mystery of the statue and nighttime visitors than she'd been a week before. She hadn't said a word to anyone about what had happened, other than the false explanation she'd given Pam.

Now, with the weekend free since Kevin had gone to be with Tom, Eve called her friend Bev to talk. She'd met Bev and her husband Tim last year when she'd taken a Freelance Writing course at a local junior college. The three had become fast friends, often visiting back and forth on weekends. "Something strange has happened," Eve said uneasily. She knew Bev had an open mind, but she wasn't sure how much she should say. "I'd like to talk to you and Tim about it, and see if you guys could come up with an explanation."

"Sounds mysterious." Bev's deep voice sounded almost like a man's. "Tim's working on the lawn this afternoon. Why don't you come over this evening around seven?"

The afternoon passed slowly for Eve, like watching a pot and waiting for it to boil. She knew Bev and Tim were interested in Psychic and paranormal phenomena. Tim himself was psychic, to a degree. Eve could think of no one else she could discuss these things with, without running the risk of someone's thinking she was crazy.

Flashing back to how she had gotten this house, even *that* was subject to scrutiny. She had asked her guardian angel, for pity's sake! She had put nine qualifications on her list, and he'd found her a house that met all nine. But if it had truly been her guardian angel who'd found it, why hadn't he known the place was haunted?

When Eve arrived at the door at seven, Bev and Tim were waiting. "So what's this mysterious thing that's happened?" Bev asked.

Bev was a large woman with short black hair and a pretty face. Her husband was even larger than she, with brown eyes, brown hair, and a closely cropped beard.

"Is it okay if we sit down first?" Eve asked with a strained smile. She really wasn't looking forward to talking about this.

"Sure," Bev said. "You two go ahead and sit down. I'll get us some Diet Cokes."

Eve hated the taste of diet drinks. The only time she drank them was when she was with Bev and Tim.

"Before Bev gets here," Tim said in a hushed voice, "does this have anything to do with the house you're living in?" He had sat down in a brown recliner and gestured for Eve to take a seat on the leather couch.

"Why do you ask that?" Eve said uneasily.

"Because when Bev and I were there last week, the hairs on the back of my neck stood on end. I kept having the feeling something Evil was in the house."

"You actually *felt* something?" Eve whispered. "It's not just me?"

"Felt what?" Bev asked. She had arrived with a tray of Diet Cokes just in time to hear Eve's question.

"We're talking about what I felt that night we were at Eve's," Tim said. "Tell her about what *you* felt that night."

Bev handed Eve a Diet Coke, then sat down in the chair across from her. "It was a really weird feeling—kind of like someone was watching us."

A feeling of panic clutched at Eve's stomach. "I know the feeling," she rasped. "Christmas Eve, I felt that way too. After I'd gone to bed, the feeling didn't go away." In a misguided effort to soothe her nerves, Eve took a swig from her Diet

Coke. "When I opened my eyes and looked around, there were two people in the doorway—a man, and a woman. When I blinked, they disappeared." By the time Eve had finished speaking, goosebumps had covered her flesh.

"You're sure you weren't dreaming?" Tim breathed. "Lucid dreams can seem awfully real."

"I wasn't dreaming," Eve answered. "I was scared from something that happened earlier in the evening, and I couldn't go to sleep." Eve's account of what had happened Christmas Eve gave her the creeps, just talking about it.

"You're sure there wasn't an explosion or something?" Tim asked with a frown. "There's no chance Kevin could have gotten out of bed and gone in to play with it, and accidentally knocked it over?"

"There was no explosion," Eve said firmly. "And Kevin was asleep. I checked on him. Besides, he didn't know I'd put the statue in my closet."

Across the room, Bev was clutching the arms of her chair.

"Then I guess there's only one explanation," Tim said. "I think it's time you called a parapsychologist—that, or an exorcist."

Speaking for the first time since returning to the room, Bev tried to force a little levity into the conversation. "Better yet, Eve could sell tickets for tours of the haunted house." When neither her friend nor her husband smiled, Bev offered a more reasonable suggestion. *"You've* been wanting to take Rachel Potter's course in the Paranormal, Tim. Why don't you and Eve take it together?"

Both Tim and Eve thought this was an excellent suggestion, but they wished Bev would come along…

The night of the first class at the community college, Eve was nervous. Standing in front of the vanity mirror, she applied a coat of mauve lipstick to match the design in her bulky knit sweater. Her blue eyes were strangely at odds with the prominence of her cheekbones. She supposed the hue of her eyes must go with her English nose. Eve was glad Tim had agreed to take the class with her. She wouldn't have taken it if she'd had to go alone. When they arrived for the class, the lecture hall was filled to capacity.

When Rachel Potter came on stage, her first request was that everyone change seats and make sure their new seat was adjacent to two total strangers.

Eve and Tim exchanged bewildered glances. There was a stir of voices as everyone in the class got up to change seats. After everyone had sat down, Rachel cautioned the class not to introduce themselves to classmates seated next to them.

Rachel was a large-bosomed woman with flaming red hair. Dressed in a flowered muumuu and dangling gold earrings, she gave an appearance of being larger than life. "I want each of you to give a personal possession to the person sitting next to you. Just be sure the item you choose belongs to you, and nobody else."

The thin freckle-faced woman seated next to Eve handed her a set of keys. Eve dug in her purse, and gave the woman a hairbrush. She suspected they were each going to be asked to do a psychic reading of the person whose object they now held in their hands.

When Rachel was satisfied that everyone was ready, she asked the class to close their eyes. "I want you to clear your minds of all thoughts and concerns," she said in a hypnotic voice. "Let your tensions go and relax. Take a few deep breaths, and let them out slowly. In, and out… In, and out… Now concentrate on the item in your hands. Touch it. Feel it. See with your mind's eye some fact or event associated with its owner. See it now."

Eyes closed, Eve tried to concentrate as she manipulated the keys. But the only things that came to her mind were an intravenous feeding bag and the incongruous word *buttons.* Try as she might, she could not attach a body to the feeding tube or an item of clothing to the buttons.

When time was up, Rachel told the class to open their eyes and turn toward their partners. "Tell your partner what you saw."

"I'm afraid I'm not very psychic," Eve told the thin woman next to her. "What I saw didn't make any sense. I just saw an intravenous bag with no body attached, and no hospital bed, and heard the word 'buttons' in my mind. Is someone in your family sick, or in the hospital?"

"No," the thin woman said thoughtfully. "My grandmother's in a nursing home, but she's not on an I.V." After thinking for a moment, the woman's eyes brightened. "But when I was a senior in college, my sorority threw a party and served drinks from an intravenous bag. Maybe that's what you were picking up on."

Eve's breath had caught when the woman told her about the party. Now, she ventured to ask about the buttons.

"I have no idea," the thin woman said. "When I was in high school, my boyfriend used to call me Buttons as a pet name, but—"

"Then that's it," Eve said excitedly. "Two matches have to be more than a coincidence."

Eve couldn't believe she had actually done it. She had held this woman's keys in her hands and picked two unrelated events out of the woman's past. She could hardly wait to hear what the woman had sensed about *her.*

"I saw something pretty specific about you," the woman said, "but if it's not accurate I don't want you to get mad."

Mad? Eve couldn't imagine what the woman could have seen that would make her angry. "Don't worry," she said with a smile. "I won't get mad."

"I saw you standing in front of a fireplace," the woman said. "You were wearing some sort of silky gown, and the firelight showed through the fabric to make a silhouette of your body."

The memory of a night from just last month flashed into Eve's mind, bringing an attractive blush to her cheeks. In her mind's eye she could see herself in the pale blue gown, standing in front of the firelight.

"You were waiting for someone—I guess it was your boyfriend. I heard a motorcycle, and when you answered the door, I saw a tall well-built man with a beard and a leather jacket."

Johnny. The night the thin lady was describing had been a romantic interlude between Eve and a special friend from the dance club she often attended. Eve believed he was quite possibly the sexiest man she'd ever met; and this sexy man had wanted *her.* It had been a giant step in gaining back her self-esteem as a woman. For Johnny, who was on the rebound, it had gone a long way toward

13

rebuilding his masculine ego. "I know the night you're talking about," Eve said quietly. "You don't have to tell me anything else."

A deep blush stained the thin woman's cheeks. "That's alright," she said quickly. "I didn't see anything else anyway. *Honest.*"

Eve appreciated the woman's discretion, but didn't believe her for a moment.

After the tactile readings were finished and everyone had shared their results, Rachel asked for a show of hands from students who'd received an accurate reading. At least two thirds of the class raised their hands. "Good," Rachel said. "We're going to try something a little different now. I have a stack of pictures in my hands. I'm going to turn my back and pick one so you can't see what I've picked. Then I'm going to lay the other pictures face down on the stage and concentrate on the picture I've chosen. I want you to close your eyes and relax like you did before, and try to see the picture in your mind."

The auditorium grew very quiet as everyone in the class closed their eyes and concentrated on picking up on the message Rachel was sending. At first Eve saw nothing. Then an image began to form of a staircase made of white steps with dark shadows: rectangles of black and white.

After five minutes, Rachel showed the class the picture, and Eve was once more amazed. The picture was a photograph of a piano keyboard. The white steps with black shadows Eve had seen had been the piano keys. Eve wondered how Tim was doing with *his* images. If she, who didn't have a psychic bone in her body, could do this well, *he* must be doing terrific! Eve could hardly wait to see what Rachel would teach them next. She wasn't to be disappointed.

"How many of you know what an aura is?" Rachel asked. About half the class members raised their hands. "How many of you have actually seen them?" This time no hands went up.

"No one? Then how would you like for me to teach you?"

A chorus of "Yes!" and a smattering of applause greeted the question.

"Alright then," Rachel said. "First, I want you to let your eyes go a little out of focus, and concentrate on looking at the outline of my body... You should see a white line—It's called the life light—outlining my body; and one or more colors layered on top of that." Here, Rachel paused to allow the class to try what she'd just described.

Eve had seen examples of heat photography once in a magazine, but hadn't realized auras could be seen with the naked eye. When she allowed her eyes to go out of focus as Rachel instructed, and stared at the outer edge of the psychic's arm, she saw the white band Rachel had described. Beyond the white band, she saw a band of yellow. Beyond the yellow was a thicker band of violet. Wow! This was amazing! To think that every person in this room was surrounded by colors that no one normally saw...

"How many of you can see it?" Rachel asked.

Sixty percent of the class raised their hands.

To prove that what her students were seeing was real, Rachel brought a male student onto the stage and instructed the others to look at his aura and write down what they saw. One hundred percent of those who saw his aura agreed that it was yellow.

"Would you like for me to demonstrate how I can make my aura bigger and brighter?"

A chorus of "Yes!" and more scattered applause provided the encouragement Rachel needed. Drawing several deep breaths, she walked to center stage and closed her eyes. Eve and the rest of the students blurred their vision and stared at the outer rim of Rachel's body against the backdrop of light. Adjacent to her body was a band of white, as expected. But what began as a thin outer band of yellow bordered by a band of violet began to spread until it had reached a width of ten inches or more extending out from her body. As the fascinated students continued to watch, fingers of green shot out like flames.

"Is my aura getting bigger?" Rachel asked.

"Yes!" the students shouted. Mixed with the excited shouts was a burst of applause.

"Would you like to know how I did it?" Rachel asked. For a moment, the psychic paused for effect. Then she continued on: "I was praying, and saying the twenty-third psalm in my mind... Now watch behind me as I exit the stage." Three hundred eyes watched Rachel walk off that stage. Heard throughout the auditorium was a collective gasp. Trailing behind Rachel like a silken banner was a stream of colored bands four to five feet long. The banner could still be seen for at least fifteen seconds after Rachel had left the stage!

A round of thunderous applause exploded and filled the room.

When at last the applause had died down, Rachel returned to the stage and announced that next week's topic would be earthbound spirits. "We're going to talk about haunted houses, people. So come prepared to tell your stories."

Chapter 4

It was Friday night—Eve's night for dancing. But today Tom had called to say he and Lorraine wouldn't be available to take Kevin. So when Pam had come to pick her boys up from daycare, Eve had asked if Pam could take Kevin for the evening. Eve would pick him up at Pam's apartment after the dance.

It was the first time Eve had worn the black jumpsuit. For six months it had lain in the bottom of her bureau drawer. But tonight Eve felt daring. It wasn't just the plunging neckline. The nylon jumpsuit was *backless*, with slightly flared legs that gave the illusion of a floor-length skirt. When Eve had first tried it on, she'd been shocked to see that it really looked good on her. The stark contrast between the black fabric and the fairness of her skin, rather than making her look pale, had made her look—well, *sexy*. Tonight, that's how she wanted to feel. It had been a hard week. She deserved some fun.

Eve had picked up her wrap and evening bag and was on her way out the door when the phone rang. "Hello, Eve? This is Johnny. Just thought I'd better call you in case you hadn't heard: The dance won't be at the usual place tonight. They've rented a hall downtown."

Eve didn't like the idea of having to drive to downtown Sacramento at night—not with her poor sense of direction and the quality of her night vision. Irritated that no one else from the club had called to notify her before this, she asked Johnny to hold on while she got a pencil and paper.

After giving Eve the address of the hall, Johnny told her she'd probably have to park a block away. "I doubt that there'll be any meter spaces available, so you'll probably have to park in the lot around the corner."

Eve cringed at the thought of walking a block *alone at night* in downtown Sacramento. But she wanted to go dancing, damn it! They wouldn't have rented the hall if they'd thought the area was dangerous. If other women could go there, she could go too. Besides, if she went early, she might find a space. She might not even have to park in the lot around the corner.

Eve was back in good spirits when she dropped Kevin off at Pam's. She always felt good when she knew she was going dancing.

"You'd better be careful in that outfit," Pam teased. "Johnny's liable to carry you right off the dance floor."

"The way I feel tonight," Eve teased back, "I just might let him."

Traffic on the freeway was light. Eve found the street without any problem, but it was poorly lit, and she couldn't make out the addresses on the buildings. Considering that it was a one-way street, she would have to circle the block.

Just to make certain she had taken the address down correctly, Eve stopped at a convenience store and went in to ask directions. The clerk behind the counter couldn't have been more than eighteen, but his eyes looked her over appreciatively. As Eve walked out, the young man suddenly called after her, "Miss! Please don't get out of your car!"

That was odd. Eve couldn't imagine why he'd said a thing like that, but she didn't go back to ask him. Instead, she got into the silver Datsun and started the engine.

The second time around, she spotted the building. But Johnny had been right about the parking. Every spot within a block of the building was taken. She would have to park in the lot around the corner. With a sigh of disgust, Eve circled the block again and headed for the parking lot. Just as she signaled to pull over, a sportscar cut her off, and she found herself circling the block *again*. At this rate, the dance would be over before she got there!

Turning in at the parking lot entrance *should have been* a simple matter. But this time a truck not only cut her off, but forced her onto the freeway on-ramp headed home! Eve was beginning to feel more than a little strange. First the store clerk, then the sportscar, now the truck forcing her onto the freeway…

Determined not to say "die," Eve took the first off ramp and approached the parking lot again. In an episode of déjà vu, a *delivery truck* cut her off and, for the second time, forced her back onto the freeway!

Alright, Eve thought. *Enough is enough.* She wouldn't try again to park in the parking lot. She would drive by the hall one final time. If there was an open space, she would stay. If all the spaces were still taken, she'd throw in the towel and head for home. *Please let there be a parking space.*

Someone must have heard her plea. When she turned onto the street where the dance was being held, there was an empty space directly across the street! She wouldn't have to walk any distance after all.

Muttering a silent prayer of thanks, Eve put the Datsun in park and picked up her bag. When she opened the car door, music blared from across the street, through the open door of the hall. But as she stepped out of the car and closed the door behind her, an eerie feeling assailed her: It was as if a wall of energy were blocking her way. Through the open door at the top of the concrete stairs, Eve could see couples dancing and having a good time. But when she tried to walk forward, the energy wall stopped her. Frightened now, she unlocked the car and got back inside. The convenience store clerk's words sounded in her mind: "Miss! Please don't get out of the car!"

Eve's whole body was trembling as she put the Datsun in gear and pulled out of her parking space to head back toward the freeway. *Just get me back to Pam's safely,* she prayed in her mind. Suddenly it occurred to her that maybe the force hadn't been trying to stop her from going dancing at all. Maybe it had been trying to tell her she needed to get to Kevin! *Please just get me there safely,* she prayed frantically. *Please protect Kevin. Let him be alright!*

Twenty minutes later, she arrived at Pam's apartment.

When Pam opened the door and saw Eve, she put an arm around Eve's waist for support, and helped her inside. "What happened to you? You're white as a sheet!"

"Is Kevin alright?" Eve asked breathlessly. "Has anything happened to Kevin?"

"Kevin's fine," Pam said in a puzzled voice. "He and my boys are sleeping. What are you doing home so early?"

Sinking onto the brown striped sofa, Eve poured out the story to Pam. "I was so scared, Pam. I didn't know what was going on. The only thing I could think of was that maybe something had happened here, and God was trying to make me come back."

Somewhere between the convenience store and the apartment, Eve had forgotten she was an Agnostic.

"Stay right here," Pam said. "I just need to go in the bedroom and make a quick phone call."

Eve watched as Pam left the room, then sank back against the sofa and closed her eyes. It was then that she saw it. In the vision, the dance was nearly over and she'd decided to leave early. As if in a trance, she watched herself emerge from the hall, clutching the black evening wrap under her chin. She saw herself skip down the concrete stairway and head toward her car across the street. And then she saw the derelict—a man in dark clothing, with a cap pulled over his eyes and a knife in his raised hand! She watched in horror as he ran up behind the Eve in the vision, and plunged the knife into her back.

When Pam returned from the bedroom, her face was ashen. "I just talked to my aunt. She lives about a block from where the dance was being held. Apparently there was a *reason* you were kept away. My aunt said there's been a rash of *stabbings* in that area. God or your guardian angel must have known that if you went to that dance, *you'd* be the next victim."

Badly shaken, Eve allowed herself to be convinced to spend the night on Pam's living room couch.

Before going to bed, she went to the guestroom to check on her son. Kevin was sleeping peacefully. If Eve could somehow manage to do the same, things were bound to look better in the morning…

Not surprisingly, Eve found herself looking forward to Rachel Potter's next class. She was finally going to get an answer to what was going on in her house and her life. Despite the fact she'd seen no further visions or apparitions, the memory of Christmas Eve and the derelict vision were still strong in her mind.

When Eve and Tim arrived at the lecture hall, class members who had now gotten to know one another were buzzing about tonight's topic of discussion. "The reason *I'm* here," one gray-haired lady said, "is that Abraham Lincoln's ghost has taken over my guestroom. My whole family has seen him. He never moves or says a word. He just sits on the straight-backed chair in the corner, staring into space."

Eve couldn't imagine why *Abraham Lincoln* would want to stay on earth and vegetate in this lady's guestroom. It didn't make sense. Maybe a ghost was playing a practical joke.

"I have one I've never seen," a man with thinning hair said. "He writes backwards messages on steamy mirrors. At first I thought my wife was doing it, and she thought it was me. But then we steamed up the bathroom on purpose, and went out together for five minutes. When we went back in, there was a message that said 'sloof.' Viewed in a second mirror, the word said 'fools.'"

Eve wanted to ask if the man and his wife had ever tried writing messages in return, but at that moment Rachel walked out onto the stage.

"Well," Rachel's voice boomed through the microphone. "I see you're all anxious to tell your stories. But first I'm going to tell mine." She told first of the fact that she'd been able to see the future even as a child. "My mother told me it was a gift, but I saw it as a curse. It made me different from everyone else. I didn't fit in with my family or any of the kids in my neighborhood."

Rachel went on to tell the story of a spirit who'd lived with her family when she was growing up. Sometimes it would hide things to get her in trouble—"like the time it hid my mother's car keys in my baby sister's diaper. My mother wouldn't believe I hadn't taken her keys until the time I was gone to visit my cousin, and my father's missing wallet showed up in her purse. After that, she believed me. When my parents finally called a parapsychologist, he said we had an earthbound spirit that needed to be released."

When Rachel had finished her story, she called for a show of hands. "How many of you are here tonight because you have one or more earthbound spirits in your home?"

Right hands of a third of the class went up, including Eve's.

"How many of these earthbound spirits are mischievous or destructive?"

Right hands of a fifth of the class went up, including Eve's.

"Tell us about yours, briefly," Rachel said, nodding toward Eve.

Eve hadn't expected or wanted to be singled out. But now that she had, given the present company, she wasn't really embarrassed. "I've seen two: a man and a woman. On Christmas Eve, I think they were responsible for breaking a statue I had painted as a gift."

The psychic nodded, then asked what sort of statue it was.

"It was an Indian chief," Eve replied.

The psychic pursed her lips and frowned before expressing her opinion. "It's possible a spirit was in the statue when you bought it and brought it home. He may have destroyed the statue himself. It might not have been the couple you saw at all. Have these spirits done anything else destructive?"

When Eve said they hadn't, Rachel nodded. "Then most likely, they were just trying to let you know they were there. If all they had done was show themselves or give you an eerie feeling, you might have dismissed them as imagination or as a lucid dream."

Eve left class that night armed with instructions of what to do in the event the apparitions should reappear. But their next appearance didn't come until weeks after she'd finished the class...

Chapter 5

Kevin's fourth birthday had come and gone. Daycare was running smoothly. Eve had fallen into a routine of dating and dancing on the weekend nights Kevin was with Tom and Lorraine. Like the proverbial kid in a candy shop, Eve was making up for lost time, enjoying to the limit the dating frenzy she'd dreamed of as a teen but had never experienced till her breakup with Tom. It seemed men in general didn't agree with Tom's assessment of her desirability, or of her ability to dance. It was a heady change for Eve.

An outsider who didn't know better might have believed she'd become obsessed with dating and dancing. But anyone who'd lived with her would have known that was only part of the story. Yes, dancing and social activities fed her ego and kept her in shape. But they also got her away from the house and kept her mind occupied with things other than ghosts.

It was a Wednesday night, and Tom had just brought Kevin home. After giving her son a bath and reading a bedtime story, Eve had put him to bed with a song and a backrub.

Since there weren't any good movies tonight on HBO, Eve took a hot bath and decided to go to bed herself. She'd been asleep for perhaps two or three hours when the now familiar feeling of unease awakened her: the sixth sense that told her she was being watched. This time Eve didn't wait. She sat up in bed and opened her eyes. The man and woman were back, standing in the bedroom doorway, dressed as before. Only now they'd apparently grown bolder. When she blinked, they didn't disappear. Frantically trying to recall what Rachel had said to do, Eve demanded to know who they were and why they were here. *"What do you want?"*

Like a holograph that had suddenly been switched off, the silent couple vaporized. Rushing to Kevin's room to make sure he was alright, Eve congratulated herself for having had the presence of mind to challenge the apparitions. She'd managed to get the upper hand for now. But where could she go from here? Though Kevin rallied for a moment when Eve bent to kiss his cheek, he went back to sleep immediately. Eve was glad *he* wasn't feeling the same anxiety as she.

Back in her own bed, it took a long time for Eve to calm her erratic breathing and quiet the thudding of her heart. The couple hadn't stayed long enough for her to finish. Next time she would tell them they were dead, and it was time to be released.

Eve had fallen into an uneasy sleep when she was awakened again—this time by Kevin's voice. "Mom? Mom, I peed my bed."

Peed his bed? Kevin hadn't wet the bed since he was a year and a half old! "I'm coming, Sweetheart." Knuckling the sleep from her eyes, Eve stumbled down the hallway and into Kevin's room.

Tears had welled in Kevin's eyes and his lower lip was quivering. "I'm sorry, Mommy. I didn't mean it."

Eve gathered her son into her arms and kissed him on the cheek. "Don't worry about it, Punkin. It's no big deal. I'll wash you and get you into some dry pajamas and you can sleep in the guestroom tonight. We'll keep both doors open so I can hear you if you need me, and I'll change these sheets in the morning." It occurred to Eve to let Kevin sleep with *her*, but she didn't want to start a precedent that later might be hard to break. Better to just leave the doors open. Besides, if the couple appeared in her doorway again, she didn't want Kevin to see them.

It puzzled Eve that Kevin had wet his bed. As she tucked him into the double bed in the guestroom, she nuzzled his cheek "Night night, Sweetheart. I love you very much."

"Night night, Mom. I love you and like you."

When Kevin had first learned the meaning of the words 'love' and 'like,' he'd decided neither word alone was sufficient for expressing his feelings. Ever since that time, he'd made a point of telling Eve he loved her and liked her before going to sleep.

Back in the master bedroom, settling into the comforter on her queen-sized bed, Eve tried to shake the fresh feeling of unease that had settled over her. She had been asleep perhaps an hour when she was awakened again—this time by an overwhelming sense of doom. Something besides the silent couple was in the house—something Evil—and it was coming down the hall. Eve could feel it as surely as she could feel her own heartbeat. The progress of the presence seemed to pause. It was looking for Kevin! She had to get to her son to protect him!

But when Eve tried to get out of bed, she couldn't move. She was paralyzed! She tried to scream to Kevin to come to her, but no sound would come out of her mouth. Terrified, she screamed a mental prayer: "God, I can't protect him by myself. Please help me!"

In her paralyzed state, Eve watched in horror as an apparition of herself sat up in her body. It was wearing the same violet baby doll pajamas as she. Its size and hair color were also the same. The apparition was sitting up, but still a part of her body. Though Eve tried again to speak, no sound would come out. Her arms and legs were stiff as stone. *What's going on?* her mind screamed. The apparition swung its bare legs out over the bedside and just for an instant, its face—*her* face—looked back.

In the hallway, the Evil presence was on the move again. The Eve in bed could sense it. 'Hurry!' her mind screamed.

22

Springing into action, Eve's other self broke away and ran from the room, pausing only long enough to glance back at Eve. When the apparition paused, it suddenly thought, *What's happening to me? I can see myself in my bed. But I know I'm there. How can I be* **here**? *I have to get to Kevin*!

For an instant, the human Eve still frozen in bed heard and saw nothing outside her room. "Dear God," she prayed. "What's happening out there?"

As instantly as her mind had returned to her paralyzed body, it switched to the spirit-Eve now running toward the guestroom. In her apparition state, Eve could feel the dark presence looming through the hallway toward her, but she refused to look in its direction. If she looked, she too might be paralyzed with fright. Kevin was on the guest bed sleeping soundly. Throwing her body over his, the spirit-Eve closed its eyes, then her mind was gone—back to the physical Eve frozen in her bed.

What is happening to me? the physical Eve thought frantically. An overwhelming feeling of claustrophobia gripped her, robbing her of the ability to breathe without panting as she realized she was virtually quadriplegic! Clammy beads of perspiration dotted her forehead. Her ears began to ring. *What if I stay this way from now on? What if while I'm in the guestroom protecting Kevin, the Evil force comes in here and I can't move?* Beneath her she could feel the sheets growing damp from perspiration.

And then her mind returned to the spirit-Eve sprawled on the guest bed covering Kevin's small body with her own. *It's in this room,* her spirit thought tensely. *I mustn't turn to look.*

A clammy coldness permeated the room. Eve's spirit self felt the cold, but did not shiver. *I won't look,* her spirit chanted. *It can't hurt my son. I won't let it. I won't look. It can't hurt my son...I won't let it...*

Despite the fact her eyes were closed, Eve's spirit self sensed the light of dawn. "It's over," she muttered. She had shielded her son for more than three hours. The evil presence was gone.

Rising from the guest bed, the spirit-Eve looked down at her son and thanked God for protecting him, before returning to the master bedroom. Still paralyzed in the queen-sized bed, the human Eve watched through fearful eyes as her spirit sat down in her body at the site of her groin and navel, then swung its legs up onto the bed and lay back. As Eve's spirit lay down in her body, it melded into her physical self and disappeared. As suddenly as she'd become paralyzed, Eve was able to move. The relief that swept through her was beyond belief.

Frantic, Eve leaped out of bed and ran to the guestroom. Kevin was still sleeping soundly. Whatever had been here had left without harming him. Eve knew she had to find help before it returned.

Though she went through the motions that day of caring for the daycare children, Eve's mind was on the events of the previous night. What was happening here seemed beyond Rachel Potter's scope of experience. In desperation, Eve thumbed through the Yellow Pages in search of a listing for a parapsychologist. When she found one, she marked the number but didn't make the call till she'd put all the children down for their naps.

The voice that answered the phone was pleasant and informal. Eve felt comfortable with the man immediately—or at least as comfortable as it was possible to feel, given the reason for her call.

"Start from the beginning," Dr. Peterson said. "Tell me in detail exactly what happened."

When Eve had finished her account of the strange phenomenon, Dr. Peterson's calm voice told her not to be afraid. "What you experienced was what's known as Astral Projection. Put in simpler terms, you had an Out of Body Experience. Don't worry. You're not going crazy. Hundreds of people have these experiences everyday. Some people have them at will."

Have them at will? "Why on earth would anyone *want* to have an experience like that?"

"I don't have an answer to that question," Peterson said. "But trust me. They do."

Eve wanted to move on to another topic and tell the parapsychologist about the couple in the doorway, but Peterson wasn't finished. "Tell me," he said. "Did you see anything else? Perhaps a silver cord?"

"A silver cord?" Eve echoed.

"A silver cord attached to your navel. A cord that attached your out of body self to your physical self in the bedroom."

"No," Eve said. "I don't remember anything like that. No. I'm sure there was no cord."

"It's really not important," Dr. Peterson said. "Some people see the cord, and some don't. Those who *do* refer to Astral Projection as going 'out on the strand.' Many believe that if the cord gets severed, they won't be able to return to their body. In other words, they'll die."

Die? Eve hadn't even intended to *go* out of body. Was he telling her that by doing so, if the Evil presence had severed the invisible cord she could have *died?*

Don't worry about the fact that you didn't see a cord," Peterson said. "Just be thankful you were able to protect your son."

Eve's heart was still thudding from the thought that she could have died. Forcing herself to focus on what Peterson was saying, she honed in on the phrase *protect your son.* "Do you really believe something was here?" she asked in a hushed voice. "Do you think it meant to hurt him?"

"I definitely believe something was there," Peterson replied. "Whether it intended to hurt your son or not, we'll never know. I think it's more likely it intended to scare him. I find many cases where these entities appear in children's rooms, and when the children tell their parents, the parents don't believe them."

"What you're saying," Eve said in a sick voice, "is that when kids say they've seen a bogeyman, it's not always their imagination." How many children, she wondered, had been the victims of spirit harassment, and couldn't get help because their parents refused to believe them?

"Sometimes it's a ploy for attention," Peterson said. "And sometimes it's simply fear of the dark. But often, I believe they're telling the truth—particularly when a parent or grandparent has experimented with the occult at some time or another—for example, in the form of a Ouija Board."

24

Eve had experimented with both a Ouija Board and Automatic Writing, but that had been years ago. Could these unwise choices have been responsible for an evil spirit coming into their home and seeking Kevin out?

Chapter 6

Unable to quell the feeling she was being watched any time she went into the master bedroom at night, Eve made the decision to confront whoever or whatever was watching her—regardless of whether she could see it or not: "Who are you?" she asked shakily. "What do you want?" No answer. "This is *my* house, and you don't belong here. I want you to leave. Get out of my house!" The sensation of being watched grew even stronger, causing the hairs on Eve's skin to prickle.

Her heart was pounding as she edged her way out of the bedroom and closed the door. There was no way she could sleep in her own bed tonight—not with the presence watching her. And she couldn't sleep in the guestroom either. Ever since the night she went out of body, she'd been unable to enter the guestroom. The energy field barring the guest doorway was strong: almost as strong as the force field that had prevented her from going dancing the night of the vision.

Kevin's bed was positioned against one side of the living room wall; the hide-a-bed sofa was on the other. If Eve slept on the sofa against Kevin's wall, at least she'd be able to hear if he woke during the night.

At one in the morning, Eve snapped awake and squinted at the fluorescent dial of the clock on the birch end table. It took an instant to get her bearings and realize she wasn't in her bedroom; she was on the living room couch. A movement across the room caught her eye; then she saw him. He was a distinguished looking man with wavy brown hair and a graying moustache, standing by the fireplace with his left arm resting on the mantle. Seen in profile view, his strong nose served to emphasize the ruddiness of his complexion. Head bowed as if in sorrow, he reminded Eve of Paladin in the old T.V. series Have Gun Will Travel. She wasn't frightened by the apparition. Instead, she felt an overwhelming sense of sadness. When she could hold her eyes open no longer, she blinked, and Paladin vanished.

It was odd that when apparitions appeared, she could see them without need of a lamp or overhead light. Not that the living room was totally dark. There was a certain amount of light filtering through the patio door drapes—not enough to distinguish facial features from across the room, but enough to distinguish shape and size. Dim lighting notwithstanding, she'd seen this man's features as clearly as if she had seen him in light of late afternoon.

The following night, the Paladin apparition appeared again—head bowed, standing in front of the fireplace, this time holding a pipe. This time, instead of merely trying not to blink, Eve held her eyes open with her thumbs and forefingers. When the urge to blink became unbearable, the apparition vanished.

The next day was Saturday. Eve waited till what she considered a decent hour to call, then dialed the parapsychologist's home number. "Dr. Peterson? This is Eve Tarlton."

"Good morning, Eve. How are you?"

"Not too well," Eve replied. "There's something in my bedroom and the guestroom across the hall. It's an eerie feeling, like the air is thick."

"But you haven't actually seen anything more?"

"Not in the bedrooms," Eve replied. "But I started sleeping on the living room couch, and twice I've woke up in the middle of the night to see a man standing by the fireplace, with his arm on the mantle."

"And both times you saw him from the same point of view?"

"In profile," Eve replied. "Hanging his head, and looking very sad. I know I didn't dream him, because I forced my eyes to stay open. I was wide awake when I saw him."

There was a moment of silence as Dr. Peterson processed this information. "From all that you've told me, it sounds as if you may be living in a house where there's been a violent death. Maybe the couple you saw were having an affair. Maybe this guy by the fireplace killed them, then turned the gun on himself."

"No," Eve said. "This man doesn't look to me like someone who was capable of killing anyone."

"Regardless of why this spirit's in your house," Dr. Peterson said, "He's earthbound, and he needs to be released. This man may not even realize he's dead. He may be confused as to why you're living in *his* house! If you want to make absolutely sure you're not dreaming, and find out if this apparition is real, I'd advise you to move your couch to another spot in the room. If you see him again, but from a different angle, you'll know he's real and that you're not just dreaming."

"And then?" Eve's voice was so quiet even she could hardly hear it. "Suppose I find out for sure that he's real. What do I do then?"

"Talk to him," Peterson said. "Comfort him. Let him know you don't mean him any harm. After you've won his confidence, you can break the news to him that he's passed away, and hopefully release him."

Eve's nerves were stretched to the breaking point as she dragged the sofa to a spot between the living and dining rooms where it could serve as a divider.

That night, she slept without incident. Sunday night, she awakened with a start. The sad man was there again, standing by the fireplace. Only this time he was looking directly at *her* and he didn't disappear when she blinked. The resemblance to Paladin was astounding—right down to the horizontal lines in his forehead. He even had the deep cleft in his chin. Drawing a deep breath, Eve sat up on the couch. Her heart went out to him, and she wasn't afraid. "You look so sad," she said softly. "I know you must be wondering who I am and why I'm here. My name's

Eve Tarlton. My son and I bought this house from the Jansons, who lived here before." Here, Eve paused in search of the right words. "I'm not sure how to tell you this, so I'm just going to have to blurt it out." Her heart ached over what she was about to say. "You've apparently died," she whispered. "You've passed away, but your spirit has stayed here."

The sad man showed no change in facial expression. He simply looked at Eve through moist brown eyes.

"I don't know why you stayed," Eve went on. Her voice seemed to gain strength as she spoke. "Maybe because this house is familiar; maybe because you have some sort of score to settle. But that score is with someone else. Not with me. Not with my son. It's time for you to leave—not just this house, but to leave the *earth*." Her words sounded callus, but she didn't know any other way to say it. "There's a better place waiting for you..." Her voice faded away, and the room fell silent.

The sad man took his arm down from the mantle. Eve's mouth was dry, but she wasn't afraid. She felt only empathy and love for this man. Before she realized what she was doing, she reached out her arms. "It's alright," she whispered. "If you don't want to go yet, I understand. If you want to, you can stay for a little while longer."

Eve's heart was racing as the Paladin look-alike crossed to where she was sitting, and knelt to meld into her embrace. His somber brown eyes gazed into hers, but it was as if she were holding air in her arms. For an instant, she detected the masculine scent of fine wine and pipe tobacco. Then he was gone.

Sitting alone in the darkness with her heart thudding in her ears, Eve tried to make sense of what had just happened. *Did I, or did I not, just hug a ghost?*

For the rest of the night, Eve slept fitfully—and for the next, and the next, and the next after that. Then came the night when voices awoke her. "Eve," the chorus said, "We're trying to contact you. Why are you resisting us?"

Eve flashed back to the night years ago when the angelic lady in white had visited her room when Tom was away. *She* had also said "they" were trying to contact her. Who was this "they"? And what did they want with *her*?

"Can't you understand I'm not one of you?" Eve whispered. "Can't you understand I don't *want* to be contacted?"

"Mom?" Kevin called from the other side of the wall. "Mom? Are you okay? Is something wrong?"

"There's nothing wrong, Sweetheart," Eve called back. "You were just dreaming. Go back to sleep."

Eve lay awake long into the night, wishing it were that simple.

The next several months were miraculously free of paranormal experiences. At least that's what Eve believed until many years later when Kevin told her about the cloaked figure who used to come into his room at night and stand at the foot of his bed. The one night Kevin had mustered the courage to try to run to her for protection, the cloaked figure had cast a web of energy over him, stinging his skin and rendering him paralyzed till dawn. Kevin hadn't told Eve about the visits when they happened. Unaware that she, too, had been having ghostly experiences, he hadn't thought she'd believe him.

Chapter 7

The next six years of Eve Tarlton's life were punctuated with bad luck and unexplainable events. Following the night she hugged the so-called earthbound spirit, she was involved in three rear-end traffic collisions, spaced approximately one month apart. Each collision resulted in a whiplash. If she hadn't known better, Eve would have wondered if there was a subliminal sign on the back of her car that said in huge letters: "Hit me."

Unable to make a decent living in daycare, Eve was eventually forced to turn to an office job, and put Kevin into a church sponsored Preschool/Daycare. She'd always believed it was a mother's role and responsibility to stay home and raise her own children, at least till they were old enough to go to school. But faced with the choice of going under or taking an outside job, she did what she had to do.

Evenings and weekend days when Kevin wasn't with Tom, Eve showered him with attention—reading stories, playing games, working on art projects together… As long as she kept busy every minute of her waking hours, she didn't have time to think about who or what was sharing her home. Of course there was the time when Michael, the son of a donut chain manager she was dating, claimed to have seen a lady similar in age to his Granny, walking down the hallway to the guestroom. Another time, when he and Kevin were playing, Michael saw a man standing over them with a hat pulled over his eyes and a gun in his hand. He told Eve about it in confidence, but said he knew the man wasn't real, because Kevin couldn't see him. When Michael tried to tell his dad what he'd seen, Nick chalked it up to a vivid imagination. *Eve* saw no reason to argue.

When Nick asked Eve and Kevin to combine families with him and Michael and move to a town in Central California where he'd accepted a job as a restaurant manager, Eve made the decision to go for it.

"Going for it" in this case involved quitting her job, taking Kevin out of his current kindergarten, moving to Petersville to be a stay-at-home wife and mother, taking advantage of the opportunity to write during school hours, and eventually trading her house for the restaurant Nick was managing. Life was good. It appeared that Eve's luck had taken a turn for the better.

Appearances were deceiving.

No sooner had Eve settled into her new home and begun to feel secure, than a heavy tread on the stairway awakened her in the night. *Oh God*, she thought frantically. *Someone's in the house!* Terrified, Eve sat up in bed and nudged the bearded man sleeping beside her. "Nick," she hissed. "Wake up. Someone's on the stairway!" When Nick continued to snore, Eve nudged him again. And then she heard the voice.

The sound of it filled the mountain cabin, but still Nick continued to sleep undisturbed. "Eve." The intruder on the stairs knew her name! "There's Evil in this house," the deep voice thundered. Frozen with fear, Eve stared at the wall shielding the stairway from view. How could Nick continue to sleep when the voice was so loud it practically rattled the windows? Why hadn't it awakened the boys? When the voice continued, Eve realized that she alone could hear it. "Only *you* can do what has to be done to rid this house of the Evil that dwells within." And then the voice fell silent, leaving Eve trembling and soaked with cold sweat. Her fingers and toes felt like slivers of ice as she clutched the down comforter under her chin.

What evil was the voice talking about? A spirit? A person? Was the cabin haunted? Had the voice of *God*—who she wasn't even sure she believed in—just spoken to her, telling her *she* was responsible for doing something about it? Eve knew from her Christian background that God had reportedly talked to Noah to warn him of the flood. He had talked to Moses, to give him the Ten Commandments. But she'd never heard of Him talking to housewives about ridding their homes of evil!

Within three months after combining families, Eve's stepson Michael hit Kevin over the head with a log. Days later, he pushed Kevin down the stairs and screamed at Eve that he wished *she* were *dead*. Could *this* be the evil the voice had been talking about?

Six months after she traded her house for the restaurant Nick was managing, an arsonist burned it and framed Nick for the crime. Eve lost not only the restaurant, but her savings, her car, and everything else of value she'd ever owned.

After the fire, things only got worse. At the end of seven years, fearful that staying with Michael would prove fatal, Eve took Kevin and left for Southern California. There, she found a job, and Kevin found a number of lasting friendships. Now that Kevin was old enough to stay alone for a few hours at a time, Eve fell back into the routine of dating and dancing. Their budget was tight, but she had no complaints.

Throughout it all, her close relationship with her son remained constant. Together, they'd made it through some tough times. But the one thing missing for Kevin was a close relationship with his dad. It wasn't entirely surprising to Eve when Kevin asked permission to move to Sacramento and live with his dad for high school…

The first month Kevin was gone was torture to Eve. All she could think about was the fact that she was missing her son's high school years. Of course there was phone contact, but that wasn't enough. Eve wanted to attend Kevin's football games. She wanted to be there for his proms and graduation.

When Eve made the decision to quit her job and move, she knew she was taking a huge risk. The economy wasn't in the greatest shape, and she had no idea where she would find a job in Sacramento. She didn't even have a place to live. All she knew was she had to be near her son. When she returned to Sacramento, the spirits were waiting.

Chapter 8

"Why is your son so angry?"

Eve was seated in a darkened living room lit only by candlelight. On the couch directly across from her, a large woman with short blonde hair was shuffling a deck of Tarot cards. Eve hadn't told the psychic she had a son. "I don't know what you're talking about."

"Your son," Myra said. "He's extremely angry. I don't think his anger is directed at you—or even at his father. I get the feeling it's directed at someone at school who's been picking on him—a bully. I see a weapon..."

Cold fear took root in the pit of Eve's stomach. She had come to Myra Paulson for a psychic reading to ask when and where she could find a job. After a month of house sitting and putting her application in all over town, she was no closer to finding work than she'd been when she arrived in Sacramento. Her meager savings were running out. "What kind of weapon?" she asked in a faint voice. Kevin didn't know anything about fighting! If the boy who was bullying him was carrying a weapon—

"Something sharp," Myra said. "Maybe a knife."

When Eve had first arrived for the reading, the psychic had picked up some sort of a wand filled with clear liquid and what looked like glitter, and shaken it in all four directions. Though Eve had asked her why she was doing this, Myra had brushed the question aside without answering. Now, she shook it again.

"Who has the knife?" Eve breathed.

"It's *both* of them," Myra answered. "I'm getting mixed signals. I see a fight in the near future: two boys jabbing at each other's faces with pointed objects, but the objects don't seem to be knives. Someone could lose an eye!" Clutching her head, Myra stood and began to pace. "He's too powerful. I can't take it."

Eve was leaning forward now, on the edge of her seat. "Who? *Who's* too powerful? What can't you take?"

"Your spirit guide," Myra said weakly. "That's who's been talking to me. He wants to talk directly to you. I can't do this anymore."

*Spirit guide? **What** spirit guide?* "My experience with spirits has not been good," Eve said shakily. "I don't want any of them offering me advice."

As Eve spoke, a pair of beige cats slinked into the room and leaped onto the couch where Myra was sitting. Based on their blue eyes—similar to hers—Eve at first suspected the cats were Siamese. But their velvet hair was so short as to make them appear almost hairless.

Without warning, the bolder of the two leaped down from the sofa and into Eve's lap. Though she inwardly cringed, Eve tried not to show it—even when the twin feline jumped down from the sofa and onto the back of the chair she was sitting in.

"I knew when I first saw you that you were psychic," Myra said. "Your eyes— so pale blue—in the candlelight, they could almost be mistaken for silver. Now that I see how my cats react to you, I'm certain. You need to develop your psychic abilities. You could be a very powerful lady."

Eve's eyes were light blue because her father's had been light blue, but they certainly weren't silver. When she was a little girl, her father had used to say her eyes were robin egg blue to match the blue of their Buick. "I don't want to be powerful," Eve replied. "I just want to protect my son and find a job." The cat on the back of Eve's chair had now moved onto her shoulder and was rubbing against her cheek. It was all Eve could do to keep from squirming. On the move again, the twin in her lap crawled into the sleeve of the coat she'd draped across the chair arm.

"This is unheard of," Myra said. "My cats have never taken to anyone like this, other than me."

Eve knew Myra's words were meant as a compliment, but she wished the cats would just leave her alone. When she didn't reply to the comment about the cats, Myra sat down and once more picked up the wand.

"How will you know how to protect your son if you don't let your guide tell you the danger he's in?" As she posed the question, Myra shook the wand in each of the four compass directions.

"What are you *doing*?" Eve asked uneasily.

"A dark spirit came into the room," Myra said. "I could tell by the flicker of the candle flame when no air was moving. But it's gone now. Now listen to me. Before you talk to any spirit, you need to close your eyes and surround yourself with a protective white light. Then ask the spirit to declare himself—whether or not he's of the light. Always remember: *a spirit can't say he's of the light if it isn't true.*"

Eve could tell by looking at Myra that her head was still throbbing. She couldn't understand why the spirit guide, if he existed, couldn't communicate without giving someone a massive headache. The lady in white hadn't had any trouble speaking. Neither had the chorus of voices. *They* hadn't given *her* a headache. Why was this one giving Myra one now?

"Your guide's saying you've closed him and the others out," Myra said weakly. "They've tried time and again to talk to you, but you've closed your mind against them."

Could that really be possible? Eve had told the angelic woman and the chorus of voices that she didn't want to be contacted. Could it be that her brain had truly

33

shut them out? If that was the case, if she wanted to hear from them *now*, how could she open the path to communication? It was clear she would have to do *something*. Kevin was in danger!

On the verge of panic, Eve left Myra's house and drove back to the partially furnished house where she was staying. Ever since the day he was born, Kevin had been the most important thing in her life. Now a psychic was telling her he was in danger. Eve's hand was trembling as she punched the buttons to dial Tom's number. It was early enough in the day that Tom and Lorraine would still be at work. 'Please, Kevin, be there…Please…'

"Hello?"

"Kevin?" Eve said. "Sweetheart, there's something I need to talk to you about. Are you in some sort of trouble at school?"

There was a moment of silence before Kevin replied. "Why would you ask that?"

"You already know I haven't found a job yet," Eve said uneasily. "Today I went for a psychic reading to get advice on where else I could apply. But the psychic spent most of the hour talking about *you*. She said you're very angry about something at school. She said knives or some sort of sharp weapons are involved."

There was another long silence. When Kevin finally spoke, his voice was defensive. "It's true that I've been pretty mad. There are a couple of dudes at school that have been giving me a ration of shit."

Eve had never allowed Kevin to swear when he was growing up. Hearing him now, it was hard to hold her tongue. "Do these boys have weapons?" she asked in a hushed voice.

"I'm sure they carry knives," Kevin replied. "But so do I."

Oh dear God, Eve thought weakly. *Myra was right.* "The psychic said you were carrying a knife. But I didn't believe her. Why are you carrying a *knife*?"

"Chill out, Mom," Kevin said irritably. "I didn't say I was going to use it. I'm just carrying it for protection."

"You don't know how to fight with a knife," Eve protested. What had the world come to that a freshman in high school needed *a weapon* for *protection*? "If you pull out a knife, you could get yourself killed! I want you to get rid of it, Kevin. I want you to promise me you won't carry it with you again."

"I can't promise that, Mom. And if you tell my dad about it I'll deny it and won't ever tell you anything again."

Eve's mind was reeling. This couldn't be her son talking! "Sweetheart, you know I'm only saying this because I love you. If someone at school is giving you problems, you need to tell the principal. Or at least tell your *dad.*"

"There's nothing my dad can do. And I can't tell the principal. Don't worry about it, Mom. They were hassling me pretty badly for awhile. But the past few days, they've left me alone."

"Sweetheart," Eve said, "Why didn't you tell me about this before? Why would you keep something like this to yourself?"

"Because I knew you'd just worry and act like you're acting now," Kevin snapped. "This is something I just need to take care of on my own."

This was not what Eve had wanted to hear, but to argue at this point would only make matters worse. "The psychic said there's going to be a fight. Two boys jabbing at each other's faces with pointed objects." Eve knew that telling Kevin this would probably just make him more angry. But she couldn't let it drop.

"I don't know who this psychic lady is," Kevin snapped, "but she's got everything screwed up. It wasn't a fight; it was a game, and it already happened. Me and Tony were having a play fight jabbing at each other's eyes with ball point pens. But then we realized how dangerous it was, so we stopped."

Jabbing at each other's *eyes*? Eve and Kevin had only been apart for four months. Could this actually be her son talking nonchalantly about a game in which someone could have lost an eye? "What could you have been *thinking*?" she asked incredulously. "Didn't you realize one or both of you could have been blinded?"

"Chill out, Mom. Nothing happened. I already told you: When we realized how dangerous it was, we stopped. What's this psychic's name and number? I'd like to talk to her."

In hopes that Myra could talk some sense into him, Eve gave her son Myra's name and phone number. After they hung up, she drew a deep breath. Myra had said she should surround herself with a protective white light before attempting to contact a spirit guide. She had done creative visualization in the past. This should pose no problem.

Closing her eyes, Eve imagined herself filled with and surrounded by light. "If I have a spirit guide—a spirit of light—who's been trying to reach me to talk about my son, please talk to me now. And I'd appreciate it if you'll try not to give me a headache."

Except for the distant sound of a car engine, the room was deathly silent. Frantic to find a way to communicate, Eve went to the bureau drawer where she'd stored her meager belongings, and took out a gold chain and pearl drop earring. When she returned to the living room and sat down on the sofa, she attached the chain's clasp to the earring to form a pendulum.

She knew from what she'd learned in a Psychology class in college—and later experimented with on her own—that a pendulum could be swung in any direction (presumably by the subconscious mind) without conscious effort of the person who was holding it. If the subconscious could swing a pendulum, surely a *spirit* could do it. With this thought in mind, Eve took a pen and pad from her purse. Using the coffee table as a desk, she made an arc of letters similar in arrangement to the letters on a Ouija Board, plus the words "yes, no, and maybe," and an array of punctuation marks. Her heart was thudding so loudly in her ears that she could no longer hear the car engine next door.

"Okay," she said when she was ready. "Here goes." Heart in her throat, she imagined herself surrounded by light. Apprehensive, but *not truly expecting anything to happen*, she knelt on the rug beside the table and held the pendulum over the arc of letters. "If there's a spirit of light who wants to talk to me about my son, this is your chance. I'm holding a pendulum over this paper. If you'll swing it to the letters to spell out the words, we'll be able to communicate."

The pendulum instantly began to swing. Startled, Eve dropped the pendulum onto the table. When she picked it up again, her hand was shaking. "Sorry about that. I guess I'm a little jittery."

The pendulum again began to swing. It swung unerringly to each letter, and halted dead still at the end of each word. "My name is Gideon," it spelled out. "And I'm of the light. I am your guardian angel."

Chapter 9

Unable to fathom what had just happened, Eve dropped the pendulum in her lap and raised her hands to her face. "Oh—my—God…"

The pendulum and alphabet arc lay silent on the table. Seated in the dusky shadows of the living room, Eve stared at the alphabet arc as if it had sprouted wings. Her stomach growled in protest of the fact that it was late and she hadn't eaten. From outside she could hear the competing sounds of a honking horn and a barking dog. She sat there till the horn and dog grew silent and lengthening shadows gave way to darkness. Then she turned the three-way lamp on low and closed the living room curtains.

When she picked up the pendulum this time, she didn't have time to ask a question before it began to swing. "What was *that* all about?" Gideon demanded. "As your guardian angel, I try to call you for forty-three years, and when I finally get through you put me on hold?"

This was unreal. Either Eve Tarlton was losing her mind, or her guardian angel had just cracked a joke! "I'm sorry," Eve said. "If you've been with me for forty-three years, you must realize you gave me quite a shock."

"Lesson Number 1," Gideon said sternly: "Never pick up that pendulum unless you've surrounded yourself with the protective white light. Lesson Number 2: When you picked up the pendulum and I made it start swinging, you accepted without question that it was me. How did you know I wasn't a dark spirit? Did you *ask* if I was of the light?" Eve knew that he'd put emphasis on the word 'ask' because the pendulum swung harder on that particular word. "I believe I asked you a question," the pendulum spelled out. "When I ask a question, I expect an answer."

Apparently her guardian angel wanted to make as many points as he could before she was tempted to put the pendulum down.

"No," Eve replied. "I didn't ask."

"Surround yourself with the light, then ask."

Laying the pendulum on the coffee table, Eve closed her eyes and imagined herself surrounded by a glowing light of protection before reopening her eyes and picking up the pendulum again.

"Ask if I'm of the light."

"This is ridiculous," Eve muttered. "I know who you are. If you weren't who you said you are, you wouldn't have insisted that I protect myself."

"Ask."

"*Okay*! Are you of the light?" The instant she'd spoken, Eve regretted her impatience.

For a moment the pendulum didn't swing, and Eve felt her heart leap into her throat. At last the chain and earring swung to the word Yes. "You lucked out this time. I am Gideon, and I'm of the light. And don't ever talk to me in that tone of voice again."

Recognizing that the chastisement was deserved, Eve apologized and controlled her tone of voice through the rest of this unlikely conversation, even when Gideon voiced his complaints on how difficult she could be to deal with. Point in case: the night of the dance when the stabber was skulking in the area of the hall, and Gideon had had to create an energy field to protect her.

The more they talked, the more Eve felt as if she'd known Gideon all her life—which, in a way, she supposed she had. No longer feeling uncomfortable, she ventured to ask about Kevin, and what was going on with him and the bullies at school.

"Kevin has given his guardian angel more than a few gray hairs," Gideon said. "He's turned into a rebellious teen, Eve. But you did a good job of raising him. He's basically a good kid."

"What about the *knife* he's been carrying? What about those boys who've been bullying him? What about that ridiculous fight, jabbing at each other's eyes with ball point pens?"

"That was a hairy one," Gideon said. "Abdul Ben Hana and the other boy's guardian angel managed to abort it by getting through to Kevin and Tony how dangerous it was."

Eve knew what the pendulum had spelled, but felt there must have been some mistake. "Kevin has an *Arab* or *Islamic* guardian angel?"

The pendulum quivered, as if Gideon were laughing. "Guardian angels have no nationality. We choose our own names, independent of what our names were when we were human."

It had never occurred to Eve that, other than in the movies, guardian angels might be people who had died and gone to Heaven.

"Abdul's doing a great job," Gideon assured her. "Kevin's in no immediate danger."

Eve was relieved to hear that Kevin wasn't in danger—at least for the moment.

"I have another one of your guides here," Gideon said. "His name's Caruso. He's a spirit guide trainee that feels he owes you an apology. I told him until he gets his act in gear, he can only talk to you through me."

How could a spirit guide Eve wasn't even aware of owe her an apology?

Reading her mind, Gideon answered that Caruso was new at this, and didn't have the hang of it yet—living in a realm where past, present, and future exist simultaneously. He also needed work on controlling his newfound power. "That's why he gave Myra such a headache. It's also why he jumped the gun, telling her about the pen incident as if it hadn't already happened. He was trying to be helpful, but all he did was cause you to panic."

"Panic and get in touch with *you*," Eve shot back.

"That's one good side effect," Gideon agreed. "The other is that Caruso has learned a lesson. Next time he'll think twice before he starts shooting his mouth off."

This was blowing Eve's mind—destroying any perception she might have had of how guardian angels were supposed to talk.

"You'd rather I used words like 'thee' and 'thou'?"

It suddenly dawned on Eve that Gideon had been reading her mind.

"If I *couldn't* read your mind, my hands would be tied," Gideon said glibly "And I don't particularly approve of what you're thinking right now. So cool it."

The thought that had just occurred to Eve was that she resented this invasion of her privacy. The thought that occurred now—which she was certain Gideon could read, was that she liked him, but he was awfully bossy.

"You're going to have to learn to live with it," Gideon said. "We're in this together for the long haul."

This was definitely going to take some getting used to—knowing someone was listening to her every thought. Eve would have to be careful in the future of what thoughts came to mind. In the meantime, she asked what had become a main concern. "I've been here in Sacramento almost a month, and I haven't found a job yet. I've put my application in all over town. I don't know what else to do."

"Just be patient," Gideon said. "The job is out there, but the timing's not right."

That was easy for him to say. He wasn't the one who was running out of money. "When is the timing going to be *right*?"

"Have a little faith," Gideon said. "I'm not going to let you starve. Just give me some time."

It was a comfort for Eve to know her guardian angel was working on trying to find her a job. She had thought she was in this alone. But she didn't like the fact that it didn't seem to be bothering Gideon that the job search was taking so long.

When at last Eve glanced at the clock, she realized they'd been talking for nearly three hours.

"It *is* getting late," Gideon commented. "Maybe you should put the pendulum away for the night. I'll still be here in the morning. And when you talk to me tomorrow, don't forget rules 1 and 2. Goodnight, Sweetheart."

Sweetheart? Had he called her *Sweetheart*? This was so neat! She had actually made contact with her guardian angel, and he had called her Sweetheart! How many people in this world had that sort of relationship with their guardian angel? Eve slept better that night after talking to Gideon than she'd slept in weeks. She felt like a kid who'd met Superman, and Superman had said they were in this thing together.

Chapter 10

To celebrate her newfound relationship, albeit with a spirit guide, Eve decided to go dancing. The problem was she had no one to go with. The dance club she'd belonged to when she'd lived in this area before didn't schedule dances in the middle of the week. She really wasn't worried about going alone, now that she knew she had Gideon to protect her. But just the same, she would prefer to go with another woman.

Breakfast tasted better this morning than Eve could ever remember its tasting. She felt like a smoker who had given up the habit and was now getting back the benefit of taste buds. "Does this have anything to do with you?" she asked, pausing by the coffee table to pick up the pendulum. Just in time, she remembered to surround herself with light.

"Very good," the pendulum spelled out. "What comes next?"

Eve was glad he had reminded her. "Please identify yourself," she said. "And are you of the light?"

"Very good," the pendulum spelled out. After identifying himself, Gideon quickly moved on. "Try calling a dance club downtown and ask if they have a policy for matching single women."

It wouldn't have occurred to Eve to call a dance club. But after talking to the proprietor of a club by phone, she was glad she had. She was a little nervous about going to a club she'd never been to. But the voice on the phone had assured her there would be other women there without escorts, and he'd make sure she was paired with one.

It had been awhile since Eve had donned her dancing clothes and taken special care with her make-up. She had asked the proprietor the average age of the club's patrons, and been told the age ranged from twenty-five to fifty. She'd be in the lower half of the upper decade, but that was alright.

From the parking lot, when she arrived, Eve could hear the steady beat of the music blaring inside the club. Stepping out of her beige Shadow, she shivered in the November chill!. The skirt she was wearing wasn't exactly intended for warmth.

Even at forty-three, her legs looked good in mini-skirts. Her figure was trim, and her face was free of wrinkles. She could easily have passed for thirty-five.

The cigarette smoke hung heavily in the air as Eve stepped into the club. Looking at the stir of humanity around her, Eve clutched her evening jacket to her chest. Maybe this wasn't such a good idea after all. When she saw the gray-bearded bartender motioning to her, she almost turned to leave.

"Are you the lady who called? If you're Eve, there's a lady here named Carla who already has a table. I told her I'd steer you her way when you got here. That's her over there."

The woman the bartender was pointing to was even more petite than Eve, and several years Eve's senior. Her face had a hard quality, as if she'd led a troubled life. Her features reminded Eve of an actress from the forties—Betty? Barbra? Yes Barbra. The woman looked like a smaller version of Barbra Stanwyck, except that she had long platinum hair that Eve suspected was a wig.

Approaching Carla's table, Eve debated what to say. She wasn't at all sure about this. She'd never known of a club before where they matched unattached women for safety's sake or to make them feel more comfortable. "Excuse me," she said, raising her voice to be heard above the Michael Jackson song. "Are you Carla? The bartender said—"

"You must be Eve," Carla said loudly. "Have a seat."

Judging from the fifty or so couples gyrating out on the dance floor, Eve commented that they were lucky to have a table.

"I came early," Carla shouted.

Settling in, Eve hung her evening jacket over the back of her chair and laid her evening bag on the table. The volume of the music was deafening.

During the next three hours, the newfound friends danced several dances. But mostly they chose to sit and shout to make themselves heard above the music. Eve was amazed at how many things they had in common. By the end of the evening, they had formed a budding kinship, and agreed to have Thanksgiving dinner together. Eve would have preferred to cook dinner for herself and Kevin, but Kevin was going with Tom and Lorraine to spend Thanksgiving with Lorraine's relatives in Stockton.

Throughout the time she and Carla were visiting, Eve kept an eye on the blonde man at the next table. He couldn't have been taller than five feet eight. But his smile reminded Eve of Robert Redford. When he finally asked her to dance, Eve returned his Redford grin with a dazzling smile of her own.

"I wanted to ask you to dance earlier," Ted said. "But you and your friend were talking, and I didn't want to interrupt."

As they climbed the steps to the raised dance floor, Eve said a mental "thank you" to Gideon for talking her into coming tonight...

By the time Eve was ready to leave the club, she and Ted had exchanged phone numbers, and he'd promised to call tomorrow. Back at the table, Eve waited for Carla to return from the restroom.

"That guy you were dancing with was kind of cute," Carla commented. "Did you give him your phone number?"

"I gave him mine, and he gave me his," Eve replied. "He said he'll call me tomorrow."

"Famous last words," Carla groaned. "Do you really think he'll call?"

Before Carla's skeptical comment, it hadn't occurred to Eve that he wouldn't. "I hope so," she replied. "I don't know any eligible men in this area. It would be nice to have someone to date."

When Eve got home that night, the first thing she did was kick off her shoes and sit down on the floor by the coffee table. The pendulum began to swing as soon as she picked it up. "How did you like Carla?"

Surprised that Carla, not Ted, was to be the topic of conversation, Eve shrugged. "I liked her. We exchanged phone numbers, and we're going to have Thanksgiving dinner together. She doesn't have any family around here either."

"How do you know you're not talking to Satan?"

Stunned by the question, Eve put down the pendulum long enough to close her eyes and surround herself with light. When she picked the pendulum up again, she asked the speaker to identify himself and to state whether he was of the light.

"That's more like it," Gideon said. 'I'm Gideon, and I'm of the light. And I want to introduce you to Caruso."

The statement surprised Eve. She recognized the name, and knew Caruso to be the spirit guide in training who had trouble controlling his power and distinguishing between past, present, and future; the one who had presented a past event in Kevin's life as something that was going to happen in the future.

"Thank you so much for giving me the honor of letting me talk to you through this pendulum," Caruso gushed. "I've never talked through a pendulum before. As a matter of fact, you're the first human I've talked to since I was alive on earth." As fast as the pendulum was swinging, Eve wondered if Caruso ever paused for breath. "I wanted to tell you how sorry I am for worrying you when there was no need. I never would have worried you like that if I had known. I can't believe I could have been so—"

"It's alright," Eve interrupted. "Gideon explained."

"I'm sorry," Caruso said. "Sometimes I get carried away. It's just that I'm such a klutz. I'm never going to get to another level if I can't even learn to control my power or tell time! You just don't know what it's like here, having everything happening at once. I mean right now, for me, you're talking to me through the pendulum, but you're still at the dance club, and you're laying in bed dreaming about the book you want to write. It's so confusing. Is it cold where you are? You have goosebumps on your skin."

Eve did indeed have goosebumps. Though the owner of the house she was staying in had left her most of the furniture, she had turned off the gas, so the house had no heat. Judging from the rate the temperature was already dropping, tonight was going to be a cold one. Eve would have to use her hair dryer again to heat the sheets before she climbed into bed. She was grateful that Tom and Lorraine had found this house sitting position for her right next door to them, where all she had to pay was the phone and electric. But she would be glad when she found a job so she could get an apartment and have her brother-in-law ship her furniture here. She was lucky to have been able to store her furniture indefinitely in one of the trailers at his

Southern California truck yard. As soon as she was ready, he would deliver her things.

Eve had made the move back to Sacramento on a wing and a prayer to be near her son. Up to this point, the relocation had proven to be disappointing. Kevin was into his high school friends, and rarely seemed to have time for her. He hadn't even spoken up and suggested to his dad and Lorraine that he spend Thanksgiving with his mom. Who did Tom and Lorraine think she'd be spending the holiday with? Didn't they realize she was *alone*? She had no real friends in the area. Add to this scenario the fact that she was still unemployed, and it didn't exactly add up to security.

But now things were looking up. For starters, she had Gideon—and Caruso, for what he was worth. She'd had them all along of course, but hadn't been aware till now of their existence. Tonight, she'd made a new friend in Carla, and had met a man she might be dating by the weekend.

Suddenly realizing she was still on the board and hadn't been reading a word Caruso was saying, Eve apologized. "I'm afraid I got distracted, Caruso. Would you please put Gideon back on?"

There was a moment of 'silence,' then the pendulum began to swing. "This is Gideon again. I'm glad you took my advice tonight and went to that dance club so you could meet some new people. My job is much easier now that I can talk directly to you instead of trying to put feelings and thoughts into your head. And Sweetheart, I know it's bothering you that this is the first Thanksgiving you'll be spending without Kevin. But don't worry. You're not going to be alone."

It occurred to Eve that Gideon had broken his own rule by just calling himself by name and not requiring her to ask if he was of the light. Having to be so careful was already becoming a pain. But it was comforting to hear from her guardian angel that things were going to be alright.

Raising a hand to stifle a yawn, Eve glanced at the wall clock above the beige sofa. She would probably be warmer if she changed into her flannel nightgown and robe, but she didn't want to interrupt the conversation. A blush stained her cheeks as it suddenly occurred to her that Gideon would be with her when she changed. It wasn't fair that he knew what *she* looked like—both with and without clothes—but she had no idea how to picture *him*.

Reading her thoughts, Gideon apparently couldn't resist a comment. "You look beautiful both with and without clothing. I was *wondering* how long it was going to take you to start wondering what *I* look like."

The blush on Eve's cheeks turned a deeper shade of pink.

"You're cute when you're embarrassed."

Who ever heard of a guardian angel telling his ward she was beautiful—or that she was cute when she was embarrassed? It was almost as if he were *flirting* with her! Something was definitely wrong with this picture. "Are you of the light?" Eve asked suspiciously.

"Yes, I'm of the light." The pendulum shook as if Gideon were laughing. "And the reason most guardian angels don't say that sort of thing is that either they can't communicate with their 'ward,' as you called it, or else they've been an angel so long that they can't appreciate the sight of a good-looking woman."

43

"So are you going to tell me what you look like?" Eve asked. "Or do I have to guess?"

There was a pregnant pause before he began to speak. "I don't have a body as you know it. But when I did have, I was a big man—over six feet tall; not overweight, but muscular. I had sunbleached brown hair and a beard, and I always wore flannel shirts and jeans. I was a farmer back then when I was married to you."

"When you were—*What did you say?*"

For a moment the pendulum hung still, as if Gideon were hesitant to speak. Then it began to swing. "*Damn.* I didn't mean for that to slip out. I wasn't ever supposed to tell you that. Now I'm going to be in trouble with the Boss."

The last thing Eve wanted was for Gideon to get in trouble, but she couldn't just let this drop! "What did you *mean* when you said we were *married?*"

From next door, Eve heard Tom's car turn in at the driveway. Apparently he and Lorraine had been out tonight too. What would Tom think if he knew what she was doing right now? The pendulum, as yet, had not moved in answer to her question. When it did, it had quite a story to tell:

"We were married in the early eighteen hundreds. We lived on a farm, and Kevin was our son. His name was Matt then. He died in a terrible accident. When he was twelve years old, he fell into the grain bin and—He fell into a grain bin and suffocated."

Suffocated! What a horrible way to die! And what did Gideon mean, saying Kevin had been Matt? Eve had never believed in reincarnation. Was Gideon saying it existed?

In her mind, Eve could picture Gideon's face: the strong jaw line, the ruddy complexion above his well-trimmed beard, the tears that had welled in the depths of his brown eyes... "If we were married two hundred years ago," she said quietly, "and Kevin and I were reincarnated, how does it come that *we* had to come back, and *you're* a *guardian angel?*"

"When you died, you could have stayed here and worked your way through the ranks like I did," Gideon replied. "But there were things you felt you could have done better during your life on earth—lessons you felt you should have learned. So you asked to be allowed to try it again. Matt chose to come back so he could experience growing up."

"Give me a break," Eve said. "You can't really expect me to believe this."

"Remember the dreams you used to have as a teen-ager? The ones where you were living in the Old West? You lived on a farm, and your husband looked the way I described myself a little while ago. Why do you think that, even now, flannel shirts turn you on, Eve? Why do you think nearly every man you've been attracted to has brown eyes and a beard?"

Blushing once more, Eve ignored the reference to flannel shirts and beards. She had forgotten the dreams. But she did indeed remember them, now that Gideon mentioned them: dreams of being married to a bearded man in a flannel shirt and form fitting jeans. Gideon hadn't mentioned that his jeans were tight, but that's how Eve had dreamed them. Surely the dreams couldn't have been memories: memories of a previous life!

"You were so beautiful," Gideon said. "You had blonde hair then. Your eyes were the same blue as they are now. And you had the same figure. Your voice even sounded the same: sweet, and sort of sultry. I loved you more than life itself. I still do, Eve. That's why I asked to be your guardian angel."

A sensual stirring began in Eve's loins, causing her to drop the pendulum. It wasn't right that she should be feeling this way about a Heavenly being—or that he should be feeling this way about her! This wasn't the ghost and Mrs. Muir, for Heaven's sake!

Picking up the pendulum again, Eve drew a calming breath. "If what you're saying about how you became my guardian angel is true—and I'm not saying I believe it is…" Her words were cut short by the ringing of the phone. Putting the thought on hold, she picked up the receiver.

"Hey, Mom. You weren't asleep, were you?"

Eve's mind was still reeling from what Gideon had told her. She had to force herself to concentrate on what her son was saying.

"No," she answered. "I went out dancing, and just got home. I'm—I'm wide awake."

"You just sound a little strange," Kevin said. "Are you sure you're okay?"

"I'm fine," Eve lied. "Just a little tired. What's up?"

Remembering the sensual thrill that had swept through her body when Gideon told her he loved her more than life itself, Eve blushed. He'd been speaking purely in a spiritual sense. She knew that. So why did she feel as if he'd just asked her to make love? *Get a grip*, she chided herself.

"I called that psychic, Myra," Kevin said. "She jumped all over my ass, telling me to stay away from the dudes I hang out with. What have you been telling her?"

Myra? Eve thought numbly. *Jumping on Kevin's ass?* "I haven't been telling her *anything*, Kevin. Whatever information she got, she didn't get it from me."

"Well whoever she's getting it from," Kevin said irritably, "I wish they'd stay out of my business."

Eve could hear the anger in her son's voice. But she was certain she heard frustration as well. "Whatever Myra said to you, she was only trying to help."

"Yeah, well, I wish you'd call her tomorrow and tell her I don't want or *need* her help."

Eve hadn't expected Myra to come down so hard on Kevin. It was obvious Myra had no teen-agers of her own. If she did, she would have been more tactful. "I'll call her," Eve said quietly. "Right now, how about if we change the subject? Where did you go tonight? What have you been doing?"

"Just hanging out," Kevin said evasively. "I thought maybe you'd want to have lunch together this weekend since we won't be having dinner together on Thanksgiving."

Once again Eve was struck by the lack of sensitivity on Tom and Lorraine's part—planning to take Kevin to have Thanksgiving with Lorraine's relatives when his real mom would be eating alone, if not for her newfound friendship with Carla.

"Yes," Eve said tiredly. "I'd like to do lunch. In the meantime, you could drop over for a visit now and then. I'm just next door, you know." She might have added that she couldn't very well go over *there* to visit, considering that it was Tom and Lorraine's house now.

"Yeah, well… Maybe I'll stop in after school tomorrow," Kevin said. "I love you."

"And I love you, Sweetheart. Very very much." Even though she sometimes felt she no longer knew him, Eve felt a flood of warmth for her son. "Sleep tight, Sweetheart. Goodnight."

That night Eve dreamed she had written a novel and become a best selling author. With the $50,000 advance and royalties rolling in, she no longer needed to look for a job. When she woke in the morning to the ringing of the phone, she was still on the brink of destitution.

The voice on the other end of the phone was Ted's, asking if she'd like to go to lunch. He'd left his own car in Europe when he was working overseas, so she'd need to pick him up…

Chapter 11

The Tuesday before Thanksgiving began with a phone call from the personnel department of a legal firm where Eve had applied for a position of Word Processor/Dictaphone Transcriptionist.

"Could you come for an interview this afternoon?" the receptionist asked.

Could she? She'd be there with bells on!

The large white building took up half an acre in the outskirts of the city. The gold carpet smelled new. Combined with the modern art on the walls, the plushness of the carpet gave a feeling of wealth. Eve had dressed in a gray suit with a red silk scarf and red heels that matched her shoulder bag. Stepping up to the reception desk, she identified herself and waited for the blonde receptionist to notify the personnel director she'd arrived.

The interview went well, and Eve was hired on the spot. She would start work a week from Monday. It wasn't a prestigious position. She'd be working under Lauren, the executive secretary who reported indirectly to the president of the firm. The salary would be less than what Eve had been used to as a secretary in L.A., but at least she'd be bringing in a paycheck. And the benefits were good.

When Carla called that evening, Eve had just hung up from talking to her mother, and was seated at the dining room table munching a take-out burrito. "So?" Carla said. "Did you get the job?"

"Yes!" Eve said excitedly. "I was going to call and tell you, but I didn't think you'd be home yet. I start a week from Monday." When she'd talked with her mother, Eve had said nothing of having visited a psychic to ask advice on her employment situation. She had no such compunctions about mentioning it to Carla. Carla had told her at the dance club that she, herself, had had a number of psychic experiences. "The psychic told me I'd been working before the end of the month," Eve said. "It looks like she was right."

"Who did you go to?" Carla asked eagerly. "I've been thinking of going for a reading, myself. But I don't want to go to anyone that's not reputable."

They talked on the phone for nearly two hours. Before she knew it, Eve found herself telling her new friend the details of her psychic session with Myra, and how Myra had said she must find a way for her spirit guides to communicate.

"That sounds pretty far out to me." The tone of Carla's voice was wary. "Are you going to try it?"

Despite the fact there was no one to hear, Eve lowered her voice to a whisper. "I already have. I couldn't figure how else to do it, so I made a pendulum from a chain and an earring."

The proverbial pin could have been heard dropping as Eve described how the pendulum had begun to swing over each letter of the arc, and how precisely it had stopped at the end of each sentence. Even now, the feeling was surreal, to think that she'd actually carried on a two-way dialogue with her guardian angel.

"Do you think I could talk to mine?" Carla asked in a hushed voice. "I mean, do you think this would work for everyone?"

"I don't see why not," Eve said with a shrug. "If mine can swing a pendulum, I suppose yours could too. But there are rules you have to follow. Apparently you can get into trouble if you don't follow the rules."

Talking to Carla was so easy. Eve felt as if they'd known one another for years. The last thing discussed before they hung up was the menu for Thanksgiving dinner.

When Ted called after Eve and Carla had hung up, he said he'd been trying to get through for over an hour. They talked till well after midnight, and ended by agreeing to have lunch together tomorrow. Eve would have to take *her* car, of course. Not only did Ted not have a car: he didn't even have an apartment yet. He was living in a motel in the outskirts of Sacramento until he made a decision of whether to stay in the States or return to Europe. In the meantime, since he had no family or friends in the area, he told Eve he was glad he'd met her, and only wished they'd met before she'd made plans to spend Thanksgiving with Carla.

It occurred to Eve to invite Ted to join them, but she didn't want to do that until she'd had a chance to ask Carla how she felt about it. When she asked, she could tell by Carla's response that she wasn't comfortable with the idea of making it a threesome.

As luck would have it, Carla called to cancel just a day and a half before Thanksgiving. Her son had called from San Jose and asked her to have dinner with him and his family. If Eve had been in Carla's position, she would have told her son and his family that she'd already made plans with a friend for dinner, and suggested that she drive to San Jose for the weekend to visit. Apparently that didn't occur to Carla.

Submerged in a case of the doldrums, Eve considered calling Ted. But he'd probably made other plans by now. She didn't want to put him on the spot. The last thing she wanted was his pity.

She could see it all now, just her and the spirits, having Thanksgiving dinner together. Conversation would be a little one-sided, with Eve having to lay down her fork and pick up the pendulum at the end of each sentence...

Thanksgiving morning, Ted called to wish Eve a happy holiday. When Eve told him about Carla's change of plans, Ted asked her to have dinner with *him* at an all-you-can-eat buffet. It seemed he hadn't made plans after all. Gideon had been right about Eve's not having to spend Thanksgiving alone.

Thanksgiving with Ted was fun. Eve enjoyed looking at his pictures of Europe, and hearing stories of his adventures in Spain. Ted enjoyed hearing the plot of Eve's novel that she'd begun years ago, but placed on hold. The turkey was dry, and the pumpkin pie was awful. But compared to the turkey potpie Eve would have been eating if she'd stayed home, the meal was a real feast.

The next few days moved very quickly for Eve. With Ted's help, she found an apartment just three blocks from her new job. It was a large apartment complex with a rec building and Olympic sized pool. Eve's apartment was on the second floor, overlooking a park-like area of grass and hot pink rose bushes.

Dressed in jeans, baggy sweatshirts and tennies, Eve and Ted were sitting on the living room floor, leaning against a bare white wall. The apartment's only furnishings—a birch end table, a twenty-eight inch T.V. with stand, a portable stereo, and a brass table lamp were lined up against the opposite wall. "I can hardly wait for my furniture to get here," Eve said with a tired smile. "I hate the thought of sleeping on the floor in an empty apartment." Her voice sounded hollow in the nearly empty room.

"What all do you have coming when your furniture gets here?" Ted asked. Seen at close range, Ted didn't really resemble Robert Redford. His hair was shorter than Redford's, and he was built on a smaller scale. But he still had that winning smile.

"When my son Kevin and I were living in L.A., we were renting my sister's furnished condo," Eve said. "My bedroom and living room furniture went to my ex. So all I really have coming that I couldn't fit into the car when I came is a single bed, a dresser, a coffee table, another end table, and a dining room set."

"Then you don't actually have a couch or a chair?"

"Not till I get a paycheck," Eve groaned. "I suppose when it gets here I could put some big pillows on the single bed and use that as a sofa till I can afford to buy one." Eve wondered what Ted must think of a woman who'd given up a well-paying job to move to a city where her future was so uncertain. She supposed if he'd ever had children, he might understand.

"I know where you can pick up an easy chair for twenty-five dollars," Ted said. "I saw it in the window of a used furniture store. If you can swing the twenty-five dollars, we could drive by this afternoon and see if it's still there."

"If *you* can get it up the stairs to this apartment, *I* can swing the twenty-five dollars. Maybe we could stop at a craft store on the way back, and pick up some silk plants for the living room."

For a used chair, the brown recliner was in excellent condition. The only flaw Eve could find was a small scratch on the wooden trim on the front of one padded arm. A little dab of scratch remover would take care of that. Maybe she could even sleep in the chair until her bed arrived.

It took both of them to carry the heavy recliner up the stairs. Halfway up, Eve wondered if they were going to make it all the way without snagging the chair on the stair rail or knocking off one of the small wooden legs. When they got to the landing, Ted told her to let go. He could carry it the rest of the way himself. Eve didn't argue the point.

When the chair had been deposited in the living room, Eve scooted the end table next to it, and put the brass lamp on the table. On the opposite wall, she positioned the T.V., and put the portable stereo on the shelf underneath the stand. It wasn't exactly the Ritz, but at least she'd be entertained.

When the time came for Ted to leave, Eve hugged him and would have given him a kiss for his help, but theirs appeared to be slated to be a platonic relationship.

After Ted had gone, Eve surrounded herself with the imaginary white light and picked up the pendulum. "Oh, Gideon," she said with a sigh. "Who would have thought it would come to this? I've got a boyfriend who has no desire to touch me. I'm living in a virtually empty apartment. I've found a job, but my income will only be half what I was making as a secretary in L.A."

"This is Gideon, and I'm of the light. Feeling sorry for yourself won't accomplish a thing," the pendulum spelled out. "There are plenty of people worse off than you. You have a roof over your head, a girlfriend who loves to talk on the phone, a man who wants to help you, and you're within half an hour's distance of your son. True, Ted doesn't have a pot to piss in himself. But that's because he's new to the area just like you are."

Doesn't have a pot to piss in? What kind of talk was that for a guardian angel?

"Ted's guardian angel and I are pals," Gideon said. "We figured if we put you two together, you could drive Ted where he needs to go, and he could buy *your* meals."

Eve had thought she'd attracted Ted on her own! She didn't like the idea she'd had supernatural help. "If you were going to choose a man for me, at least you could have picked one who'd be physically attracted to me. Today we spent the entire day together, and he didn't even try to hold my hand. I'm wondering if he's gay."

"Don't look a gift horse in the mouth," the pendulum spelled out. "Ted needs you. You need him. Make the most of it. And no, I didn't pick him because I'm jealous."

The thought that had just occurred to Eve, which Gideon had apparently read, was that he had deliberately chosen a man he knew wouldn't want to get romantically involved with her.

Later that evening, Eve put the phone next to the recliner, and lay back as far as the chair would recline to try to clear her mind. She would need all the sleep she could get tonight. She was starting her new job in the morning. At one a.m., the phone rang. "Mom? 'Sorry to call you so late. I just got home. I hope you weren't asleep."

Eve didn't understand why Tom and Lorraine were allowing Kevin to stay out so late. But Kevin was living with *them* now. She didn't feel she had the right to interfere. "I was asleep, but that's okay."

"Something really cool happened today," Kevin said. "I just wanted to share it with you…'

They talked for well over an hour. It wasn't the same as living in the same house, but phone calls and weekly lunches were better than living three hundred miles away, even if the phone calls *were* normally at midnight or one in the morning.

Three months later:

With Lauren on vacation, Eve had been filling in for the week, reporting to the executive assistant who served as a middleman between Lauren and the firm's president. It seemed to Eve things were going well. Today, despite the constant ringing of the phone, she'd already typed nine memos and more than a dozen error-free letters, which she had placed in the basket for Margaret's approval.

But Margaret wasn't pleased with her performance. A memo from yesterday had apparently been typed on the wrong form. Eve had not been trained in what forms to use. She was expected to choose the appropriate form, based on the content of each memo. Likewise, she was expected to infer the appropriate greeting and salutation for each recipient. It seemed to Eve a bit much to expect that she would never make a mistake. Now she'd been called into Margaret's office, and Margaret was definitely not happy.

"When you were hired, it was with the understanding you had the skills to take over if Lauren couldn't be here," Margaret said coldly. "So far you've proven to be totally incompetent."

The false statement hit Eve squarely between the eyes. "How can you say I'm incompetent when I've finished every Dictaphone tape you've put in my basket, and more?"

"I didn't say you couldn't *type*," Margaret said, dismissing Eve's protest with a wave of her hand. "But for what we're paying you, I expect more than a typist. Lauren is supposed to have trained you. I don't have time to go over instructions half a dozen times and still have you make mistakes!" Eve thought the gray-haired woman was through, but that was wishful thinking. "Two of this morning's memos have to be done over," Margaret spat. "One was missing a comma, and one had two spaces under the heading when there should have been three." Shoving the memos in Eve's direction, Margaret averted her head.

The memos had been marked in red ink. A huge circle had been drawn at the insertion point for the missing comma. Having majored in English in college, Eve knew that a comma in this case was optional. A note in large bold letters had been written in the margin regarding the missing space.

"I'm sorry," Eve said. "I'll try to be more careful in the future." It galled her to have to kowtow to this woman when the missing comma was unnecessary, and the memo was perfectly balanced just as she'd typed it. If she'd thought Gideon would do it for her, she would have asked him to zap her out of this mess without having to listen to anymore of Margaret's bull.

"Sheridan wants to see you in her office," Margaret said curtly. "I don't know what she wants, but I can assure you, she's not happy." Sheridan was the executive vice president, and Margaret's immediate supervisor.

How could a day that had started out so well have degenerated into this? Before Lauren had gone on vacation, there hadn't been a single complaint about Eve's work in the nearly three months she'd been here. On the contrary, she'd become accustomed to praise. Now, it seemed she could do nothing right. Heart in her throat, Eve crossed the hall and tapped on Sheridan's door. "You wanted to see me?"

The V.P.'s office was richly paneled, furnished with a large oak desk and credenza. "There was no coffee at the staff meeting this morning," Sheridan said in a clipped voice. She was a thin woman with a severe hairstyle and a suit that looked like it had been designed for a man. "When I started to make a pot myself, there was mould in the coffee pot!"

Eve had no idea what she was expected to say.

"Well?" Sheridan said. "I'm assuming you must have some sort of explanation."

"No," Eve said softly. "I don't know what all this has to do with me."

"It's Lauren's job to see that there's a fresh pot of coffee for bi-monthly executive staff meetings," Sheridan said with exaggerated calmness. "When Lauren's not here, that responsibility falls to you."

"But no one told me that," Eve protested. "How was I expected to know?" Eve had noticed Sheridan's cologne when she entered the office. Now the scent of Today's Woman was overwhelming.

"Did it ever occur to you to check Lauren's calendar? If you had, you would have seen that it said Executive Staff Meeting at nine."

Eve hadn't even known Lauren *had* a calendar. "Even if I'd known about the meeting, I wouldn't have known about the coffee."

"Lauren and Margaret should have told you," Sheridan said curtly. "You can go now, Eve. I'll take this up with Margaret."

It wasn't long after the incident with the coffee pot that the position of Lauren's assistant was eliminated, and Eve received her final paycheck. There were other personnel shifts as well, including demotions and transfers to other departments. But since Eve had the least seniority, she was the one to go.

Sobbing and totally demoralized, Eve slumped onto the platform rocker and tearfully filled herself with light, then leaned forward to reach for the pendulum on the snack tray serving as a table. "How could you let this happen without warning me, Gideon?"

"This is Gideon, and I'm of the light. Sweetheart, there was nothing I could do. Margaret needed a scapegoat. When Sheridan called her on the carpet, she blamed everything on you."

Eve's eyes were swollen, and her cheeks were splotched, the forerunner of a sinus headache. "You must have seen this coming," she sobbed. "You shouldn't have kept it from me."

"Sweetheart, calm down," Gideon said. "I hate to see you like this. You know I had no way of talking to you at work. As of last night, I saw the possibility of this happening. But the probability was less than seventy-five percent. There was no point in getting you upset over something that might not even happen."

It was the first Eve had been told about "probabilities." It would not be the last.

Within a week of Eve's job loss, Ted was transferred back to Europe. Ted had been a good friend. Eve would miss his company and his Redford smile.

Though Eve turned her application in with several firms and signed up with five temporary agencies, she was lucky to get two days' work a week.

Discouraged and despondent, she still continued to go dancing at a local singles club. Sometimes she went with Carla. Sometimes she went alone. Dancing and the positive attention she got there were all that saw her through.

One particularly dreary evening, Carla called and asked if Eve was going to go to the open dance at Parents Without Partners. Once a month, the singles club Eve and Carla both belonged to held an open dance that non-club-members could attend. Eve didn't normally care for open dances. "I don't think so," she said gloomily. "You know how those open dances are. Anyone there worth dancing with is already married."

"I'm going with my apartment manager and a friend from my apartments," Carla said. "Why don't you come and join us?"

When Eve demurred, Carla continued to press. "Think about it," she said. "Even if there aren't a lot of single men to dance with, you'll be part of the group and it'll be fun to talk."

Too depressed to accomplish anything at home, Eve made the decision to put on her dance clothes and at least put in an appearance. She had an entire array of flared dance skirts and matching turtleneck tops in varying colors, but she always wore the same pair of shoes: a pair of black one-inch heels with a strap across the heel. Giving her appearance a last once-over in the mirror, Eve picked up her evening bag and headed for the door. If she didn't enjoy herself once she got there, she could always leave and come home. "Okay, Gideon," she said with a forced smile. "Let's go dancing."

When Eve arrived at the Mechanics Hall, more than half the tables were already full, but there were a couple of empty tables up front. Eve liked sitting in front, and always came to the dances early to be assured of a good seat. She was headed for a front table when she heard someone call her name.

"Eve! Over here!" It was Carla, and she was seated at a table with a full-bosomed brunette and a large red-bearded man. Smiling, Eve crossed the room to the table where Carla was sitting, and sat down in the chair Carla had saved for her.

"Eve," Carla said with a bright smile, "This is Ella. She's the manager of my apartment complex. And this is Whit Neucomb. Whit's our handyman."

Carla was looking unusually pretty tonight. Instead of her usual platinum wig, she had chosen a shorter frosted style. The plunging neckline of Ella's red jumpsuit left nothing to the imagination. Whit was wearing a sports jacket and slacks— overdressed for regular P.W.P. functions, but appropriate for an open dance.

Eve's seat was directly across from Ella's, with Carla to her left, Whit to her right. Apparently Ella had a thing for Whit. At any rate, she was making an effort to monopolize his attention, leaning forward as she spoke, to give him an unobstructed view of her breasts.

Eve had been there perhaps an hour chatting with Carla, when Whit finally turned away from the apartment manager and asked if she would like to dance. Surprised, Eve accepted the invitation and walked ahead of Whit to the dance floor. The song was a slow one. When Whit pulled her close, the top of Eve's head reached the center of his chest. The faint scent of his cologne was pleasant, but not overpowering. For such a large man, Eve was surprised at Whit's grace. "You follow really well," he said into her hair.

It wasn't the first complement Eve had received on her ability to follow. She took it as a point of pride to be able to follow any man on the dance floor. She and Whit danced to several songs—not doing much talking; just enjoying the way their bodies seemed to meld.

"I'm going to ask the D.J. to play an East Coast Swing," Whit said. "Stay right here. I'll be right back."

By the time the swing dance was finished, Eve was winded. Whit was a strong leader, and had led her through every swing dance step she knew, plus a few combinations she'd never seen. Exhilarated, she allowed him to lead her back to the table. This might turn out to be a fun evening after all...

When Eve got home that night, she took out the pendulum and filled herself with light. "What do you think, Gideon? Do you like Whit?"

The pendulum began to swing. "You didn't ask if I'm of the light."

"Okay, okay," Eve said tiredly. "Please identify yourself, and tell me whether you're of the light."

"Yes, I'm of the light," Gideon answered. "Whit's okay, I guess. He's not my favorite of the men you've been with, but he'll do till someone better comes along."

Gideon's comment was less than enthusiastic, but at least he hadn't said anything totally negative.

Eve and Whit went dancing the following night, and the next night they went out to dinner. Conversation with Whit was easy. Despite the fact he was a bit of a bigot, he and Eve shared a lot of the same goals and philosophies. Before either of them realized it, they had fallen into the habit of talking every evening on the phone and seeing each other at least four times a week. What had begun as a casual acquaintance turned into an affair.

Eve knew that sooner or later she was going to have to talk this thing out with Gideon. Having a boyfriend was one thing. Having an affair was quite another. It wasn't like Gideon to avoid a subject—particularly one as important as this.

Finally, Eve could take it no longer. "Alright, Gideon. Talk to me. I know you have to be dying to comment on the fact that I'm having an affair with Whit. This is your chance. I'm asking you. Tell me what you're thinking."

"Gideon here. I'm of the light. Does it really *matter* to you what I think?"

It sounded to Eve like Gideon was jealous.

"I heard that," Gideon said. "You seem to have forgotten, I'm your *guardian angel*."

"I haven't forgotten," Eve replied. "It's just that I know how you feel about me. I feel the same about you. But you're there, and I'm here, and we can't change that. As a *human*, I need to have *physical* relationships, even though you might not approve."

"That's why I haven't stopped you," Gideon said, "though I'll have to admit I've been tempted."

"Tempted because you don't like Whit? Or tempted because you're jealous?" Eve teased.

"Don't get smart," the pendulum spelled out. "Whit's a decent enough guy. He likes a lot of the same things you do, and he won't do you any harm."

Eve was glad they had had this little talk, but there was one thing more that needed to be said. "Sometimes I get the feeling you're watching my every move, even when Whit and I—even when I'd rather not be watched."

"I'm you're guardian angel," Gideon said. "It's my job to watch over you. Do you want me to get in trouble for not doing my job?"

Though Eve didn't argue the point, she couldn't help feeling that his job could still be done without having to get so up close and personal when she wasn't even in danger...

Over the next six months, Eve got by financially by going out on temporary job assignments. In every case, the employers liked her work and put in a request to have her back, in the event they needed another temp. But none of the companies were hiring full-time.

There were numerous interviews in which Eve wasn't even considered because she was over-qualified. In three interviews, she was one of the two finalists. Two potential employers made the "difficult decision" to hire her competition. The other said the job was Eve's if she could just pass one more test. Eve passed it. But the applicant with the flirtier smile got the job.

"What's wrong with me, Gideon? In Southern California, I was doing fine. But since I left to come here, everything's gone downhill."

"How can you say everything's gone downhill?" Gideon chided. "You have your furniture here now. You've bought a love seat and a decent bed, and fixed up your apartment to look really cozy. You have a steady boyfriend, a woman friend, and you're seeing Kevin twice a week." Here he paused, as if for breath. When Eve didn't comment, Gideon went on. "Temporary work assignments are getting you through. What do you have to complain about?"

"I'm living from hand to mouth!" Eve said emotionally. "I need a decent job with benefits and a steady paycheck!"

"The job you're destined for is coming," Gideon assured her. "You just need to be patient awhile longer. Unfortunately, patience has never been one of your stronger suits."

Chapter 12

With a renewed determination to find something more than temporary work, Eve walked down to the newsstand in front of the rec center the next morning and bought a newspaper. In the want ads column was a job as a legal secretary. "No legal experience required."

Eve called to schedule an interview, and went in that afternoon.

The law offices were unimpressive. The carpet was wearing thin in spots, and office personnel other than the attorneys had metal desks. The attorney in charge was a tall, thin, balding man with wire-rimmed glasses and a Midwestern accent. "We're really in a bind here," he said. "The workload is several months behind. But with your typing speed, I think you could do it. You should be able to get us caught up in a couple of weeks."

Eve had been given a typing test before the interview, and had scored 85 words a minute with no errors. If typing was the main thing they needed, she was definitely up to the task. But she had no knowledge of legal forms and terminology.

"Don't worry about that," Stanton said. "The secretary who's leaving will train you."

The harried secretary, though she did her best to find time to train Eve, did well to have five minutes at a time between phone calls. Not even enough time to familiarize Eve with the forms, let alone train her to do the job. "I really apologize for leaving you this mess to start with," June said. "You see what it's like with these phone calls. I can barely get the dictation and Dictaphone correspondence typed. That's why that stack of forms on the credenza is over twelve inches tall! I can't believe Stanton told you no legal experience is needed."

When June told Eve she was leaving day after tomorrow, Eve nearly choked. "I can't take over doing these legal forms, when I don't even know what they are!"

"I'm sorry to leave you in the lurch like this," June said. "When I gave my notice a month ago, I told Mr. Stanton he needed to get someone in here in time to get them trained before I leave. Even if he'd brought a girl in today to handle the *phones*, it would have *helped*. But no. He thinks the job is a piece of cake. That's how much he knows."

That evening, Eve stayed two hours after quitting time in an effort to catch up on the routine typing. When she got home, Whit was standing by her carport waiting.

"Whit!" Eve said in surprise. "What are you doing here?"

"We were supposed to start country western dance lessons tonight," Whit said angrily.

Damn. Eve had been so stressed over work she'd forgotten all about it. "I'm sorry, Whit. Today was my first day on my new job, and I had to work over. I forgot all about the dance lesson." Even to her own ears, it sounded like a lame excuse.

By the time they arrived at the dance club, the dance lesson was nearly over. Though he went through the motions, Whit was in a foul mood the entire evening, and made no effort to hide it.

As weeks passed and they continued the dance lessons, there were other times Eve was late or had to cancel. Finally, Whit issued an ultimatum. "I can't take this, Eve. This is three times this month you've been late. If this keeps up, we might as well drop the class."

The night air was cold, and Eve was shivering beneath her coat in the carport outside her apartment. "I'm sorry, Whit. You know how much I enjoy the class. But I *have* to make a success of this job, and I just can't seem to get caught up—not with the phones, and Stanton adding to the stack of forms everyday…"

"This can't go on, Eve. I'm not going to play second fiddle to anybody's job."

Eve felt that Whit was being unreasonable. It wasn't her fault she was overwhelmed at the office. He knew her financial dilemma. Why couldn't he at least try to understand?

The next time they were due to go for a dance lesson, it was Whit who called to cancel. "I had an accident today. I fell off a roof." His voice sounded weak—barely audible.

Eve's stomach constricted in a knot of concern. "How badly were you hurt?"

"I don't know," Whit said. "I think I may have broken some ribs."

"I'll be right there," Eve said tensely.

The drive to Whit's apartment took approximately fifteen minutes. By the time Eve arrived, Whit had gone to bed.

"Tell me what happened," Eve said. "Was it the roof of your apartment building? How did you fall?"

The roof Whit had fallen from had been one he was repairing for a friend who lived in a residential area near the mall. "She's that old lady I told you about that's psychic," Whit said. "It was really weird. I slipped on some wet leaves and fell off her roof, but instead of hitting the ground I landed over a redwood fence before I fell the rest of the way. It hurt like hell, and knocked the wind out of me. But Nell took me into her house and put her hands on me. She said a bunch of words I couldn't understand, then she told me to go home, and said I'm going to be alright."

"But you may have some broken bones," Eve argued. "You need to go to the emergency room for x-rays."

Though Whit protested, Eve finally won out. Besides his ribs and shoulder, he had hurt his knee and ankle. So getting him down the stairs and into her car was almost more than Eve could manage. When she got to the hospital emergency entrance, Eve got out of the Shadow and asked an orderly to help.

The wait in the lobby seemed interminable to Eve. Finally a nurse came out to tell her Whit wanted her to be with him. Eve hated the sights and smells of hospitals. She'd hated visiting hospitals, even as a child. She couldn't imagine how anyone could work in this atmosphere day after day. When she saw Whit lying there with his shirt off and his ribs taped, she crossed to his bed and laid a cool hand on his arm. "How are you feeling?"

"Sore," Whit said. "But there are no broken bones. The doctor said he can't understand it. He couldn't even find a bruise. I guess it must have been that mojo Nel did when she took me in her house and said those words over me."

An eerie feeling crept up Eve's spine. She didn't know what sort of 'mojo' Whit was talking about. But whatever it was, it was no substitute for medical attention. "Are they going to keep you overnight for observation, or will they let me take you home?"

"I'm supposed to lay here till the doc comes back to tell me I can go," Whit said weakly. "I don't think I'm going to be dancing for awhile."

Eve was disappointed to hear that they wouldn't be able to continue their dance lessons, but her main concern was for Whit. It was well after midnight by the time she got home. But she went directly to the board to talk to Gideon. "What about this old woman, Gideon? Whit said she said a bunch of words over him that he didn't understand."

"This is Gideon, and I'm of the light. Sweetheart, it was black magic. Whit doesn't know it, and it won't do any good for you to tell him, but Nell is in it up to her ears. I want you to stay away from her. Don't let her do a psychic reading for you even if Whit suggests it."

The next morning at the office, Eve could hardly keep her eyes open.

As the days wore on, despite heroic efforts on her part, Eve fell farther and farther behind in her work. If only the phones would stop ringing for ten minutes! The constant tension was wearing on her nerves.

And then Whit's mother died. Two days later, Gideon asked if she could talk to Eve through the board. "I'll have to swing the pendulum for her. But she's worried about how Whit's taking the news. That's why she wants to talk to you."

Nell had already asked Whit if he wanted to talk to his mother through her. The thought of being contacted by his dead mother's soul had freaked Whit out, to the point of causing a rift between him and his psychic friend.

"His mom already knows you can't tell Whit that you've spoken to her," Gideon said. "But she wants to talk to you anyway."

Eve couldn't believe she was being asked to converse with the soul of a woman whose body was still in the funeral home.

"I'm glad Whit has you to be with him in his time of sorrow," the pendulum spelled out. "I was in a lot of pain on earth, but I'm better off now. I hope you'll be patient with Whit while he's trying to come to terms with his grief."

"Of course I will," Eve said softly.

"Thank you," the pendulum spelled. "You're very sweet." And then the pendulum was silent.

Over the next several days, Eve spent countless hours either *with* Whit, or talking with him on the phone. But still the long hours at work continued cutting into the time Whit wanted to spend together.

Finally he couldn't take it any longer. "I told you once before that I won't play second fiddle to any woman's job. You need to make a choice, Eve: the job, or me."

Eve was sitting at the dining room table in her baby doll pajamas, sipping a hot chocolate and holding the phone to her ear. She couldn't believe what Whit had just said. "You can't be serious, Whit. You know I need this job. If I don't put in the hours needed to get the work done, I'll get fired!"

"The job or me," Whit repeated.

There was a moment of silence as Eve digested Whit's words. So this was it. He was giving her no choice. "I'm sorry, Whit. But I guess that means we won't be seeing each other anymore."

When Whit replied, his voice was frigid. "Then I guess this is it." Without another word, he hung up the phone.

Though Eve was bewildered by Whit's attitude, and regretted having their six-month relationship end on a sour note, she couldn't say she didn't feel at least a little bit relieved. Whit had reached the point of dropping hints about the possibility of getting married. He had never once said he loved her, and Eve certainly wasn't in love with *him*. There was no way she'd ever have considered marriage. She just wished it hadn't had to end like this.

The next day Eve called Carla to tell her what had happened. It was Saturday, and Carla drove to her apartment to commiserate. "Let's ask Gideon *his* take on all of this," Carla suggested.

Carla and Gideon had grown to be friends. Gideon often teased with her, through Eve. "Before you take out the board, I think we ought to light a candle," Carla said. "Myra says you should never talk to spirits unless you have a candle so you'll know if there are any dark ones in the room."

Carla had gone for a reading with Myra, and the two of them had clicked. Myra had given Carla a heart-shaped rock that Carla carried with her everywhere.

Eve didn't feel that a candle was necessary, but she took one down from the sconce on the wall and lit it to make Carla feel better. Setting the lighted candle on the coffee table, Eve reached for the board and pendulum. She had long since discarded the tablet page and made a cardboard replacement. Listed in the corner were the names of all the spirits Eve knew to be of the light, and a statement that said: "I'm of the light." This way when one wanted to speak, all he need do was swing the pendulum to his name and then to the statement about the light. It saved a lot of time, and a whole lot of aggravation. The list had actually grown quite long. It seemed Eve had a throng of guiding spirits on various levels, and all were clambering to talk through the board. Gideon had been patient with them thus far, but Eve didn't know how much longer his patience would last.

Gideon didn't have much to say to Carla about Eve's breakup with Whit, other than what he'd already said to Eve in private. "Whit acted like a self-centered jerk. Eve's better off without him."

"I like the way Gideon's so down to earth," Carla said. "You don't need a translation to know what he's saying. I wonder if my guardian angel's like that."

The pendulum swung to Gideon's name, and then to the phrase "I'm of the light." "Tell Carla if she wants to speak to her guardian angel, Joan's right here."

"Joan?" Carla said. "You mean my guardian angel's a woman? I *knew* it!"

"Yes, I represent myself as a woman and I'm of the light," the pendulum spelled out. "Please add my name to the list."

Carla was thrilled to be given the opportunity to talk to her guardian angel. "Let me try to hold the pendulum," she said eagerly.

Eve handed Carla the pendulum, and it began to swing—slowly and laboriously. "It's going so slow that by the time the words are spelled out, I forget what she's trying to say," Carla said. "Here, Eve. You take the pendulum. Let her talk through you."

For the next fifteen minutes, Joan answered Carla's questions, reminding her of incidents from childhood when Carla's rebellious nature had worked for her own good, unwittingly cooperating with Joan's efforts to protect her. "I felt so bad for you when you were growing up," Joan said. "I did my best to protect you, but Satan was working against me every step of the way—in the form of your uncle. You don't know how often I wished I could give you a loving hug."

Carla had shared certain things with Eve from her childhood. But the events Joan referred to were new to Eve. Her heart melted at the tears in Carla's eyes when Joan expressed the desire to hug her.

"You could give me one now," Carla said in a tiny voice.

"Alright," Joan said. "Close your eyes and fold your arms across your chest."

Carla was sitting on the floor by the coffee table. Rising to her knees, she closed her eyes and folded her arms. At first, she apparently felt nothing. But then her lips curved in a dazzling smile.

"I feel a soft touch," she whispered. "Almost like feathers all around me..." Tears were now dribbling down Carla's cheeks. "It's warm, and very comforting. It feels like—It feels like *love*."

Eve couldn't remember when she'd felt so touched. It made her feel like—"Gideon, do you suppose you could give *me* a hug?"

"Sure I'll give you a hug, *bitch*. But first, look at the candle."

What? Speechless with shock, Eve dropped the pendulum. The candle flame was flickering wildly. A dark spirit had apparently managed to get into the apartment. But how? And *why*? What had she done to attract the attention of a spirit of darkness?

"It's the dark spirit that's been following me all my life," Carla said bitterly. In the flickering light from the candle, Carla's face looked as if it had just aged ten years. "All my life, every time I've tried to go to church or take an active part as a Christian, bad things have started to happen. Now it's happening again because I got in touch with my guardian angel."

"It must be because we forgot the protective white light," Eve said shakily. "Blow the candle out, and we'll light it again after we've surrounded ourselves with light."

Carla did as she'd been bidden.

When Eve returned to the board, Gideon identified himself. "I'm sorry you had to experience that Sweetheart. It's time you learned to talk telepathically so we don't have to depend on this damned board."

"But I can't speak telepathically," Eve protested.

"Yes you can," Gideon said urgently. "A guide you haven't met yet has been working with you without your knowledge. You're already halfway there." Ignoring Eve's expression of shock, the pendulum swung on. "This board is too cumbersome, and as long as you have to depend on it, we can't talk to you when you're away from home. You've drawn a lot of attention in the spirit world, Eve. That interruption a few minutes ago was just one example. It's imperative that we be able to get through to you when you need us."

"But I *can't talk telepathically!*"

A previously unknown spirit named Abahdi identified himself and said he was of the light. "As Gideon told you, I've already been working with you. The next step is to speed up communication." Abahdi then began to swing the pendulum with lightning speed, speaking both of things that were familiar to Eve, and of things that were unfamiliar. Eve didn't miss a word.

"You don't even realize it," Abahdi said, but I didn't spell out the words you were reading. I only gave you the first letter of each word. You've been doing this for weeks."

The pendulum swung to Gideon's name, and to the statement "I'm of the light."

Put down the pendulum," Gideon said. "Put down the pendulum and talk to me."

Hands trembling, Eve laid the pendulum on the table.

"Can you hear me?" Gideon said. "This is the sound of my voice." He was speaking to her in her mind—like her own thoughts, only different. His voice was strong and reassuring. It sounded to Eve like the voice of love.

"I heard him," she whispered. "He spoke in my mind, and I heard him, Carla!"

Carla's eyes were as big as silver dollars. "What did he sound like?" she whispered back. Eve was just about to answer, when Carla gasped. "The candle! Look!"

Rising from the candle was a dense pillar of black smoke. The candle was barely half an inch thick, but the pillar was four to five inches in circumference, narrower at the shaft, and thicker at the end. Eve watched from the loveseat, frozen in morbid fascination as the black pillar rose several feet into the air and began to curve.

Viewing it from the side, Carla's face contorted in fright. "It's a black penis!" she gasped. "And it's coming for you!"

How could this be happening? She'd surrounded herself with light!

From Eve's vantage point, as the giant penis came toward her, its tip was as large as a grapefruit! Fear gripped her stomach, and a whimper started low in her throat. As the black penis tip drew closer to her face, Eve shrank against the loveseat. Tears were streaming down her cheeks, and her hands were shaking violently. For one horrifying moment, Eve feared the demonic thing would rape her. Where was Gideon? Why wasn't he protecting her?

"Get out from under it!" Carla shouted.

Inching across the sofa with her back pressed against the cushion, Eve slithered out from under the demon penis and leaped from the couch. Like a periscope, the smoke pillar rose and bent, turning quickly from side to side, in ominous search of its prey.

In a sudden bold move, Carla gathered her courage and streaked across the room to snuff out the candle. The black penis disappeared. But before they could fully comprehend what had happened, Gideon was talking inside Eve's head. "It's still in the house! It's on the loose! You've got to get it out of there!"

"Gideon says it's still here!" Eve shouted.

"Take Carla's hand," Gideon said urgently. "I'll be with you, even though I won't be talking to you. I want you to light another candle for each of you. Don't worry. I won't let anything get in them. Together I want you and Carla to carry your candles with one hand, and hold hands with the other. Walk through each room of the apartment, and watch your candle flames. If the candle flames flicker, I want you to say these words: 'In the name of Jesus, I command you to leave this apartment.' Just stick together, and don't let them scare you."

"Gideon wants us to light a couple more candles," Eve said in a hushed voice. Her blue eyes were enormous, and her skin was as pale as snow. "We're supposed to hold hands and take the candles through each room. If a flame flickers, we're supposed to say 'In the name of Jesus, I command to you leave.'"

Afraid to follow Gideon's advice, but more afraid not to, the two friends did what he had said. "Remember," Carla whispered. "If anything starts to come out of that flame, just snuff it out."

Together with their candles held high, the women held hands and walked through the hallway to the bedroom. The flames didn't flicker till they came near the closet. "It's in there," Carla breathed.

A cold chill crept up the length of Eve's spine. "In the name of Jesus…"

The candles stopped flickering.

"Let's go in the bathroom." Carla whispered.

The candle flames burned steadily through the hallway and in the bathroom. But when they returned to the living room, the flames went crazy. Each time they started to say the words, the spirit would move, and the flames would grow still. It reminded Eve of a fly flitting about the room and coming to rest first on one object, then on another. Finally it settled in a picture on the wall. The print was of an American Indian. It was one of Eve's favorites. She'd had it for years.

"Look at the eyes," Carla whispered. "They're watching us."

It was true that when they moved, the Indian brave's eyes seemed to follow. Strange that Eve had never noticed that before. The candle flames flickered and sputtered. Black smoke rose from the candles and was drawn inexorably to the picture. "In the name of J-Jesus," Eve whispered hoarsely, "We c-command you to l-leave."

When the smoke finally dissipated and the candle flames had been still for five minutes or longer, both Eve and Carla sank onto the loveseat, weak with relief, too exhausted to move.

"This is Gideon," a voice said in Eve's head. "And yes I'm of the light. I'm very proud of both of you, Sweetheart. You can relax now. The dark one's gone."

Elated that they'd succeeded in clearing the apartment, Eve was nevertheless upset that a dark spirit had been here in the first place, and that Gideon had done nothing to keep it from rising out of the candle. What would have happened if they hadn't been able to make it leave? The experience with the smoke penis had affected her deeply, as had having the dark spirit call her a bitch. "Why, Gideon? I haven't done anything to make a dark spirit want to attack me. Why didn't you stop it?"

"I'm sorry," Gideon said. "I lost my concentration, and it caught me off guard. I promise it won't happen again. Fortunately, Joan was able to get through to Carla to give her the impulse to snuff out the candle."

"I want you to come home with me and spend the night at my apartment," Carla urged.

Eve would have liked to take Carla up on her invitation. Two frightened women together would be stronger than one alone. But she couldn't allow herself to become dependent.

"Thanks," Eve said, "but I can't do that. You live too far away from my work. Besides, if it's me this dark spirit hates, what's to say it wouldn't follow us there?"

Carla finally left at ten o'clock, with the understanding she'd call to check in the minute she got home, and that they would both sleep with the light on and a phone beside their bed.

It didn't occur to Eve that Gideon hadn't answered her question about why a dark spirit would have wanted to harm her.

Chapter 13

The night was blessedly uneventful, but the next day when Eve was pulling on her nylons, she noticed that her vision was blurred. That was odd. She hadn't been reading or using the computer without her reading glasses before she went to bed last night.

"Good morning, Sweetheart. This is Gideon, and you know I'm of the light. I want you to call in sick today."

"Why should I call in sick?" Eve asked. "I feel fine."

What had begun as a slight blurring of vision now became more pronounced as Eve stepped into her black straight skirt and pulled her rose sweater on over her head.

"You need a rest," Gideon insisted. "I want you to make the call."

The blurred vision by now had reached the point that Eve could barely walk across the room without tripping. *What's going on?* she thought frantically. *Am I having a stroke?* She couldn't think of any disease that began with the onset of blindness. "What wrong with my eyes, Gideon? *What's happening to me?*"

"Make the call," Gideon replied. "Tell them you got pollen in your eyes and had an allergic reaction. Tell them you'll let them know when you can come back to work."

"*You're doing this to me?*" Eve shrieked. "What kind of guardian angel *are* you, that you would pull a dirty stunt like this? I thought you *loved* me."

"I do love you," Gideon replied. "That's why I'm doing it."

Left with no choice, Eve bit back the words that had sprung to her lips, and shakily did as she'd been told. It was a good thing she'd put her work number on speed dial. Otherwise, she wouldn't have been able to see the numbers. The phone was answered by a machine. When the call had been made and the message left, Eve's vision returned to normal. "How could you have done this to me?" she cried.

"You need a rest," Gideon said. "It was for your own good."

"You had no right to interfere with my work!" Eve shouted to the air. In her mind's eye, she could see Gideon standing over her in his jeans and flannel shirt.

His brown eyes, though loving, were stern. "Sometimes you can be a real *bastard*, Gideon."

"I'd advise you to watch your tongue," Gideon replied. "There are limits to what I'll put up with, even from you."

Eve didn't know what that threat implied, and she didn't want to find out. If she was going to be forced to spend the day at home, she might as well take advantage of it and work on a craft project. Maybe she'd start early on her Christmas gifts for next year...

The following day was a repeat of the day before. "Call them," Gideon ordered. "Tell them your vision is still blurred and you can't see to type."

The third day when Eve awoke, her vision was normal. "Make the call," Gideon said.

"Forget it," Eve argued. "This has already gone too far." Instantly, her vision began to blur.

"Make the call."

When on the fourth day Eve was able to return to work, Gideon told her to write a letter of resignation and turn it in immediately. "I can't do that," Eve protested. "I need this job!"

"It's not the job for you," Gideon replied. "Turn in your resignation."

There was no one Eve dared talk to about this except Carla. Anyone else would think she was schizophrenic. She had called Carla the first day it happened, and had been unpleasantly surprised when Carla took Gideon's side. Now, Carla was taking his side again. "The job is making you a nervous wreck, Eve. And it's not going to get any better. You need to turn in your resignation. I've been thinking of looking for a roommate anyway. You can move in with me while you're looking for another job."

"But I can't—"

"Yes you can, Eve. I want you to promise me you'll *do it*."

Seething at the fact that she was being coerced into quitting her job, Eve wrote the letter of resignation when she arrived at work that morning. "Hurry," Gideon prodded. "You need to have the letter done when the office manager arrives."

Eve had finished the letter and just printed it out when the office manager came in with an envelope in hand. She was a woman of approximately Eve's height with a sweet face and long straight brown hair. Her dowdy clothing seemed to add to her sweetness. Eve had liked her from the first day they met. "I'm glad to see your eyes are better," Caroline commented. "I was getting a little worried about you."

"Before you say anything else, I need to give you this," Eve said quietly. She could feel Gideon's eyes upon her when she handed the letter to Caroline.

The office manager accepted the letter and read it through with a somber face. Her reaction was neither anger nor surprise. It was relief. "I am so glad you gave me this before I had a chance to do what I came here to do," Caroline said. There were tears in her eyes as she held up the envelope. "You didn't have a chance, Eve. No one without a legal background could have come into this job and taken over without proper training. I would have trained you myself, but I'm overworked too. I have your final paycheck in this envelope. I was supposed to fire you today on the grounds of missed deadlines and excessive absence."

Too stunned to speak, Eve made no reply.

"Since you submitted your resignation first, I can tear this up and pretend I never had to tell you about it," Caroline said. "Mr. Stanton wrote it, and it really wasn't very nice. I'll write you a letter of recommendation before you leave this morning. And if you need a verbal reference, you can refer the calls to me."

So that was it. Eve was unemployed again. Gideon had done this to her by forcing her to miss three days of work without a doctor's excuse during her first three months on the job.

"It would have happened down the line anyway," Gideon said. "Stanton was dissatisfied when you couldn't get ahead, and the work kept piling up. He's a cheapskate, Eve. He never would have hired extra help. The probability that he would have fired you was ninety-eight percent. I didn't want you to have to go through the trauma of being fired, and I couldn't see letting you ruin your health while that jerk was making up his mind."

There they were, back to probabilities again. "I guess I should thank you," Eve said gloomily. "But what am I going to do now?"

"You could move in with Carla like she asked you to."

"My rent here is paid till the end of the month," Eve argued. That gives me three weeks to save up enough for next month's rent. If I re-activate my file with the temporary agencies, maybe I won't have to move."

Eve had grown to like her apartment. She didn't want to move into a single room, which is basically what it would be if she moved in with Carla. Carla was used to having her apartment to herself. If Eve took advantage of her generosity, she would need to be as unobtrusive as possible. "You know what, Gideon? I don't think I can stand to think about this anymore tonight. There's an open dance at the Red Lion Inn. I'm going to go there and have a good time."

"Then ask Carla to go with you," Gideon urged. "I have my reasons for not wanting you to go alone."

Though Eve doubted that Carla would want to go, she called anyway to issue the invitation. Lately Carla didn't really seem to enjoy going dancing with Eve. When the two of them were together, Carla rarely got invitations to dance. The fact of the matter was that Carla lacked confidence in her own femininity. Years ago, she'd been a police officer. Her suspicious nature and take-charge attitude often drove men away.

To Eve's surprise, Carla said she would go. "But can I wear your black ruffled skirt?"

The skirt Carla wanted to borrow had a stretchy knit midriff, with wide rows of cotton ruffles from the hips to a few inches above the knees. Eve had planned to wear the skirt herself, but readily agreed to lend it to her friend.

"I'll come there to get dressed," Carla said. "Which wig do you think I should wear? The platinum, or the frosted?"

Eve replied that she thought Carla should wear her own hair, but Carla felt more attractive when she was wearing a wig. "I guess I'll go for the frosted..."

Rather than be among the first to arrive, the two friends timed their arrival for precisely nine o'clock. Since most of the seats at the tables were already taken, they checked their wraps and evening bags, and joined the group standing on the sidelines. It wasn't long till Eve was asked to dance.

When the song was over and Eve returned to the sidelines, Carla cupped a hand and whispered in her ear. "Don't look now, but Mitch is here, and he's been watching you ever since we arrived."

Mitch was Carla's former boyfriend. They had broken up six months ago.

Odd that Carla would think Mitch was watching *her*. Eve had had the same feeling herself at another dance. Now that she considered it, she realized she'd seen Mitch at every dance she'd attended in the past several weeks. Unable to resist casting a glance in his direction, Eve confirmed for herself that Carla was right. Mitch *was* watching her, and making no bones about it. Eve knew that Carla was over Mitch. But it still wasn't good to have Carla's ex-boyfriend ogling *her*.

After the dance when Carla drove Eve home, she came upstairs for a Coke. "You don't know what Mitch is like," she said. "He fantasizes about petite fragile women with blue eyes and light skin. He dreams about what he'd like to do to them, and it isn't pretty."

Silent till now, Gideon joined the discussion. "This is Gideon, and I'm of the light. Carla's right, Sweetheart. Mitch isn't what anyone would call 'Mr. Nice Guy.' And he *was* watching you and having perverted thoughts."

"Those perverted fantasies are the main reason I broke up with Mitch," Carla said. "Those, and his drinking. When we were together, any time he'd been drinking he'd complain about *my* olive complexion. He'd complain about the fact that my eyes were brown, and that I was almost as strong as him. When he was drunk, he used to watch women on T.V. who looked like you, and tell me what he'd like to do to them. Most of the time, Mitch is a really nice guy, Eve. But when he's been drinking, he's downright dangerous."

Just thinking about what Carla was saying made Eve's skin crawl.

When Mitch was at the next dance Eve and Carla went to, and the next dance after that, Carla's police instincts kicked into full gear. Back at Eve's apartment, she spoke to Gideon. "Gideon, tell me if I'm wrong. But from my standpoint, the way Mitch was looking at Eve tonight was the same way I've seen him look at women on T.V.—the ones that when he's drunk, he refers to as stuck up bitches."

"I wish I could say you're wrong," Gideon said. "But Mitch is a sick man, Carla. The thoughts he was having tonight could land him in prison. Eve, I don't want you going to anymore dances alone. In fact, I'd prefer that you lay low for awhile. That, or find another place to dance."

It galled Eve to think that one man's sick fantasies should restrict where she could go and what she could do. "You're my guardian angel," she challenged. "Why can't you protect me?"

"Because this is Satan's realm," Gideon answered. "There are limits to how far I'm allowed to go."

Eve couldn't believe what she was hearing. Gideon had basically said that his hands were tied when it came to defending her. What was the point of having a guardian angel if he was going to bow out when the going got tough?

"I hear your thoughts," Gideon said, "And I don't like what you're thinking. I hadn't intended to tell you what sort of thoughts Mitch was having tonight. But I think you need to know, Eve. He was fantasizing about slashing your face."

Eve flinched as if she'd been punched in the gut. She felt like she was going to be sick.

"That sounds like Mitch, alright," Carla said. "When he's been drinking, it's almost as if he's possessed."

"There's more," Gideon said ominously. Eve didn't know what was coming, but whatever it was, she didn't want to hear it. "Mitch has a friend who just moved into this apartment complex. Carla, I believe you know him. He's a big man with a clean-shaven head. His name starts with the letter R."

"Rizzo," Carla breathed. "He was in prison on a narcotics conviction. But I heard he's out on parole." Raking a hand through her frosted wig, Carla rose from the chair and began to pace. Eve was seated on the loveseat, hands clenched in her lap. "Rizzo and Mitch were best friends," Carla said. "If Rizzo is living here in this complex, that's not good. That means Mitch will be coming to see him. If Mitch sees *you* here, he'll know where to find you."

"The probabilities of Mitch doing anything himself are less than 35%," Gideon said. "Even when he's been drinking."

"You're right," Carla agreed. "But all he'd have to do is give Rizzo the word. Rizzo is an animal. He wouldn't think twice."

Tears of fright had welled in Eve's eyes. Her heart was thundering in her ears.

"You have to get out of here and move in with me," Carla said urgently.

"She's right, Sweetheart. You'll be safe with her."

"My rent is paid through the end of the month," Eve said shakily. "I'm not going to let *paranoia* force me to move before then."

Two evenings later, Carla again came to Eve's apartment. She was wearing her own hair today, and beige slacks that complimented her slender figure. Obviously agitated, Carla rushed in when Eve opened the door. "I need to talk to Joan or Gideon."

Alarmed by the sense of urgency, Eve offered Carla a seat and took out the board. Eve had just finished a hot bath, and her skin was still flushed and smelled faintly of lemon bath oil. For a brief moment, Eve closed her eyes to surround herself with the protective white light. "Joan?" she said. "Carla's here, and she needs to talk to you."

The pendulum swung to the appropriate phrases, then began to spell out Joan's message. "Carla, what happened to you on the way here was done by the dark spirit that normally attaches itself to Mitch."

"You mean Mitch is involved with a dark spirit?" Carla said uneasily. "Is that why he acts so strange when he's been drinking?"

"That's not why," Joan said, "but the drinking certainly encourages it to stay. Even normal people are more easily influenced when they've been over indulging."

Confused by the course of the conversation, Eve asked what was going on. "What happened on your way here, Carla?"

"The bastard tried to make me have a wreck!" Carla shouted. "My car kept trying to pull to the right, but I knew it wasn't anything that had to do with the car.

So I said 'Leave my car alone, you son of a bitch. After that, the car was fine.'"
Obviously overwrought, Carla perched on the edge of the brown recliner. "There's
something I haven't told you Eve."

The tone of Carla's voice caused Eve's muscles to tense even more than they
already had.

"When I turned into the parking lot tonight, I saw Mitch. He was in his car,
headed for an apartment on the other side of the complex."

"Carla's right, Sweetheart. Now that Rizzo lives here, Mitch comes here on a
regular basis," a voice said in Eve's head. "Fortunately, he doesn't know your car."

"Did Mitch see you, Carla?" Eve asked in a hushed voice.

"When I spotted him, I turned down another row," Carla said. "I parked behind
the trash bin. I don't think he saw me."

"That was keen observation and quick thinking on your part, Carla," the
pendulum spelled out. "Your instincts make it easy for me to be your guardian
angel."

Something akin to rage flashed in Carla's eyes, and she rose to pace in angry
strides. "Put down the pendulum, Eve."

"Why?" Eve asked hesitantly. "What's wrong?"

"Put the pendulum down!"

Startled by Carla's forcefulness, Eve did as she had asked.

"They're all a bunch of damned liars," Carla grated.

"*Who* are a bunch of liars?"

"Gideon, Joan, Caruso…"

Eve couldn't believe Carla was saying this. Gideon had blurred *her* vision just
for refusing to make a phone call. What might he or Joan do to Carla if she was
calling them *liars*? "Why would you even say that, Carla?"

"I didn't see Mitch's car," Carla spat. "I just made that up to test them, and
they didn't even know the difference."

It didn't make sense that Carla could fool both Gideon and Joan. As her
guardian angel, Joan should have been with her every minute. At the very least, she
should have read Carla's mind and known when she was lying.

"Sweetheart, this is Gideon, and I'm of the light. Pick up the pendulum."

Eve picked up the pendulum, and it immediately began to swing. "Carla, this is
Joan, and I'm of the light. That wasn't me talking a few minutes ago. It was the
same spirit who was interfering with your car. It's very powerful, and it managed to
block my communication so it could talk to you itself."

"If you're my guardian angel," Carla said angrily, "then why the hell didn't you
kill it?"

"Because I'm not allowed to use excessive force," Joan replied. "It's a *mental*
war between spirits of light versus spirits of darkness. We're stronger than they are,
but we're not allowed to use full power against them. The earth is Satan's realm,
Carla. All it takes is one break in concentration on my part to let them sneak in…"

Chapter 14

Moving Eve's things into Carla's two-bedroom apartment meant doubling up on sofas and chairs, and filling every inch of space in the second bedroom with floor to ceiling boxes. It wasn't exactly a palace. But at least Eve still had a roof over her head.

"Phew!" Carla said, mopping her brow. "I don't know about you. But I'm beat! How about if we go out for fast food—my treat—then come home and watch a movie?"

Carla was a true friend. Eve didn't know what she would have done if she hadn't had Carla to turn to. But she didn't want to take advantage of their friendship. "You're doing enough already, by letting me move into your apartment. I don't want you buying me dinner. I brought some sandwich makings. Why don't we just kick back in front of the T.V. and eat at home?"

Later, after watching a tearjerker on HBO, Carla suggested that Eve get out the board so *she* could talk to *Joan*. "I want to ask her some questions."

The questions Carla wanted to ask were about some childhood memories that had been resurfacing lately. Hers had not been a pleasant childhood. After her mother's death, her father had been unable to cope with parenthood. He'd sent her to live with his brother's family, and basically washed his hands of her except to send a check every month to pay for her support. Once there, Carla had lived a Cinderella existence—never having clothes of her own that weren't hand-me-downs from her cousins; never having a new toy—not even a doll. She had envied her cousins, who seemed to have everything a child could want. When she'd asked her Aunt Hattie why she couldn't buy a doll with a small portion of the money her father was paying, she'd had her face slapped for insolence, and been sent to the room she shared with her cousin to think about her ingratitude.

The pendulum swung to Joan's name, then to the phrase "I'm of the light."

"I've brought these troubling memories back for you because it's time for you to deal with them," Joan said. "When you didn't have a way of talking with me, I wouldn't have taken the risk. But now you're in a position where we can talk them out together."

Eve felt like an intruder, having to act as a go-between. But Carla assured her she didn't mind.

"Other than the abuse you suffered, which you're not ready yet to delve into, what is your strongest childhood memory?" Joan asked.

Without hesitation, Carla said it was the doll. "My cousin Sara had a doll that I thought was beautiful," she said wistfully. "It had blonde curls and pink cheeks, and a pink dress trimmed with lace. I wanted to have a doll like that so badly I could taste it. When my cousin was around, she wouldn't even let me touch it, but I used to sneak and play with it sometimes when I was alone."

Eve's heart went out to the child in her friend that had wanted a doll, but never had one.

"I want you to go to the toy store and buy a doll tomorrow," Joan said. "You can afford it. I want you to buy the prettiest doll you can find: one you would have loved when you were a little girl. Will you do that for me, Carla?"

Surprised at the request, Carla said that she would.

The next day was Saturday. Together, Eve and Carla went to Toys 'R' Us to look at the dolls. When Carla found it, she knew instantly which doll she had to buy. Her instinct was supported by Joan, who told Eve that the child portion of Carla's subconscious was ecstatic at the prospect of owning the doll, but fearful of allowing itself to hope.

"It's fifty nine bucks!" Carla protested.

"How much is it worth to you to heal the subconscious wounds of your childhood?" Joan replied. "Buying this doll for the little girl in you would go a long way toward the healing process."

The doll had golden curls and long dark eyelashes that opened to reveal azure blue eyes when she was picked up, and closed when she was laid down. She was dressed in a white lace pinafore over a rose satin dress, with lace-trimmed socks to match. The buckle shoes on her tiny feet were white patent leather.

"What are you going to name her?" Eve asked when they got home.

"Darla," Carla mumbled. "That's as good a name as any. But you'd better ask Joan what my *subconscious* thinks."

"This is Joan, and I'm of the light," Joan said with a smile in her voice. "Tell her that her subconscious likes the name just fine." It suddenly dawned on Eve that for the past several days, Joan had been speaking to her telepathically. "It's much simpler," Joan said. Then back to Carla: "Carla, honey, you've taken the first step. But there's one more thing I'd like you to do for your subconscious. When you were at the video store yesterday, your subconscious noticed a copy of Pete's Dragon on the shelf. If you were to rent it, and hold the doll while you watch it…"

"No," Carla said. "Forget it."

"How important is it to you that you heal your subconscious?"

With what limited knowledge Eve had of Psychology, what Joan was saying made perfect sense to her. She just wished Carla could see it.

Later that day, dressed in a stylish pink sweatsuit, Carla was seated at the dining room table munching a tuna salad sandwich. "I have some orange and beige afghans we can put on your loveseat and chair to tie them in with my furniture. But I think we need to hang some pictures on the wall. What do *you* think?"

71

"We definitely need to do what we can to make the furniture match," Eve agreed. "But the only pictures I have are the Indian brave and some smaller prints that wouldn't go with the orange and beige of the afghans."

"I have some pictures in the hall closet," Carla said. "Let's take a look at them and see what you think."

Eve stayed at the table nibbling at her sandwich while Carla rummaged through the contents of the closet. "Here's one I've never hung up," Carla called. "It's never seemed to go with anything I had. What do you think?"

What Eve thought was that the surrealistic flowers were just shy of being ugly. "I can't imagine where we'd hang it," she said diplomatically. "The colors don't really match."

"Could I make a comment?" Joan put in. "By the way, this is Joan, and I'm of the light."

Surprised, Carla said that she'd be interested in Joan's opinion.

"Why don't you try hanging the picture on that small corner wall by the sliding glass door?"

The two friends exchanged dubious glances, but Carla carried the picture across the living room and held it up by the door for Eve's opinion.

Eve stopped chewing, and gaped at the picture. "It's perfect!" she cried. "I wouldn't have believed it, but it's the perfect touch to tie the whole room together! Let me hold it for you to look!"

Carla stood back while Eve held the picture in place. "Just a little higher," she suggested. Carla looked at the picture for a long critical moment, and then she smiled. "It doesn't even look like the same picture. Why didn't I ever think of hanging it there?"

While Carla dug in a kitchen drawer for a hammer and nails, Eve returned to her lunch and took a sip of Coke. "Maybe Joan was an interior decorator in a former life."

"Close," Joan said. "I was an artist."

Intrigued, Carla asked Joan to tell more about herself. "What did you look like? How did you die?"

"I had hair the color of yours," Joan said softly. "Yours when you allow your real hair to show. I don't know why you always insist on wearing wigs when your own hair is so pretty."

Ignoring the comment about her wigs, Carla asked about Joan's appearance, other than the color of her hair.

"I was tall and slender," Joan replied. "I had an olive complexion, much like yours, with a thin nose and rather prominent cheekbones. My eyes were hazel."

"I can see her," Carla breathed. Carla had closed her eyes, and her lips were curved in a brilliant smile. "She's beautiful. She's dressed in a white flowing robe of some sort, and she's smiling at me! I wish you could see her." The brilliance of Carla's smile glowed even brighter. "Now she's hugging me. I can feel her arms around me. I can feel how much she loves me."

Eve's heart was touched, and her eyes grew moist, but she willed her tears not to fall. When the moment had passed, she carried her plate and glass to the kitchen and loaded them into the dishwasher. It was amazing how much her life had changed since the day she went for a psychic reading and was introduced to Gideon. Now Carla was experiencing the same thing with Joan.

"She still didn't answer my other question," Carla said. "Ask her how she died."

Without waiting for Eve to pose the question, Joan replied. "This is Joan, and I'm of the light. I died in the gas chamber of a Nazi concentration camp. I know what it means to be abused. That's why I was assigned to *you.*"

Chapter 15

Though Eve signed up with a number of temporary agencies in the area of the apartment complex where she and Carla were now living, she didn't receive a single call for work. Daily checks of the want ads proved equally fruitless. Meanwhile, Eve's meager savings were dwindling.

In an effort to hold on to some sense of normality, Eve continued to go dancing. Only now Gideon was insisting that she only go with Carla. The problem was that, even with Carla, Eve couldn't get away from Mitch. The man apparently had nothing else to do but attend every singles function within a thirty-mile radius! Everywhere Eve went, he was there—watching from the sidelines.

And then came the night Mitch asked her to dance. Cringing on the inside, but smiling on the outside, Eve allowed herself to be led onto the dance floor. When Mitch tried to pull her close, her back stiffened.

"Relax," Mitch said. "You're stiff as a board."

Making a conscious effort to relax her muscles, Eve counted the seconds till this dance would be over.

"I was thinking maybe you and me might go out for breakfast."

Warning sirens shrieked in Eve's head. "Thanks," she said with a nervous smile. "But I can't. I'm here with someone."

"You're here with Carla, just like you always are," Mitch said. "That's no problem. *I* can take you home."

Eve's hands had grown clammy, and her heart was thudding so hard within her chest that she was certain Mitch could feel it. "Gideon?" she said in her mind. "Gideon? What should I do?" No answer. "Gideon?" her mind shouted. "Please answer me!"

"He's not here, bitch."

Oh God, Eve thought frantically. *Oh God, what should I do?* Forcing herself not to let her panic show, Eve curved her lips in what she hoped resembled a smile. "Thanks, Mitch. It's nice of you to offer. But I make it a policy never to leave with anyone I didn't come with."

Eve's legs felt like they were made of water as she made her way back to the table where Carla was waiting. "I've got to get out of here," she said weakly. "I've got to get home so I can talk to Gideon."

In the car on the ride home, the dark spirit continued to harass her. "Now that you know how to talk through telepathy, what made you think we couldn't talk to you too? You turned him down, bitch. Now you'd better watch your back. You never know who might be waiting, just around the corner…"

"In the name of Jesus," Eve whispered. "In the name of Jesus, I command you to leave this car."

"I'm not in the car, bitch. I'm inside your head."

Terrified, Eve continued to pray. "Dear God, in the name of Jesus, please make him leave me alone."

By the time she and Carla arrived home, Eve's face was drained of color. "Let's get you inside," Carla said. "We'll imagine the apartment filled with white light, and you can try to get Gideon to talk to you on the board."

Seated on the living room floor with two candles burning and the board on the coffee table between them, Eve and Carla stared at the board, each with her own thoughts and fears. When Eve finally reached out and picked up the pendulum, it immediately began to swing. "This is Gideon. I'm of the light. Sweetheart, what happened tonight was only the beginning. You don't know what you're destined for, but the dark spirits do. They know Jesus has chosen you, and they're going to do anything in their power to prevent you from doing His will. That's why we've got to get you away from the city."

"Hold it," Eve said shakily. "What do you mean, Jesus has chosen me? Chosen me for what?"

"That will be revealed to you after you've moved to Placerville."

"*Placerville*!!!" Eve shrieked. "If you think I'm moving to Placerville, you're out of your mind!"

The small historic town of Placerville was located in the mountains above Sacramento. Eve had gone there once to attend a psychic fair. All she could remember about it was the Hangtown Saloon and the fact that the streets, aside from the fair, had been nearly deserted.

"You'll be safe in Placerville," Gideon insisted.

Eve's stomach was churning, and her head had begun to throb. If she moved to Placerville, she'd be isolated! She would have to drive thirty-five miles each way just to have lunch with Kevin! Calls to Kevin and Carla would be long distance. Not to mention the fact there would be nowhere to go dancing… "No," Eve said. "The answer is No. I don't believe it's Jesus' will for me to move somewhere I don't want to live, away from my friends and family. If He has something in Placerville He wants me to do, I'll just have to commute from here. He can protect me."

"Sweetheart," Gideon argued, "That's not how it works. If Jesus picks you to do something, *you* don't call the *terms*!"

When another month had passed and Eve still hadn't found a job, Gideon apparently decided the time had come to sweeten the pot. "Would you like to hear more about probabilities?"

"Not if it has to do with moving to Placerville."

Eve was seated in the recliner trying to read a novel by Steven King. Carla was on the sofa holding Darla on her lap, watching a video of Pete's Dragon. It was the third time Carla had been forced to watch the video as part of her therapy for healing her damaged self-conscious.

"The probability has to do with a man in your life," Gideon said. "The man you're destined to marry."

Laying the book aside, Eve gave Gideon her full attention.

"If you move to Placerville and take the job Jesus wants you to have, the probability of your meeting this man is ninety-eight percent. If you stay in the valley, the probability goes down to thirty percent or lower."

Intrigued but skeptical, Eve told Carla what Gideon had said.

"I've been thinking about Placerville," Carla replied. "It's pretty obvious to me that they're not going to let you find a job in the valley. Think about it, Eve. How many times have you come this close?" Here, she held up a thumb and forefinger. "If what Gideon says is true, and there's a job waiting for you in Placerville where you'll be safe, I think you ought to consider it."

The expression "Et tu, Brute?" came to mind, but Eve didn't say it. "Do you have any idea what it would be like, living in Placerville?"

"It would have to be better than living here," Carla said. "You can't find a job here. You can't go out dancing. Half the time when you try to talk to Gideon, the dark ones interfere so you can't tell who you're talking to anyway. If it's Kevin you're worried about, you only see him once a week *now*. You can do that even if you're living in the mountains. If you had a job and didn't have any real bills other than the basics, we could talk on the phone everyday just like we used to. I think you ought to quit being so stubborn, and go."

"And I think you should listen to Carla," Gideon said.

"Even if I were willing to go, I can't afford to rent a place," Eve said miserably. "I'm down right now to my last two hundred dollars. I can't pay rent and a security deposit up front!"

"Yes you can," Carla said quietly. "If it means getting you a job, whatever that may be, I could lend you the money. But I'd have to have a guarantee from Gideon and *God* that you'll have the money to pay me back."

Stunned by the offer, Eve stared at Carla. "I can't take your money, Carla. I don't have any idea when I'd be able to pay it back."

"Get out the board," Gideon said. "The boss wants to talk to you."

"If this is a dark spirit," Eve said, "I command you in the name of Jesus to leave me alone."

"Sweetheart, this is Gideon. And you know I'm of the light. Now get out the board. *God* wants to talk to you. And you don't have to worry about His being of the light. No dark spirit would *dare* claim to be God. God gives them a lot of leeway, but that's one thing He won't tolerate."

Speaking to Carla, Eve repeated what Gideon had said.

"Why would *God* want to talk to *me*? I can't believe He would want to talk through a pendulum and an alphabet board." Eve recalled from her Christian upbringing as a child that anyone who dared even look on God's face would *die*. If he started sending his power through this pendulum, she might very well get electrocuted! "This doesn't sound right. I'm not going to do it."

"It doesn't sound right to me either," Carla said nervously. "But if God wants to talk to you, you can't just say 'No.'"

"I think I just did."

"I *know* you just *did*," Gideon thundered. "And I can't believe you did it. Now pick up that pendulum before *I* decide to do something drastic!"

Eve's hand was trembling as she picked up the pendulum and muttered a silent prayer for God to be gentle. Suddenly the pendulum began to move in huge forceful swings, so forceful the pendulum was nearly torn from Eve's hand. "This is the lord God, Jehovah, and I *created* the light! I'm going to use you to speak to Carla, Eve. So don't put the pendulum down, or I'll have to speak directly to your mind."

Gripping the pendulum for dear life, Eve waited for God to speak.

"Carla," the pendulum spelled out, "I'm very proud of you. That was a selfless gesture, offering to lend Eve the money to finance the move to Placerville. It was also an act of faith. Faith in Eve that she would do everything in her power to pay back the debt, and faith that if *I give my word* that the debt will be paid in full, it will be done. You have my word, Carla. When you need the money, it will be there."

"Could I please say something?" Eve put in.

"Speak."

"I'd like to have some assurance that if I borrow the money from Carla, when the time comes to pay off the debt, it won't involve my mother." Eve's mom had been a real trooper, never failing to come through for Eve during the hard times. It wasn't her mom's fault that Eve couldn't find a job in the valley. Eve didn't want her mom to have to foot the bill for moving to Placerville.

"When Carla needs the money, it will be there," the pendulum spelled out. "Independent of your mother."

"Then it's settled," Carla said, reaching out to engulf Eve in a hug. "We'll wait till you get the job before I give you the money. After you start getting a paycheck, you can make payments—whatever you can afford. I just needed a guarantee that the money would be there if I need it. Now that I have that promise, I'm not worried. Why don't we take a drive up to Placerville this weekend? We could look around to see what kind of rentals are available, and check out the job ads..."

On the day that Eve and Carla planned to make the drive, Gideon informed them there was a problem. "The dark ones don't want you to move to Placerville," he said. "It's a lot like Superman and kryptonite. When the dark ones are around gold, it drains their strength. Since there's gold under much of Placerville, once you've moved there, it will be harder for them to harass you. That's why they're planning an accident for you in the outskirts of town. You have to be very careful, Sweetheart. One thing you should be aware of is that the ones who are planning the accident are not higher beings. These particular demons see through your eyes and hear through your ears. If you don't see or hear something, they don't either. Carla, I'm sure you get my point."

Eve was glad Carla did, because *she'd* totally missed it.

"Leave it to me," Carla said confidently. "I'll do the driving."

Once inside the blue sedan, Carla told Eve to close her eyes. "Don't ask questions. Just close your eyes, and keep them closed."

As they drove onto the freeway heading *East toward Placerville*, Carla maintained a running monologue, ticking off the names of off ramps as if they were headed *west toward Redding*. "Business loop 80…"

At first, Eve was confused. But once she'd caught on, she went along with the game. If the dark spirits who were after her saw through her eyes and heard through her ears, the ruse would throw confusion into the scene…

"Interstate 5, Los Angeles, Redding…There's the first sign for the Airport…" Ten minutes later, Carla called out that they'd just passed the Woodland turn-off…

When they arrived in the outskirts of Placerville, one lane of the freeway was closed, due to a collision. "You can open your eyes now," Carla said. *"There's the* accident that was intended for *us."*

Gideon later explained that the dark ones waiting outside Placerville, told telepathically by the ones hearing through Eve's ears that she and Carla were headed toward Redding, had caused the accident to happen to someone else, rather than scrap a good accident plan. Eve found this very hard to believe. But she had been warned that an accident was being planned in the outskirts of Placerville. It seemed too much of a coincidence that an unrelated accident would occur in exactly the same place at exactly the time *they'd* been slated to arrive. Eve muttered a silent prayer of thanks that she and Carla were safe, and to bless anyone who'd been hurt in the collision.

It came as no real surprise to Eve that the only affordable rental in Placerville was an efficiency apartment in the town's only hotel. Eve's heart, already not in this expedition, sank at the thought of *living* in the musty old hotel with its Victorian lobby and rickety elevator. The woman behind the reception desk had to be at least seventy years old. According to what she told Eve when she showed her and Carla the apartment, the average age of tenants at the hotel was sixty-five and older. This scenario didn't exactly inspire Eve to run out and submit her employment application. Not that there were a lot of places to submit it.

A visit to the town's one employment agency netted no job leads at all. Still, Eve took their typing and I.Q. tests, and thanked them for their assurance that they'd call, in the event that anything became available. The next step was to buy a local newspaper.

Skimming through the job ads, Eve groaned. "The only thing I see here is an ad for a certified nursing assistant at a convalescent hospital. There's not a single office job listed."

"Guess we'd better pull off in a quiet spot and get out the board," Carla replied.

Gideon had told them to take the board along, in case they had difficulty getting through to him. Telepathic signals, he had explained, were easily muffled or interrupted, and it was likely the dark ones would be doing their best to break down communications today.

Carla pulled the car over in a shady spot and Eve took out the board. After mentally surrounding themselves with a protective white light, she picked up the pendulum. The pendulum swung to Gideon's name, then to the phrase "I'm of the light."

"Call the convalescent hospital," Gideon spelled out. "This is the job."

Eve stared at the pendulum as if Gideon had gone berserk. *This* was the job she'd been waiting for? She'd been forced to quit a secretarial job that paid nearly two thousand a month so she could apply for a *hospital* job that paid little more than *minimum wage*? "You've got to be kidding. There's no way I'm going to put in an application for this job. You know I hate hospitals. They give me the creeps!"

When Eve's father had been ill with A.L.S., she had hated going to the hospital to visit him; not because she hadn't wanted to see her father, but because of the smells and sounds of the hospital. The misery and helplessness there had deeply disturbed her.

"You know what happened when you didn't do what Gideon said before," Carla said glumly. "I think you'd better make the call."

Eve was tempted to say "To Hell with Gideon," but prudence held her tongue.

"I heard that thought," Gideon spelled out. "Don't push it."

When Eve placed the call to the hospital, the director of certified nursing assistants answered. Once the preliminaries had been exchanged, the nurse asked Eve if she had a strong back.

"No," Eve said. "As a matter of fact, I think this call was a mistake. I'm sorry I wasted your time."

"Hold on," the nurse said. "I'm free right now. I'd like for you to come in for an interview."

Covering the receiver with her hand, Eve made a face of revulsion. "She wants me to come for an interview!"

"Why doesn't that surprise me?" Carla quipped.

The convalescent hospital was easy to find. Carla waited in the parking lot, while Eve went inside. The first thing to hit Eve when she opened the door was the ammonia smell of urine and the stench of diarrhea. To the left was what appeared to be a combination dining room and living room, presumably for visiting with family and friends. On the back dining room wall, in line with the door, was a bulletin board displaying pictures Eve assumed to have been drawn by elementary school children; that, or by elderly adults who didn't know how to draw.

Stretching straight ahead past the dining room was a long corridor lined with open doors. An old lady in a wheelchair emerged from her room and headed straight toward Eve. The odor of urine grew stronger as she approached. "My, you're a pretty girl," the old lady said. "What's my name?" Smiling broadly, she covered her nametag and looked up at Eve expectantly. Her cheeks were heavily rouged, her lipstick slightly smeared. Mischievous eyes sparkled through black-framed glasses.

Eve hadn't seen the name tag before the woman covered it up. "That's a tough one," she teased back. "Is it Martha May?"

"No," the old lady said. "Guess again. I'll let you know when you get close."

From a distance, Eve could hear a woman's voice crying out for "Mama" to please take her home. Through an open door ahead and to the left, a different voice was moaning, "Help me! Someone please help me!"

Alarmed, Eve looked around for a nurse or C.N.A. Finding none, she approached the open door. The wheelchair patient followed close behind. A woman the size of a rhinoceros was lying in bed, stuffed between two guardrails. "Help me," she said pitifully. "They're trying to kill me."

Eve's heart was thudding as she entered the room and touched the woman's hand. *"Who's* trying to kill you?" she asked softly.

"No one!" the old lady in the wheelchair shouted. She had wheeled her chair into the room behind Eve and was glaring at the whimpering mass of humanity lying in bed beneath a rumpled sheet. "Tell her to shut her damned mouth before someone decides to shut it for her!"

It was amazing to Eve that, in the space of a minute, the sweet childish old lady in the wheelchair had been transformed into a foul-mouthed shrew!

"It's my daughter," the bedridden patient whimpered. "I killed *her*, now she's going to kill *me*. Can you please help me?"

Oh God, Eve thought in a panic. *What am I doing here?*

"Forget about the old bitch," the wheelchair patient snapped. "What's my name? Do you like my earrings? My son gave them to me."

Shaking her head to clear the fog, Eve rushed into the hallway, intending to go back out the way she'd come in.

"You must be Eve," a blonde nurse said with a smile. "I see you've met Florence and Norma. My name's Doreen."

"Now you've gone and wrecked it," Norma groused. "She was supposed to *guess* my name, but you told her! Do you like my earrings? My son gave them to me."

"Yes, Norma. The ear rings are very pretty," the nurse said. "Now why don't you go find your aide? Tell her you need to be changed. Eve and I are going to go into my office. We need to talk in private."

I don't belong here, Eve thought frantically. *Gideon, damn it, you can't make me do this.* Determined to botch the interview, Eve followed the nurse into her sterile office. Eve had worn a black skirt and red turtleneck sweater with matching red shoes and purse, thinking that at the most she'd be filling out an application at an agency today. She was painfully aware that *here* her top and accessories were the only touches of color in the room, unless one wanted to count the brown desk and chairs, or the tiny gray specks in the white tile floor.

Doreen's blonde hair was short, barely covering her ears. Despite the fact that her eyelashes were short and pale, the only makeup she wore was a thin coat of pink lipstick. She was wearing white slacks and a white pullover top, covered by a white smock, open at the front. Eve had spotted a couple of C.N.A.s in the rooms they'd passed on their way to Doreen's office. They, too, were dressed in white, but had been wearing a white button up smock, white jeans, and white shoes. Both had also had their hair pulled up in a ponytail, and neither had been wearing jewelry.

The smell in the office was more pleasant than in the hallway, in that it smelled of flowers instead of urine; but it caused Eve's sinuses to tighten. Considering that the only flowers in sight were a bouquet of silk daisies on the desk, Eve surmised that Doreen must have sprayed the room with air freshener.

"Tell me about yourself," Doreen said, gesturing toward the single chair in front of her desk.

Eve perched on the edge of the chair that was offered and pulled her black skirt down over her knees. "What would you like to know?"

The nurse settled back into her chair with a smile. "For starters, tell me about your work experience."

This ought to discourage her Eve thought with a smug grin: "I used to be a teacher. When I left teaching, I allowed my credential to lapse, and became an Executive Secretary. That's pretty much it, except for a little freelance writing. I really don't have the appropriate background for this job. There's no point in wasting anymore of your time." This said, Eve stood up to leave.

"Don't be silly," the nurse said, motioning Eve to sit back down. "There's no experience necessary. We do the training right here at the hospital."

Great, Eve thought venomously. *This is just great.*

"The training course lasts three months. During those three months, you'll work with C.N.A.s who already have their credentials. At the end of that time, we would hope you'll stay here, but you'll be qualified to work anywhere in the state."

Until today, Eve hadn't even known what C.N.A. stood for. She still wouldn't, if it hadn't been spelled out in the paper. "Actually, I think coming here was a mistake. I really don't like hospitals. They give me the creeps."

"I feel the same way," Doreen said with a friendly smile. "It's something you get used to. Here's an application for you to fill out. It's just a formality so we'll have it on record. I'll just go check on Norma, and then I'll be back."

Left alone in the office, Eve stared at the application blank. She was tempted to write that she had a felony conviction. That would serve Gideon right. But no. She couldn't lie…

"All finished?" Doreen asked when she returned. Glancing over Eve's application, she nodded.

"You asked on the phone if I had a strong back," Eve said. "Actually, it's very weak. If a strong back is needed for this job, I don't think—"

"I'm sure that after a few weeks on the job, your back will get stronger," Doreen interrupted. "We'll train you in the proper way to lift. When our C.N.A.s have to lift, they work in teams. So that won't be a problem."

What's going on here? Eve thought, on the verge of panic. *She should have sent me packing when I answered her first question! What's it going to take to get the point across that I'm not right for the job?*

"The pay is five seventy-five an hour, topping out at seven after a year on the job. Out of this will come mandatory union dues. Any questions?"

"No," Eve said quickly. "I don't have any questions. Thank you for taking the time to talk with me, but—"

"When can you start?"

"When can I—You mean you're *offering me the job*?"

"It's hard to come by good C.N.A.'s," Doreen said. "In a small town like this, we don't have that many applicants. Your employment record shows that you're a responsible person. Of course I'll have to check out your references, but I'm sure everything will be fine."

On the way home, in an effort to get Eve's mind off her misery, Carla suggested they talk to the spirit guides. She had a few questions she'd like to ask them.

"What do you want to know?" Eve groused.

They had turned onto the freeway, and were driving past open fields of dried grass, dotted by an occasional tree. "I want to know if people who've died can talk to us," Carla said.

"Gideon?"

"This is Gideon, and I'm of the light. It all depends on whether they've gone to Heaven, or Hell, or been reincarnated. Who did she have in mind?"

"Elvis," Carla said simply. "I want to talk to Elvis."

There was a chuckle inside Eve's head as Gideon processed Carla's request. "Hold on," he said. "Let me ask the Boss." When Gideon returned, he said that Elvis had elected to go back to earth and try to live a better life—without the drugs this time around.

This whole idea of reincarnation was puzzling to Eve. "If everyone gets a second chance to do things right and get into Heaven, what's the purpose in having a Hell? Why did Jesus have to die on the cross?"

"Not everyone gets a second chance," Gideon replied. "Hell is full of mass murders and child molesters, and people who've committed terrible crimes. But people like Elvis who've basically lived a good life, often still wish they could have done a little better. It's up to the boss to make the decision of whether to let them try again or not."

While Eve and Carla were discussing what Gideon had just told them, Gideon interrupted to tell Eve there was a new spirit of light who would like to talk to Carla. "He's not an original angel, and he's never lived on earth. He's from another galaxy. His name is Orlo."

A spirit from another galaxy? It had never occurred to Eve that Heaven might contain spirits from a planet other than earth.

Flattered that a spirit from another galaxy would ask to talk to her, Carla said she would *love* to talk to Orlo. "Ask him about life on his planet. How does their society compare to ours?"

It was a bit awkward passing messages back and forth and having to go through Gideon as a translator. But gradually a picture emerged of a distant planet where there is virtually no crime because anyone who commits a crime is ostracized from society and cut off from the food supply to starve to death. We have only two classes: farmers, and teachers. Farmers are necessary for the survival of the body. Teachers are necessary for the survival of the mind. Thus, the two classes are equal. Since everyone on my planet is either musical or artistic, the soul is nourished as well."

"Everything we do is for the good of the whole," Orlo continued. "Anyone who can't or won't conform is ostracized and cut off from the food supply."

Wow, Eve thought. Half the people she knew would have starved to death by now if they'd been born on Orlo's planet, instead of planet earth. "What about equality of the sexes? Are men and women treated equally on your planet?"

"There is no opposite sex on my planet," Orlo replied.

"*No opposite sex?*" Carla echoed. "You mean you're all—"

"We're like a plant on earth that is self-pollinating," Orlo said. "We are bi-sexual in the sense that we are two sexes contained in the same body. The period of gestation is days, rather than months. Because there is no virtually no sin on our planet, there is no pain associated with childbirth."

"Self-*pollinating?*" Carla echoed. "Nothing like taking the fun out of it... That was a joke, Orlo."

"I do not understand your humor," Orlo said. "Please explain."

"Never mind," Carla groaned. "It wasn't that funny."

When Carla asked her next question, Eve knew she was thinking of her granddaughter who was having problems in preschool. "What about the kids on your planet? Are parents and teachers there more strict than here on earth? What happens there if a child talks back or disobeys?"

Neither Carla nor Eve was prepared for the answer.

"There is no love or emotion on my planet. A child who disobeys is cut off from the community food supply and starved to death. Thus, on my planet, children rarely disobey."

Stacie Spielman

Chapter 16

Eve had told Doreen she needed two weeks to get her affairs in order and make arrangements for the move to Placerville. It wasn't that she actually had that many affairs to get in order. She just wanted to postpone the move as long as possible. She still hadn't adjusted to the idea that she was being forced into working in a convalescent hospital—the one place in the world that she could not even imagine herself *visiting* on a regular basis, let alone working.

She was wearing jeans and a baggy red sweatshirt, sitting crosslegged in the middle of her bed. "I just don't understand how you could do this to me, Gideon. You led me on for months, telling me about this great job I was destined to have, and *this* is what it turns out to be?"

"I never said it was a great job," Gideon said. "What I said was it's the job you're destined to have. Trust me, Sweetheart, there's a reason for this. You have some life's lessons to learn, and this hospital is where Jesus wants you to learn them. I can't tell you what He has planned for you. But take my word for it, it will be wonderful."

Life's lessons? Hadn't she learned enough lessons for one lifetime? "I really wish I could see you face to face, Gideon. I'd like to see your eyes when you're telling me these things, so I'd know whether you're putting me on. Why can't you just appear to me, so I can see you?"

"Sweetheart," Gideon said, "It's not easy for a guardian angel to appear in human form. It's extremely draining. Taking care of you is a big job. I need all the energy I can get."

Apparently Eve's disappointment was evident. At any rate, Gideon thought it worthy of a suggestion. "I'm not an artist like Joan," he began, "But what if I could—"

"Could what?" Eve asked glumly.

"What if I could alter the grain in your coffee table to make a picture of myself the way I looked when we were married? I could do one of you as you looked back then too, with your blonde hair pulled back and pinned up on top of your head."

84

"You could actually do that?" Eve asked in awe. Eve knew he could swing a pendulum and stop it on a dime. She knew he could predict the future to an extent, and do whatever it took to blur her vision and bring it back again. But change the grain in a table to make a self-portrait?

"You have to be patient," Gideon said. "I've never tried this before. It may take a few days."

Excited, Eve leaped from the bed and raced to the living room where Carla was seated in front of the T.V., cradling the doll and watching yet *another* replay of Pete's Dragon. "This is it," Carla grumbled. "I've paid to rent this damned thing three times. The child part of my subconscious had better store up the memories. Because once I've turned the film in this time, I'm not checking it out again."

Eve had watched the film with Carla once, and sympathized with her dilemma. Weary of watching the same film over and over, Carla had put the videotape in the machine and picked up a book to read. Within seconds, Joan had been "on the line" telling Eve to give Carla the message that her subconscious couldn't see the *movie* if her eyes and conscious mind were reading a *book*.

At last count, Carla had seen the film five times. This time was number six.

"Guess what?" Eve said excitedly. "Gideon's going to change the grain in my coffee table to make a picture of himself! Can you believe it?"

For the next three days, the roommates checked the table every time Gideon's promise came to mind. Though Eve checked the table hourly while Carla was away at work, this was one watched pot that was very slow to boil.

They had gone to a fast food restaurant for dinner, and were commiserating with one another about Eve's upcoming move. "Too bad Gideon didn't get his portrait done in time," Carla said. "I think he may have bitten off more than he could chew."

It was already dark by the time they got home. When they arrived and clicked on the light, Carla glanced at the table. "Look!" she gasped. She was pointing to the cabinet supporting the tabletop. Her hand was trembling with excitement. "He did it!

Eve's heart skipped a beat as she dropped to her knees for a closer view. "Where?"

"Right there," Carla said. "See? He's wearing a hat. But there's his face with his moustache and beard. He looks just like he described himself!"

The three-inch-tall face and neck were in profile, looking down into the eyes of a woman to the left and several inches below. The woman, also shown in profile, had her hair pinned atop her head, and appeared to be wearing a high-necked gown.

"Look!" Carla said. "He's still working on the one of him right now. I just saw him fill in the eyebrow!"

Eve couldn't see the difference, but Carla swore she'd seen the change occur as surely as if a brush had just painted the final stroke. "Gideon?" Eve said. "Is this just our imagination? Or did you really succeed in changing the grain?"

"This is Gideon, and I'm of the light. I told you I'm not much of an artist," he reminded her. "But I did my best. Joan did the eyebrow. That's what Carla just saw."

When Carla spoke again, her voice was filled with awe. "Look at the dress you were wearing, Eve. Except for the neck, it looks just like the one I have folded in the chest in my bedroom. It belonged to my grandmother."

"The one in the portrait is your wedding dress," Gideon said. "Most of the time, you kept it packed away. But sometimes you'd put it on and model it for me because you knew how much I loved to see you in it. I've often thought if I could just come back to be with you again, I'd give up all—"

"But you *are* with me, Gideon."

"That's not what I mean," Gideon said softly. "As a guardian angel, I can never experience making love again. I'll never be able to kiss again, or feel the touch of a woman's hand—your hand—running your fingers through the hair on my chest... I'd be in trouble if I even got caught *talking* like this."

The warmth that had washed over Eve when he'd begun to speak about making love was totally inappropriate, and Eve knew it. Banishing the thought from her mind, she blinked. When she did, the image in the table temporarily seemed to disappear, but when she peered more closely, it was definitely there. Eve didn't notice when Carla quietly got up and left the room...

"Look!" Carla said from the doorway.

Startled, Eve turned to see Carla holding up a white lace gown. The lace was slightly yellowed from age. Whoever had worn it had been tiny—hardly bigger than an adolescent child.

"Why don't you try it on?" Carla suggested.

"I couldn't fit into that," Eve said. "I couldn't have fit into it when I was a teenager, let alone now."

"Try it for *me*," Gideon urged. "Please."

Convinced that she'd never even get the gown over her shoulders, Eve took it into the bathroom and peeled off her shirt and jeans. When she emerged from the bathroom, she'd managed to get into the gown, but could only get it zipped halfway up the back. "I told you it wouldn't fit."

"Let me tuck the fabric under where it won't zip in the back," Carla suggested. "It'll make it look like the back of the gown's cut in a V." When the fabric had been turned under, the gown actually looked like it fit. "Let's pull your hair up too, like it was in the picture."

When Carla had finished her handiwork, she stood back to appraise it with a critical eye. "That's not bad," she said with a nod of approval. "If you had high-topped shoes instead of bare feet, I could almost believe you stepped out of the eighteen hundreds. Go in my bedroom, and take a look in the mirror."

Feeling more than a little self-conscious, Eve went into the bedroom to stand in front of the mirrored closet. With her hair pulled atop her head, and the white lace gown, she'd been transformed. Smiling, Eve did a pirouette. So this was basically what she'd looked like on her wedding day. She wondered what Gideon had worn. Had he worn a suit with a high-collared shirt and white gloves, and carried a top hat? She preferred not to ask. Some things were best left to the imagination.

"Come out here and model it for Gideon," Carla called from the living room. Eve knew Gideon could see her right where she was, without her having to go to the living room. But since Carla was really getting into this, Eve went into the living room to humor her.

"So what do you think, Gideon?" Carla asked. "Does she look like you remember her?"

"He says you've outdone yourself," Eve translated. "He wants me to turn all around and pretend he's sitting there on the couch watching."

"Well," Carla said with a grin, "Go ahead and do it!"

No longer self-conscious, Eve extended her arms and slowly twirled around and around.

"You look beautiful," Gideon breathed. "Except for the color of your hair, you look just like—"

Speaking in a whisper, without even hearing what Gideon had said, Carla completed the thought: "You look just like you did in the picture."

Chapter 17

Soon after the incident with the picture and the gown, Eve told Gideon they needed to talk. She was lying in bed, staring at the ceiling, listening to a tape of Crystal Gale. "This isn't healthy for either of us," she said in her mind. "The way you're always remembering what it was like when you were here on earth… What it was like when we were together… It's going to get you into trouble. And if anyone but Carla knew about *me* they'd think I'm certifiable! I'm on the verge of *falling in love with you*, Gideon, and you're not even human! How am I ever supposed to find a *man* to spend the rest of my life with, if I'm in love with my guardian angel?"

There was a moment of mental silence before Gideon spoke. When he did, there was an uncharacteristic resignation in his voice. "Just for the record, Sweetheart, being in trouble is nothing new for me. You'll never know how many times I've been in hot water over my methods of taking care of you. I'll probably have to be a guardian angel for a hundred more years to make up for it, before I can move on to the next higher rung. But don't worry. It's been worth it. And don't worry about competition either. Once the right man comes along—which will be soon—I'll bow out of the picture."

"But I don't *want* you to bow out of the picture," Eve protested. "I love you, Gideon. Promise me you'll never back away to the point that I can't talk to you when I need to—regardless of whether there's a man in my life, or not."

"I'll always be there in the background," Gideon assured her. "But no man is going to stick around if he feels like he has to compete for your affections—especially with a rival he can't even see. No, Sweetheart, we can't go on indefinitely the way we have been. I want you to have a man in your life. There's nothing I want more than for you to be happy."

As if to prove that he meant what he said, the next night Gideon asked Eve if she felt ready to meet the man she was destined to marry. He had mentioned before that this man lived near Placerville, but Eve had suspected he was just saying that to get her to make the move.

"He has a favorite eating place in Placerville that he goes to twice a week for brunch. If you were to drive up there tomorrow while Carla's at work, you'd get a chance to see him, and let *him* get a good look at *you*."

Intrigued at the prospect, despite her sadness over the fact that if this really *was* the man of her future, her relationship with Gideon was destined to change, Eve asked Gideon to describe this mystery man.

"He's tall and well-built," Gideon said. "I know from experience that you like hairy chests, so you're going to love *his*. He has dark, longish hair and a moustache and beard—short, and well trimmed, just the way you like them."

It occurred to Eve that Gideon could have been describing Johnny, from the dance club years ago. *So far, so good,* she thought with a delicious shiver. *What's his name?*

Gideon told her that for security reasons, he couldn't divulge her soul mate's real name. "I *can* tell you he lives on a ranch, and has horses. He likes movies, and going out to dinner. And he loves to dance—especially country western. For now, we'll just call him Chad."

"What's the catch?" Eve said suspiciously. "This guy sounds perfect for me. But I know there has to be a catch. There always is."

"The catch is he's recently divorced," Gideon said, "and right now he doesn't have a whole lot of self-esteem. These past few months, he's been pretty much a hermit. His friends have been trying to get him to date, but he's gun shy. He doesn't think he's ready."

The next morning, Eve took special care with her hair and makeup. Since Chad lived on a ranch, she pulled her shoulder length hair back in a banana clip and chose to wear jeans and boots, rather than jeans and tennis shoes. In the absence of a Western blouse, she wore a white pullover sweater. She arrived at the country restaurant fifteen minutes before Chad was due to show. Seated in a corner booth gnawing her lower lip, Eve played with her napkin and tried not to look at her watch.

"Can I take your order?" a dark-haired waitress asked, "Or are you waiting for someone?"

"I'm waiting for someone," Eve said with a nervous smile, "but I'll have an orange juice. No, on second thought, make that a Coke."

Eve had finished her Coke and ordered another. By any stretch of the imagination, Chad should have been here by now. Rather than risk drawing the attention of the dark ones, Eve hadn't yet spoken to Gideon since her arrival. Now, she broke the mental silence. "So where is he?" she asked worriedly.

When Gideon replied, it was not what Eve wanted to hear. "He got up this morning and got dressed to come, but when he went out to his truck, all his tires were flat. I'm sorry, Sweetheart. Apparently the dark ones overheard our conversation and figured out who he was. He's at a gas station right now getting his tires replaced, but it doesn't look like he's going to make it for brunch."

Angry and disappointed, Eve finished her Coke and paid the bill, then went out to her car. What the—Running along the driver's side door was a scratch more than eight inches long. Eve had had the Shadow for two years, without a single dent or scratch. It sickened and infuriated her that someone had apparently done this while she was in the restaurant.

"Who was it?" she grated.

"Sweetheart, it was a couple of teenagers."

"Why didn't you *stop them*?"

"This is Gideon, I did cause the boy with the key to drop it. But he picked the key up and scratched your car anyway."

Furious, Eve rubbed a finger over the scratch. Wait a minute... Rubbing a little harder, she frowned. What was going on here? Without saying a word, she spat on her finger and used the spit to wipe the area clean surrounding the scratch. Her car hadn't been *keyed*. It hadn't even been *scratched*. With a little bit of elbow grease, the mark had wiped right off!

The hair on the back of Eve's neck stood on end with the realization that Gideon had lied to her—or that the spirit talking to her wasn't Gideon at all. "Who are you?" she asked shakily.

"Did you really think I didn't know where you were going, just because you didn't talk to Gideon on the way?" a voice in her head asked.

Frightened by the voice and its absolute calmness, Eve got into the Shadow and pulled onto the main street. "Why do you hate me so much?" she cried. "I've never done anything to you. I don't even know who you are!"

"That's a simple matter to rectify," the voice said. "This is Satan."

Eve's stomach lurched violently and her breath caught in her throat. Her heartbeat, already erratic, now began to race. For an instant, the car swerved, but she quickly brought it under control.

"Careful, Eve," the silken voice said. "You wouldn't want to have an accident, now *would* you?"

"Leave me alone," Eve said shakily. "I don't want to talk to you. Just leave me alone!"

The soft voice reminded her of the voice of a child molester in a film she'd once seen, trying to seduce a teenager. "You haven't heard what I'm offering," the voice crooned.

Eve wasn't certain she believed this was Satan. But if not the devil himself, it was one of his disciples. "Whatever you're offering, forget it!" Eve said forcefully. "I don't want anything from you. Not now. Not ever!"

Her words of denial had no effect, and the voice continued to speak as she pulled onto the freeway. "I've known you since the first time you spoke to me through a Ouija Board. It's quite possible that I know you better than you even know yourself."

"That was *you*?" Eve gasped.

"It really makes no difference whether it was me or one of my demons," the voice replied. "The end result is the same. Whether you realize it or not, you want what I'm offering, Eve. I can give you more power than you ever dreamed of."

The statement brought Eve's thought pattern up short. "I don't want *power*," she replied. "Even if I did, I wouldn't accept it from *you*."

"Everyone wants power," Satan replied. "And you're no exception."

"Then you're not the mind reader I thought you were," Eve scoffed. Where would Satan have gotten the idea that she had a desire for power? She'd never dreamed of being in a position of authority; never wanted to control other people around her...

"Let me look into your mind," Satan challenged. "Let me look into your innermost thoughts and desires. If you truly don't want power, I'll be able to see it."

"Look away," Eve said. "I don't have anything to hide."

Several minutes of silence passed. Sunrise Ave., one mile. Signaling to change lanes, Eve breathed a sigh of relief that the voice was apparently gone.

But a moment later, the voice returned. "You're right. You *don't* want power in terms of controlling others. You prefer to get your way by diplomatic means if possible. But you do want *money*, Eve. And what is money, if not power? I can make you rich, Eve. I can make you a millionaire. All you have to do is say what I want to hear."

Eve felt like the Eve from Bible times in the Garden of Eden. "I don't deny that I'd like to be rich," she said uneasily. "And I suppose you're right when you say money's a source of power. But that's not why I want it. I want it to *survive* and live a normal lifestyle. I want it to help the people I love and care about."

"Tell me you love me," Satan said. "Tell me you love me, and it's yours."

"I *don't* love you!" Eve shouted. "I never will!" Her skin crawled with revulsion at the *thought* of saying the words.

"You don't have to mean it," the hypnotic voice breathed. "All you have to do is say it, Eve. Three little words, and I'll make you rich beyond you're wildest dreams. Say it, Eve. Tell me you love me."

Eve's hands clutched the steering wheel in a white knuckled grip. When she spoke at last, her voice was trembling, but firm. "In the name of Jesus, I command you to leave. Get thee behind me, Satan."

Chapter 18

There was no possible way to get all of her possessions into the furnished efficiency apartment, so Eve didn't even intend to try. She was fortunate in that Kevin and his dad had volunteered to help with the move—first to put the bigger items in storage in Shingle Springs; then to move selected items to Placerville, to the hotel apartment. Now, as she looked at the expression on Tom's face, Eve was wondering if she'd made the right decision in accepting his offer of help. Not that she could blame him for having his doubts. He must think she'd taken leave of her senses.

Eve could barely control the urge to laugh at the look in his eyes behind his dark-lensed glasses when they loaded the coffee table onto the antique elevator and closed the accordion door. Tom was an athletic man with short brown hair and a well-trimmed moustache—the stereotype of a country club jock. In a job interview, he had once described himself as a jock, and her as a scholar. "It's a good thing we sent Kevin on up ahead," Tom commented. "I don't think this elevator could have made it with all three of us, and the table, too.

It took five trips from Tom's van to the third floor apartment to unload the last of Eve's belongings. Acutely aware that Tom had avoided making any comments about the apartment, Eve thanked him for his help, and asked if he'd like a drink.

"No thanks," Tom said. "We need to get home. I'll wait out in the hall while you two say 'Good-bye.'"

Engulfing her son in an affectionate hug, Eve spoke into his neck that she would call him in a couple of days, and be in the valley next weekend to take him to lunch. It was hard to believe he had grown so much in the past year. He'd long since passed Eve up in height. The stubble on his chin when Eve lifted her face to kiss him scratched her cheek. "Looks like I'll be buying you an electric shaver for Christmas."

"My dad already bought me one," Kevin said with a grin. "I was planning to hit you up for a watch."

Eve's first night in her new home wasn't lonely. She had too much to do for that. Of course Carla called and they talked for over an hour. But beyond that, there were boxes to be unpacked and things to be put away.

The main room served triple duty as a living room, dining nook, and a kitchen nook in the front right corner. The threadbare brown sofa had cushions barely two and a half inches thick. The dinette set was a cheap service for two. And the kitchen, such as it was, contained a half-sized gold refrigerator, a half-sized sink, a counter top electric stove, and six inches of counter space. Eve was glad she had brought her birch coffee table with the grain portraits of herself and Gideon, and the matching end table for the T.V. At least *something* felt like home.

The bathroom next to the kitchen nook was wide enough for a tub and a toilet, and that was it. The towel rack was on the wall behind the tub. The bedroom was about the same size as the living room, with a double bed, a white French Provincial dresser, and a matching nightstand with the ugliest lamp Eve had ever seen. Fortunately, Eve had brought her own brass lamp. The first thing she did after hanging her pictures was to put the furnished lamp on the floor in the closet. When she did, her mind flashed back to the Christmas Eve in the valley when the Indian statue she'd painted had been smashed beyond repair.

Shaking off the memory and the bad feelings it evoked, Eve lined the dresser drawers with scented shelf paper and unpacked her clothes. She would have to go shopping tomorrow and buy white jeans and smocks for work. The portable stereo sound of Kenny Rogers kept her company as she arranged her meager kitchen supplies in the tiny cupboard beneath the stove. When she'd finished, she flopped onto the sofa and imagined herself surrounded by a protective white light.

"This is Gideon, and I'm of the light," a familiar voice said in her head. "Welcome home, Sweetheart. You can't imagine how glad I am to finally have you here where you're safe. I have someone I'd like for you to meet, but first would you please turn off the music? The singing is a distraction, and I want your full attention."

Considering that she was about to meet someone new, Eve said she'd prefer to talk through the board.

"This spirit is not a guardian angel," the pendulum spelled out. "He's several rungs on the ladder higher than that. You're going to be spending a lot of time with him from now on. His name is Saul."

Eve had a feeling she was about to find out why she'd been brought here. It was about time.

"Hello, Eve," the pendulum spelled out. "My name is Saul, and I'm of the light. I'm going to be your Healing guide."

Healing guide? Did he say *healing guide*? What was this guy talking about?

"I know Gideon has told you that you've been chosen," Saul said. "I've been chosen too, to train you in your work as a healer on your path to becoming pure light."

Pure light? Eve didn't know what he was talking about, and didn't intend to ask.

"Would you mind if I talked telepathically? It would be much faster, and I promise not to give you a headache."

For the next two and a half hours, Saul talked in Eve's head, explaining to Eve what her destiny was to be. He told her she was destined to become a great healer. To illustrate the point, he compared the healing touch to pumping gas, with God being the oil well and refinery, Jesus the pump, and Saul the hose. "You'll be the nozzle. Through your hands will pass the healing energy just as the nozzle funnels gas into a car. The car represents the patient."

Eve couldn't believe what she was hearing. *This* was why she'd been brought here? She, who had never shown even the slightest interest in being a nurse or doctor was being pushed into becoming a *natural healer*? She didn't even believe in natural healers! "Why *me*?"

"Because you've never taken drugs. You've never drunk or smoked. You've never taken any substance into your body to defile it. You're a good person..."

"But I haven't lived a celibate life," Eve protested. "I'm a junk food junkie..."

"Nobody's perfect," Saul said. "Past sexual relations haven't affected your health, so they're not a factor. And your diet can be changed."

"But I don't want to change my diet," Eve protested. "I *like* the things I eat."

"We'll deal with that when the time comes," Saul said. "For now, I want you to buy a deck of Tarot cards."

"*Tarot cards!*" Eve protested. "Those are used in witchcraft and the occult!"

"Yes," Saul agreed. "They are. But they can also be used for good. Tarot cards are like electricity. Used properly, electricity will light your house and cook your food. Used improperly, it can kill you. With Tarot, as with many things, it all depends on who's using them, and for what purpose."

Eve was flattered that she rated her own personal Healing guide, and she liked Saul. She really did. But she hadn't asked for any of this, and she wasn't at all sure she liked what came with it.

For starters, there were reserved parking spaces for hotel guests, but none for residents of hotel apartments. For those who'd been here long enough to rate parking passes in the garage down the street, this wasn't a major problem. For Eve, it meant having to park on the street, and move her car every two hours till seven p.m. After that, she was free to park in the lot behind the hotel, as long as she moved her car back to the street by seven the next morning. The parking lot was accessible by a narrow alleyway that ran between the hotel and the neighboring building.

The musty smell that permeated the hotel overpowered even the lemon wax Eve had applied to her furniture. Tomorrow when she went shopping, she would have to make a point of looking for an air freshener strong enough to fight it. While she was at it, she would buy a foam pad to put on top of the uncomfortable mattress.

Tossing and squirming in the moonlight that streamed through the thin drapes covering her bedroom window, Eve pulled a pillow over her head to muffle the drunken shouts from the alley below. Whoever was shouting had the foulest mouth Eve had ever heard. But even that was preferable to the grunts, squeaky springs, and wall thumping that were going on in the room next door.

When the alarm went off, signaling that it was time to move her car to the street, Eve opened one eye and groaned. "I can't do this, Gideon. I can't live in a place where sleep is a luxury. If I'm going to have to work in this town, you have to find me another place to live."

"This is Gideon, and I'm of the light. Good morning to you too, Sweetheart. You'd better get a move on if you don't want to get a ticket."

Muttering beneath her breath, Eve stepped into her jeans and pulled on a sweatshirt and tennis shoes. Considering that the elevator gave her the creeps, she took the stairway past the laundry room and went out the back door onto the narrow sidewalk that led to the alley. The damp morning air caused her to shiver. In two weeks, it would be Halloween. For the first time in her life, she wouldn't be celebrating.

She never would have believed this could happen: that she—Eve Tarlton— would draw the attention of Satan himself, that this attention would lead to her having to move to this Podunk town, or that she would be chosen by the *Master Healer*, and pressured into working in a convalescent hospital. She supposed she should feel honored to have been chosen. Instead, she felt persecuted and cheated. She cursed the day she had ever gone to the psychic and learned that she even *had* a crew of *spirit guides*.

Eve had no doubt, had she never been exposed to the spirit realm, that she would be living a normal life like everyone else around her. She would have come to the valley and found work like any normal woman of her age with her particular skills and talents. Yet here she was, skulking through the alley at six o'clock in the morning, praying she wouldn't be mugged before she got to her car!

After moving the Shadow, Eve walked back to the hotel and went back to bed. She wasn't due to start work till day after tomorrow. She'd been awake half the night. This morning, come hell or high water, she was going to sleep in. When she finally awoke four hours later and went down to move the Shadow, there was a parking ticket under the wiper.

Anger and self-pity warred for dominance in Eve's mind. She'd lived here less than twenty-four hours, and already she hated the town of Placerville. She hated the hotel and its musty smell. She hated the demons that a year ago she hadn't even believed in, but who now seemed to be forever at her door. She hated the fact that she couldn't live with her son. She hated that dancing, the activity she enjoyed most, was now apparently a thing of the past. She hated that she didn't have an assigned parking space, and was burdened with having to move her car all day long. And perhaps most of all, she hated the job that she had yet to start.

A phrase from her childhood came to mind: "I cried because I had no shoes till I met a man who had no feet." What did that have to do with the price of tea in China? It was a phrase Eve's mother used to use when Eve got depressed prior to menstrual periods as a teenager. It had never occurred to her mom to just buy her a bottle of Midol.

Pull yourself together, Eve chided. *At least you have a job and a warm place to live, which is more than can be said for the poor soul you saw on the street when you went out to move your car.*

What she needed was a good breakfast. A glass of orange juice and a plate of bacon and eggs at Bob's Big Boy would do wonders for her outlook. At least that's what Eve told herself.

95

By noon, she had eaten and gone to K Mart, where she'd bought five pairs of white jeans, a pair of work shoes, and five white smocks—one work outfit for each day of the week. Next, she'd gone to the grocery store for bread, eggs, milk, cheese, and hamburger. It might not be a gourmet selection, but at least she wouldn't go hungry. The next item on the agenda was a deck of Tarot cards.

A check of the phone book revealed that there was one metaphysical store in town. Rather than drive to the store and have to parallel park by a meter, Eve called first to ask if they had Tarot cards in stock. Apparently there'd been a recent run on Tarot. That or they hadn't ordered enough in the first place. At any rate, there were none to be had. The Tarot would have to wait till she made a trip to visit Kevin.

Eve had noticed when she drove through town yesterday that a movie she'd been wanting to see was playing at the theater. Maybe a matinee would help lift her spirits. Eve had never gone to a movie alone, but she needn't have worried about anyone's thinking it was strange. The theater was practically empty.

"This is Gideon, and I'm of the light," a voice in her head said.

"And this is Saul. I'm of the light."

"Hi, Guys," Eve said in her mind. "I'm glad you're here. But I'm really not in a very good mood today, and I'd prefer not to get into any big discussions at the moment. The movie's about to start."

"This is not the movie," Gideon said. "It's a preview. I just wanted to tell you for future reference that if we ever need to have a private conversation, this is the place to do it."

"Yes," Saul agreed. "I'm sure Gideon has told you that gold drains dark spirits of strength. There's enough gold in the ground under this theater to make it virtually impossible for them to interfere."

It was good to know there was at least one place in the world where Eve could commune with her guardian angel without having to worry about being interrupted. "That's good to know," she mouthed silently. "But for now, how about if we watch the movie?"

The movie was a Kevin Costner film. Except for an occasional comment on the story and on Eve's reactions to Kevin Costner, the guides honored her request not to talk till it was over.

After the movie, Eve drove back to the hotel and parked the Shadow. She'd been right about the matinee. It had helped her mood. But it still galled her to know that she'd have to move the car in two hours.

That evening, Eve called her mom to let her know she'd gotten moved in and was doing okay. After that, she called Carla.

"So how was your first night?" Carla asked. "I already miss you. I kind of got used to having you around."

"I miss you too," Eve said. "You wouldn't have believed the noise around her last night. Some drunk was staggering around in the alley yelling 'Fuck you!' and on the other side of my bedroom wall, a honeymoon couple was doing just that. They kept bumping against my bedroom wall. They even knocked my pictures crooked."

"Sounds like you had a more exciting night than I did," Carla said with a laugh. "I just washed my hair then fell asleep in front of the news."

Mindful of the fact that this was a long distance call, Eve kept one eye on the clock. After ten minutes, Carla said she would call her back so they could share the bill.

When they had hung up, Saul told Eve it was time for a demonstration. Curious, Eve asked what kind.

"Actually," Saul said, "It's God who's going to do the demonstration. He wants you to make a fist."

Puzzled, and a little frightened, Eve made a fist of her right hand. What had she done to rate God's taking such an interest in her at this point in her life? First, thanking Carla for lending her the money and making it possible for her to come to Placerville. Now, wanting to do a demonstration? She had thought God stopped doing this sort of thing back in the days of Moses!

"Hold the fist as tight as you can," Saul instructed. "This fist represents your heart, and how it's been closed to God ever since you were in college."

Forced to own up to the fact that she'd allowed her faith to falter, Eve was overcome by a sense of guilt. "My heart isn't closed against Him anymore," she protested. "I went through an agnostic period for awhile, but I believe in Him now. I thought He knew that."

"You *believe* in Him, but you think of Him as some sort of ogre," Saul said. "You're not even *trying* to have a relationship with Him. That's why He feels your heart is closed. That's why He wants to do this demonstration."

Eve was thinking through what Saul had just said when she was startled by a finger's breaking broke loose from her fist. She hadn't released the finger. She was still holding the fist as tightly as she could. She hadn't felt anything touch her—no sense of muscle weakness, or of the finger's being pried loose. When she tried to close it, the finger wouldn't stay down. Suddenly another finger popped loose. From outside in the alley, Eve could hear the drunken voices of a man and a woman quarreling, oblivious to the fact that upstairs in this hotel, a miracle was taking place.

"Keep the other fingers tight," Saul said. "As tight as you can."

Though Eve renewed her effort to keep her fist closed, straining to the point that her arm was trembling, her fingers and thumb broke loose from the fist one by one till her hand was outspread in an open palm. If she hadn't experienced it, she wouldn't have believed it. God, the creator of the universe, had asked her—Eve Tarlton—to make a fist, and had personally opened her hand.

"Your open palm is your heart as He wants it to be," Saul said. "Open to receive Him. Open to a personal relationship with Him."

Awestruck by what she had just experienced, Eve began to tremble. Tears filled her eyes and spilled out onto her cheeks.

"God wants to know what it would take for you to be comfortable having a personal relationship with him," Saul said. "You read a lot of books, and watch a lot of movies. If you were to think of a story character or celebrity who, to your mind, represents a father figure who loves unconditionally yet commands respect and authority—who would it be?"

A number of actors came to mind from family programs Eve had seen on T.V. both as a child and as an adult, but the one who stood out in her mind was Lorne Greene as Ben Cartwright on Bonanza... "I guess I'd have to say Ben Cartwright."

"Then, when you pray to God, if it would help, why not picture Him in your mind as looking like Lorne Greene, if that's what it would take to make you comfortable?"

Somehow the thought of picturing God as Lorne Greene took away from the specialness of what had just happened. "I don't know," Eve said. "Somehow that doesn't sound very respectful."

"If that's what it takes to make you comfortable, just explain to God that you mean no disrespect," Saul said. "And by the way, God isn't the only one who's unhappy with you. Jesus isn't too happy with you either."

"What did *I* do?" Eve protested. "I moved here where He wanted me to move. I took a job I didn't want, to train for what *He* wants me to do. I don't drink. I don't steal. I don't lie or cheat or commit adultery. *What have I done* to make Him unhappy?"

"It's not what you've done," Saul said patiently. "It's what you haven't done. You're very comfortable talking to Gideon or to *me*. But you've hardly talked to Him since you were a child. Jesus wants to be a part of your life. But He doesn't crash parties where He hasn't been invited."

Chapter 19

The first week on the job was a nightmare filled with sights and smells that prior to this Eve had never even imagined. *Textbook* training began at 2:00 p.m., and took up more than a third of each workday. The training was held at a long table in the conference room, and consisted to a large part of Doreen's reading the text aloud in a droning voice devoid of inflection. Having worked as a teacher before Kevin was born, Eve was appalled at this teaching method. But others in the class knew nothing of Eve's teaching experience. She preferred to keep it that way. Of the eight other women in the class, all were younger than Eve. Most were barely out of high school, and had as their educational goal in life to obtain their three-month credential as a certified nursing assistant. Eve had hoped to make friends at work that she could socialize with in her off-duty hours, but this was obviously not going to happen. The only woman here even close to her age was Doreen, and she was married.

Each of the nine trainees was assigned to care for eight patients, under the watchful eye of the nurse in charge. Beds had to be stripped and changed each morning, patients sponge bathed or showered, and their hair and teeth brushed before dressing for breakfast. Breakfast for residents who were ambulatory was served in the dining room. For those who were bedridden, breakfast was served in bed. Patients unable to feed themselves had to be fed.

A four-tiered cart of breakfast plates was wheeled into the hallway each day at 7:30 a.m. At that time, all C.N.A.s were expected to be finished with their pre-breakfast chores and ready to begin serving. The food wasn't all that hot to begin with, but at least it was warm for the first patients served. By the time the cart reached residents at the end of the hall, it was lukewarm to room temperature at best.

Once patients had been fed, it was the C.N.A.s' job to wash their hands and faces and collect the bibs and trays. By then, it was time to make the rounds taking temperatures and blood pressure, and changing soiled sheets and gowns. Patients who could sit up or be belted into wheelchairs were wheeled to the dining room or into the hallway, where they stayed till after lunch. Soiled sheets were to be placed in a plastic bag the size of lawn bags for collecting cut grass. Sometime between breakfast and two o'clock each day, each C.N.A. was expected to take her soiled laundry to the washroom and rinse the sheets and towels by hand before putting them into the canvas laundry bags stationed at each end of the hallway. At twelve noon, lunch was served, and the whole process began all over again except that by now the patients were dressed, and the process was reversed.

After lunch trays and bibs had been collected, water jugs filled, and beds freshly made, it was time to make the rounds doing Range of Motion exercises. In a normal routine, the C.N.A.s would have time between two and three p.m. to wheel their patients back to their rooms and put them to bed. But because of time restrictions during training, this process was by necessity moved up. As a result, Eve found it difficult if not impossible to get all her soiled sheets rinsed before class. The entire first week, she was forced to leave her bag of foul-smelling bed linens on the floor in the washroom with a note attached saying they were her responsibility to rinse, and that she would return to rinse them after class. Considering that training class went right up to punch-out time and no over-time was allowed, that meant Eve was forced to clock out at five, then return to the washroom for whatever time was needed to gag her way through the rinsing process before going home to dinner.

Her first five days on the job, Eve went through two bottles of hand lotion and five dozen disposable pairs of plastic gloves. At night, she would dream of the residents in her care—sixteen in all, due to the fact that each C.N.A. had one group of patients three days a week, and another group for the other two: There was Nadean, the young woman who'd been hit by a drunk driver and reduced to the mental age of six months; Thelma, the seventy-year-old woman who cried round-the-clock for her mother; Norma, who was perpetually asking "What's my name? Do you like my ear rings?" Darby, the double amputee; Mrs. Stillwell, crippled with Rheumatoid Arthritis; her constant whiner roommate, Mrs. Japetto; Carlo, the young man who'd tried to out race an oncoming train… The list played on and on in Eve's head. She couldn't even eat and appreciate her food. In her nostrils was the constant stench of stale urine and diarrhea.

Though Carla called each evening, and Eve had Gideon and Saul for company, Eve was totally drained—both mentally and physically. As a favor to Joan, Eve secretly drew a cartoon of a dragon to give to Carla, and colored it to Joan's specifications. By the time the weekend came, Eve was ready to see her son and go dancing. "I know I can't go to any of the places Mitch goes," she told Carla. "But isn't there any other place we can go that we wouldn't have to worry about Mitch showing up?"

"I hate to say this," Carla said, "But I think you're going to have to wait awhile before you can get back into dancing. Why don't you just come down and we'll visit and take in a movie? You can spend the night, then take your son to lunch tomorrow, and go shopping for anything you need before you go back up the hill."

Though Eve hated to admit it, she knew Carla was right. *Damn Mitch Titus.* Why did he have to get a fixation on *her*?

"I can get there by six thirty if I don't eat before I come. Do you feel like going out for fast food?"

"How about if we just send out for Chinese," Carla suggested. "My treat."

Chinese sounded good to Eve. She hated to have Carla foot the bill, but she knew Carla knew about her budget constraints. She also knew better than to argue. "Okay. Gotta go. I'll see you after while."

By the time Eve arrived at Carla's apartment, she was feeling a little more relaxed. Handing the dragon drawing to Carla with a grin, Eve told her Joan's suggestion that she hang it on the wall so her subconscious mind would be able to see it every time she walked through the apartment, and wouldn't feel deprived at being unable to re-watch the film.

"It's cute," Carla said. "But I can't hang this up. Anyone who comes to my apartment will think I'm crazy."

"Not if you tell them your granddaughter colored it."

And so it was settled, and the cartoon picture of Elliot was taped to the wall in the hallway enroute to the bathroom.

When the Chinese food arrived, Saul asked Eve to introduce him to Carla. "He's the healing guide I told you about," Eve said, opening the chow main carton and dumping it onto a serving plate. The aroma of sweet and sour pork made her mouth water. "He prefers to represent himself as a black man because he says I've never thought of black men in positions of power before now."

Carla had set flatware and two paper dinner plates on the table, then gone back to the kitchen for sodas. "So what does this black guide look like? Are we talking Sidney Poitier? Harry Balafonte? Martin Luther King? Cassius Clay?"

When Saul answered, there was a definite smile in his voice. "This is Saul, and I'm of the light. Tell her I'm a cross between Poitier and Balafonte, but with silver hair."

"Oooo. He sounds handsome," Carla said after Eve had repeated Saul's words. "Saul, Eve told me why you're one of her guides. But she didn't say who you used to be when you were human."

"I was a physician more than five hundred years ago," Saul replied. "Now I'm a being of light, working my way up the ladder toward the ultimate goal."

"Which is?" Carla asked, taking a bite of chow mein.

"What everyone in Heaven is working toward," Saul answered through Eve. "To become pure light."

At this, Eve popped a chunk of sweet and sour pork into her mouth. "Sounds boring to me, doing nothing but shine all day."

"That's because you don't understand the concept," Saul said. "When you get to heaven, you'll understand that there is no greater aspiration. The only thing beyond it is Jesus Himself."

Carla didn't say anything, but Eve had yet to be convinced.

Before leaving with Carla for the movie, Eve placed a call to Kevin and left a message to let him know she was here, and available to take him to lunch at Togo's tomorrow. Later, when she and Carla returned from the movie, Joan identified herself and asked if Eve would mind if she talked to Carla.

"Eve will be leaving tomorrow to go back to Placerville, Carla. If there's anything you want to ask me, now's the time.

"No," Carla said tiredly. "I can't think of anything offhand. Except how's the childlike part of my subconscious doing?"

"I'm glad you brought that up so I wouldn't have to," Joan said. "Your subconscious was very upset with you for putting Darla away in the closet. To your subconscious mind, putting the doll away where it can't be seen or touched is the same as when you were a child and weren't allowed to play with your cousin's doll."

"Oh," Carla said tonelessly. "I didn't think of that. What do you think I should with it? Put it out on the couch?"

"That would be a good start," Joan said. "But it wouldn't hurt to also lay it in your bed at night and pick it up and hug it every now and then."

Eve didn't know about Carla and Darla, but that night, *she* slept better than she'd slept in a week. It was great to have a comfortable bed, and not to have to worry about getting up at six in the morning to move her car.

In the morning, Eve and Carla had a breakfast of fruit and cereal before Eve got dressed in her jeans and bulky sweater and left to go to the Metaphysical Book Store.

Having no knowledge of Tarot cards, Eve was dismayed to find that there were so many different types of decks available. "Choose the one you like best," Saul said.

The deck Eve chose was by Motherpeace. She chose this particular deck because the cards were round. When she walked out of the store, an elderly man hailed her. "Why are they afraid of you?"

Glancing back over her shoulder, Eve didn't see anyone *else* coming out of the store. "Are you talking to *me*?"

"Yes," the man said. "Why are the dark ones afraid of you?" Eve was glad there was no one else around to hear what the man was saying. Judging from the Psychic Reading sign on the table in front of the store window, Eve assumed the gray-haired man must be psychic. "The dark ones are *not* afraid of me," she assured him. "Though I wish they *were*."

The old man gestured toward a straight chair by the table. "Then they're afraid of what you're going to become," he said. "Please sit down and let me take a reading."

"Thanks," Eve said uneasily. "But I have to get home."

Unwilling to be put off, the old man took her arm in an attempt to lead her to the chair. "This will only take a minute…"

Eve had had psychic readings done in the past, but never one like this. Instead of looking into the future, the man closed his eyes and passed his hands close to her body, apparently sensing her energy field. When he'd finished, he opened his eyes. "I was right the first time," he said quietly. "The dark ones hate you, and for very good reason. Once your powers have been fully developed, you're going to be a force to be reckoned with."

On the way to pick Kevin up, Eve thought about the things the man had said. This wasn't the first time she'd been told of her power. She really didn't know what was going on, and wasn't at all sure she liked it. When the man had passed his hands close to her, it had given her the creeps.

"This is Saul, and I'm of the light. This one was my fault," Saul said in her mind. "I should have warned you about allowing psychic people to touch you. You're at a very vulnerable stage in your development. When one psychic touches another, as this man did when he took your arm, energies are exchanged. You were lucky this time. No harm was done. But if the one who touches you is tied to the dark side, you could absorb the dark energy, and he could sap the positive energy from you. Don't ever let a psychic touch you again. And the same goes for touching a dead body—or even a person who's near death."

Working at a convalescent hospital, Eve didn't know how she was expected to avoid death and near-death conditions, but she promised Saul she'd be careful.

Later when Eve picked Kevin up, he asked her on the way to Togo's how she liked working at the hospital.

"I hate it," Eve replied. "But at least it's a job."

"My dad says he can't understand why you can't get a teaching job at a private school, or work in an office for decent pay. He can't figure why someone with your education would quit a good paying office job to move to Placerville and work for minimum wage."

Eve could readily understand why Tom would be puzzled. She was a little puzzled herself. "Sweetheart, you remember when I first moved here, I went to see Myra? And you remember she told me that 'spirit guides' had told her all those things she knew about you? Well, the spirits who told her those things were *my* spirit guides. Am I freaking you out by telling you this?"

"No," Kevin said. "But your spirit guides don't know shit about me. They told Myra things were going to happen that were already in the past."

"Yes," Eve said. "I know. That was Caruso. He hasn't learned yet how to cope with time. In the spirit dimension, past, present, and future exist at the same time."

Turning in at Togo's, Eve found an empty parking space right in front of the door. "I can't tell you anything more if you're going to repeat this to your Dad. If he knew any of this, he'd think I'd lost my mind."

Eve had always been able to talk to her son about virtually anything. Even when Kevin was in junior high at the age when kids typically withdrew from their parents, they'd talked openly about topics that in many families were avoided or even taboo. Eve remembered well the day she had caught Kevin studying the drawings in The Joy of Sex. The paperback volume had been included in a box of books Eve had purchased at a garage sale. Instead of going berserk and taking the book away, Eve had sat down next to her son on the sofa, and they'd looked through the book together—from a *clinical* perspective. Later, Kevin had told Eve she spoiled the thrill of sneaking to look at dirty pictures.

They'd been equally open on the topic of religion. Eve hadn't raised Kevin as a Christian, but she'd always made certain he knew stories from the Bible. The fact that a professor in college had caused her to doubt her own beliefs, didn't mean she was willing to chance steering her son wrong. While living in Southern California two years ago, Kevin had raised the question of angels. "Something happened to me and my friends today," he'd said. I want to know what you think of it."

Kevin had gone on to say that he and his friends had been walking along the main boulevard when a longhaired man dressed in a robe-like garment and sandals had seemed to appear out of nowhere. "He stopped us and asked if he could talk to us for a minute." Kevin had then told how the man's face had glowed as he'd quoted New Testament scriptures and told them the word of God. "When he asked if we wanted to give our hearts to Jesus, we all said we did. After that, we walked away. But a few seconds later, I turned around to see him again, and he was *gone*. There was no place for him to go, Mom. There's a cement block fence along the sidewalk on both sides of the street, and he couldn't have walked or run fast enough to get out of sight that fast. We looked all around for him, but he'd just disappeared. Do you think he was an angel?

Eve hadn't really known what to think. But her son's face had been transformed by the experience, and she hadn't wanted to spoil it for him by saying she didn't believe. "What do *you* think, Sweetheart?"

"I think he was. And I think the reason he was dressed like that was because that's the way people dressed in Bible times. Do you believe in Jesus, Mom?"

Eve had been tempted to skirt the issue, but she'd always been honest with Kevin in the past. He'd had the right to expect no less of her now. "Sweetheart, you know that I grew up believing Jesus was God's son, and that after He was crucified, He came back to life. What you don't know is that when I was in college, a professor made an assignment that made me begin to doubt. Now I'm not really sure what I believe. I know Jesus existed. But I'm just not sure about the rest. I do believe in a force of good, and an opposite force of evil, and that we can choose to align ourselves with one or the other. I choose to align myself with good."

"But that's not good enough," Kevin had argued. "To get into Heaven, you have to believe that Jesus was God's son, and that He was crucified for our sins, and that He came back to life. You have to believe that He did it so people like us can be forgiven for their sins and go to Heaven. It was His gift to us, Mom. If you don't want to go to Hell, you have to accept it."

"Is that what this angel told you?"

"Yes," Kevin had said, "And I believe him."

That had been two years ago. Now Eve believed in both God and Jesus, and here they were in Togo's talking about psychics and spirit guides. "How about if you grab that booth over there, and I'll place our orders?" Eve suggested...

Back at the table, munching her turkey and ham on rye, Eve reminded Kevin that he mustn't tell Tom any of what they were talking about.

"You know I never talk to my dad about this stuff," Kevin said. "My dad's an atheist. He'd think I was a nut."

"Alright then," Eve said. "It isn't that I *wanted* to quit my office job. It isn't that I didn't try to find another one." Eve hadn't planned to tell Kevin about her direct contact with spirit guides or how Gideon had forced her to quit her job at the law firm. But he already knew the spirits had talked to Myra, claiming to be Eve's spiritual guides. She saw no reason to keep it from him that they were involved in her "choice" of jobs.

"They say I'm in danger here in the valley," Eve said with a tired sigh. "There's a man who's been watching me when I go dancing, and they say he wants to hurt me. They say I'm safe in the mountains."

Kevin was a handsome boy with thin features and blue eyes. Like his mom's, his blonde hair had darkened with age. Looking at Eve now with the intensity of youth, he struggled in vain to understand. "Why didn't you just stay here and not go dancing? Then you could be safe *here*."

Taking another bite from her sandwich, Eve debated how to respond. "They say I'm destined to become a hands-on healer," she said carefully. "They say I have a healing touch, and they want to train me to use it. That's why they want me to work in the hospital."

Kevin raised his Coke to take a long drink, then set it down with a thoughtful expression.

"You healed *me*. When I fell off my bike doing that trick jump, and landed on my face... You sat on the couch for hours everyday with my head in your lap, rubbing my forehead. Remember what the doctor said? He said he'd never seen anyone with an injury that serious heal as fast as I did. He was amazed."

Eve remembered the accident well. Kevin's mouth had required twenty-eight stitches. His face had been swollen beyond recognition. She had stayed home from work with him for two days. Cradling his head in her lap, she had gently stroked his hair and forehead, talking to him all the while about anything she could think of to get his mind off his injuries. She had secretly feared Kevin's face was ruined. But he'd healed without a noticeable scar.

When Eve dropped Kevin off at home, she hugged him and handed him the other half of her turkey sandwich. "You might as well take this. I'll never eat it." Eve knew Kevin had fully expected to eat half of hers. That's why he'd only ordered one for himself. "It will be two weeks before I have another weekend off," she said into his neck. "I have to work next Saturday, but I'll have Sunday off. I'll call you to let you know what time I'll be down. I love you, Sweetheart."

"I love you too, Mom. If that spirit guy Caruso tells you anything else about me, don't believe him."

When Eve got back to her apartment that evening, Saul asked her to open the Tarot cards. "I'll be training you in the Tarot, but not the traditional method or meanings. You won't be using it to tell fortunes. The cards are strictly for your own use, for keeping in touch with your destiny."

Chapter 20

Eve actually found herself looking forward to her first lesson in the use of the Tarot. It would be a new experience working with Saul. She liked the healing guide very much. In many ways, he reminded her of Gideon.

The hours spent at work the next day seemed to drag even more than usual, with the high point being when an overweight toothless patient with chronic B.O. refused to swallow the pureed spinach Eve shoveled into her mouth, and sneezed it in her face. Eve had thought she was going to be sick. Though she'd washed the spinach from her face and managed to get it out of her hair, her smock had been stained, and she'd had no choice but to wear it to class at the end of the day. "I see you've been initiated," Doreen said when Eve walked into the training room. "Believe me, we've all been there."

That evening, Saul commented on the incident and Eve's reaction to it. "How much do you think Velma knows?" he asked. "Do you think she recognizes you when you walk into the room? Do you think she knows her name when you speak to her? Is she aware when she soils her diapers?"

"As nearly as I can tell," Eve replied, "she doesn't even know her name. She doesn't respond to anyone I know of. The only thing I've ever seen her respond to is food. When she sees a spoon coming near her face, she automatically opens her mouth."

"Now we're getting somewhere," Saul said. "Tell me, Eve, does she *always* open her mouth when she sees a spoon? Or are there times when she refuses?"

"Sometimes I have to coax her," Eve replied. "Usually for vegetables, I have to coax her by touching the spoon to her mouth and talking to her like she's a little girl. Sometimes once she tastes it, she pushes it out with her tongue. But for pureed fruit or ice cream, she opens wide every time."

"Do you think she likes spinach?"

"No," Eve replied. "It takes forever to feed it to her. That's why when she finally opened her mouth today, I gave her a really big bite to get it over with."

"Which she refused to swallow?"

"Which she refused to swallow," Eve agreed. "She sneezed it right in my face."

"And how did it make you feel when that happened?" Saul's voice was filled with loving patience as he continued his line of questioning.

"It pissed me off," Eve replied. "She ruined my smock. And it grossed me out."

"Exactly," Saul said. "Now let's take another look at Velma. You said the *only* thing she responds to is food. Is that right?"

"Yes," Eve answered. "But the spinach stained my smock. And we only have so much time for feeding. If we take too long—"

"The fact that she only responds to food must mean food is very *important* to her," Saul interrupted. "Particularly foods that she *likes* to eat. How do you think it made her feel when she opened her mouth expecting ice cream, and you gave her a bite of spinach instead? Imagine yourself in *her* place. Suppose you had to rely on someone else to feed you, and instead of giving you the foods you love, they gave you the foods you hate! What would you feel like doing?"

"Spitting it in their face," Eve groaned. "It's a wonder *Velma* didn't spit it at me instead of just holding it in her mouth till she sneezed."

"Point well taken," Saul said. "Now get out the cards and a pencil and paper."

They worked for over an hour, with Saul assigning meanings to the cards and Eve making notes of the description of each card, along with the meaning assigned. Though she didn't count the cards, Eve knew there were more than fifty.

"Tomorrow we'll start your training," Saul said. "We've done enough for today. The next time you go to a metaphysical bookstore, I want you to look for a book on white witchcraft, and also a book that tells the psychic meaning of colors."

"White witchcraft!" Eve protested. "Why would you want me to get a book like that?"

"In the spiritual realm, you have the light and the dark," Saul said patiently. "Sometimes, if they hate you enough, dark spirits cast spells. In the event that a spell is cast on you or someone you love, it would be good if you knew how to counteract it."

A disturbing thought suddenly came to Eve's mind. "I need to talk to Gideon a minute."

"I'm here, Sweetheart. And I'm of the light."

"Gideon," Eve said urgently. "Do you remember when Kevin's dad and I got a divorce, and Kevin and I moved into that house where I saw those ghosts? There was one that I felt sorry for, and hugged. After then all sorts of bad things happened for *years*. Was he—Did he—"

"Yes, Sweetheart. It was a dark spirit. Dark spirits can choose to appear any way they want to: as people, as animals—even as objects. They even choose whether to give an eerie feeling. And yes, the one you hugged caused most of your problems. It's still causing trouble, even now."

Even the *memory* of the spirit hug gave Eve the creeps. She was glad she had Gideon and Saul in her life now. Except for Carla, they'd become her best friends.

The next day at work, when Eve fed Velma her lunch, instead of alternating bites of fruits and veggies, she experimented with mixing the peas with the fruit to make them a little more appetizing. In the meantime, she made a point of standing to the side, just in case Velma decided to sneeze...

Now that she'd basically adjusted to the routine, Eve's job wasn't as *hard* as it had been in the beginning, but she knew she would never get used to the misery. One day had a way of running into the next, and the next, and the next, and the next after that: everyday different, yet everyday the same...

Stretching to relieve her back, Eve groaned. Just two more weeks, and her training would be through. Then maybe she'd be better accepted. She hoped so.

In the beginning, the other C.N.A.s had seemed to resent her. She didn't know why, unless it was her age and the educated way she talked. She couldn't help the fact that she was forty-four years old, or that she had the vocabulary of an educated woman. Nor could she help the fact that she'd never done this type of work before and needed help in turning or transferring the heavier patients. According to Doreen, asking for help with transfers was standard procedure. Yet three fourths of the time when Eve asked for assistance, the other C.N.A.s were too busy to help, or told her to go ask Johnathan. Johnathan was a twenty-seven-year-old C.N.A. no one seemed to like—not even his patients. Johnathan was of normal intelligence, but had an unusual look about him with his dark eyes that were set too close together, his thick neck, short legs, and feet that seemed too small for his body.

In exchange for Johnathan's grudging willingness to assist her, Eve always made herself available to help *him* with Iola, his most difficult patient. Iola hated Johnathan, to the point of often spitting in his face when he bathed her, or trying to scratch him when he took her to the toilet. In contrast, *Eve* had managed to establish a shaky rapport with her.

Eve's one actual *ally*, on the two days a week that he worked, was Ed Schaeffer. Ed was older than Eve, and had been a C.N.A. for over twenty years. He was built like an aging basketball player, with graying hair and a thin moustache. When Ed needed assistance, he turned to Eve. In return, when she needed *him*, he was always available. Thank God for Ed. But that was enough thought about work...

A check of the half-sized refrigerator revealed that Eve had the outs. She would have to run down to Raley's to get something for dinner and tomorrow's breakfast.

At Raley's, Gideon suggested that Eve pamper herself tonight and take one of the whipped cream baths she used to love. During her single years between Kevin's dad and her second husband, when she'd felt like being pampered, Eve had enjoyed sitting in steaming bubble baths, eating whipped cream from a champagne goblet. The thought that Gideon had been with her even then—apparently watching when she took her baths—brought a blush to Eve's cheeks.

By the time she'd had dinner and was ready for her bath, it was already seven o'clock.

"Not quite yet," Saul said. "First the Tarot. Then the bath."

It had become a nightly routine for Eve to go through the Tarot deck reciting the meaning of each card. If she missed one, she had to start over again, and couldn't quit till she'd gone through the entire deck without making a single mistake. Saul was a hard taskmaster, but his methods worked. Tonight, Eve was ready to do a reading.

"We're not going to worry about the traditional way of reading the Tarot," Saul said. "First I want you to shuffle the cards, then count out forty-two and discard the rest. Then I want you to deal five cards face down in a stack. Deal the next card face up. Keep doing this till you've used all the cards. If you don't have enough left at the end to count out the full amount, discard the extras."

Eve took out the cards. Sitting on the floor by the oval coffee table, she dealt the cards as she'd been instructed.

"Now tell me the meanings of the cards that are turned face up," Saul instructed.

The first face-up card was Spiritual Contemplation. The second caused Eve to draw a startled breath; the picture was a Skeleton that signified Death. The third was an old crone that symbolized Deception; the fourth, the Wanderer who represented going forth into the world with a mission; the fifth, Romantic Love; the sixth, the wolf that stood for Evil at her door. And the final card stood for Prosperity.

"This is your destiny," Saul said. "Throughout your life you'll commune with your spiritual guides, as well as with God and Jesus. The Death card has nothing to do with physical death. It signifies the death of your old life, and the beginning of the new." Eve was relieved to hear *that*. "But in your new life you must always be wary of deception," Saul went on. "Any time you see the Wanderer, this is a sign that you will use your healing powers far and wide. This doesn't mean that you'll have to travel. But wherever you go, you'll heal the sick and injured. The Romantic Love card represents the relationship you'll soon find. Evil at your door obviously represents the dark sprits who are always there hoping to thwart you. And finally, the Prosperity card stands for the wealth that will eventually be yours. Any questions?"

Actually, if it weren't for the dark spirits, this fortune didn't sound bad at all.

"Put the discards back in the deck and shuffle the cards, then count out forty-two and deal them again," Saul ordered. "Change the number of cards you turn face down."

Eve did as she'd been told, and to her amazement, the same cards as before were turned face up, only in a different order. Enthralled, she dealt the cards again. Only one card had changed. Instead of Romantic Love, she turned up Sexuality.

When Eve glanced at the clock, it was after ten! Emotionally charged, she put away the Tarot cards and ran a hot bath full of bubbles. From the tiny refrigerator, she took out a can of whipped cream, then took a champagne goblet down from the overhead cupboard. She definitely had cause for celebration! Squirting the whipped cream into the goblet, she hummed beneath her breath.

"Don't forget the candles," Gideon reminded her.

Eve had almost forgotten that the bubble bath/whipped cream ritual had to be done by candlelight.

Bathed in the light of votive candles placed on the four corners of the bathtub, the tiny bathroom was transformed. Before stripping off her clothes, Eve pinned her shoulder-length hair atop her head.

"I want you to do exactly as I tell you," Gideon said softly. "I'm going to talk to you, but I don't want you to answer. Just play along with the game, and do exactly as I say. Okay?"

"Whose bath is this?" Eve teased. "Yours? Or mine?"

"Just do it," Gideon said with mock severity. "Humor me on this one."

Following instructions not to talk, Eve dipped her foot in the foaming bath and winced. It was a good thing she'd allowed space to add some cool water. Still silent, she knelt on the fluffy blue throw rug and swirled a hand in the water to test. When the water had reached a comfortably warm temperature, she stepped into the tub and sank beneath the suds.

"Now sit up," Gideon instructed, but cover your breasts with suds... Good... Now dip the spoon in the whipped cream and bring it slowly to your lips... Good...Now close your eyes and take a bite. Make it sensual..."

Enjoying the game, Eve closed her eyes and drew a deep breath before slowly inserting the spoon of cream into her mouth. Closing her lips, she exhaled with a moan as she slowly and sensually withdrew the spoon.

"You're doing great," Gideon said. "Now take another bite. Then I want you to look up and pretend you see your soul mate standing there. I want you to smile your sexiest little smile, and say "Well, hel-lo." Do it in that throaty voice you used on your answering machine recording."

Eve was beginning to feel ridiculous, but she went along with the game.

"Perfect!" Gideon said. "Now you can relax and finish your bath."

Though the water temperature had cooled a little, it was still warm enough to be relaxing. Sliding down into the water, Eve took another bite of whipped cream. Now if she were just getting ready to go dancing, everything would be perfect...

When Eve had finished her whipped cream and gotten out of the tub, she reached for a fluffy towel and blew out the candles. She didn't know how long she'd been in here, but she'd be sorry in the morning if she didn't get to bed.

"I have something to tell you, and I don't want you to get mad," Gideon said.

"What could you possibly say that would make me mad?" Eve asked. She realized the ridiculousness of the question as soon as she'd asked it.

"Remember several years ago when you had an out of body experience?"

It was something Eve didn't like to think about. But she clearly remembered it.

"Then you know astral projection is possible..."

Eve didn't know where this line of conversation was going, but she didn't like the sound of it.

"Chad's guardian angel and I have been collaborating on how to get you two together," Gideon said carefully. "As you know, it hasn't been easy. The dark ones have stepped in at every turn to keep you two from meeting."

"You're not suggesting that I go out of body..."

"Oh no. Nothing like that," Gideon said quickly. "What I'm saying is that after Chad went to sleep tonight—This is why Saul insisted that you read the Tarot cards *before* your bath—After Chad finally went to sleep, his guardian angel took him out of body and brought him here to see you taking a bath." Gideon had dropped the news as casually as if he were telling her it was going to rain.

"He did *what*?" Eve squealed.

"Don't worry," Gideon assured her. "You were completely covered. When Chad wakes up, he'll think he had a sensual dream about a sexy lady having a bubble bath. When he eventually sees you, he'll recognize you as the woman of his dreams."

Chapter 21

Since Eve didn't have a weekend day off this week, she decided not to drive down to the valley. She could accomplish more by staying in Placerville than by driving to the valley when Kevin was in school and Carla was at work. For starters, she needed to shop for more work clothes. Two smocks and one pair of jeans had been stained beyond repair.

After shopping for clothing, Eve planned to go to the library. If she couldn't find what she needed there, she would visit the metaphysical bookstore.

A search of the library card catalogue turned up nothing on white witchcraft or on the psychic significance of colors. By the time Eve was finished with her research, it was lunchtime. Rather than go back to the hotel for lunch, she went to the country restaurant where Chad liked to eat brunch. One never knew when he might show up. If she came here often enough, she might just get lucky. Based on the description Gideon have given her, Eve felt confident she would recognize Chad if she saw him.

The chicken salad had too much pickle for Eve's taste, and a strong after taste of onion. The Coke was flat and watered down. If this was typical of this restaurant's usual fare, Eve wondered what the appeal could be. Maybe Chad just liked the atmosphere, or maybe they made a mean cup of coffee...

The smell of incense wafted through the doorway as Eve stepped into the bookstore. Behind the glass counter were crystals in various shapes and colors, along with gold and silver chains of both traditional and Celtic design. Standing in the middle of the store was a rack displaying incense, fragrant oils, zodiac cards, and boxes of candles. But none of these were of interest to Eve. Attempting to appear nonchalant, she drifted over toward the bookshelf along the right wall. She was engrossed in thumbing through a paperback from the shelf, when a man with thinning hair and wire-rimmed glasses approached her. "Hi. I'm Paul. Did you find what you're looking for?"

"Well, no. Actually—" Eve didn't want to say she was looking for a book on white witchcraft. Instead, she said she was looking for a book on the psychic significance of colors. "I know green is the color for healing, but I don't know anything else about psychic colors, except for the color of auras." She knew about green because Saul had told her that when working with healing energy she must always see green when she closed her eyes.

"We don't have a book specifically about colors," the store manager said. "But there is a book on this shelf that has a *chapter* about colors. I could try to find it for you if you think that would be of help."

"I'd appreciate that," Eve said with a smile. She was about to give up on finding a book on white witchcraft, when she decided on impulse to take a chance and ask. "I'm not interested in the dark side of the occult, but I'm doing a paper on white witchcraft. Do you happen to have any books on it?" The part about the paper was a lie, but Eve figured it would be better to tell a white lie than to risk having the store manager think she was a witch.

"Nothing on white witchcraft," the thin-haired man said. "But there's someone here I think you might want to meet. I'm picking up that you're a very psychic lady, and you need to know how to protect yourself. Wait right here…"

When the man returned, he brought with him a black-haired woman who appeared to be Native American. She was approximately thirty years old, dressed in black slacks and a black turtleneck sweater. "Paul tells me you need to learn about protection. Would you like to step into the next room with me?"

Eve really didn't know what to expect. Surely this woman wasn't planning to teach her how to fight off an attacker.

The adjoining room was empty, except for the threadbare gold carpet on the floor. The Indian woman took a leather pouch from her pocket and emptied four purple stones into her palm. "My name is Rhonda," she said softly. "I'm going to teach you how to call the spirit energies to protect you against negative forces."

Eve had met a woman once who claimed crystals could be used for healing. But she'd never heard of using them for protection.

"Hold this stone, and tell me what you feel," Rhonda said.

Eve took the purple stone that was offered, and closed her eyes to shut out distractions. In the hand holding the stone, she felt a slight tingling sensation. "I'm not sure what I'm feeling," she said. "It feels like a faint vibration."

"That's the stone's natural energy," Rhonda answered. "It's good that you can feel it. That tells me you're very sensitive. Now give me the stone. Stand facing me, and watch."

While Eve watched and listened, Rhonda did a ritual of sorts, calling the energy of the *Spirit of the East* into the stone. "In the East, the sun rises," Rhonda intoned. "It is the direction of renewal and rebirth. The Spirit of the East draws his energy from fire. I call upon the Spirit of the East to infuse this stone with the energy of fire…"

"*Now* hold the stone and tell me what you feel," she said.

Eve took the stone and closed her hand over it as before, then closed her eyes to concentrate on what she was feeling. The "slight vibration" had increased a hundred fold. "That's amazing!" she cried. "It feels like the stone has electricity running through it!"

"The energy of fire is very powerful," Rhonda agreed. The fact that you can feel it shows that you are very spiritual." Rhonda then continued the ritual, calling in a monotone for the energy of the West, South, and North to come into the stones she was holding.

When she had completed her recitation, her voice returned to its normal inflection. "Unfortunately, we're out of amethysts at the moment. But I want you to go to another metaphysical store and buy at least four amethysts for yourself. Test them first to make sure they're pure. Hold them in your hand to feel the vibration. The stronger the vibration, the purer the stone."

Eve hoped the other customers wouldn't think she was crazy, holding stones in her hand and closing her eyes, as if she were in some sort of trance.

"Take the amethysts home, and put one in each direction of your house," Rhonda said. "Due East, due West, due North, and due South. Call the energy of the appropriate spirit into each stone, then put the stones out of sight so no one will touch them. You'll be amazed how much more serene your home life will become, and how much better you'll feel in general."

Uncertain of what to make of what she'd just experienced, Eve expressed her thanks and returned to the main store where Paul was waiting.

"I have to tell you," Paul said in a voice too low for other customers to hear, "When you walked into the store, our protection pyramid came down. At first I thought you were involved with the dark side. But then my guide told me it wasn't you. The pyramid had been disrupted by the dark spirit who followed you in."

A dark spirit had *followed her into the store*? Eve had thought dark spirits couldn't *survive* here. What had happened to the fact that the gold in the ground supposedly sapped their energy?

"You must be a very powerful lady to have drawn the attention of a dark spirit powerful enough to disrupt our pyramid," Paul said. "Our pyramid's very strong. It takes a strong spirit to disrupt it." Paul's scalp shined through his thinning hair in the fluorescent light from above. His blue eyes were intense behind the lenses of his wire-framed glasses. "Would you and your guide like to join us in the back room and help us re-establish our pyramid?"

Eve couldn't very well refuse, considering that the man believed she'd been influential in *disrupting* their pyramid in the first place. Besides, her curiosity had been piqued. She wanted to see what he was talking about.

The back room, like the room Rhonda had taken Eve to, was devoid of furniture. Gesturing for Eve to have a seat on the floor, Paul sat on the floor as well. "My spirit guide is Lone Wolf," he said. At this point, Rhonda joined them and took a crosslegged seat facing Eve. "Rhonda's spirit guide is Dancing Water," Paul continued. "Would you like to introduce yourself and tell us the name of *your* guide?"

Following Paul's example, Eve gave only her first name. "My name's Eve. And my healing guide's name is Saul."

"You realize, of course, that Saul is not his real name," Paul said.

"I know it's the name he *chose*," Eve replied.

"I've met your healing guide before," Paul said. "But under a different name."

Surprised at this statement, Eve asked how Paul knew it was the same spirit guide, when Saul couldn't be seen.

"I recognized his energy," Paul replied. "And my guide confirmed it. Saul, under different names of course, has been the teacher of many great natural healers. The last time I met him, he was known as Thundercloud. He's an extremely powerful guide. You're fortunate to have him assigned to you."

This was good news. Eve wouldn't have wanted Paul's spirit guide to describe her guide as a wimp. She wondered why Saul had made the transition from a name like Thundercloud to a name like Saul. But now was not the time to ask.

"Let's all close our eyes," Paul said softly.

Closing her eyes as instructed, Eve listened as Paul chanted his reverence for the spirits, and concentrated on calling the energies of fire, trees, rocks, and animals into the amethysts that had been spaced throughout the shop, including calling *all of them* into the amethyst at the apex.

"The apex is the point at which all the energies connect to complete the energy pyramid," Paul explained. "It might be in a light fixture in the middle of the house, or on top of a hutch... Ours is taped to the ceiling. The closer to the center the apex is located, the greater the degree of protection."

Eve had had no idea when she entered the shop that she was entering a "pyramid" of protective energy. "Do you have to go through this ritual everyday?"

"Sometimes several times a day," Paul replied. "But it's worth it. Fewer bad things happen in your life when you have the energies to protect you."

Before Eve left, Paul asked for her phone number. There was a natural healer he thought she might be interested in talking to, but he wanted to call the woman first before giving out her phone number. "If she's agreeable, I'll call you, and you can get in touch with her."

Eve had never met another natural healer. She hoped the woman would want to talk to her. In the meantime, Paul and Rhonda had given her a lot to think about. She was glad she hadn't driven to the valley today, but she felt a compelling urge to go there this evening and tell Carla what she'd learned. Tomorrow, she would go to the metaphysical store in the valley and buy enough amethysts for both of them.

When Eve arrived, Carla was still at work, so Eve used her key to get in. She was watching a movie on HBO when Carla arrived home.

"I didn't expect to find *you* here. I didn't think you were coming this week, since it's not a weekend." Carla's shoulders were drooping, and there were circles under her eyes.

"I came to tell you what I learned today," Eve said. "But that can wait. You look like you had a hard day at work. Are you feeling okay?"

"I'm fine," Carla groaned. "I could just use a stiff drink."

This is Saul, and I'm of the light. Ask her if she wants *me* to mix her one.".

Now what was Saul up to? When Eve relayed the suggestion, Carla shrugged. "Sure. Why not?"

"Tell her to go get a can of Sprite." Sprite, as Saul knew, was Carla's soft drink of choice. "Just wait, Eve. You're going to enjoy this."

Heading for the refrigerator, Carla scoffed. "I was talking about an *alcoholic* drink. Not a can of Sprite!"

When Carla returned with the soft drink, Saul told Eve to pop the top and put her hand over the can. When she did, Eve felt the carbonated soft drink popping beneath her palm, followed by a wave of energy that made her hand and arm tingle from her fingertips to her elbow.

"Ask what kind of mixed drink she wants."

Intrigued by the request, Eve relayed it to Carla.

"Strawberry daiquiris are my favorite," Carla said with a teasing grin. "But unless I make a trip to the liquor store, I'm afraid he can't do much about that."

"Don't be too sure," Saul said through Eve. "One strawberry daiquiri coming up." The soft drink began to pop once more beneath Eve's palm, and a renewed flash of energy rushed through her hand. "Ask her to taste this, and see what she thinks."

Handing the can to Carla, Eve told her to taste it and let Saul know what she thought of it. Carla raised it to her lips with a skeptical grin, and took a sniff. When she did, her eyes widened in awe. "Eve! You've gotta *smell* this!"

Eve took the can from Carla's hand, having no idea what to expect. When she raised it to her nose, she gasped. The Sprite in the can had apparently been transformed. Wafting from the can now was the mouth-watering aroma of freshly cut strawberries! "Taste it," Eve whispered.

With a look of wonder, Carla took a tiny sip—and then another. A smile of delight spread across her face. "This is perfect!" she cried. "It's delicious! In fact, I'd say it's more than delicious. This is the best strawberry daiquiri I've ever had!"

"You're kidding," Eve said. "You mean it actually tastes like alcohol?"

"If you don't believe *me*, taste it for yourself." Carla had already downed half the daiquiri, and was grinning from one ear to the other. "Ask Saul to mix me a screw driver. But wait—" Rather than waste a perfectly good daiquiri, Carla finished it off, then crushed the can. "Let me get another Sprite…"

The screwdriver Saul mixed was a little weak for Carla's taste, so he beefed up the strength and nearly knocked her on her ear. "Whew!" she exclaimed. "Another one of these, and I'll end up with a hang-over!"

Eve felt like a magician's assistant in a Las Vegas show. Next to her fist popping open, what she was witnessing here was the most amazing thing she'd ever seen.

"Let's play a game," Saul suggested. "I'll make the flavors and tell you what they are, then Carla can guess."

When Eve told Carla about the game, Carla readily agreed.

"Let's start with coconut," Saul said.

Eve put her hand over the top of the can and again felt the now familiar popping against her palm. The rush of energy flowed through her hand, then stopped. "I guess it's done…"

Carla lifted the can to her lips and took a sip. "Definitely coconut. But I don't like coconut. Make me something else."

The next flavor was grape, followed by chocolate.

"Let's see if we can fool her," Saul said. "We'll just make it taste like ice."

Expecting some exotic flavor, Carla took one sip, then another. Her eyebrows knitted in a puzzled frown. "It doesn't taste like anything," she said with a shrug. "If I didn't know better, I'd think I was drinking—*ice*."

116

Chapter 22

The next morning, since Carla didn't have to go to work till noon, she went with Eve to the metaphysical store. Carla had never been to a store of that type, and was curious to see what sort of things they carried. The store here was larger than the one in Placerville. Entering the store, they were faced with a divided bin of stones and crystals of various kinds. To the right was a glass jewelry counter displaying earrings, bracelets, rings, and pendants, along with an array of silver and gold chains of various lengths. "Let's take a look," Carla suggested.

Gazing at the pendants in the display case, Eve's attention was drawn to a pale green stone in an oval 12c gold setting. "That pendant's beautiful," she commented.

"This is Saul, and I'm of the light. Most people don't realize it, but the peridot is a powerful stone. It would be good for you to buy the pendant to wear for protection."

Apparently Saul had forgotten about Eve's budget constraints. The peridot alone would cost two days' pay, let alone the chain to hang it from. "Let's check out the amethysts."

Though Carla tried testing the amethysts for purity, she wasn't really sensitive to the vibrations. Testing first one stone and then another in the palm of her hand, Eve chose the ten strongest: five for her, and five for Carla. Rhonda hadn't mentioned needing a fifth stone, but Eve knew from Paul that they each needed an extra to use for the apex.

"You've done well choosing the amethysts," Saul said. "Now I think you should buy the peridot. You can put it on a credit card."

Against her better judgment, Eve bought the pendant along with the amethysts. Making minimum monthly payments, it would probably take her a year to pay if off.

When they got back to Carla's apartment, Eve taught Carla to set up a pyramid. Together, they called the energies into the stones for East, West, North, and South, and hid the stones throughout the apartment, then hid the apex in the light fixture in the hall. Next, Eve placed a call to Kevin, but he wasn't home, so she just left a message.

Eve dreaded having to return to Placerville, despite her efforts to look at things in a positive light. Returning to Placerville meant returning to the hotel apartment she hated, with its threadbare sofa, lumpy bed, thumbnail sized kitchen, and noise from the street. Returning to Placerville meant returning to the job she despised, with its smells of urine and fecal material. Returning to Placerville, in many ways, signified in Eve's mind a return to Hell.

"How about if I drive up with you after work?" Carla suggested. "I haven't seen your apartment yet, and I don't mind having to drive home after dark."

Eve's countenance brightened immediately. To date, no one except her son and ex-husband had seen the apartment, unless one wanted to count the spirit guides— and of course Chad, when he came out of body to visit. It would be fun to cook dinner for Carla and have her company for the evening…

In the rearview mirror, Eve could see Carla at the wheel of the blue compact sedan. She was glad she'd tidied up her apartment before driving down to the Valley. As small as it was, one carelessly tossed item of clothing could make the entire apartment seem a mess.

When they arrived in Placerville, it was late enough to park their cars in the lot behind the hotel. Rather than go through the alley and circle the hotel to go in through the front door, Eve used her key to go in through the back, and they climbed the three flights of carpeted stairs.

"This isn't so bad, except for the musty smell," Carla puffed. "If you're climbing these stairs everyday, at least you're getting your exercise."

When they reached the third floor, Eve raised a finger to her lips. "The walls are very thin," she whispered.

Except for the number on her door, there was nothing to distinguish Eve's apartment from the other apartments on this floor. The only way to distinguish between single rooms and apartments was the amount of space between the doors.

"This is it," Eve whispered. She didn't talk in a normal tone of voice until she'd unlocked the door and they were inside the apartment. "Voices carry in this place like you wouldn't believe. The old lady who owns the hotel lives right down the hall. I don't like for her to know when I come and go."

Eve had learned early on that the hotel owner didn't miss a trick when it came to keeping tabs on her tenants. She had also learned not to say anything to the gray-haired receptionist that she didn't want to have repeated.

Looking around the efficiency apartment, Carla rolled her eyes. "It's not exactly what you've been used to in the past, but at least having a few pieces of your own furniture helps."

"Being *chosen* definitely has its drawbacks," Eve agreed. "If I'd never met my spirit guides or been chosen to become a healer, I'd probably be living in a nice apartment right now, working at a job that pays two thousand a month. Sit down and relax. I'll get started on the pizza."

Given the miniscule size of the kitchen, and the fact that counter space was virtually non-existent, it was impossible to make a pizza without pulling the small dining table over to work on.

Before dinner, Saul told Eve to see if she could do anything to help Carla's headache. Normally when Carla had a migraine, Eve could tell by her eyes. But this evening, she hadn't noticed anything amiss. "Do you have a headache, Carla? Saul said you do, and that I should see if I can do anything about it."

"My sinuses have been killing me all afternoon," Carla replied. "I took a couple of pills, but they didn't do any good."

Following Saul's instructions, Eve told Carla to sit on one of the dinette chairs. Then she put her hands around Carla's head and closed her eyes to try to see the green. Instead of the usual black that accompanied closed eyes, Eve was amazed to find that what she saw tonight was a brilliant shade of emerald green. "*Now* what do I do?"

"There are two ways for a natural healer to eliminate pain," Saul answered. "She can put positive energy *in*, or she can pull negative energy *out*. Pain is nothing more than a concentration of negative energy. I'm going to make a magnet of your hands to attract that negative energy. Once you've pulled it out, the pain will be gone."

When, after a few seconds of cupping Carla's head, Eve pulled her hands away, it was if they were attached to a rubber band. A force—the force of the negative energy—was pulling her hands back toward Carla's head. Pulling harder, Eve felt the negative energy trying to maintain its grip. It was like a tug of war with an elastic band. When the negative energy suddenly snapped loose, Eve almost lost her balance. "Now take it outside," Saul instructed. "Go away from the door, and brush it off your hands."

"The headache's gone," Carla said in amazement. "I actually felt you pulling it out of my head!"

Eve was as astonished as Carla, to think she had actually *pulled a headache out of someone's head*! When she went outside to wipe the negative energy off her hands, it felt as if her hands and forearms were covered with cobwebs. It was like nothing else Eve had ever experienced. It was a real trip.

"It was really weird," Carla said when Eve returned. "When you pulled your hands away, I could feel the pain being pulled out of my sinuses. Then your hands would get closer and the pain would be back, but not quite as bad as before. When you suddenly jerked back, the pain went with you. Too bad you can't get a patent on this!"

When the friends had talked this experience and its potential through from all angles and finished their pizza, Carla reluctantly stood and picked up her purse. "I guess it's about time for me to be heading home. It'll be eleven o'clock by the time I get there."

Eve really didn't want Carla to leave, but she understood her reluctance to stay any later. "Too bad Chad couldn't have visited while you were here," Eve said. "That would have *really* blown your mind."

"Maybe he could *still* come," Carla said with a shrug. "Why don't you ask Gideon?"

"This is Gideon, and I'm of the light. I've already checked. Chad's guardian angel said Chad'sleeping. He could bring him over for an out of body visit before Carla leaves."

"Chad's asleep," Eve said excitedly. "Gideon said if we want him to, his guardian angel will bring him over now."

Carla's eyes were shining like a kid's at a carnival. "I'm not *about* to miss this one."

Gideon set the stage by instructing Eve and Carla what to do. A few minutes later, when Chad "arrived," they were seated on the sofa in the dimly lit living room discussing their future plans to go dancing.

"He's here," Gideon said. "Touch Carla to let her know, then look up toward the T.V. That's where he's standing. I'll let *you* take it from here."

Eve touched Carla on the knee, then turned toward the T.V. and looked up to where she assumed Chad's face would be. "Hi!" she said brightly. "It's nice to see you. I was hoping you'd come again. This is my friend, Carla."

Looking in the same direction as Eve, Carla smiled. Then, to Eve's surprise, Carla rose and extended her right hand. When she didn't feel an immediate response, Carla crossed the floor to where Chad was 'standing.' "I *feel his hand*," she whispered. Shaking the invisible hand, once she'd recovered from her shock, Carla told Chad it was nice to meet him.

Carla might have returned to her seat at that point, but her curiosity got the better of her. Reaching out with her left hand, she touched his invisible chest. "I can feel him," she whispered.

Eve didn't know why Carla was whispering. If Chad was indeed here, he could certainly hear her. What must he be thinking, having a strange woman he's never met before shake his hand then start feeling his body? It was a good thing he'd remember this only as a dream!

"His chest feels like a wall of energy," Carla whispered. Using both hands to sense Chad's presence, she worked her way outward toward his arms, then felt all the way up his arms to his shoulders. "He's tall," she said. "And his shoulders are broad."

"You can actually *feel* the width of his shoulders?"

"Come over here and feel for yourself," Carla said.

"This is Saul, and I'm of the light. Don't do it. She's making him feel like some sort of specimen. He's ready to bolt."

When Eve didn't respond to Carla's suggestion, Carla lowered her hands and patted her way down the length of Chad's out-of-body torso. Suddenly, she yelped, and jerked her hands away!

"He's gone now," Saul said. "But I'll guarantee you one thing. This was one dream he'll never forget."

When Carla returned to the sofa, her face was flushed and her hands were shaking.

"What happened?" Eve asked. "Why did you jerk away like that?"

"Because," Carla said, *"He had a hard on*!!"

120

Chapter 23

Before putting the peridot around her neck, Eve called the energies into it as Saul had told her to do. "Wear it under your smock so the patients can't grab it. Under no circumstances are you to let anyone but you touch it."

Eve was hesitant to even wear the necklace to work. The residents in her care were like children when it came to wanting to touch and feel…

If the energy of the peridot was making a difference in Eve's day, she certainly couldn't sense it. To start off the morning, Iola called Eve into the room and offered her a chocolate bonbon. Iola's thinning hair and beady eyes reminded Eve of a troll. Eve could easily imagine her waiting beneath the bridge, trying to catch the Billy Goats Gruff. It was out of character for Iola to offer to share her candy. Sitting up in her hospital bed, she showed her yellowed teeth in a crafty smile. "Don't be shy, Dear. Come over here." As she spoke, she held out a bonbon in an effort to entice.

The chocolate bonbons did look delicious. But despite the fact her sweet tooth was begging her to say "Yes," Eve smiled and said "No thank you." She knew Iola had to have touched the bonbons to put them out on her tray. There was no telling where her hands had been. The bonbons were probably teeming with germs.

Back out in the hospital corridor, Eve encountered Doreen. "I couldn't believe it," she said. "Iola actually offered to share her chocolate bonbons with me."

"Is she doing that *again*?" Doreen said with disgust. "I'd better go have a look." Eve waited by the door while the nurse went in to speak to Iola. "That's just what I thought. I'm sorry, Iola. I'm going to have to take your bonbons away." Eve was surprised when Iola didn't protest when Doreen took a Kleenex and picked the bonbons up off the tray. "You know what I have to do with these, don't you?" Doreen asked. "I have to flush them down the toilet. I'll send your aide to clean your hands and wash your tray. After this, *no more bon bons*. Do you understand me?"

"She was going to eat one," Iola said, tossing her head toward Eve with a wink. "I almost talked her into it."

Between each of the rooms was a closet and a small bathroom. When Doreen had flushed the bonbons, she returned to the hallway. "It's a good thing you didn't take what Iola was offering. Do you know what those things were?"

Iola had called the candy bonbons. But to Eve, they had looked more like chocolate malt balls.

"They were *turds*," Doreen said. "She got them out of her diaper."

Eve's stomach heaved, and she thought she was going to be sick. She was headed for the restroom when another patient hailed her. "I know you're not my aide. But I'm wet. Can you change me?"

"Let me look for your aide first, Mrs. Japetto. Someone will be here in a minute."

A quick check of the rooms revealed that Mrs. Japetto's aide was nowhere to be found. With a sigh of resignation, Eve took a washcloth and diaper from the hall linen closet and returned to Mrs. Japetto's room. At this rate, she'd never have her own patients ready in time for breakfast…

Racing around like a woman possessed, Eve made the rounds, bathing and dressing her female patients and taking them to the bathroom. She'd formed the habit of carrying a pencil and tablet in her pocket to make note of bowel movements' size and consistency. On days like today, there was simply no time to record the BMs at the nurse's station when they occurred. She would have to record them this afternoon before she reported to class.

Breakfast tray delivery went smoothly until Eve delivered Carlo's tray. Grinning broadly, Carlo made a happy noise of greeting. One hand was down the front of his diaper, playing with his penis. The other was covered with fecal material, flailing in the air like an odorous brown flag. "Oh Carlo," Eve moaned. "Couldn't you have waited till after breakfast?"

"Just leave him and finish delivering the trays," a young C.N.A. said from the hallway. "You're already behind schedule, and I can't feed all these patients by myself."

Eve was damned if she did, and damned if she didn't. If she took the time now to clean Carlo up and change his diaper, breakfast would be half over by the time she had finished, and the other C.N.A.s would report that she hadn't been there to help. On the other hand, if she left Carlo sitting in his own poop, she'd get written up if a nurse found out about it. Caught up in the dilemma, Eve compromised. She would leave Carlo till the trays had all been delivered, but come back and change him before she fed anyone.

She was delivering the last of the trays when Doreen's voice came over the speaker. "Patient in room 8 needs assistance. Will the C.N.A. for room 8 please report to the front nurse's station?"

The patients in Room 8 were not normally Eve's responsibility. She had them today because Ed was sick.

"Will the C.N.A. for room 8 please report to the nurse's station?" Doreen repeated.

In response to the call, Eve walked rapidly down the corridor, past the open doors of Wing A. As she passed Thelma's doorway, Thelma called in a pathetic voice. "Mama? Take me home. I want to go home."

Two doors away, Norma was laying on the buzzer.

"I'll be with you in a minute, Norma," Eve said from the doorway. "I'm wanted at the nurse's station."

"What's my name?" Norma asked. "Where are the ear rings my son gave me?"

By the time Eve arrived at the nurse's station, Doreen was losing patience. "Would you please get in there and clean Carlo up? You really need to keep a better eye on your patients, Eve. We're dying out here from the stench."

Eve accepted the admonishment, and said nothing in her own defense. She couldn't very well say that she'd known Carlo had soiled himself, but a C.N.A. had told her to leave him. At least Doreen hadn't written her up.

Covering her nose with her hand, Eve went into Carlo's room. "It's about time you got here," the man in the next bed said. "Another minute, and I'd have changed him myself!"

Eve could never understand why the hospital would put a patient like Mr. Williams in the same room with someone like Carlo. Mr. Williams had diabetes and emphysema. But his mind was as sharp as a twenty-year-old's. "I'm sorry, Mr. Williams. I couldn't be in two places at once. What do you say if after I change Carlo, I rub some lotion on your back?"

"You don't have to soft soap me," Mr. Williams said. "I can see that you're overworked. They should call in a substitute when a C.N.A. gets sick, instead of doubling up."

Eve couldn't agree with him more. But she knew there was no way the hospital would call a substitute unless two or more aides were absent at one time.

When lunchtime finally arrived, Eve took out her chicken salad sandwich and bought a canned Coke from the soft drink machine. The lunchroom was empty except for Eve and the red-haired C.N.A. sitting across the table from her. "Are you feeling alright?" Eve asked. "You're looking a little pale."

"I twisted my knee last night, and it's killing me," Marcie replied.

Leery of telling Marcie or anyone else at the hospital about her healing touch, Eve cautiously mentioned that she might be able to help.

"I already took some Aspirin, thanks," the C.N.A. said with a wave of her hand. "It didn't do any good."

Eve had taken a bite of her sandwich. Now, as she chewed, she considered what to say. "I'm not talking about Aspirin. If you'll let me put my hands on your knee—"

"Whoa," Marcie said. "You're not gonna put some kind of mojo on me, are you?"

"No mojos," Eve said with a smile. "I've been told I have a healing touch. I'm just going to try to take your pain away."

Marcie turned around in her seat and glanced toward the door to make certain no one could see.

Kneeling in front of Marcie, Eve put her hands on Marcie's knee and closed her eyes to see the green. A tingling sensation immediately began in her hands.

"My knee feels kind of prickly," Marcie said. "Is it supposed to feel that way?"

Eve didn't respond immediately. Instead, she pulled her hands away slowly, pulling against the elastic effect of the negative energy causing the pain.

"It feels like you're pulling something out of my knee," Marcie said, looking at Eve with an expression of wonder.

"I am," Eve replied.

As the pain in her knee dissipated, the strain in Marcie's face melted away. "Let's not tell anyone about this," she whispered. "We can just keep it as our little secret."

"That sounds good to me," Eve said. "I was going to suggest that myself. Would you excuse me for a minute? I'll be right back."

Leaving a smiling Marcie to enjoy the rest of her lunch, Eve went out onto the patio. When she was certain no one could see her, she flung her hands and wiped off the cobwebs of negative energy. Reflecting back on what had just happened, Eve understood some of the natural high *Jesus* must have felt when He healed the sick centuries ago.

If only Eve had had this ability as a child, she might have been able to help her dad…

Chapter 24

On Graduation Day, Eve stood in line with the rest of the newly accredited C.N.A.s to receive her stethoscope. It was hospital tradition to give a stethoscope to everyone who completed the C.N.A. training. After the applause and refreshments, the C.N.A.s returned to their wing to make their rounds taking blood pressure and doing range of motion exercises for those who were unable to move for themselves.

At lunchtime, Eve was taking her turn feeding wheelchair patients in the dining room who were unable to feed themselves. Though she'd learned to rather enjoy feeding time in general, she was *particularly* enjoying Marjorie, the white-haired lady in the pink velour bathrobe and matching hair bow. There was something about Marjorie's face that seemed to shine with an inner beauty. Eve wasn't certain why Marjorie was unable to feed herself. But she wouldn't be at this table if she didn't need assistance.

"That's it for the mashed potatoes," Eve said. "Which do you want next? Peas? Or corn? Or would you rather I took turns?"

Marjorie opened her mouth to reply, then her eyes suddenly widened as she looked over Eve's head at something behind her. "Is that your husband standing behind you?"

Though Eve looked back over her shoulder, she saw no one. "Where? I don't see anyone."

"Right behind you," the white-haired lady said. "There are two of them: a tall man with a beard, and another man with him—a black man. They're both wearing suits and look very handsome. Did they come to attend your graduation?"

"This is Saul, and I'm of the light," Saul said. "Tell her 'yes.'"

It had been them! Marjorie had seen Gideon and Saul standing behind her! Eve felt an overpowering surge of love at that moment. "Yes," she said with a tearful smile. "They came for my graduation." She only wished they had shown themselves to *her* instead of Marjorie. She didn't ask telepathically why they hadn't allowed *her* to see them. She didn't want to risk having a dark one interrupt, and ruin a lovely day. *Thanks for coming,* she said in her mind. *As a graduation gift, I have a request. How about giving Don and Mrs. Stillwell a break today?*

Since developing the ability to infuse a patient with positive energy, Eve had formed the habit of visiting two particular patients whenever she found herself with a free moment. One was a cancer patient named Don, and the other was Mrs. Stillwell. Both were fully lucid, and with them Eve had formed an attachment beyond what she felt for her other patients. She always made a point of being the one to feed them, and enjoyed hearing their stories from the past.

Eve's heart ached for Don when his legs cramped to the point of being pulled up toward his chest, and for Mrs. Stillwell, whose Rheumatoid Arthritis had converted her hands to gnarled knots. Often, with her healing touch, Eve was able to relieve some of Don's leg pain. Twice, she'd succeeded in completely taking the pain out of Mrs. Stillwell's hands. It distressed her to know that the relief wasn't permanent. It lasted longer than painkillers and anti-inflammatory drugs, but the pain invariably came back.

On a high from the certain knowledge that her spirit guides had come to attend her graduation, Eve stopped in to see how Mrs. Stillwell was feeling. Despite the fact that an aide had styled her gray hair and colored her cheeks with rouge, the old lady looked even more frail than yesterday. "The pain's pretty bad today," she said weakly. "I was afraid you wouldn't have time to see me, with graduation. But I was hoping you'd come by."

Taking the elderly woman's gnarled hands in hers, Eve closed her eyes to see the green and feel the flow of healing energy. After a minute or two, she released them. "How do your hands feel now, Mrs. Stillwell?"

"The pain's gone," the old lady said with a tired smile. "You're an angel. Bless you."

After Mrs. Stillwell, Eve went to see Don. His face was drawn, and his dim eyes were sunken. "If you could just put your hands on my knee…"

That evening on Eve's way home from work, Saul suggested she stop at a store to pick up a newspaper. Eve didn't know what he had in mind. But she knew sooner or later he'd tell her.

After a dinner of broiled fish, salad, and a baked potato, Eve turned on the stereo and took out the Tarot cards. As always, she felt a thrill when the cards came up assuring her she was destined to become a great healer, and that romance and prosperity were just around the corner.

When she had finished with the cards and was on her way to the bathroom to take a bath, Saul identified himself and told her to wait. "I want you to look in the job ads. There's one I want you to see."

"But I don't have the time or energy to take a second job," Eve argued. "I can barely drag myself around now, as it is."

"Just trust me on this and read through the damn ads." As soon as the word 'damn' had slipped out, Saul apologized. "I have to learn more patience."

Eve hadn't minded the use of the word 'damn.' It had just made Saul seem more human—like Gideon.

Glancing through the ads, Eve's attention was caught short by an ad for a C.N.A.: "C.N.A. needed for A.L.S. patient. Four hours each night…"

A horrible feeling of sadness engulfed Eve as she tossed the paper aside. Her father had died of A.L.S.—Lou Gehrig's Disease. Helpless, Eve had watched the disease destroy her father's nervous system, taking with it his dignity, destroying all but his ability to think. In the end, he'd died of suffocation. Eve had felt guilty for years after his death. If only she'd done more to help… But she knew in her heart that it wouldn't have made a difference. "I want you to call this number," Saul said.

"What's the point, Saul? I can't be working half the night and still having to go to work at the hospital."

"Call the number, and tell the nurse you're a natural healer."

Nervous about what sort of reception she'd receive, Eve placed the call. When a female voice answered, Eve told the woman she was calling about the job ad in the paper.

"Are you a certified C.N.A.?"

"Yes I am," Eve replied. "But I'm not calling to apply for the job. I'm calling to see if I might be able to help in another way. I'm a natural healer."

The woman on the other end explained that she was a registered nurse, and that she'd quit her job and brought this patient home from the hospital to care for her personally. What she really needed was a C.N.A. to spell her for a few hours of sleep each night. But at this point, she would welcome any help she could get.

Eve took the nurse's address and directions to her home in Shingle Springs, and promised to come on her next day off. When she'd hung up the phone, Eve buried her face in her hands. Memories of her father's illness flooded into her mind. "Am I really going to be able to help this woman, Saul?"

"Sweetheart, there's nothing that can be done to cure this woman unless Jesus Himself decides to take a hand. You can't cure A.L.S., but you *can* relieve some of her discomfort."

"*Sweetheart,*" Eve said. "Saul, did you just call me Sweetheart?"

"Yeah!" Gideon put in. "Sweetheart's *my* name for her! What are you trying to do? Cut into my territory?"

"I'm sorry," Saul said. "I've been working closely with Eve these past few weeks, and I've come to love her too. It just slipped out."

"Well don't let it slip out again," Gideon said.

"You don't have sole right to the name," Saul argued. "If you—"

Eve couldn't believe this. Her two spirit guides were having an argument in her head! "Guys!" she said. "Cool it!"

On the way to Shingle Springs two days later, Eve couldn't help laughing at the memory of the argument. Her guides were like a couple of kids!

The directions the nurse had given Eve proved to be easy to follow. The turn-off in Shingle Springs took her to a narrow tree-lined country road. Squinting to see the numbers on the mailboxes, Eve drove slowly till she came to the gravel driveway that led to the two-story farmhouse.

Parked at the side of the house were three old cars in various states of disrepair. The hood on one was open. From her vantage point, all Eve could see were a pair of jeaned legs and a male derriere. "Is this where a nurse named Jill Burstyn lives?" she called loudly.

"Yeah," a voice called from under the hood. "That's my mom. You can go on up."

The house had no doorbell. Eve had to knock several times to be heard. When the door opened, a wan woman with short blonde hair smiled an exhausted greeting. "You must be Eve. I'm Jill."

Eve had expected to be greeted by a nurse in a white uniform. What she *hadn't* expected to find was a sleepy-eyed woman in jeans, bare feet, and a baggy gray sweatshirt. Eve was glad she'd decided to wear jeans and a mauve sweatshirt of her own. When the nurse moved aside, Eve stepped into the entryway. The living room to the right had been converted to a hospital room. Except for a blue chair in the corner and a step stool by the bed, the entire room was taken up by the hospital bed and other medical equipment.

"I was just suctioning Evelyn's lungs when you came to the door," the nurse said. "That's why it took me so long to answer. Come in, and let me introduce you to Evelyn."

Eve followed Jill to Evelyn's bedside. The woman in bed appeared to be in her mid- forties. Instead of a traditional hospital gown, she was dressed in a floral print gown trimmed in lace. "This is Evelyn," Jill said. "Doesn't she look beautiful today? Evelyn, this is Eve, the natural healer I told you about."

"If you'd like to touch her," Jill said in a side whisper, "It's okay to take her hand."

Eve approached the bedside with a lump in her throat, and reached for the puffy hand lying on the mattress. As she did, Saul identified himself and warned her to draw back. "If you touch her when she's this weak, she'll drain your strength."

Realizing that she'd just had a close call, Eve made a mental vow to wait for Saul's instructions next time. "Hello, Evelyn. I hope you'll understand if I don't touch your hand just yet. Until you're stronger, I need to maintain a little distance. But it's very nice to meet you."

There was no movement in Evelyn's hand, no sound from her mouth. Only the gurgle in the suction tube as Jill suctioned the mucous from her lungs. Standing next to the bed was a pole with a feeding bag. When Eve looked into Evelyn's face, her ears began to ring and a cold sweat coated her brow.

Evelyn had probably once been an attractive woman. Her black hair framed her puffy face, emphasizing the pasty pallor of her once beautiful complexion. Eve recognized the puffiness as a sign of fluid retention. Evelyn's jaw was slack, and her mouth hung open: a grotesque caricature with painted red lips. Her dark eyes rolled pathetically in Eve's direction. Other than this simple movement, Evelyn showed no sign of life.

"Her eyes are the only thing she can move," Jill said. "They're how we communicate. She blinks once for Yes, twice for No." Having offered this explanation, Jill asked if Evelyn was glad Eve had come to see her.

A slow blink indicated the answer was "Yes."

"There's not a trace of positive energy in her body," Saul said. "I don't want you to worry about relieving pain today. I just want you to give her a transfusion of positive energy."

Eve couldn't do this. It was not going to work, having Saul give instructions, and letting Jill and Evelyn think *she* had the power to heal. She had to tell them about Saul and let *them* make the decision of whether they wanted to go any farther.

128

"There's something I have to tell you both," Eve said nervously. "The healing touch—the energy source—doesn't come just from me. I know this sounds strange, but believe me, it sounds just as strange to me as it does to you. I have a spiritual healing guide who talks to me telepathically and gives me directions of what to do." Now that she'd said it, they probably thought she was certifiable, but it couldn't be helped. They had to know the truth. "Why don't I go out in the kitchen, and let you two decide whether you want to go on with this?"

"You don't have to leave," Jill said. "Ask Evelyn yourself. If she's agreeable to go on, it's okay with me."

Jill's reaction was not what Eve had expected. Eve wondered if perhaps Jill had had past experience with the paranormal. "Evelyn," Eve said quietly, "I guess it's up to you. My power to relieve pain doesn't come from *me*. As I understand it, the healing power is channeled from Jesus *through my healing guide*, through me. My guide's name is Saul. He's who convinced me to answer Jill's ad in the paper."

A single blink said Evelyn understood.

"If you still want me to try to help you, I'm willing," Eve said. "If you just want me to leave, and not come back, that's okay too. It's up to you. Do you want me to leave?"

Double blink: "No."

"Then does that mean you want me to stay and try to help?"

Single blink: "Yes."

"Then that settles it," Jill said. "Let's get started."

Eve couldn't believe it had been that simple. She'd at least expected a reaction of shock. But both Jill and Evelyn had taken her explanation in stride.

"Is it alright if I put my hands over you?" Eve asked Evelyn. "I'm not going to touch you. I just want to share some positive energy with you. Will that be alright?"

Slow blink.

Before attempting to transfuse Evelyn with positive energy, Eve asked if Jill would like to feel the energy herself. Eager to experience what Evelyn would be feeling, Jill reached out her hand.

The instant Eve placed her hand near Jill's, Jill felt a rush of positive energy through her arm and hand. "I feel it," she whispered. "It feels like a faint current of electricity. You're telling me this is positive energy, and you can put it into Evelyn's body?"

"Her disease has depleted her reserves of positive energy," Eve explained. "Before I can do anything to help with her pain, I need to replenish what's been depleted."

With Saul's guidance, Eve placed her hands an inch or so above Evelyn's body and began to move them in slow clockwise circles. When she did, she felt the energy being sucked from her hands. "Be careful," Saul said. "Don't touch her. Just keep moving your hands over her, and see the green…"

When Eve had finally completed today's session, she sank into the blue chair—exhausted.

"How do you feel, Evelyn?" Jill asked. "Could you feel anything happening when Eve was moving her hands over you?"

Slow blink.

"Are you feeling any better at all?"

Slow blink.

"Do you want Eve to come again?"

Evelyn rolled her eyes in Eve's direction and did a slow blink.

The hope in the brown eyes tore at Eve's heart. Should she tell Evelyn she couldn't cure the disease? That the best she could offer was relief from discomfort? Or should she say nothing, and let Evelyn have her own thoughts? Surely Evelyn must realize that once the nervous system has been destroyed—"I'll be back soon," Eve said. "I promise."

Slow blink.

Eve had donned her coat and was preparing to leave when Jill asked if she thought she could do anything for *her.* "It's from all the lifting I do. I have chronic pain in my lower back."

"Sure," Eve said tiredly. "I'll do what I can."

"Before you work on her back," Saul said, "I want you to do a diagnostic search for areas of pain. This will be good practice for you. Have her stand in front of you, and with your eyes closed pass your hands over various areas of her body. You're looking for areas of green, red or black."

"My healing guide wants me to do a diagnostic experiment. Would you mind? It just involves passing my hands close to you and trying to sense the areas of pain."

"Not at all," Jill said. "This will be a new experience for both of us. Did you hear that, Evelyn? Eve's going to try to sense where my body has pain, by putting her hands close to me."

Slow blink.

Standing before Eve, Jill held very still as Eve knelt at her side and closed her eyes. Moving her hands slowly within inches of Jill's body, Eve could feel the energy field emanating from Jill's skin. Using the energy field as a guide, she explored Jill's body front and back, without once coming in contact. As she did, with her eyes closed, she saw gradations of color from dark green to lighter green, to red, to black.

"The colors you're seeing have nothing to do with auras," Saul explained. "Green, for your purpose, indicates areas of good health. Dark green is best, but light green is still good. Red is for moderate to strong pain; black if for severe." Saul went on to explain that what he and other spirits saw was similar to Kurlean photography. They could tell problem areas at a glance when they chose to look beneath the surface. This, by the way, was how *dark* spirits were able to pinpoint a person's areas of vulnerability. "Now go over each part of her body again, and tell Jill what you see."

This time Eve alternated, opening and closing her eyes so she'd be accurate in telling Jill exactly where she saw the pain. "I see medium green for your feet, and for your lower legs and left knee. There's no pain there. But there's medium red— that's moderate pain in your right knee... I also see medium red in your left elbow...I'm seeing light green in your left shoulder, neck, and head—that's okay— and dark red in your right shoulder: That means a lot of pain...Your chest and stomach seem to be alright; so is your upper back. But I see black in your lower back. That's where it hurts the most."

When she'd finished, Jill spread her hands in amazement. "Everything you said was right on. I'm impressed."

It made Eve feel good to hear that her first reading was accurate. "I don't have time to work on everything tonight. So let's get to work on your lower back. How about if we move that footstool over in front of the chair…"

While Jill sat on the stool bending forward, Eve put her hands on her back and pulled them slowly away. The elastic pull of the negative energy was incredibly strong. It took three trips outside to dispose of all the energy Eve had pulled from Jill's back. When she had finished, Eve asked Jill how she felt.

Twisting from one side to the other, Jill smiled. "The pain's gone! Evelyn, this stuff really works! The pain's gone from my lower back!"

Driving back to Placerville, Eve felt as if she were floating on a cloud. She had enjoyed taking the pain from Jill's back. But her real excitement was over the prospect of working with Evelyn. She hadn't been able to help her Dad when she was a child. But she was going to help Evelyn, even if it was only to the extent of relieving her discomfort. "Thank you, God…"

The next time Eve saw Evelyn, it was to work on a bedsore. Despite the fact that Jill turned Evelyn every hour, Evelyn's skin was beginning to break down. The sore on her right hip was six inches across: extremely inflamed, and oozing. For this, Eve placed her hands—encased in plastic gloves—directly over the sore and closed her eyes. Not content to see merely green, she forced herself to *focus* until the green she saw was emerald and her hands felt like they were electrified.

Eve worked on the bedsore until she was exhausted. And then she worked on Jill's knee and shoulder. When she was ready to leave, she said goodnight to Evelyn, but received no response. Evelyn's eyes were wide open, staring at the ceiling. "Evelyn? Can you hear me?" No response. Turning toward Jill, Eve whispered, "Is she—"

Jill had picked up Evelyn's wrist and was taking her pulse. "She's just sleeping. She's lost the ability to close her eyes. Her eyes get so dry. Do you think you could work on them?"

"Sure," Eve agreed. "But I'm kind of drained right now. The healing works best when I'm not so tired. Maybe you could use drops for tonight, and remind me next time I come."

The following day, Saul suggested that Eve call to ask Jill if there'd been any improvement in Evelyn's bedsore. "I think you'll find there's been an improvement of about twenty-five percent."

When Eve called, she didn't tell Jill what Saul had said. She simply asked her to check. When Jill returned to the phone, she reported that there had been a significant improvement.

"How much?" Eve asked. "Ten percent? Twenty?"

"No," Jill replied. "I'd say it's improved by at least twenty-five percent."

Bingo.

When Jill called Eve three days later, it was to say that Evelyn had come down with Pneumonia and might not last the night.

Saul talked to Eve all the way to Shingle Springs, describing to Eve what she must do when she got there to break up the congestion. When Eve arrived, Jill didn't come to the door. She hollered for Eve to come in.

"The suction tube keeps getting blocked," Jill said. "There's something in there that won't come out. If we can't get the mucus out of her lungs—" Jill's voice cracked with emotion. "Is there anything you can do?"

Eve took her jacket off and laid it on the chair, then immediately set to work, moving her hands over Evelyn's rib cage as Saul had directed. "See the green," Saul said softly. "Remember your healing power's at its peak when you see the emerald."

Eve's hands continued to move in broad circles as she closed her eyes and envisioned a field of green. *You've got to focus,* she said in her mind. *Focus, and see the emerald.* "You're doing fine," Saul said. "Just try to relax, and the emerald will come. Good. Now reverse directions. There's a mucus plug in her bronchial tube about four inches long, but it's breaking up."

"Saul says there's a four-inch long mucus plug, but it's starting to break up." As Eve spoke, she continued to move her hands, only now she moved them closer to Evelyn's body.

"That's it," Saul said. "You've got it now. The plug has broken into four sections, each about an inch long. Tell Jill to suction again. The plugs will be coming out any second."

Eve passed on the message, and Jill began to suction. No longer closing her eyes to see the green, Eve watched in fascination as one by one the inch-long mucus plugs came through the tube—bing, bing, bing, bing—just as Saul had predicted.

The sigh of relief that escaped Jill's lips was a reflection of Eve's own emotions. "Her tubes are clear! You did it! Now she can breathe!"

For the next three days, Eve drove to Shingle Springs every evening after work. The going was slow. But little by little Evelyn's condition improved until eventually the antibiotics kicked in. The crisis was over.

When Eve returned the following weekend to check on Evelyn's progress, Jill had a friend there she wanted Eve to meet. "This is Marsha. She had an accident last week. She dropped a bag of cement on her toes. Marsha's a skeptic, but I thought maybe you could help her."

Marsha was a short stocky woman with brown hair pulled back in a ponytail. Jill said she was a nurse, but she wasn't wearing a uniform. She was wearing baggy jeans and a Levi jacket open at the front to reveal a flowered blouse. Her feet were too swollen for normal shoes, so she was wearing thick white socks and sandals.

"Would you like to sit down in the chair over there?" Eve suggested. "If taking off the sandals poses a problem, you can leave them on. But it would be better if you could take both them and the socks off."

When Eve knelt before Marsha and cupped the swollen toes of one foot in her hands, she felt an immediate outpour of positive energy. "Do you feel anything?"

"I'm not sure," Marsha answered. "I think I feel something: maybe a little tingling sensation."

When five minutes of positive energy did no apparent good, Eve decided to reverse her tactics. "Up till now, I've been sharing positive energy with you. But it's negative energy that's causing your pain and numbness. I need to pull the negative energy out." Based on the way Marsha rolled her eyes, Eve halfway expected her to get up and run—or hobble from the room, as the case may be. When she didn't, Eve set to work. Slowly and methodically, she proceeded to pull the negative energy from Marsha's feet and carry it outside to the porch to dispose of it. After ten minutes or so, Marsha said that feeling had returned to the two toes on her right foot that had been numb.

"What about the pain in your other toes?" Eve asked.

"It's not as bad as it was," Marsha said. "I really didn't think you'd be able to help. But about half of the pain's gone."

"Did you hear that, Evelyn?" Jill asked excitedly. "The feeling came back in two toes that had been numb. And the pain in her other toes is half gone!"

"We're not finished yet," Eve said. "I think I can take the rest of the pain away."

"Thanks," Marsha said, standing and beginning to button her coat. "But I have to go. My husband will be coming home, and I didn't leave a note telling where I'd gone. I'm sure the pain and numbness will be back before the day's out, but thanks for trying."

"I told you she was a skeptic," Jill said with a grin. "Don't let her get to you. You helped her, and she knows it. She just won't admit it."

Marsha had just left when another friend of Jill's arrived. "This is Bud Michaels," Jill said. "I've been telling *him* about you, too. Bud is a skeptic, just like Marsha. So I asked him to come and meet you."

Bud was a male nurse in his early thirties, dressed today in a white t-shirt and jeans. His lips were curled in a mocking smile. When he shook Eve's hand, he commented that he didn't feel anything unusual.

"What did you expect to feel?" Eve asked.

"The way Jill's been talking about you, I was hoping to feel some sort of magic. But to tell you the truth, I don't believe in this natural healing stuff. I think it's all in Jill's imagination."

Eve didn't like Bud Michaels. He was a know-it-all with an attitude. "Do you have any pain anywhere in your body? If you do, you could find out firsthand whether it works or not."

"You tell *me* whether I have any pain," Bud said with a smirk. "You're the one who's supposed to be a natural healer."

Closing her eyes, Eve passed her hands over the area of Bud's head, arms, and torso. In all except his upper right arm, she saw shades of emerald green. "I see moderate pain in your right upper arm. The rest of your upper body seems to be in good shape."

"Lucky guess," Bud said. "Now let's see you take it away."

If that was the kind of attitude he was going to have, Eve would have preferred to let Bud *keep* his damned pain. But Evelyn could hear what was going on, and she couldn't afford to let Evelyn's confidence in her falter. Closing her eyes to see the green, she placed her hands on Bud's arm.

For pain that was supposed to be moderate, the tenacity of the negative energy was extremely strong. Each time Eve tried to pull it out, it would be drawn back into his arm. After struggling with the pain for five minutes or more, Eve finally gave it a sudden jerk, breaking away perhaps half the negative energy field. Once she had disposed of it, she returned for the rest. "Is your arm feeling any better at all?" she asked.

"You tell me."

Eve was tempted to tell Bud to forget it. Instead, she placed her hand on his arm again and drew it away, feeling the strong elastic pull of the negative energy, but not as strong as before. When the last of it had broken away, she went back outside to brush it off. *That was the toughest one yet, Saul. I thought for a minute there it wasn't going to work.*

"You did just fine," Saul said. "Don't be too hard on the guy. He's part of the medical community. They're trained *not* to believe in natural healing."

When Eve went back inside, Bud was smiling. "I have a confession to make. While you were trying to pull the pain out of my arm, I was fighting against you with all my might. I could feel the pain being pulled out, but I was using my will power to pull it back in. The pain's gone now, so I guess you won."

Glancing at Jill, Eve could see the relief in the nurse's face. Apparently, Jill valued Bud's opinion. It had been important to her that Eve prove a point. Eve was glad not everyone was as skeptical as Bud and Marsha. If they were, it would take all the fun out of healing.

Now that Bud's skepticism had been somewhat defused, Jill brought up the subject of a spirit who lived at Bud's house, and had become like a member of the family. "Tell her about Kram, Bud."

Bud had a *spirit* who was like part of his family, yet he was skeptical about the possibility of *natural healing*? "Kram?" Eve said. "This spirit's name is *Kram*?"

"That's not his actual name. His name is really Mark. But when he first wrote it in the steam on the bathroom mirror, it was backwards—as if he was writing it from inside the medicine cabinet. So instead of calling him Mark, we decided to keep the name Kram."

Warming to the subject, Bud told Eve about how Kram often played with his young daughter, and how when she'd gotten a helium balloon for her birthday, it had floated up the stairs and *back down again.* "It's kind of fun having Kram around. When we move to another house, we're going to take him with us."

Eve had thought the natural *healing* was unusual. But things were getting weirder and weirder. "Kram never does anything scary or destructive?"

"No," Ted said. "He's a friendly ghost. I guess he's our family's version of Casper."

Before Eve left that night to go back to the hotel, Jill wrote a phone number on a slip of paper and handed it to her. "This is a C.N.A. who comes here to help me three times a week. *She* wants to talk to you about guardian angels." Apparently Jill had been telling everyone she knew about Eve and her spirit guides.

When Eve went a few days later to meet Jill's friend Sandy, she felt an outrush of healing energy the moment Sandy touched her hand. "Come in," Sandy said. "Jill has told me a lot about you."

Sandy was Eve's height with short brown hair and an acne-scarred complexion. She was dressed today in baggy peach sweats, the same shade as Eve's bulky sweater. Eve couldn't really judge her size, other than to know she was a little overweight. "Jill said you can find out the name of my guardian angel."

"I might be able to find out for you," Eve said. "But first I need to know why I felt an outrush of energy when you shook my hand."

Amazed that Eve had felt it, Sandy said she'd felt it too.

"Ask her about her colon," Saul said.

"My healing guide wants me to ask you about your colon. Is there some sort of a problem?"

Eve had sat down on the sofa, and Sandy had taken a seat on the matching loveseat. A look of shock registered on Sandy's face. "That's amazing! How did your guide know I have a spastic colon? I haven't had a B.M. for over a week."

"Tell her you can mix her a drink," Saul said.

When Eve explained to Sandy that she could put the natural healing energy into a soda for her to drink, Sandy didn't question. She simply excused herself and went into the kitchen. Apparently Jill had made her a believer. Before returning to the living room, Sandy popped the top on a can of Pepsi and poured the foaming liquid into a glass.

Placing a hand over the glass of soda, Eve closed her eyes and waited for the green. When she saw the field of emerald, the soda began to splash. "I think your drink is ready."

Sandy took the glass of Pepsi and returned to the loveseat. While Eve explained how she had gotten in touch with her guardian angel, Sandy drank the soda down. If Eve had counted the seconds from the time the glass was empty to the time Sandy leaped from the loveseat and raced for the bathroom, she was certain it couldn't have been more than three…

Chapter 25

It was Monday evening, and Eve had just gotten home from work when the phone rang. Expecting it to be Carla, she was surprised when she answered to hear Paul's voice. "This is Paul from the Metaphysical store. I talked to Margaret, and she said she'd like to meet you."

Eve had forgotten about Paul's saying he knew someone she should meet. First the lady with the smashed toes, then the male nurse, then Sandy, now Margaret... If people kept introducing her at this rate, she'd have met the whole town by the end of the month!

Despite the fact that she'd been living in Placerville for more than three months, Eve was unfamiliar with the streets in town, other than the streets from the hotel to the hospital, and from the hotel to the shopping mall. Fortunately, Margaret lived within three blocks of the hospital.

The house she lived in was a single-story frame house surrounded by trees. When she opened the front door, Margaret greeted Eve as if they'd been friends forever. "Come in. I have lemonade and cookies on the enclosed patio. I thought it might be nice to sit out there and talk."

Margaret's short gray hair and matronly figure were at odds with the hippy image Eve had formed in her mind. So was her immaculate house. The patio, enclosed by glass and surrounded by trees, gave a feeling of being outdoors, but without the frigid temperature.

Taking a seat in the wicker chair that was offered, Eve watched as Margaret set two glasses on the table and poured the lemonade. "I've never known anyone else who does what I do," Margaret said. "You're the first I've met."

"That makes two of us," Eve said, reaching for a shortbread cookie. "How did you get into natural healing?"

"I read an article about this woman who practiced hands-on healing," Margaret replied. "I figured if she could do it, why couldn't I? So I started trying it on my family whenever they got hurt or had aches and pains.

"What's it like for you?" Eve asked. "Do you feel a tingling when the healing energy goes through your hands?"

Margaret said she did, like her hands were on the verge of going to sleep.

When Eve asked if she also provided pain relief by pulling negative energy out of the person's body, Margaret said she did, and that she often had trouble getting it off her hands and arms. "I don't know how to describe the feeling. It's like—"

"Cobwebs?"

"Yes!" Margaret said. "I never thought about it like that."

When Margaret questioned Eve and found out that Eve had a spiritual healing guide, she said there were a couple of ladies she thought Eve might be interested in talking to. She didn't say why she thought Eve should speak to them; only that she would like to hear Eve's opinion of what they had to say.

Eve placed the call the minute she got back to the hotel. "Is this Wynona?" When the woman said she was, Eve identified herself and said that Margaret had suggested she call. "I don't know what Margaret felt we might have in common," Eve said. "I'm a natural healer."

"I don't know why she suggested you call either, unless—Are you in touch with your spirit guides?"

"Yes," Eve said. "That's how I got into natural healing."

"My job's a little more unusual than that," Wynona said. "I don't mean the job I work at to earn a living. I mean the one I do evenings and weekends."

Curious, Eve asked what this unusual job was.

"I chart the winds," Wynona replied. "My sister charts the waters."

Eve had never heard of any person other than a weatherman charting the winds and waters. "Do you mean you and your sister are meteorologists?"

"No," Wynona said. "I *control* the winds. My sister controls the world's waterways."

Now Eve had heard everything. What kind of a nut had Margaret hooked her up with? "What makes you think you control the wind?" she asked quietly.

"I don't just think it," Wynona said. "I know it. My spirit guide trained me, and I've tested it. When I will a breeze to blow, it blows. When I will it to change directions, it changes."

Eve wondered how this woman had come this far without being committed to an insane asylum.

"If the wind and water charts aren't why Margaret suggested you call me, maybe it was my out of body experiences."

"You have out of body experiences?" Eve asked cautiously. "Do you do this willingly, or does it just happen?"

"Oh, I do it willingly," Wynona replied. "You'd be amazed the interesting people you can meet when you go out of body."

Eve felt like she'd been beamed into a spaceship, and was talking to an alien creature. "These people you meet can't see you. Right?"

"Oh, they can see me," Wynona said. "Because they're out of body too. I've even had a love affair out of body."

Gideon, Eve said in her mind. *Tell me this isn't happening. I don't even know what to say to this woman.*

"This is Gideon, and I'm of the light. Don't say anything. Just listen."

As Eve listened, Wynona went on to describe the out of body affair she'd been having for months with an Asian man from her office. "He's very shy," she said. "To see us together at work, you'd never guess. But out of body, he's a wonderful lover. I finally decided to confront him last week and make him admit what's been going on."

"And what did he say?"

"He denied it. He even denied any attraction to me. But that's because he's shy, and not ready to bring our affair out in the open."

For a long moment, Eve was silent. But then she asked the questions that had been on her mind ever since Wynona started talking. "These people that you meet when you're out of body: Do you talk to them? Are they friendly? If people are out there having sex somewhere in space, where's the privacy?"

"Yes, I talk to them," Wynona said. "But you have to be careful when you're out of body. Not everyone who goes out of body is nice. Sometimes they want to fight."

"Have *you* ever had to fight out of body?" Eve asked weakly. She could not believe she was even having this conversation.

"Yes," Wynona answered. "But usually when anyone gives me any trouble, I will myself back home to get away from them."

Eve wondered what would happen if they followed her home, but didn't ask. She didn't feel that she could continue this conversation any longer. "I've been so distracted that I let my potatoes boil dry," she lied. "I'm going to have to get off the phone and clean up the mess."

"It's been nice talking to you," Wynona said. "Maybe we can talk again sometime…"

As soon as Eve got off the phone, she asked Gideon for an explanation.

"Wynona doesn't know enough to make spirits tell whether they're of the light," Gideon said. "She's gotten in with some dark ones, and they're making a fool of her. But I don't want you calling her back and telling her that. You have enough dark spirits working against you without taking on *hers*."

Eve thought about Wynona and her sister for the rest of the evening. Couldn't they see how ridiculous it was to think *they* could control the elements? Eve was still thinking about them when she moved her car to the back parking lot and went to bed. Around midnight, the phone rang.

In an effort to get to the phone in the dark, Eve got her feet tangled in the bedspread and fell to her knees. *Damn.* "Hello?"

"I'm sorry to wake you," Carla said. "But I need to talk to Joan."

"What's wrong?" Eve asked.

"There's something wrong with my eyes. I'm seeing colored lights all around me: blue, and green, and purple. They're rectangular lights all around my head."

"This is Joan, and I'm of the light. Tell Carla not to be afraid. They're spirits of light that have taken refuge in her apartment. That's just how they choose to represent themselves."

Joan went on to explain that not all spirits of light were as powerful as guardian angels. And those who had jobs on earth often had to contend with the forces of darkness. "Sometimes they get drained of energy and need a rest. Normally they go to a church. But in this case, they went to Carla's apartment."

"They're beautiful," Carla said. "They look almost like a wind chime of lights. I have the overhead light turned off, and they're lighting up my dining room!"

"Well at least you know they're nothing to be afraid of," Eve said with a stifled yawn. "I can understand why you were freaked out at first. But now maybe you can get some sleep."

"Thanks," Carla said. "And tell Joan I love her."

It occurred to Eve after she'd turned out the light and gone back to bed that she'd experienced so many amazing things in recent months that she'd almost begun to take them for granted.

Eve felt as if she'd just gone to sleep when she snapped awake with the eerie feeling that she'd just been levitated and dropped back onto her bed. "This is Saul, and I'm of the light. Get up and get ready for work. Mrs. Stillwell needs you."

When Eve arrived at the hospital, she went directly to Mrs. Stillwell's room before even punching in. The old lady's face lit up the minute she saw her. "Last night I was in so much pain. It was worse than it's ever been. I said a prayer for God let you know I needed you, so maybe you'd come to work early. Then God spoke to me in my head. He said, 'This is from Eve.' And my pain went away."

The feeling of exhilaration that flooded through Eve at that moment was a natural high beyond any she'd felt up till now. Closing her eyes, she said a mental prayer of thanks.

That evening when Carla called, it was to say that she'd had an accident. Walking across the parking lot, she had tripped and fallen. Her left thigh had been badly bruised, she had abrasions and bruises on her fingers, and the cut on her forehead had required four stitches. "The doctor gave me pain pills, but I sure wish *you* were here."

There was no way Eve could drive to the valley this late in the evening and still make it back in time to get any sleep before work tomorrow. "I'll come tomorrow evening," she promised.

"Too bad you can't send the healing energy through the telephone wires," Carla teased. "Can you imagine if you were able to do that? Someone could get hurt on the East Coast, and you could send healing energy from California to take away their pain."

"Tell her to get a Sprite and pour it in a glass," Saul said.

When Eve passed on the message, Carla asked if he was planning to mix her a stiff drink to make her forget the pain.

"Don't be cute," Saul said. "Just get the Sprite."

Carla put down the phone, and Eve could hear the refrigerator opening and closing. She could hear as Carla opened the cupboard door and took out a glass. When Carla returned, Eve could hear the fizz as she filled the glass.

"Okay," Carla said. "I've got the drink. What's next?"

"Tell her to put her injured fingers in the Sprite," Saul ordered. "Then I want you to concentrate on seeing the green, and tell *her* to do the same. If both of you can see it, this just might work."

Both Eve and Carla did as they'd been told, and Carla reported that she could feel the fizz popping on her hand. When Eve had a clear view of emerald green in her mind's eye, she concentrated on "sending" it to Carla, and asked if Carla could see it.

"I see some green spots," Carla said. "No—Wait—They're getting bigger…"

"Keep your eyes closed," Eve instructed. "Try to fill your whole field of vision with emerald green."

"I see it!" Carla said excitedly. "It feels like an electric current's is going through my arm and hand. The Sprite's popping all around my fingers."

After two or three minutes of concentration, Eve suggested they take a rest, and Carla pushed the glass of Sprite aside. To get Carla's mind off her injuries, they talked about a recent movie starring John Travolta.

Suddenly Carla stopped mid-sentence. "You're not going to believe this, Eve. Are you sitting down?"

Eve was sitting at the tiny dinette table with her bare feet propped on the second chair. "I'm sitting down. Why?"

"You're *not* going to believe this. I'm not sure I believe it myself."

"So tell me!" Eve prodded. "What's going on?"

Carla could barely control the excitement in her voice. "You know the fingers I put in the Sprite? The knuckles were totally black and blue. Right? Well, they're not anymore. The bruises are gone!"

Speechless, Eve listened as Carla gushed on. Eve had thought she'd heard some amazing things, but this had to take the prize.

The next day, her day off, Eve drove to the Valley to see Carla's hand for herself, and do what she could for the cut on Carla's head. Just as Carla had said, her fingers were free of bruises. Eve put her hand on Carla's forehead to infuse the cut with positive energy, then Carla pulled down her slacks to show Eve her leg. A dark black bruise at least six inches long and four inches wide covered the thigh she had landed on. "Good grief," Eve said. "You're lucky you didn't break your leg!"

They had made sandwiches for lunch and were seated at the table visiting when Eve suddenly had a brainstorm. "If the Sprite worked for the bruises on your fingers, why not try it on the black bruise on your thigh?"

"I'm out of Sprite," Carla said. "All I have is Coke."

"The brand name doesn't matter," Eve said. "How can we do this?"

For want of a better idea, they filled a hairspray cap with Coke, and Eve put her hand over it to infuse it with positive energy. When the Coke had reached the equivalent of a cold rolling boil in the cap, Carla took her slacks off, and Eve inverted the cap in the middle of the bruise. Holding the cap tightly in contact with Carla's skin, she maintained the pressure for thirty seconds or so, closing her eyes all the while to see the green.

When Eve had finished, Carla put her own fingers on the cap to hold it in place till she could get to the bathroom and release it in the bathtub. When she returned to put her pants back on, she commented that if the Coke was working, it certainly wasn't working as fast as the Sprite.

An hour or so later, Eve suggested they check the bruise. When Carla pulled down her slacks, they both gasped. In the middle of the black bruise was a perfectly round patch the size of the hairspray cap—of normal skin. The bruise that had been in contact with the soft drink was gone!

Three days later, Carla called to tell Eve she had already had her stitches removed. "The doctor said he's never seen anyone heal so fast…"

Chapter 26

Thanksgiving Day, 1991 was Eve's second Thanksgiving since returning to Northern California.   Once again, Kevin was spending the holiday with his stepmother's family, and Carla had gone to San Jose to spend the day with her grandchildren.   Rather than spend the holiday alone, Eve went to the hospital to have Thanksgiving dinner with Mrs. Stillwell.

Eve had expected to have to feed Mrs. Stillwell before eating her own dinner. But when she took the old lady's hands in hers, a temporary miracle occurred. Instead of the pain merely going away, Mrs. Stillwell's fingers began to uncurl! Excited, Eve closed her eyes and concentrated on seeing the emerald green. A rush of healing energy coursed through her veins. Just as her own fist had been opened the night of God's demonstration, Mrs. Stillwell's arthritic fingers straightened. The joints were still enlarged, and her fingers were still misshapen.   But for Thanksgiving dinner, she was free of pain and able to feed herself without help. Too bad the food was cold.

Eve was just getting ready to leave when a C.N.A. came to Mrs. Stillwell's door and asked Eve to help her transfer a patient. "I know you're off today, but I can't find anyone else to help, and Mr. Smith needs to go to the bathroom."

Eve hated transferring Mr. Smith. The last time she'd had to help transfer him, he'd asked her to open her shirt so he could take a look at her *teats*. "I'll stop in again to say Good-bye before I leave, Mrs. Stillwell."

Following the other C.N.A. down the corridor to Mr. Smith's room, Eve glanced in the rooms as she passed, to wave at the patients who were eating in bed.

Mr. Smith was a large man with thick lips and unfriendly eyes. Eve guessed him to be around seventy years old.   Except for the fact that he couldn't walk, he was capable of helping take care of himself, if he would do it. But he wouldn't. As he was so fond of telling anyone who would listen, he was paying a fortune to live in this G.D. place. He might as well get his money's worth.

The C.N.A. who'd asked for Eve's help swung the old man's legs over the edge of the bed and raised him to a sitting position so she could snap a safety belt around his waist. "I got Eve to help me transfer you to your wheelchair, you old coot. We don't want any of your hanky panky today."

"Who said anything about hanky panky?" Smith asked, looking toward Eve with a leer.

Eve should have suspected he was planning to try something. Instead, she was totally unprepared. When she approached to help lift him, his arm shot out and his hand grabbed her between the legs. "Stop it!" Eve squealed. Though she tried to knock his hand away, he was stronger than she was, and wouldn't budge. Eve wanted to knock the old goat's false teeth down his throat. But physical violence was against the rules.

Refusing to relax his grip, the old lecher fondled Eve's crotch through the fabric of her jeans. The other C.N.A.'s hands were occupied, supporting him so he wouldn't fall. "Get your hand off of me," Eve spat, "or so help me I'll—"

"What's going on here?" Doreen asked from the doorway. "Mr. Smith, stop that. What would your wife say if she knew you were fondling the girls who are here to take care of you?"

The guilt trip worked, at least for the moment. The old man released his lecherous grip, and Eve was able to back away.

"Eve, you're not even supposed to be helping when you're not clocked in," Doreen said. "Go on home and enjoy your Thanksgiving. *I'll* take care of Mr. Smith.

Later, Eve questioned Saul, demanding to know why the pain relief she provided for Mrs. Stillwell couldn't be permanent. "I help these people at the hospital, and four hours later they're as bad off as they were before. They could get the same results from taking morphine. What's the point in healing, if it isn't going to last?"

"This is Saul, and I'm of the light. Sweetheart,"—This time Eve didn't draw attention to his use of the pet name—"Your healing abilities aren't fully developed. You're doing great, and you're really helping these people. But the ability to *cure* is going to take time."

That night, Eve experienced the final lesson she'd been sent to Placerville to learn. She was lying on the sofa resting with her eyes closed when the phone rang. The normal reflex to open her eyes failed, and her eyes remained closed. Despite her efforts to move her arms and legs, she was paralyzed as surely as she had been the night of her out of body experience. From the dining nook, the phone continued to ring. *What is going on*? Eve's mind screamed.

"It's time for another lesson," Saul said. "What you're experiencing now is the equivalent of being in a coma. You can hear. You can feel and smell. But you have no control over any part of your body. Your thought processes are unaffected. This demonstration will help you understand any coma patients or so-called 'vegetables' you might ever have to take care of."

Whoever had been on the phone apparently hung up. Though Eve tried desperately to move and open her eyes, her body remained paralyzed. Instead of seeing the green she'd grown accustomed to seeing, her closed eyes now saw nothing but black. She felt as if she'd been shut up in a coffin. Her breathing became shallow, and her heart began to race. *Saul!* her mind cried out. *Please stop this!*

No answer.

"Saul!"

The claustrophobic panic Eve was feeling was overwhelming. If her heart beat any faster, she feared she would have a coronary. *I can't stand this,* she thought frantically. *If it goes on much longer, I'll die!* Beads of perspiration dotted her forehead and soaked the armpits of her cotton smock. *If I don't show up for work in the morning,* her mind reasoned, *someone will come to check on me. Oh God. If they take me to the hospital, they won't know what's going on. Suppose they give me electric shock to revive me!*

The simulated coma lasted an hour: an hour of pure Hell. "This is Saul, and I'm of the light. It's over now, Sweetheart. You can open your eyes now, and get up."

At that moment, Eve hated her healing guide. She hated Gideon for allowing him to do this to her. She didn't do the Tarot.

"Can I talk to you for a minute?" Caruso asked in her head. "I know you're mad at Saul and Gideon, and I don't blame you. That coma thing was a rotten thing to do. But it taught you a lesson most people never learn. How many other nurses and C.N.A.s can put themselves in the shoes of people who've had strokes that turned them into vegetables? Now that I think of it, they did you a real favor. I'm not saying it wasn't mean and all, but try to see it through their eyes. How else could they—"

"*Alright,*" Eve interrupted. "You've made your point."

The next morning at work was relatively uneventful, but when Eve decided to go out for lunch, her car was not where she had parked it. Her first panicky thought was that the Shadow had been stolen. But she had the key in her hand. Anyone who had taken it would have to have hotwired it.

A sick feeling gripped Eve's stomach as she slowly turned around. There was the Shadow on the other side of the parking lot, it's rear bumper smashed into the fender of another car. Apparently the Shadow had drifted backward across the lot and banged into the white Ford as it picked up speed. Thank Heaven she'd been able to keep up her insurance.

If the Ford hadn't been in the way, the Shadow would have left the parking lot and gone into the street. How could this have happened? It wasn't possible that Eve had left the car in gear. If she'd done that, she wouldn't have been able to get the key out of the ignition. She had left the car unlocked. Was it possible a vandal had gotten into the car and shifted gears? No, of course not. In order to do that, he would have to have had a key—the key she was holding in her hand at this moment. A check of the gearshift showed that it had been in neutral when the car drifted backward across the lot.

"It was a dark one," Gideon told her. "I'm sorry I wasn't able to stop him. If the Boss would just let us use the powers He gave us... But no: He ties our hands, and the dark ones get away with doing things like *this.*"

"*Why?*" Eve asked tearfully. "What did I ever do to them to cause them to hate me so much?"

"You don't have to have done anything to them, Sweetheart. They hate you because you've been chosen."

Chapter 27

Eve had just finished the dishes, and popped open a can of Coke. The more she thought about it, the more convinced she became that it was time to get out of this town with its parking tickets and drunks in the alley, and move back to the valley where at least she could go dancing on the weekends. All the gold in *them thar hills* hadn't been enough to protect her car. She wished to high Heaven she'd never been "chosen."

On the other hand, if she hadn't been chosen, she would never have experienced the thrill of having *God* open her closed fist, or of breaking up the congestion in Evelyn's chest, or of pulling pain out of people's bodies... She guessed she wasn't really sorry she'd been chosen. But she still wanted out of Placerville.

In the valley, at least she'd be able to go dancing. Mitch was no longer a factor. Eve had asked Carla, and been told Mitch had stopped showing up at the dances weeks ago. She'd already been trained in hands on healing. And she'd already learned whatever lessons the hospital job had been intended to teach her.

As far as she could see, the only thing keeping her here was the fact that Chad supposedly lived in this area. Considering that in the three and a half months she'd been here, her guides had sent her on at least a dozen of what had turned out to be wild goose chases, she'd be just as likely to meet Chad living in the valley as she would if she stayed here. His guardian angel could bring him *there* out of body just as easily as he could bring him to the hotel. There was no good reason why she shouldn't move back. *This* time instead of *standing in her way*, her guides could help her find a decent job for decent pay.

"I'm quitting," she told Saul. "I've hated my job from the day I came to work here. I like the healing, but I can do that anywhere." To Gideon, she had considerably more to say. "I'm sick of living in a Podunk town where there are no men my age except drunks and hayseeds. I'm sick of spending my evenings at home doing Tarot cards and learning *lessons*. And I'm sick of living in this smelly old hotel where I have to move my car every two hours and have to fear for my life every time I walk through the alley to get back from the parking lot! I want to spend more time with Kevin. I want to go dancing. I want a decent paying job so I can save some money. And I don't want to be badgered by dark spirits who have it in their heads that I'm on some sort of power trip."

"This is Gideon, and I'm of the light. Are you quite through? Can I say something now?"

"Not if you're going to try to talk me into staying." This said, Eve folded her arms and plopped down on the sofa.

"We've seen this coming," Gideon said. "That's why Saul speeded up the lessons. We agree that the main danger in the valley is past now. You can make the move with our blessing."

If Eve had known it would be this easy, she'd have rebelled a month ago. The following day, she gave her two-week notice.

"You realize, of course, that I can't write you a letter of recommendation when you've worked here less than six months," the personnel director said.

"I don't plan on looking for work as a C.N.A.," Eve said. "I'll finish out the two weeks, and then that's it."

When Eve left work that day, it was pouring rain. Without an umbrella, she was soaked by the time she made it from the car to the hotel. After dinner, she called to check on Evelyn.

"I was going to call you tonight," Jill said. "Evelyn has taken a turn for the worse. Her son flew in today from Alaska to see her one last time while she's still able to recognize him."

"If I leave right now, I can be there in half an hour," Eve said tensely.

"I don't want you to have to drive in this rain," Jill said. "The wind's picking up, and I just saw a streak of lightening…"

The truth was that Eve was terrified of driving in the storm after dark, trying to find Jill's farmhouse on a two-lane road with no streetlights. But if there'd been someone who could have helped her father, and they'd let a rainstorm keep them away… "Tell Evelyn I'll be there as soon as I can."

For all the good the windshield wipers did, the Shadow might as well not have had any. Sheets of rain swept across the freeway, pelting the car and blinding Eve to oncoming traffic except for the glare of headlights. "Please let me get there safely," Eve prayed. "Please let me get there in time to help Evelyn."

When she arrived at the farmhouse, the gale force wind rendered her umbrella useless. She was drenched by the time she made it to the door. Inside the sickroom, the scene was grim.

"She's lost the ability to communicate with her eyes," Jill said.

Evelyn lay on the hospital bed with a tube trailing from her nose and an I.V. dripping into her arm. Her eyes were wide open, staring at the ceiling. Her open mouth no longer drooled. Standing next to her bed was a bearded man in his early thirties.

"This is Evelyn's son, Jim," Jill said. "Jim, this is Eve, the natural healer that's been trying to help your mom."

Eve had barely said "Hello" when Saul began to speak:

"This is Saul, and I'm of the light. Tell Jim you need him to help you. Tell him the positive energy is stronger when it comes from a family member related by blood."

When Eve relayed the message, Jim's eyes took on a fearful expression. "There's nothing *I* can do to help. I don't know anything about healing."

"Start by filling his body with positive energy," Saul ordered. "Close your eyes so you can see the progress."

Reaching for his hands, Eve told Jim what they needed to do. Standing at the foot of his mother's bed, she took his hands in hers and closed her eyes. The surge of positive energy was immediate.

"I feel it in my hands," Jim said. "It's moving up my arms."

Through closed eyes, Eve could "see" the progress of healing energy surging into the bearded man's body. "It's in your chest and torso now, and I can see it moving into your legs..."

"You're right," Jim said. "Even my toes are tingling.

"Now it's moving upward from your chest, through your neck—"

When the energy reached his head, Jim jerked his hands away. "I can feel the charge all through my body," he said shakily. "What do we do next?"

For the next hour, Eve instructed Jim in how to move his hands in conjunction with hers. Together, they covered every inch of Evelyn's body.

After they'd finished, Eve offered to work on Jill's back. "I can tell by the strained look on your face that your lower back's hurting."

Jill sat on the stepstool and laid her head on Evelyn's bed. Eve sat on the floor behind her and placed her hands on Jill's back, above and below the waistline. The negative energy jumped to her hands. When Eve had taken the negative energy out to the porch and disposed of it, she returned to infuse Jill's back with *positive* energy.

Outside, the wind had died down but it was still storming. In some strange way, Eve felt one with the storm. The lightning that flashed across the sky was a visual representation of the positive energy coursing through her veins.

Kneeling to place her hands on Jill's back once more, Eve closed her eyes to see the green.

When she sensed that Jill's body was no longer absorbing, Eve stood and crossed to the fireplace where a black longhaired dog was lying quietly on the hearth. Thoroughly relaxed now, Jill continued to rest her head on the bed. The black dog raised its head to lick Eve's hand. "What's your dog's name?" Eve asked.

Leaping to her feet, Jill whirled to face Eve. "How did you get over there?" she shouted. "I thought you were still here! I could still feel your hands on my back!"

It wasn't the first time Eve had experienced this phenomenon of having someone think she was still touching her when she wasn't. It wouldn't be the last.

That night Saul broke the news to Eve that there was nothing more she could do for Evelyn. "It's time for her to let go, Sweetheart. Jill has kept her going far too long. To try to help her anymore now would simply drain your energy."

Despite the fact that she'd known it was coming, the news came as a harsh blow to Eve. She had felt from the beginning that Jill was going against nature by bringing Evelyn into her home and devoting herself 'round the clock to keeping Evelyn alive. She knew from her own research on A.L.S. that, once the disease had progressed, there was no turning back. But Jill had convinced Evelyn if they prayed hard enough and didn't give up, their miracle would be granted and she would get better. Eve admired Jill's determination to give Evelyn quality of life right to the end. Jill had even purchased an old van with a hydraulic lift so she could take her patient on outings. But to Eve's way of thinking, there came a time when a line should be drawn. If Evelyn liked music, Jill could bring the music to *her*, rather than taking her out to a club and making her the object of stares and whispered comments.

In Eve's opinion, even with the limited quality of life Jill was trying to provide, Evelyn would be better off dead. Still Saul's news came as a blow. When Eve called Jill to tell her what Saul had said, Jill refused to accept it. "I can't tell Evelyn that. I can't ask her to give up hope. We're still praying for a miracle. I believe that one day God is going to answer our prayers, and Evelyn's going to get up out of that bed and walk."

"But Jill, her nervous system has been destroyed," Eve argued. "She's fought a good fight. Now it's time to give in."

"Evelyn's afraid of death," Jill said simply. "She's a fighter. She's managed to hold on this long. She's not ready to let go now."

Eve found herself wondering why Jill was doing this. Was it only because of Evelyn's fear of death? Or did it have to do with the fact that for two years Jill had let this take over her life? For two years, she had lived the life of a martyr. With Evelyn gone, what would she do?

"I'm sorry, Jill. I know you're just doing what you believe you have to do. But I can't work with Evelyn anymore. She's too close to death, and it would just drain my energy. I'll still come to visit her as a friend, but there's nothing more I can do to help her."

"Tell her to tell Evelyn she doesn't have to fear death," Saul said. "Tell her she's lived a Christian life, and there's a place in Heaven waiting for her."

Though Eve passed on Saul's words, she wondered if they were falling on deaf ears.

It was a few days after her session with Evelyn that Eve was chosen to go to the other wing of the hospital and assist in preparing the body of a patient who had died. When Eve arrived at the deathbed, the senior C.N.A. had already rolled the patient onto his side and was washing his back and buttocks.

"Why is the back of his body turning purple?" Eve whispered.

"The blood has already settled," Crystal replied. While Eve stood back and watched, Crystal turned the man onto his back and closed his eyes. "We need a couple of coins to put on his eyelids to keep them closed."

There was a handful of change lying on the patient's nightstand. Careful to maintain a distance, Eve picked up a couple of quarters and handed them to the senior C.N.A.

"We have to wash him before rigor mortis sets in," Crystal said. "I'll get a pan of water. You get the washcloths. You can do his arms. I'll do his legs."

At the thought of washing the dead man's arms, the blood drained from Eve's face. "This is Saul, and I'm of the light. Don't do it," Saul said. "I'm telling you, Eve. Don't do it."

I have to, Eve said in her mind. *I don't have a choice.*

Saul said nothing more. When Eve picked up the man's arm closest to her and began washing it, she felt a whoosh of energy sucked from her body as if a an energy vacuum hose had attached itself to her hands. Her head was spinning as she rounded the bed and picked up the other arm.

"Are you alright?" Crystal asked. "You don't look so good."

"I'm okay," Eve gasped. "Let's just get finished here so we can go outside and get some air…"

Five minutes later, when Crystal came to look for her, Eve was slumped on a bench outside on the patio, drained of energy, sobbing and panting for breath. "The first time's always the hardest," Crystal said. "Just take some deep breaths. You'll be alright…"

After Crystal had returned to the floor, Eve was still unable to function. From inside, she could hear Doreen on the loudspeaker calling for Eve Tarlton to report to the nurse's station. Five minutes later Eve forced herself to her feet and made her way back to Wing One.

The minute Doreen saw Eve, she rushed to her side and put an arm around her shoulders. Pulling a packet of smelling salts from her pocket, she broke it open with one hand. When she waved it beneath Eve's nose, Eve jerked away. Clutching the partial partition of the nurse's station for support, Eve tried to regain her composure.

"I can see that you're not going to be any good for the rest of the day," Doreen said. "There's only one more hour to go. If you've already rinsed all your soiled laundry, you might as well punch out and go home."

For a long while, Eve sat in the car in the hospital parking lot, thinking about what had just happened. When she finally went home to her hotel apartment, she braced herself for the tirade to come.

"I told you not to touch him, but you wouldn't listen," Saul fumed. "Haven't you figured out yet that you're not like everyone else? Haven't you figured out that you've been given a special gift, and that with that gift comes responsibilities? I let you go through with it today in hopes that you'd learn your lesson. But if after this long you're still taking chances, it's going to be a *long time* before you're ready to work with Jesus."

Until this moment, no one had said a word about Eve's working with Jesus.

"What do you think I'm training you for?" Saul asked. "Sweetheart, much as I love you, I'm only *temporary*. You're on a path toward working directly with Jesus. When that time comes, you won't need a middle man."

"But I love you," Eve protested. "I don't *want* to stop working with you." For the rest of the evening, Eve argued with Saul, pointing out all the reasons she would *never* be ready to work directly with Jesus. Finally Saul promised to stay—at least for a few more months. It wasn't exactly a concession, but at least Eve had bought some time.

When she went to work at seven, barely dragging, Eve stopped in to see Mrs. Stillwell. "You look awful," Mrs. Stillwell said. "What happened to you?"

Eve brushed the question off by simply saying she'd had a bad night. When she went into Norma's room, she got a similar greeting. "You look like hell. Whatever you've got, don't come near me. What's my name?"

Eve could already see it was going to be one of those days. By the time the breakfast cart was wheeled into the hall, she had bathed and dressed all her patients but one. That one was Darby Pendleton. Darby had decided to assert her rights this morning, and had refused to be bathed or allow Eve to dress her.

As a change of pace, and to give the patients at the end of the hall a taste of warm food, Eve reversed the order of tray distribution this morning. She was immediately chastised by the other C.N.A.s. "You're supposed to serve those patients *last*."

"Residents," Doreen called from the nurse's station. "We don't call them patients. We call them residents."

"Well, she's serving the wrong 'residents' first," a C.N.A. called back. "She's messing up our routine."

It seemed to Eve it would be a lot more fair to patients if the serving order were alternated from one week to the next. The poor patients at the front end of the wing had probably forgotten what hot food tasted like; not that the food was that hot to start with.

When all trays had been delivered and Eve went to room 12 to feed LuLu May Thompson, the frail old lady drew in her breath and let out a bloodcurdling scream. "Stay away from me!" she shrieked. "You're dead! Get away!"

Eve knew she looked bad, but she didn't look *that* bad. In an effort to calm LuLu, Eve approached her bed. "It's alright, LuLu May. I'm the C.N.A. who always feeds you your breakfast. See? It's me—Eve."

"Then if I can see you, that means—You mean *I'm* dead too?" the old lady squeaked. Shrinking against her bed, LuLu clutched the thin blanket in her claw-like fists and drew it up under her chin. "When did I *die*?"

Eve glanced over her shoulder to make sure no one in the hallway had heard, then told LuLu May to hush. "You're not dead, and neither am I." Picking up a spoon and scooping up a bite of oatmeal, Eve kept up a running monologue. "We're right here in the hospital where you were when you went to sleep. Nobody's died, including me. I have some nice oatmeal for you this morning. It's your favorite. Come on, now, LuLu May. Try a bite and you'll see."

"You mean this is not—Heaven?"

If this is Heaven, Eve thought with a groan, *I think I'd rather be in Hell.*

Chapter 28

On her last day at the hospital, Eve was assigned an extra patient that she'd never had occasion to care for before. The old lady's name was Esmeralda, but everyone called her Essie.

Esmeralda was ninety-four years old, with eyes that looked like pellets of steel, and a stone gray braid that hung over her dowager's hump. Due to the extent of her Osteoporosis, she was forced to crane her neck, even sitting up in bed, in order to see straight ahead.

"Hurry up and get me dressed," Essie snapped. "Today's the day I'm gonna kill that bitch."

Shocked, Eve asked who Essie was talking about.

"The bitch that attacked me the day I moved in here."

Though Eve tried to get her to reveal more information, Essie wasn't talking. When she'd been sponge bathed, Esmeralda demanded her bathrobe. "The one with the belt."

Eve debated whether or not to tell anyone the things the old lady had told her, but decided they were probably just the ravings of senility. She had helped Essie into her wheelchair and was making the bed when she glanced back over her shoulder to where the old woman had positioned herself in the doorway. Hunched forward in the wheelchair, Essie looked like an ancient vulture. She had removed the belt from her bathrobe and was holding it in one gnarled claw.

"Do you need me to push the chair to take you to the dining room for breakfast?" Eve asked.

"I can push my own damned chair," Essie snapped. "I'm waiting for the bitch. When she comes by, I'm gonna kill her."

Shaking her head with a tolerant frown, Eve moved on to the next room. She had just taken Thelma to the toilet and was in the process of wiping her bottom through the hole in the toilet chair when she heard the screams.

Thelma was strapped into the plastic chair, so Eve knew she'd be safe if left alone. The screams in the hallway were growing louder: "I'll be right back, Thelma."

Rushing out into the corridor, Eve was shocked to see *Norma* frantically wheeling her chair toward the dining room, screaming bloody murder as she went. Two feet behind her in another wheelchair, Esmeralda had somehow managed to get her robe belt around Norma's neck—that's why she'd wanted the belt!—and was pulling it tight with one gnarled fist while wheeling her chair with the other.

"She's killing me!" Norma screeched. "Somebody help!" Norma's face had turned a deep shade of red and the vein in her forehead was standing out. *My God!* Eve thought. *Essie really means to kill her!* Realizing her time was limited, the old lady with the dowager's hump wrapped the belt around her wrist and snapped Norma's head back in an effort to finish the job before anyone could stop her.

C.N.A.s emerged from several rooms along the corridor, and Doreen nearly collided with Eve in their race to get to the crime scene. It took two C.N.A.s to wrestle the belt from Esmeralda's hand, with Norma screaming all the while, and Essie snarling, "The bitch has to die."

Eve had grown up with the mistaken notion that old ladies were supposed to be *sweet.* Her internship at the hospital had proven that theory wrong. But in her wildest imagination, she had never envisioned a hump-backed ninety-plus-year-old woman trying to murder another "resident" whose worst crime was driving people up the wall by constantly asking her name.

"Take Essie back to her room and put her to bed," Doreen said. "And put that robe belt out of reach in the closet."

By lunchtime, Eve had barely stopped shaking. She had just finished feeding the last of her patients when a frazzled Johnathan came looking for her to ask for help with Iola. He still had the red handprint on his cheek from where the old lady had slapped him.

Eve had been leery of Iola since the incident with the chocolate bonbons, but knew what a problem her temper presented for Johnathan. Eve didn't know why Iola hated him so. But she could imagine how Johnathan felt, having to come to work everyday and face it.

When Johnathan returned to Iola's room, the old lady threw a spoon at him and snarled. "Don't come near me, you son of a bitch." Again, Eve was reminded of the old lady's resemblance to a troll. Looking beyond Johnathan at Eve, the troll smiled sweetly. "Come over here to see me, Dear."

"Hello, Iola," Eve said warily. "I came to help Johnathan take you to the bathroom. Is that alright with you?"

"Forget him," Iola smiled. "You can take me by yourself."

There was no way Eve could transfer Iola to the toilet chair alone. "You know I can't do that, Iola. We wouldn't want you or anyone else to get hurt. That's why Johnathan and I are going to do it together. Alright?"

While Johnathan held the old lady's hands, Eve snapped the red safety belt around her waist. Together, Eve and Johnathan each gripped the back of the belt with one hand as they positioned a shoulder beneath an armpit and grasped Iola's arms with their free hands. "Ready?" Johnathan said. "One—two—three—Lift."

The transfer went smoothly. So far so good. But while Johnathan was in the process of strapping Iola into the bathroom chair, the old lady motioned for Eve to come closer. "I want to tell you a secret, Dear. Come close, so I can whisper in your ear."

Leery of any secrets the troll wanted to tell her, Eve leaned close. When she did, Iola's hands suddenly shot out and grabbed her hair, pulling her down to the point of being bent in half. The pain in Eve's scalp felt like her hair was on fire. In self-defense, Eve grasped the old woman's wrists, but by now Iola had wrapped the brown tresses around her hands to the roots, and was twisting with all her might. "Johnathan!" Eve shouted. "Help me!"

When Johnathan reached out to try to free Eve's hair, Iola gnashed at him with yellowed teeth. "Don't you touch me, you asshole son of a bitch!"

If Eve hadn't known it was Iola's voice, she would have thought it was the voice of a demon—that, or the old crone from the Tarot deck. "Go get Doreen, Johnathan! Hurry!"

By the time Doreen arrived with another C.N.A. in tow, Johnathan had returned and Iola had spat in his face. The sputum was still dripping down his cheek.

"Iola, that's enough of that!" Doreen said sharply. "No more spitting! And let go of Eve's hair."

It came as no surprise to Eve that the old lady ignored the nurse's command.

"Johnathan," Doreen shouted, "Stay out of the way! Marilyn, you take the left hand. I'll take the right."

Bent double in the middle of the wrestling match, hot tears now streaming from her eyes, Eve clutched her scalp and prayed that she wouldn't lose an eye or be snatched bald by the time the foray had ended.

When at last it was over, Doreen told Eve to take a break. "Go put some cold water on your face, and see if you can borrow a rubber band to put your hair in a pony tail. We'll take care of Iola."

It would have been nice if someone had warned her about the hazards of long hair *before* instead of *after*. Eve was glad her peridot medallion was hidden safely beneath her shirt. If Iola had gotten hold of that, she could have *strangled* her.

All in all, Eve couldn't have imagined a worst day for her last day at the hospital. Other than Ed, Doreen, and the personnel director, no one from the staff even bothered to bid good-bye when she punched out for the final time. Before leaving, Eve stopped in each of her former patients' rooms to give them a parting hug. When she came to Mrs. Stillwell, she promised to come back for a visit.

Tears pooled in Mrs. Stillwell's eyes, and she clutched at Eve's hand. "Who's going to take care of my pain when you're gone? You were the only one who could help…"

Eve felt a pang of guilt at the thought of deserting Mrs. Stillwell, but then she thought of a possible solution. "Do you still have that tube of Aspercreme from San Antonio in your drawer?" Eve knew that the old lady didn't believe Aspercreme manufactured in New York was worth the tube it was packaged in. But Aspercreme from San Antone—Well, that was a different story.

When Mrs. Stillwell said she still had it, Eve bent to tell her a secret. "I can put the healing energy into the cream along with the Aspirin that's already in it. When I'm not here, you can rub the cream into your hands and think of me, and it will give you the same pain relief as if I were holding your hands. But you can't tell anyone about this. If you do, they'll think you're crazy."

"Don't worry," Mrs. Stillwell whispered. "I won't tell."

"I won't tell anyone either," Mrs. Japetto said from the next bed. "Could you put some of that healing energy into some cream for me too?"

Chapter 29

Two days before Eve was due to move to the valley, Carla called to say she had gone dancing and seen Mitch. "He asked me to dance, and I did. But afterward I had a really strange feeling. I haven't been able to shake the feeling since I got home."

Instantly, Joan's voice spoke in Eve's head. "Tell Carla she never should have danced with Mitch. Tell her the dark spirit who hangs around him when he's drinking followed her home last night, and it's in her apartment. She has to get it out."

Alarmed by the urgency in Joan's voice, Eve passed on the message.

"It's in the kitchen," Joan said. "It's infused itself into an *object* in her kitchen. It's behind the milk carton on the counter."

"Where?" Carla asked. Eve could tell from her voice Carla was on the verge of panic. "In the canister? In the coffee mug?"

"It's in something pink," Joan said. "I can't see exactly what it is. It looks like it's shaped like a heart."

"It's in a pink heart," Eve said. "She must be talking about the rock you got from Myra."

"Son of a bitch," Carla said. "The bastard knows how much that rock means to me. That's why he hid in there."

"*It*," Joan said. "Never dignify a dark spirit by calling it 'he' or 'she.' You have to get that rock out of your apartment."

"I'm going to pick the rock up with an oven mitt and take it out to the dumpster," Carla said nervously. "Don't hang up the phone. Promise you won't break the connection."

"I promise," Eve said. "I'll be right here when you come back."

When Carla returned, Eve could tell from her voice that she was shaking. "I knew I shouldn't have danced with Mitch. He was trying to get me to move back in with him."

"Surely you wouldn't consider it," Eve said. She knew that despite his drinking and psychological hang-ups, Carla was still attracted to Mitch.

"Don't worry," Carla said. "It'll never happen."

Eve hoped she was right...

On moving day, Jill lent Eve the van with the hydraulic lift to move her things from the hotel in Placerville back to Carla's apartment in the valley. Eve left the Shadow parked in Jill's driveway, and promised to return the van in the morning. Since her bed and many of her other belongings were already in Carla's spare room, and her love seat and chair were already in the living room, Eve was able to bring everything in one trip with plenty of room to spare. She wished Carla weren't working. She could have used her help unloading and carrying her T.V. and end table from the parking lot to the apartment.

"That T.V.'s too heavy for a little lady like you to be carrying." A longhaired man with a week's growth of beard seemed to have appeared out of nowhere. He was a foot taller than Eve, and probably half her age. "Do you have any beer?"

"No," Eve answered. "I don't drink. Why do you ask?"

"If you buy me a beer, I'll carry these things in for you. You don't even have to do it today. I'll take a raincheck."

Never one to bite the hand that feeds her, Eve thanked the man and introduced herself. "I'm Eve. Who are you?"

"I'm Chip Lathom," the longhaired man said. "I live in the apartment overtop of the one you're moving into."

Gideon? Eve asked in her mind. *Am I making a mistake by letting him help me?*

"This is Gideon, and I'm of the light," Gideon replied. "He's rough around the edges, but he's harmless. Take whatever help he wants to give."

When Chip had finished carrying the T.V. and table into the apartment, and together he and Eve had carried the boxes, Eve locked the door and went to the store for beer. When she returned, she took the six-pack up to Chip's apartment.

"I was just teasing," Chip said. "You didn't have to give me anything. Besides, I said one beer. I didn't say a six pack."

"I want you to have it," Eve said with a smile. "You really helped me out, and I want you to know I appreciate it."

The next morning when Eve tried to start the van, the engine clunked and sputtered, but refused to turn over. *Great*, Eve thought miserably. *What am I going to do now?* She needed her car back, and Jill needed the van. But even if she managed to get the van started, she was afraid to drive it the twenty-five miles up the hill.

"Sounds like you could use some help." It was the neighbor from upstairs again, looking even seedier than he'd looked before, but twice as welcome. "Mind if I take a look at the engine?"

Did she *mind*? Eve could have hugged him for even offering, if she hadn't been afraid he'd get the wrong idea.

After tinkering with the engine for over an hour while Eve looked on, Chip managed to get it started. It didn't sound good, but at least it was running.

"I don't think you should drive this thing by yourself," Chip said. "If it stalls out on you, you'll be stuck. I think I'd better ride along with you."

Gideon? Eve said in her mind.

"This is Gideon, and I'm of the light. You're judging the book by its cover. He's just a decent guy who wants to help."

It was definitely an advantage, having a guardian angel she could talk to when she had doubts. If Eve hadn't been able to ask Gideon, she probably never would have allowed Chip to ride with her. As it turned out, she was glad she had:

Halfway to Shingle Springs, the van broke down. If Chip hadn't been there to jiggle the wires, she'd have been stuck along the side of the road.

One of the first things Eve did when she got back to the valley was to pick up a newspaper so she could check the job ads. Since she had quit the hospital job of her own free will, there'd been no severance pay. As of this moment, she only had two hundred dollars to her name.

"You don't need to worry about getting a job right away," Carla said. "The rent's already paid, and you don't eat that much. After what you've been through, you deserve a week off."

It was good to be back in a normal apartment where Eve didn't have to worry about moving her car every few hours, and where phone calls to Kevin weren't long distance. It was good to have a comfortable bed, a kitchen with counter space, and a human roommate to talk to.

Eve and Carla were seated at the dining room table in their nightgowns, munching grapes and Monterey Jack cheese and making up for lost time, when Carla mentioned that she'd gone to Myra for another psychic reading, and had talked with her several times on the phone. "She gave me another rock to take the place of the one I had to throw out. I told her all about the healing, and what you had to go through in Placerville. Why don't we call her tonight to let her know you're back in town?"

Eve hadn't talked to Myra since the day of her own psychic reading. But apparently Carla had made friends with her. It would be good to get Myra's input on things that had been going on...

"It sounds to me like you're moving too fast," Myra said. "This healing guide is one of the most powerful guides in the whole spirit realm. You're new at this. You're not ready to deal with guides on his level. It's because of *him* that you're drawing so much attention from the dark side."

"It wasn't *my* idea to have Saul as a guide," Eve said. "It was Gideon, my guardian angel, who introduced me to him, and said Jesus had assigned him to train me."

"I don't care what Gideon said," Myra said sharply. "*My* guardian angel's been around a lot longer than Gideon, and she says he's an upstart biting off more than *you* can chew. I'm going to lend you one of *my* guides to help you learn the ropes. He wears a long robe and pointed hat just like the wizards in the Middle Ages, and calls himself The Magician."

Eve didn't know where Myra's guardian angel got off criticizing *her guides* and questioning the judgment of *Jesus*, or what Myra thought gave *her* the right to assign Eve another guide! Even if it weren't for the fact that Myra was being presumptuous, Eve didn't like the idea of borrowing someone else's guide. It was like using someone else's toothbrush, or drinking from someone else's glass.

"Mother Evangeline says Gideon takes too many chances," Myra said. "You wanted to commune with the big guys. This is it. The Magician is just one step below your healing guide. He'll keep both you *and* Gideon in line."

Who the hell was Mother Evangeline to be deciding what Eve and her guides needed? "I'd really prefer to stick with the guides I already have," Eve said tightly. "I'm sure *Gideon* isn't going to want the Magician in the picture, and I have enough restrictions with my own guides already. I don't need another one trying to boss me around."

"It's too late," Myra said. "I've already sent him."

Shit. Too irritated to talk to Myra anymore, Eve handed the phone to Carla and went to her room. "I'm sorry, Gideon. I didn't ask her to do it. But Myra says she's sent one of her guides to me."

"This is Gideon, and I'm of the light. The Magician and I have already met. This won't be the first time we've butted heads."

"Well can't you just tell him he's not needed, and send him back to Myra?"

"I can't do that," Gideon said. "I still have the final say about your welfare, but he outranks me. I'm afraid we're going to have to put up with him till he decides you don't need him anymore."

Crap. If the guide was here to stay, Eve supposed she'd better meet him. Damn Myra anyway. She should never let Carla talk her into calling her.

"Don't be cursing Myra, even in your mind," a booming voice said. When he spoke, Eve was struck with a sudden blinding headache. "I'm The Magician, and I am of the light. I can see that my talking to you is causing you pain. I'll try to tone down my energy level to coincide with yours, but this may take considerable time and experimentation. I had this problem with Myra the first few weeks I was with her. You'd better talk to *her*, and ask her what to do."

The pain in Eve's head was excruciating. Taking the phone from Carla's hand, Eve rasped into the receiver, "The Magician gave me a headache when he talked to me. My head's splitting! He said I should ask you what to do."

"I *told* you you weren't ready for the big guys," Myra said. It occurred to Eve that her own *minor* guide, Caruso, had given *Myra* a headache and that Saul, who was higher than the Magician, hadn't caused a headache yet. But she thought it best not to mention that right now. "Clear your mind," Myra ordered. "Now surround yourself with the protective white light and fill your field of vision with pale pink." Eve did as Myra had suggested, and the headache was somewhat improved. "Now fill your field of vision with pale blue." It took nearly half an hour of envisioning first one pastel color and then another before the headache had been reduced to the level of a dull throb. "Now you can take some Aspirin."

"Myra," Eve said carefully, "I appreciate your willingness to share The Magician with me. And I appreciate his willingness to work with me. I really do. But I was doing okay with just Gideon and Saul. *Their* energy levels are already adjusted to mine." Eve didn't want to risk angering The Magician and having him give her another headache, and she didn't want to insult him or hurt his feelings. But this thing had to be stopped before it went any farther. "Gideon can't say this because The Magician outranks him. But I'd appreciate it if *you'd* talk to The

Magician and tell him I'm just not ready for him. Ask him to come back to you until I've reached a level of being able to talk to him without getting a headache."

Apparently that was the wrong thing to say.

"And what makes you think Myra has any control over me?" the Magician boomed. "The two of you are talking about me as if I'm not in the room and can't hear what you're saying. At least give me the courtesy of addressing your comments to *me*."

Shit! The headache was back, and all because Myra thought she needed to meddle! "Look, Magician," Eve said. "Your talking to me telepathically obviously isn't going to work. If you won't agree to go back to Myra, how about if we make an agreement that when you feel like talking to me, you do it through the board?"

"That would probably work," The Magician said. "But we'll need a signal so you'll know when I want to speak to you. How about this one?"

Eve's nose twitched, and she raised her hand to scratch the itch. Scratching the itch did no good. "That's the signal," The Magician said. "Now take out the board..."

Chapter 30

"Sweetheart, this is Gideon, and I'm of the light. We have a problem."

Eve had spent the day signing up with temporary employment agencies all over town. Her feet were aching, her head was throbbing, and Carla had a Migraine that was not responding to the sandwich she was eating, or to Eve's efforts to pull it out. Eve didn't know who all the "we" included, but the last thing she wanted to hear was that *they* had a problem.

"Now that you have The Magician as one of your guides—even though he's only temporary—you've drawn the attention of a group of demons who call themselves the Sons of Satan," Gideon said urgently. "They're a terrorist group of dark spirits."

Sons of Satan! Eve shouted in her mind. *Are you telling me that Barbara's meddling has made me the target of a terrorist attack?* Eve's heart was pounding, and her palms had begun to perspire.

"I'm afraid so," Gideon said. "It's taking all my energy to get through to you right now. This group draws *its* energy from the bowels of the earth. They don't normally hurt people directly, but they influence others to do the dirty work for them. It's imperative that you and Carla surround yourselves with the light and strengthen your pyramid. Stay inside till I tell you it's safe to go out. You don't want to be exposed to people who can be influenced."

Though Eve tried to get more information, Gideon had either lost contact or been cut off. "This is the Son of Satan, bitch. I'm going to—"

"This is Saul, and I'm of the light. Gideon took care of that Son of Satan. But what Gideon didn't want to drain his strength to tell you is that there's an imp in the apartment. Imps are the lowest level of dark spirit, directly below the dark ones that interfere with phones and machinery and are always trying to stop us from communicating with you. You've been trained in powers of concentration. You can kill this imp with your mind. But imps are elusive and hard to pinpoint. It's in the living room now, over near the couch."

When Eve told Carla what was going on, Carla's migraine was forgotten. "I see it!" Carla shouted. "It looks like a little blob of brown fog moving along the carpet. There it is! It just hopped up onto the couch!"

Straining her eyes to see, Eve looked in the direction Carla was pointing. As Carla had said, a small foggy mass was moving about on the sofa. Bringing her hands together and pointing her two index fingers as one, Eve summoned her powers of concentration. The mass hopped off the sofa, and for a moment Eve lost track of it.

Carla took a nervous bite from her sandwich as she narrowed her eyes and peered about the room. A moment later, she shrieked. "It's in my sandwich!"

"What do you mean, it's in your sandwich," Eve asked in a tremulous voice. "How do you know?"

"Because the sandwich is pulsing in my hands!" Carla's hands had begun to tremble, and her eyes were as big as quarters. "What should I do? Throw it down?"

"Tell her to hold it," Saul said. "Then aim your powers of concentration and kill the son of a bitch."

The cheese sandwich continued to pulse as Carla held her arm out away from her body. Taking aim, Eve expelled a puff of air as she fired a mental round, followed by another, and another, and another. When at last the pulsing had stopped, Saul said the imp was dead.

"Do you think I swallowed any of it?" Carla whispered.

"You didn't start feeling the pulsing till after you'd swallowed the bite," Eve said. "You'd have known if it was there before you swallowed."

"This is Joan, and I'm of the light," the next voice said. "Tell Carla not to worry."

"Thanks," Carla said when Eve had relayed the message. "But I think I'll put this down the garbage disposal just the same."

The mind battle between Gideon, Joan, The Magician, and the Sons of Satan who were hanging around the apartment continued for several hours as Eve and Carla huddled inside, waiting for progress reports from Saul. When at last the battle was over, Gideon reported that it had been good to have The Magician on their side.

After their heartbeats had slowed to normal, Eve and Carla changed into their nightclothes and sat crosslegged on Carla's bed to discuss what they'd learned of dark spirits thus far. For starters, the term "dark spirit" apparently encompassed much more than they'd realized. To date, they'd learned of three levels of dark spirit in addition to Satan: the top level appeared to be the terrorist spirits who rarely did the dirty work themselves, but preferred to influence humans to do it for them. The middle level, your average run of the mill dark spirits, were the ones who disrupted communications, frightened children in their bedrooms at night, rose out of the candle in the guise of a giant penis, and were standing in the way of Eve's getting together with Chad. Eve didn't know yet where the imps figured into the scheme of things, but suspected they were responsible for things such as knocking over the statue in her closet.

Whatever the level, Eve hated them all, and cursed the day they first came into her life.

Chapter 31

Eve's first full day back in the valley was spent re-establishing the pyramid in the apartment, watching old videos on T.V., and talking to Kevin on the phone. When Carla arrived home that evening, she told Eve she'd discovered a new dance spot called the Classic Jukebox, and asked if Eve would like to go dancing tonight.

"Dancing in the middle of the week?"

"They give free lessons on Tuesday and Wednesday," Carla said. "They normally get a good crowd, and everyone gets to dance…"

Eve thoroughly enjoyed the evening of dancing. As Carla had said, everyone got a chance to dance in the free lessons. The couple doing the lessons were from a dance studio in Sacramento. The man was well over six feet tall, and his partner couldn't have been an inch over five feet. But together, they were dynamite.

It felt good to Eve to be able to put on her dance clothes and feel like a woman again instead of a drudge dressed in white.

During intermission, when there was free dancing, Eve was asked to dance to every song. She was having a wonderful time, and thought Carla was too. But eventually Carla got bored and said she wanted to go home. It wasn't that she hadn't had a chance to dance. It was just that she wasn't interested in any of the men who'd asked her, and didn't have the patience to deal with the ones who weren't skilled leaders.

Carla and Eve had a different perspective of dancing. While Eve would dance with virtually any man who asked, just for the fun of being out on the dance floor, Carla was a perfectionist. Men felt intimidated when she pointed out what they were doing wrong—no matter how tactfully she tried to do it. The only man who'd asked her a second time tonight was a man she had dated a year or so ago.

Since Eve and Carla had come to the club together in Carla's car, Eve had no choice but to leave. She was seated in the passenger seat on the drive home, debating whether to break the silence. So far since they'd left, Carla hadn't said a word. Finally, Eve couldn't take it anymore. "Is anything wrong?"

"Wrong?" Carla snapped. "What could be wrong?"

"I don't know," Eve said. "That's why I'm asking *you*." Eve could see the tension in Carla's jaw, and in her tightfisted grip on the steering wheel. "I really wish you'd tell me what's bothering you."

"It's not fair," Carla shot back. "All the men want to dance with you, and you don't even know the right way to dance. I take lessons and know all the steps, but the only men who ask me to dance are either ugly or have one foot in the grave."

Eve didn't know why Carla was saying *she* didn't know how to dance. She'd always gotten compliments from the men she danced with on how well she followed their lead.

"I was watching you tonight," Carla said venomously. "When you were swing dancing with that tall guy that asked you half a dozen times, and when you were dancing with the short guy in the Hawaiian shirt, you started out okay doing the triple step; but halfway through the song you switched to *step-touch* instead of a triple! It looked ridiculous."

"I didn't realize it looked bad," Eve said. "That's what I do when my legs feel like they're about to give out. It gives me a short rest, then I go back to the triple step. No one's ever complained about it before."

"Well it throws off their lead," Carla snapped.

How could it throw off their lead when the beat was exactly the same? Eve hadn't noticed anyone's having a problem. If she'd been throwing off their lead, surely she would have known it. Surely the men wouldn't have continued coming back to ask her to dance. Eve couldn't understand why *Carla* was complaining anyway. If she wanted to pace herself in the middle of a song, why should Carla even *care*?

"When the only man in the place I was remotely interested in asked me to dance, he spent the whole damned dance talking about you!" Carla shouted.

So that was it. Carla was jealous. "I don't even know who you're talking about," Eve said.

"I'm talking about Joe—the short guy in the Hawaiian shirt. I went out with him a few times last year."

"Carla," Eve said, "if you'd told me you were interested in him, I wouldn't have danced with him when he asked me."

"I'm *not* really interested in him," Carla spat. "I just like to keep him as a back-up, that's all."

When they arrived home, Eve said "Goodnight," and went straight to her room. Too many hurtful words had already been spoken. She saw no need to hang around for more.

The next morning before leaving for work, Carla tapped at Eve's door. "I wanted to apologize to you for last night. It wasn't your fault. I was out of line."

"Don't worry about it," Eve said sleepily. "I'm sorry too. I guess I should have been more sensitive to your feelings." Eve didn't really feel that she had anything to apologize for. But it was better to offer an unnecessary apology than to risk having problems with her best friend.

The next time Eve went dancing, she went alone to Parents Without Partners, while Carla went to a dance across town. Eve had a great time, as usual, but left before the dance was over so she'd get enough sleep to get up early in the morning.

She wanted to drive up to Shingle Springs after breakfast to pay a visit to Jill and Evelyn.

On the drive home, Eve kicked off her black dancing shoes. She was wearing her black flared miniskirt, a matching turtleneck, black nylons, and a red bolero with large black buttons. She liked wearing black. It made her feel thin. She knew she was at her ideal weight, but she liked to feel even thinner.

"Sweetheart, this is Gideon, and I'm of the light. Tonight you're going to have a visitor, so don't change your clothes right away when you get home. I want Chad to see you in that outfit. And you might want to put on another dab of that Toujours Moi body lotion. That's always a nice touch."

Chad was coming *tonight*? This would be the first time since the night Carla touched him below the belt. Carla wouldn't be coming home for at least a couple more hours. She always went out for coffee with friends after dances at the Sheraton. That meant Eve and Chad would have the apartment to themselves. Tonight she would set the stage...

It was nice when she got home, not to have to worry about a parking space. Slipping her feet back into her shoes, Eve opened the car door and smiled. She intended to make this a night Chad would remember. The heels of her shoes tick tacked on the cement as she crossed the parking lot. The night breeze caressed her face and lifted her hair in a sensual preview of what was to come.

What time's he coming? Eve asked in her mind as she inserted the key in the door. *"And what's he wearing? I want to be able to picture him in my mind."*

"He's wearing Levi jeans and cowboy boots, and a blue and white flannel shirt," Gideon replied. "His shirt's open at the throat—you'll love his hairy chest—and his sleeves are rolled to just below the elbow. He's already here, by the way. His guardian angel brought him early. He's sitting in the chair across the room."

Suddenly nervous, Eve drew a deep breath and raised a hand to smooth her hair. "No," Gideon said. "Leave your hair like it is. The windblown look is very sexy."

When Eve stepped into the living room and switched the lamp on low, she glanced toward the chair across the way. In her mind's eye she could see Chad sitting there in his boots, tight jeans, and flannel shirt—open at the throat. She could see his hairy chest, and his suntanned face with its brown eyes and neatly trimmed beard the color of coal. His dark hair, like hers, was windblown. Apparently even out of body, one's hair was subject to the elements. Eve felt a sensual stir as she smiled in recognition. "Hi," she said in a throaty voice. "I didn't expect to see *you* here when I came home. I've just been out dancing."

The dimly lit living room was cast in shadow as Eve kicked off her shoes and crossed the room in her stocking feet to turn on the stereo. "I hope you like guitar instrumentals."

"They're his favorite," Gideon said softly. "You're doing great. Now go get the Toujours Moi."

"Don't go away," Eve murmured. "I'll be back a minute."

When she got to the bathroom, Eve opened the medicine cabinet and took out the bottle of body lotion. Her heart was skittering as she unscrewed the ball-style lid and applied a single dab behind each ear. When she returned to the living room, she had the bottle in her hand. *Where is he now?* she asked in her mind. *Is he still in the chair?*

"He's moved to the sofa," Gideon said softly. "He's sitting at the end by the door with his arm stretched across the back."

For only a second, Eve closed her eyes to etch the image into her mind. When she opened her eyes, she was ready. "I see you're not so shy tonight," she said seductively. "Do you mind if I sit next to you?"

"He's looking at your legs in those black nylons and smiling," Gideon said softly. "He's talking to you, saying he would *love* for you to come over and snuggle up next to him. He's getting an erection just thinking about how it would feel to rub his hand over your legs."

So he was a leg man. That was an interesting tidbit of information. "I'm glad you like my legs," Eve teased, but my *face* is up here."

Eve's heart was racing wildly as she sat down in the center of the beige sofa. She felt the field of masculine energy as Chad scooted closer and put his arm around her shoulders. Brushing her long brown hair aside, Eve tipped her head and closed her eyes. A feather-like touch brushed her face, then trailed downward to nuzzle her neck…

A warm thrill coursed through Eve's body as the masculine energy field surrounded her upper torso and claimed her lips. "Mmmmmm," she murmured. "That's nice." The energy field grew stronger as butterfly kisses trailed across her cheek then touched her eyelids—first one, then the other. And then Chad's lips were on hers again…

When the kiss had ended, and the energy field pulled away, Gideon told Eve in her mind that Chad was gazing at her through hooded eyes, and had a seductive smile on his lips. Apparently Gideon had paid attention to the wording of the romance novels Eve loved to read.

Eve had no doubt that she would remember Chad. But if she wanted him to remember *her*, it was now or never. "Do you like the smell of Toujours Moi?" As she spoke, she unscrewed the lid. Pouring a generous dollop in her palm, she drew a deep breath, then put the lid back on and rubbed her palms together to distribute the lotion but not rub it in. "In the morning, when you wake up, I want you to know tonight was real," she said softly. "I want you to let me put this on your skin so you'll smell it in the morning and remember where you've been."

Guide my hands, Gideon, Eve said in her mind. Her hands explored the energy field, gently wiping the lotion over Chad's face, aware that she was also touching his beard. When Gideon guided her hands lower, Eve took the invisible hands in hers and wiped the lotion on them as well. "When you smell this in this morning, I want you to think of me and where you've been tonight," she murmured. "My name is Eve, and you're in Citrus Heights at the Brownstone Apartments, Apartment 3B. Say it to yourself tonight as you finish your dream: Citrus Heights, Brownstone Apartments, Apartment 3B."

Eve felt the energy field surround her once more, seeming to envelop her entire body. Then suddenly it was gone. *What happened?* she asked in her mind. *Did I scare him away? Is he still here?*

"He was starting to get a little too familiar," Gideon said. "His guardian angel zapped him and transported him across the room. He's standing there next to the chair right now, wondering what the hell happened."

Eve turned her gaze to the area beside the chair, and in a bold move, decided to take control. "I'm glad you came tonight," she said. "But we really can't keep meeting like this. I like you, and I want to have a relationship with you, but I don't want it to be a dream relationship where you don't even know how you got here." Since Gideon hadn't said anything, Eve assumed Chad was still here. "I've been looking for you for a long time, but now it's your turn. I go to the Classic Jukebox every Wednesday night to dance. If you want to meet me and see where our relationship can go from there, either come to the Jukebox this Wednesday night, or come to this apartment in person: Brownstone Apartments in Citrus Heights; Apartment 3B."

"Cut," Gideon said. "Print. You gave him all the information he needs. His guardian angel zapped him back into bed, and right now he's finishing out what he thinks is a dream."

Like a zombie, Eve walked into the kitchen and washed the lotion off her hands. She had returned to the sofa and was still sitting there engrossed in the music and re-living the phantom kiss when she heard Carla's key in the lock. "What are *you* still doing up?" Carla asked. "It was dead tonight at the Sheraton, so I went to PWP looking for you, but one of the guys there said you left over an hour ago."

"Chad was here," Eve answered. "I waited up to tell you."

"Let me get out of these uncomfortable clothes first," Carla said, peeling off her dress on her way to the bedroom. When she reached the area adjacent to the chair, Carla stopped in her tracks and sniffed. "Yuck! What is that awful smell?"

"I don't smell anything," Eve said.

Carla's response was to wrinkle her nose in distaste. "It smells like a man who's been out in the sun working all day, and tried to cover the sweat stench with perfume! Come over hear and smell it!"

Eve stood and walked over to where Carla was sniffing. Carla was definitely right about the smell. The combination of Toujours Moi and nervous perspiration was nauseating. "It smells like Chad must have gotten nervous after I wiped the Toujours Moi on him. I guess he forgot to wear his deodorant."

If this was an example of what Chad was going to smell when he woke up, Eve doubted he would want to come back. *She* certainly wouldn't. But then again, he would recognize the odor of his own perspiration. He couldn't blame that on her.

Oh hell. She shouldn't have put the lotion on him. But she'd been sitting on the couch when she did it. The odor by the chair was proof of one thing: The visit had been real, not a product of her imagination.

Eve truly had hoped that Chad would remember her address and show up at her door—that, or come to the Classic Jukebox. When neither happened, she went to Myra's house to ask the psychic what *she* thought of the situation. "I think they're lying to you about what Chad looks like, and I think they're lying about his name in hopes it will keep the dark ones from interfering," Myra said. Eve already knew Chad wasn't his real name, but she didn't want to interrupt. "When I close my eyes to see him, I don't see the man they're describing at all," Myra went on. "This man has blonde hair and dark skin." Shuddering, the psychic hugged herself. "Ooooo," she said. "I just got a warm fuzzy. I see horses. And lots of books all around him. I see this man sitting on his bed, surrounded by books. He loves to travel, and when he travels he always goes first class—and dancing. He loves to dance. When you find him, you'd better hold onto him because I promise you, Eve, this man will *adore* you."

Chapter 32

When another Wednesday night had come and gone, and still no Chad, Eve was starting to lose patience. According to Gideon, Chad had shown up at the Jukebox, but when he saw Eve dancing with so many others, his insecurities got the better of him and he didn't reveal himself. When Eve argued that he hadn't seemed to *have* insecurities when he appeared out of body, Gideon said that his current insecurities lay in the fact that he had shaved his beard and felt that he had no chin. "He was afraid you wouldn't like him without the beard."

If he had no chin without his beard, he was probably right. "So why did he shave off the beard, if he has a weak chin without it?" Eve demanded.

"It's really complicated," Gideon hedged. "He shaved it as a test to see if you'd like him without it. But then he lost his nerve when it came time to reveal himself and ask you to dance. Saul and I have talked, and just about come to the conclusion that he's not man enough for you."

Eve was a person who believed in facing problems and challenges head on. She had little patience with people who sidestepped the issue or took the coward's way out. But she was willing to give Chad another chance.

Eve and Carla were seated in the living room. Carla was cuddling Darla, and Eve had the board in her lap just in case The Magician should decide he wanted to talk to her. "This is Gideon, and I'm of the light. Pick up the pendulum. There's someone who wants to talk to you—It's not The Magician—and I don't think it would be a good idea to talk telepathically."

When the pendulum began to swing, the Energy of the East introduced itself as being of the light. "I don't normally communicate with humans," the Energy said. "You're only the second human I've ever spoken to. But don't flatter yourself by thinking I'm talking to you because I like you. I don't like humans in general, and you're no exception."

Eve couldn't believe a spirit would ask to talk to her to tell her he didn't like her—particularly when he didn't even know her! "If you're really the Energy of the East," Eve said, "how can you communicate? Energies can't talk."

"You have no idea what I'm capable of," the Energy said ominously. "I, and the Sprit of the East, are one and the same. And I don't care to chitchat with you. I have something to say, and I want you to listen. When I've had my say, *do not say a word."*

"I'd advise you not to answer," Carla said from the couch. "This one sounds like he has a nasty disposition."

"Your friend needs to learn some respect," the Spirit of the East said. "You and she called me into your home, and I came willingly. But I am *not* willing to *stay* here and be insulted, or subjected to anymore of this nonsense concerning your so-called soul mate and his insecurities! You gave the man all the information he needs to find you—an open invitation—and the best he could do is show up at the Jukebox and *watch from the sidelines.* Doesn't this tell you something? Where is your self-esteem? This man is a wimp! *Forget* about him, and get on with your life!"

"But—"

"Didn't I tell you *not to speak?*" the Energy shouted. Eve knew he was shouting because of the force of the swing. "Forget about Chad! The man is *history.* Three men will be coming into your life in the next thirty days. All three will want a relationship with you. It will be up to you to choose from among them. Choose wisely. Your future depends on it."

The sway of the pendulum stopped as suddenly as it had started. Three men? Three *new* men? But Eve didn't *want* a new man in her life. She wanted to give *Chad* a chance.

"I agree with the Energy," Carla said. "How much more time are you going to spend waiting for Chad? You know the dark ones are never going to let you two get together. You need to go out dancing with an open mind, like you used to do. If the right man comes along, fine. If he doesn't, you keep going out till he does."

It was a blow to Eve, having a powerful spirit tell her the man of her future was a wimp. It was even more of a blow to have her guardian angel, her healing guide, and her best friend agree with him. She couldn't just give up on Chad this easily. The dark ones couldn't keep stalling things forever. Sooner or later, if they went to the same places, their paths were bound to cross. How could Gideon and Saul turn tail just like that, when they'd been pushing her toward Chad for months? How could *she* turn against Chad when, based on the things she'd learned about him, she was on the verge of falling in love?

That weekend when she went to the Sacramento Singles Club with Carla, Eve spent most of the evening dancing with Bernie DeCampo, a tall man with short dark hair and a moustache. What Bernie lacked in class, he more than made up for in his ability to dance. Eve loved to dance with men who led with confidence: dips, pivots, unusual turns... It was obvious Bernie had taken ballroom dance lessons. When Bernie led, he led with flair.

"You look cute tonight in that ruffled skirt and your little white jacket," Bernie said. "And I like your hair pulled back that way with the bow and the baby's breath."

Eve had pinned her hair back with a large white bow this evening. As an afterthought, she'd added the baby's breath. She was pleased that Bernie liked it.

Not that she was interested in Bernie. But it was nice to have men think she was attractive, whether they were love interests or not.

"I've been thinking of signing up for Country Western Dance lessons," Bernie said. He had led Eve into a basket turn, and was looking down into her eyes. "I need a partner."

Sensing Eve's hesitance, Bernie rushed on. "No strings attached. Just dance partners. I'll pay your way."

"If I take the lessons with you, I'll pay my own way," Eve said. "That's not the problem. It's just that I don't normally get involved with any of the men I meet here."

Leading her into a pivot, Bernie smiled. "Who's talking about getting involved?"

Eve knew it must be her imagination. But it seemed to her that when Bernie's pencil-thin moustache smiled, his eyes didn't smile with it. "Can I think about it and get back to you?"

"I'm pretty hard to reach," Bernie said. "You'd better give me *your* number. Don't worry. I won't use it except to call you about the dance lessons."

It would be nice to take Country Western lessons with a man who really knew how to lead. If Eve learned how to two-step and do the cowboy cha-cha, that would be to her advantage when she eventually met Chad. "Okay," she said. "I'll do it."

When Eve told Carla on the drive home that she'd agreed to take lessons with Bernie, Carla expressed some reservations. "You'd better watch out for Bernie. He's a good dancer, but he has a reputation as a womanizer."

They had taken Eve's car tonight. Eve wished she'd let Carla drive. The oncoming headlights were bothering her eyes. "If I decide to take the lessons with him, that doesn't matter," she said distractedly. "I'm not interested in dating him."

"Well he's interested in *you*," Carla said. "Hasn't it occurred to you that he may be the first of the three?"

Bernie? The first of the three? The Spirit of the East couldn't be *serious…*

Though Eve checked the job ads daily, there were no office positions to be had that didn't require legal, managerial, or Data Processing experience. With limited funds and no job prospect in sight, Eve decided to *make* as many of her Christmas gifts this year as possible, starting with Carla's. Despite the fact that Eve disliked the Magician and his imperious ways, *Carla* liked him because he reminded her of Merlin. Eve had seen a Merlin statue at the hydro cal store. If she were to buy it and paint it for Carla, the gift would have special meaning.

When another Wednesday night at the Jukebox failed to produce Chad, Eve made plans to go to a Parents Without Partners dance on Friday.

Friday morning, Eve's nose twitched, but she ignored it. When the twitch turned to an itch, she began to scratch. But still, she went about the business of folding her laundry. Soon the itch became unbearable. "*Alright*," she grated. "I'll get out the board."

"I am the Magician, and I'm of the light. I don't think you should go dancing tonight. I disagree with the Energy. And I disagree with Gideon and Saul on this. You shouldn't be dancing and snuggling up to another man when you're already promised to Chad."

"You seem to forget," Eve argued. "Chad doesn't know anything about my being promised to him. He's made no effort to meet me. So why shouldn't I dance with others?"

"I want you to stay home," The Magician said.

"Well, I'm sorry," Eve said. "But it's the weekend and I feel like going out."

Eve was in her bedroom with the door closed, painting the wizard statue, when Carla came home from work. "Eve?" Carla called. "Are you home?"

"I'll be right out," Eve called back. Before leaving the room, she screwed the lid back on the royal purple paint, and hid the paint supplies and statue behind the bed. "How was your day at work?" she asked when she came out of the bedroom.

"I've had a headache all day," Carla said. "I was hoping you could get rid of it. If you can, I thought maybe I'd go with you tonight to PWP."

The negative energy of the beginning Migraine was extremely tenacious. Carla sat on a straight-backed dinette chair with her hands in her lap, while Eve stood behind her with a hand on either side of her face, pulling the negative energy out through her temples.

"The last time I went to a PWP dance, I met someone," Carla said. "I got the feeling he was interested in me. I want to see if he'll be there tonight." Carla went on to describe the man as being of medium height, with brown hair and glasses. She didn't know his name, but thought he was probably a few years younger than she. "I'd really like to get to know him better."

When Carla's migraine had been disposed of, Eve drew a steaming bath and stepped into the water. She was glad Carla had found someone she was interested in. She hoped the interest was mutual.

Eve had donned a red flared skirt and white silk blouse with large black polka dots that matched the black of her dancing shoes. As on the night of Chad's out of body visit, she was wearing black nylons. Rather than driving together tonight, she and Carla decided to go in separate cars.

"See you there," Carla said. Carla was looking unusually attractive tonight. She had bought a new red dress, and had her brown wig freshly styled. Eve suspected that wearing wigs so much of the time contributed to the frequency of Carla's headaches. But every time she tried to bring up the subject, Carla got defensive.

"I'll be right behind you," Eve said, glancing at her keys on the countertop. "All I have to do is put on my lipstick…"

Eve was standing before the mirror blotting her lipstick when she was struck with a blinding headache. She had no idea what had brought it on. Massaging her temple with one trembling hand, she rummaged in her purse for a bottle of Aspirin. "This is Gideon, and I'm of the light. Aspirin's not going to help, Sweetheart. The Magician told you he wanted you to stay home."

The pronouncement set Eve's teeth on edge. *Damn the Magician.* And damn Myra for sending him. "I'm not a little kid he can order around," she said angrily. "If he thinks a headache is going to keep me home, he's got another thought coming." Slamming the lipstick back in her purse, Eve clenched her jaw and gritted her teeth. She was headed for the kitchen to get a drink to help swallow the Aspirin, when she was caught up short. Where were her keys? She knew she'd left them on the counter. She'd seen them there, not five minutes ago. If the Magician had hidden her keys to keep her from going—"Damn it, Magician, what did you do with my keys?"

Eve's nose twitched, and her head continued to throb. When she took out the board and picked up the pendulum, the pendulum began to swing, first to the phrase "I'm of the light," and then to the name "Magician."

"You owe it to Chad to stay home tonight."

"I don't owe Chad a damned thing," Eve snarled. "Why can't you just go back to Myra, and leave me the hell alone?" It occurred to Eve that she'd done more swearing since she'd met the Magician than she'd done the first forty years of her life!

When the pendulum remained still and The Magician didn't respond, Eve went to the bedroom and dug in the bureau drawer for her extra set of keys. If she gave in tonight and allowed him to bully her, he'd be bullying her from now on. This had to stop.

By the time she arrived at the hall where the dance was being held, the dance was well under way. Lights had been dimmed, and the disk jockey was playing a medley of songs from the sixties. Carla had saved Eve a seat at a center table.

"I was beginning to worry about you," Carla said. "You said you'd be right behind me."

"The Magician hid my keys," Eve said. "I guess he didn't know I had a spare set in the bedroom."

"The guy I told you about is here," Carla whispered. "He's standing over there in the crowd by the bar. He's the one with glasses, in the blue shirt."

Looking in the direction Carla had nodded, Eve saw a tall man with short brown hair and wire-framed glasses, standing next to a large bosomed woman with blonde hair. The man's blue striped shirt had perspiration stains in the armpits. "You mean the one by the blonde with the big boobs?"

"Her boobs aren't all *that* big," Carla said. "Don't look. He's looking this way."

Though they touched bases at the table from time to time, both Eve and Carla spent most of their time that night on the dance floor. When a deeply tanned man with glasses and light brown hair asked Eve to dance, she allowed him to take her hand and lead her onto the dance floor. The faint scent of his cologne was pleasant, not overwhelming, as he pulled Eve close and snuggled her to his chest. When the dance was finished, he asked for another. "I've seen you here before and thought about asking you to dance, but I could never get close to you. My name's Gary Peters. What's yours?"

"Eve," Eve said. "Eve Tarlton."

She enjoyed dancing with Gary. He had an easy way about him—a smooth dancing style. Not showy, just nice. He was also an interesting conversationalist.

"Could I have your phone number?" Gary asked. "I'd like to call you some time soon and take you out to dinner."

When Gary took Eve back to her table, Carla greeted them with a dazzling smile. "Carla," Eve said, "This is Gary Peters. Gary, this is my roommate Carla."

"Gary and I have met," Carla said. Looking up at Gary with a flirtatious smile, she asked how he'd been.

"I can't complain," Gary replied. "How about yourself?"

While Carla and Gary were talking, Eve dug in her purse for a pen and paper to write down her phone number. Without missing a word of his conversation with Carla, Gary reached for the phone number and slipped it into his pocket. Could it be that Gary was love interest number two?

Later, back at the apartment, Carla slammed her purse down on the counter and turned to Eve with a glare. "Did you give Gary your phone number?"

"Yes," Eve said. "He asked me for it when we were dancing, so I wrote it down for him when I got back to the table."

"*How could you do a thing like that?*" Carla shouted.

Now what had she done? It seemed to Eve that in Carla's eyes, lately she couldn't do anything right. "Like *what*? What's wrong with giving a man my phone number?"

Tears sprang to Carla's eyes, but she quickly dabbed them away. "He was the one," she said pitifully. "He was the one I told you I was interested in. Until *you* came along, he was interested in *me.*"

Gary was the man Carla was interested in? But she had pointed toward the tall thin man standing next to the blonde! The guy with wire-framed glasses, and perspiration stains in his armpits. "I'm sorry, Carla. I didn't know. The man I thought you were interested in—"

"*They* knew," Carla said angrily. "They could have told you."

Eve couldn't believe Gideon and Saul had allowed this to happen. Or *Joan.* Why hadn't Joan told her? Eve never would have given Gary her phone number if she'd known it was going to hurt Carla.

"Ask them," Carla grated. "Ask them why they didn't tell you."

"Gideon?" Eve said. "You heard the question."

"This is Gideon, and I'm of the light. Sweetheart, Joan and I both tried to tell you," Gideon said helplessly. "You know that when you're in the middle of a crowd, there are times when we can't get through to you telepathically. Tonight was one of those times."

Chapter 33

"Who was that on the phone?" Carla asked. Carla had just emerged from the bathroom, her hair in a turban, and a cigarette in her hand.

"It was Bernie," Eve answered. "When did you start smoking again?"

"When I almost ate an imp," Carla groused. "You've been on the phone almost an hour. I hope Bernie isn't going to start calling here and tying up the phone."

Bernie had called on the pretense of needing to know whether Eve wanted to ride with him to the Western dance lessons, or preferred to ride alone. But that topic had been exhausted in less than a minute. The rest of the hour had been chitchat—devoted to getting acquainted. "There won't be any reason for him to be calling again until it gets closer to the start of the lessons," Eve said. "How's your head? Is the headache gone?"

"The headache's gone," Carla said. "But I have this damned ringing in my ears that's driving me crazy. Would you want to see if you can stop *it*?"

"Sure. I can try." Eve was dressed in a pink sweatsuit and white furry slippers. One hand and one ear were half asleep from talking on the phone so long. "I'll go to the bathroom while you get your chair."

In the bathroom, Eve lifted the toilet seat and pulled down the pants to her sweatsuit. She had just pulled down her bikini panties and sat down when Gideon decided to chat. "This is Gideon, and I'm of the light. You need to be careful about how much time you spend on the phone, Sweetheart. Carla checked her watch when the phone rang, and again when you hung up."

It irritated Eve that Carla was checking up on her. But it irritated her even more that Gideon was talking to her while she was on the pot! "Would you mind giving me some privacy?"

"Do you honestly think I haven't seen you go to the bathroom before?" Gideon asked. "I'm your guardian angel. I was there when you were born. I was there on your honeymoon. I was in the delivery room when your son was born. Why shouldn't I be here when you go to the bathroom? It's a normal biological function."

"It's a *private* biological function," Eve snapped. "Now get out of here, and give me some privacy!"

"Who was in the bathroom?" Carla asked when Eve came out.

"Gideon," Eve replied. "He thinks that since he's my guardian angel, nothing in my life is off limits to him."

Carla had brought a dining room chair into the living room, and was sitting in her turban and white terry robe. The instant Eve placed her hands over Carla's ears, she felt the tug of the negative energy. She knew Carla had a mild case of tinnitus, but this was something more. "When did this start?"

"The minute I walked in from work," Carla answered. "Those sons of bitches have been bothering me all day."

Eve knew that the 'sons of bitches' Carla was referring to were the dark spirits they'd recently learned so much about. When the ringing in Carla's ears had been reduced to a distant hum, Carla suggested they stop for now.

They had turned off the lights in the front of the apartment, and Eve had gone into her room and closed the door so she could paint. Through the bedroom wall, she could hear Carla on the phone talking to her friend Laura. "No—just temporary agencies—No interviews yet—talked to Bernie tonight for over an hour..."

It was obvious that Carla was talking about *Eve.* Apparently Carla didn't realize how voices carried, even when she had cupped her mouth with her hand. Eve knew Carla was worried about the fact that she had yet to find a job. But it had been Carla's idea for her to take a week off. Since that time, Carla knew she'd been calling on every ad that sounded like even a remote possibility. As for her talking to Bernie, maybe it had been inconsiderate to stay on the phone so long. But Carla had been in the bathroom most of the time. If she'd wanted to use the phone, she could have asked Eve to hang up.

Making an effort to ignore the phone conversation in the next room, Eve spread a newspaper out on the floor and took out the statue and paints. "Gideon?" she said. "Would you do me a favor and ask The Magician if I'm doing the right colors? I don't want to have to take out the board."

"This is Gideon, and I'm of the light. The Magician says the purple robe needs to be a little darker, and the sash should be gold. Instead of making the beard all white, it should be streaked with dark gray."

There was nothing like getting the color scheme directly from the source. Eve had painted the sash and was working on the pointed hat when her stomach began to rumble. Now that Carla was quiet, she didn't want to go out to the kitchen and risk waking her, so she reached for her purse on the nightstand and took out a Reese's peanut butter cup.

"That looks and smells so good," Gideon said. "You don't know how much I miss eating. There are times when I'd give my wings for a steak and a beer— figuratively speaking, of course."

Did I used to cook steaks for you when we were married? Eve asked in her mind. *Oh. Before you answer that, ask The Magician what color the stars on his hat are supposed to be.*

"He said they're silver, but that it would really be good if you mixed it with a little gold glitter."

"Obviously, the Magician was not a painter," Eve said. "If I mix glitter in the paint, the paint's going to turn it silver. If he really wants the glitter, I'll have to glue it on."

"Let's go back to your earlier question," Gideon said. "Yes. You used to cook steaks for me; but more often, we'd have chicken or pork chops, or no meat at all. You used to milk the cows and churn our own butter. Sometimes you'd skim the cream and give it to Matt to drink. Mattie loved cream as much as I loved beer."

Eve had finished painting the stars, and leaned back to admire her artistry from a distance. She hoped Carla would like it. "Tell me more about when we were married."

"We were married thirteen years," Gideon said. "Matt was born the first year we were married. He was a breech birth, and it tore you up pretty badly. We didn't have anymore children for twelve years after that. But after Mattie died, you wanted another baby." Here Gideon paused, and Eve thought she heard a tear in his voice. "You and the baby both died in childbirth."

Silent and thoughtful, Eve carefully set the statue aside and put the lids back on the paint bottles. *Did you ever remarry, after I died?* her mind asked softly.

"You were the only woman I ever loved," Gideon said. "I buried you in the wildflower garden you planted the year we were married."

"Was I a good wife?" Eve asked. "I can't imagine myself on a farm, milking cows and churning butter. What was our relationship like?"

There was a moment of silence while Gideon was thinking. "I was several years older than you," he said at last. "But I knew from the minute I laid eyes on you that I had to have you. You were singing in the choir at church. Your blonde hair was piled up on top of your head, with little wisps pulling loose around your face. You looked like an angel."

Listening thoughtfully, Eve folded the newspaper and put it under the bed. "Did I feel the same about you? Did I love you at first sight too?"

"No," Gideon replied. "Ours was an arranged marriage. But, once you got past your shyness, you enjoyed the lovemaking. And after awhile the other feelings grew. You used to read to me at night from a book of poetry. And sometimes we'd study the Bible together. After Mattie was born, we used to laugh a lot. You loved him more than life itself. After he died, you never smiled again until the day the doctor told you we were going to have another child."

Considering how Eve felt about Kevin, she could readily believe that what Gideon said was true. "At least my feelings for you didn't change—Or did they?"

"No," Gideon said. That's one reason why Chad seemed like a good choice for you. He looked a lot like *I* did when I was human. But it never would have worked, if after you'd gotten together, you'd found out he was spineless. You've always preferred men who are macho."

That was not entirely true. Eve liked men who were really masculine. But the word 'macho,' to her mind, was synonymous with stupid. It implied showing off by taking unnecessary chances.

"The Energy of the East would like to talk to you," Gideon said.

Surprised that the Energy had asked to speak with her again, after their less than friendly first conversation, Eve took out the board and pendulum.

"I am the Energy of the East," the pendulum spelled out. "And I'm of the light. I don't want you to misunderstand and think that I'm going to make a habit of this—talking to you, I mean. I've gone since the beginning of time, with one exception, not talking with humans until now. But talking through the board is simpler than having to actually speak, and there are some things I want you to explain."

The Energy of the East was asking *her* to explain something? Eve had changed into her blue nightgown and climbed into bed. She was seated crosslegged with the board in her lap. "I'm honored that you would want to talk to me," she said uncertainly. The memory of her last conversation with this spirit was still fresh in her mind. He had said at that time that he didn't like humans, and had no desire to *chitchat* with *her*. "What would you possibly want to ask me?"

The pendulum swung in huge sweeping motions, similar to when Jehovah had spoken to commend Carla for being willing to lend her the money to begin her training as a healer. "I want you to explain human emotions."

Human emotions? The spirit might as well have asked her to explain the color *red*!

"I'm not like Gideon and Saul who were human before they became spirits," the Energy went on. "I've been a spirit of energy since the beginning of time. As a spirit of energy, I have no emotions. I see humans respond to outside stimulus by laughing, frowning, crying, or screaming. I recognize that these are responses to human feelings of hate, love, pain, and fear. What I *don't* comprehend are the feelings that *spark* these emotional reactions."

This was obviously a topic the Energy of the East had spent considerable time pondering. He was an outsider looking in, trying to understand what he could never be a part of. Eve's heart went out to him.

"Take that look on your face right now," the Energy said. "What are you feeling?"

Eve hadn't realized her feelings were that obvious. "Well," she said uncomfortably. "I guess what I'm feeling is empathy, and pity."

"I understand empathy," the spirit said. "That's when you're trying to imagine yourself as me. But I thought *pity* is what humans feel when they see a hungry child or an animal that's been mistreated."

This was going to be even harder than Eve had thought. "It *is*," she agreed. "But it's also what we feel for someone who has lost something or someone he cares very much about, or for someone who wants something very much—and deserves to *have* it—but knows he never can."

For a moment the pendulum was still as the Energy of the East digested this information. "And the fact that you feel pity for *me* is an indication that you believe I can never understand human emotions."

"Yes," Eve said. "—No. It's not that I think it will never happen. It's just that—" She didn't really know how to explain what she was feeling. The Energy was obviously extremely intelligent. She could probably convey an intellectual understanding. But how could she explain the actual *feelings*? "Would you mind if I took some time to think about this? I really want to help you understand. But I just can't do that off the top of my head."

"*That* expression, I understand," the Energy said. "We'll talk again tomorrow."

"Good night," Eve said, laying the board and pendulum aside. "And Good night, Gideon. Good night, Saul." As an after thought, she also said "Good night" to Caruso and the Magician…

Chapter 34

Throughout the following week, Eve talked with the Energy of the East daily. Each day, she perused the classifieds and contacted local employment agencies, with still no sign of a job. With Country Western dance lessons slated to start next week, Bernie used any excuse he could think of to call each evening and talk to Eve. Each time he called, Carla became more irritated.

She and Eve had just finished a dinner of a salad and baked potato, and Eve was in the kitchen rinsing the dishes when the phone rang. "If that's Bernie on the phone again, I'm going to tell him you've moved out and left no forwarding number," Carla said, reaching for the receiver. "Hello."

If it was Bernie on the other end, Carla's snappish tone of voice left no doubt as to how she felt about his calling.

"*Joe?*" It was amazing how quickly Carla's tone of voice could change when the voice on the other end was one she wanted to hear. "You're the last person I expected to hear from tonight! How have you been?" The Saccharin sweet lilt of Carla's voice reminded Eve of Scarlet O'Hara trying to charm Suellen's boyfriend. "I'm just fine," Carla cooed. "I missed you at the Jukebox this week... Eve?" The tone of voice changed again. "You're calling to talk to *Eve?*"

In the kitchen, Eve stiffened. Why was *Joe* calling for her, and how did he get her number? She certainly hadn't given it to him. Carla must have told him they were sharing an apartment. "Tell him I'm not here," Eve mouthed from the archway.

"Sure, Joe," Carla said, ignoring Eve's signal. "I'll get her."

While Eve was talking to Joe on the phone, Carla was unloading the silverware from the dishwasher, slamming it into the drawer.

"...Thanks Joe, but I never date anyone who's dated a friend." Eve had no desire to go out with Joe, and she certainly hoped he wasn't the third potential love interest she was supposed to choose from. Carla was upset *enough* lately, without having *Joe* compound the problem.

"You didn't have to turn him down on my account," Carla said when Eve had hung up.

"I didn't give him my number," Eve said. "I didn't even tell him I was your roommate. I don't know how he found out." Before Carla had a chance to respond, the phone rang again. "Do you want me to get it?" Eve asked.

"Why not?" Carla sneered. "It's probably for you."

The phone call was from Gary. Talk about bad timing. "Hi…" From the kitchen, the clattering of silverware had stopped and the silence could be cut with a knife. "I really can't talk right now… Okay. Tomorrow would be fine. 'Talk to you then."

When Eve hung up the phone, Carla didn't say a word. She just walked past Eve into the bathroom and turned on the shower. When the phone rang again, it was Kevin. "Hello, Mom?"

"Hi, Sweetheart. I was going to call you tonight. But I figured you'd probably be out with your friends till nine."

"I was just calling to see how you were doing," Kevin said. "And to see if we could go to lunch Sunday instead of Saturday."

"Sure," Eve said. "Sunday will be fine. So tell me what's been happening…"

When Carla came out of the shower, Eve could tell she had a headache. But Carla didn't ask for her help, and Eve decided she'd better not offer. Later when Eve was in her room painting, she heard Carla close her bedroom door. A moment later, Carla was speaking quietly into the telephone. "…*Joe* called here this evening, and asked for *her.*"

The following afternoon, Eve went out to get a newspaper so she could look through the Classifieds. When she returned to the apartment, Carla was home from work, listening to the messages on the answer machine: "…Call me when you get in."

"Hi," Eve said. "You're home early. Did you have a good day at work?"

Carla had pulled off her wig and was taking the bobby pins off the skullcap beneath. "Work was the same as always," she said irritably. "But I think I'm going to have to buy a second message machine to handle all *your* messages."

Eve had only been gone half an hour. Surely there couldn't have been that many calls in that length of time.

"Bernie called. And that last call was from Gary. He wants you to call him when you get in. Are you really going to go out with him?"

So that's what this was all about. "I won't go out with Gary if you don't want me to, Carla."

"Why should I care?" Carla snapped. "It's no skin off my nose."

"This is Joan," a voice in Eve's head said. "I'm of the light. Please tell Carla I want to talk to her."

Eve really didn't want to pass on the message—not with the mood Carla was in. But she didn't feel that she had a choice. "Joan wants to talk to you."

"Well I'm not so sure I want to talk to *her,*" Carla snapped.

"Tell her I'm sorry I wasn't able to warn you about Gary," Joan said. "Tell her he's too young for her, and they have nothing in common. The man she's best suited for is right under her nose. She's been taking dance lessons with him for months."

Joan was obviously referring to the lessons Carla was taking at a singles spot in Sacramento. "Do you know who Joan's talking about?" Eve asked. "What's he like?"

"She's talking about *Walter*. He's sixty-five years old, and looks more like he's seventy."

Eve didn't know what to say. She'd had no idea when she'd given her phone number to Gary that he was the one Carla wanted to date. She'd given it to him because he was reasonably attractive, and seemed like a nice guy. She hadn't meant to hurt Carla. That was the last thing she'd have wanted to do.

"There's one thing more," Joan said. "Tell Carla to please hang the dragon picture back up. Her subconscious was very upset when she took it down."

Eve had noticed that the drawing of Elliot was missing. She'd wondered how long it would take for Joan to get around to mentioning it. Given Carla's current state of mind, her timing wasn't the greatest.

Later, Eve had eaten a peanut butter sandwich and turned on a T.V. movie when Carla came out of her room in her underwear, wearing a blonde wig and black panty hose. "Is it alright if I borrow your black skirt?"

Eve thought it took nerve for Carla to ask, after jumping down her throat less than an hour ago. "I guess so," she said tonelessly. "It's in the closet."

When Carla emerged again fifteen minutes later, she had put on her makeup and was fully dressed.

"You look pretty," Eve commented. "Are you and Laura going dancing tonight?"

"That's right," Carla said curtly. Digging in her purse for her keys, Carla didn't look in Eve's direction.

"Are you going to the Sheraton?" It wasn't that Eve really cared where Carla was going. She was simply making an effort to make conversation.

"We haven't decided," Carla said in a clipped voice. "Don't wait up for me. I'll probably be late."

"Have fun," Eve said lamely. She didn't know what had gotten into Carla lately, but whatever it was, she didn't like it.

With Carla gone, it was almost a relief to Eve to have the apartment to herself. This would be a good time to talk to Gary without having to worry about Carla's overhearing. Still, Eve felt almost guilty about making the call. "Hello, Gary?"

"Eve? I was just going to call you to see if you'd want to meet me somewhere tonight where we could have dinner and talk."

At first Eve declined, but when Gary persisted she decided it might not be such a bad idea after all. In the end, they decided to meet at Carrow's. "Don't dress up," Gary said. "Just jeans and a nice top. Shall we say half an hour?"

When Eve arrived at the restaurant, Gary was already there.

They chose a booth next to a window. Dressed in jeans and an Hawaiian shirt, Gary gave Eve the once-over and smiled. Eve hated Hawaiian shirts. This was the second man *Carla* was interested in who wore them. Eve wondered if Walter wore them too.

Gary had ordered a cup of coffee, and Eve had ordered a Coke. Reaching across the table to touch Eve's hand, Gary said he was glad she'd been able to make it on such short notice.

"Actually," Eve said, "Part of the reason I came is that we need to talk."

When their orders had come, Eve drew a deep breath and debated how much to say. "Before I say anything, I want you to promise me you won't say a word to Carla or anyone else at PWP."

Gary had been in the process of carving his steak. Now he looked up. "I take it this has something to do with the night you gave me your phone number."

"Yes," Eve replied. "I wouldn't have given you my number if I'd known you were interested in Carla first."

"Who said I was interested in *Carla*?" The question hung in the air between them like an unwelcome wisp of cigar smoke.

"You mean you—But Carla thought—"

"I asked Carla to dance one time," Gary said. "After that, she did the asking. If I'd been interested in dating her, I'd have asked for her phone number."

It was true that when Gary had been interested in Eve he hadn't hesitated to ask for her number. "The point is that Carla *thought* you were interested. She got upset when she saw me give you my number." Eve had ordered a salad and baked potato. Now as she took a bite, she waited for Gary to respond. When he didn't, she continued. "Carla's my best friend. I can't afford to let a misunderstanding like this come between us."

"So what do you suggest we do?" Gary asked. "I like you. I want to see you again. Am I going to have to worry about Carla answering every time I want to call you?"

This was a good question. If Gary truly was the second of the three men who were supposed to be coming into Eve's life, she didn't intend to blow it. "Right now I'm unemployed," she said. "You can call in the daytime when Carla's at work. Or you can wait for me to call *you* when she's out of the apartment in the evening."

Now that the matter had been settled, at least for the time being, Eve and Gary were free to get acquainted and enjoy their dinner. There were so many things they had in common that Eve felt as if she'd known Gary for years.

When Gary walked Eve to her car, he asked if he could kiss her. The kiss was soft and gentle, more friendly than romantic: nothing that would set the world on fire, but enough to pique her interest.

Eve arrived home before Carla, with ample time to change her clothes and talk on the board to the Energy of the East before Carla got home.

"We've talked about happiness and anger and sorrow," the Energy said. "Tonight, I want to talk about the emotion you call Love." Eve had changed into a purple sweatsuit, and was seated on the afghan-covered loveseat with the board in her lap.

"When you married your son's father," the pendulum went on, "you felt love for him. But he was untrue and made you cry, so now you don't." Apparently the Energy of the East had known Eve longer than she realized. That, or he could see into the past. "On several occasions your son, too, has made you cry, yet the love you feel for him remains unchanged. How can this be?"

Eve could readily understand why this might be confusing. Sometimes she didn't understand it herself. "The love between a man and a woman is different than love between a mother and her child," she said thoughtfully. "A mother's love is unconditional. No matter what her child does, or how badly he may hurt her, she still loves him."

"Like the love God feels for humans," the Energy said. "But exactly how does this love *feel*?

Eve had never stopped to analyze it before. Now, put to the test, she wasn't sure she could. "When you love someone, you want that person to be happy," she began. "You want him to feel good, and you don't want him to be hurt in any way. Is this making sense so far?"

"I understand what you've said," the Energy said. "But that still doesn't explain the feeling."

This was going to be harder than Eve had thought. "The kind of love a mother feels for her child makes her feel warm inside, and very comfortable. When she has this warm comfortable feeling, she wants to touch the child softly—to put her arms around him, and hug him."

"The way I saw you do with your son, when I looked into your past," the Energy said. "The way you did so often when he was growing up. But you did the same thing when he was injured, and I don't believe you were feeling warm and comfortable then. At those times, your heart was beating rapidly and you experienced the symptoms you have described as fear."

Eve had never realized until now how complicated emotions could be. "That feeling of fear grows out of a mother's desire to protect her child at all costs. If she thinks he's in danger, love will make her risk her own safety to protect him."

Pleased with her own explanation, Eve felt the way she had used to feel as a teacher when she'd managed to get a difficult concept across and had seen the dawn of understanding on the children's faces.

"But what of the times when your son misbehaved, and you punished him for his misbehavior?" the Energy asked. "Where were these feelings of love then?"

Eve had once taught a child from China to speak English. That had been no more difficult than this. "It's *because of* the love she feels for her child that she disciplines him when he misbehaves. She does it to protect him from the harsher penalties he'll have to face in later life if she doesn't teach him *now* to control his behavior."

The pendulum was still as the Energy of the East took a moment to digest what he had just been told. "And this feeling differs from the love a woman feels for her mate?"

Oh boy, Eve thought. *Here we go.* "The love a woman feels for her mate has some of the same characteristics. But it involves other sensations too—like a faster heartbeat sometimes when he touches her or kisses her, or looks at her in a certain way—and sometimes a rush of energy in the area between her legs."

"You love *Armand Assante*?" the Energy asked.

Puzzled, Eve said that she thought Armand Assante was an excellent actor, but that she'd never met him. And no, she didn't love him.

"Then why did you have this same rush of energy when you saw him on the movie screen with his shirt off?"

Hot blood rushed to Eve's cheeks. "That," she said uncomfortably, "is a feeling that can be part of the love a woman feels for her mate, or she can feel it for a man she thinks is attractive, even though she doesn't love him."

"I'm beginning to understand," the Energy said. "But you also say you love dancing and pizza. How is this possible?"

"That one's easy," Eve said. "When a person says he loves a food, or a movie, or a sport, or a good book, he just means he likes it very very much. He means it gives him pleasure…"

By the time Eve heard Carla's key in the lock, the Energy of the East was satisfied that he had gained some grasp on the concept of love. Looking up from the board, Eve asked if Carla and Laura had had a good time.

Carla tossed her purse onto the dining room table and reached up to unpin her wig. "I suppose so."

"Did you see Walter?"

"No."

It wasn't like Carla to be so curt. Apparently an evening of dancing hadn't been enough to defuse the anger she'd been feeling before she left home.

"If you're still upset about Joe's calling me, you don't have to worry," Eve said. "I'm not going to go out with him."

"What's the matter?" Carla spat. "Isn't he good enough for you?"

The question was uncalled for, and didn't deserve an answer. If Carla was spoiling for a fight, she was in for a disappointment. "Good night," Eve said. "I'll see you tomorrow."

Chapter 35

The next day was Saturday. When Eve returned from having lunch at Togo's with Kevin, she brought with her a newspaper. She was browsing through the classifieds crossing out some ads and circling others when she came across an ad for a nanny.

"This is different," Eve said. "Here's a doctor that's looking for a *nanny* to take care of his kids. It says here it's a salaried position with full benefits."

"You're good with kids," Carla commented. "Why don't you put in an application?"

Apparently whatever had been bothering Carla had either blown over or she'd brought it into perspective.

"I'll call first thing Monday morning," Eve said. Picking up the pendulum, she addressed a question to the Energy of the East. "What do *you* think?"

"This is the Energy of the East, and I'm of the light. Do you want this job?"

"I *need* this job."

"Then the job is yours."

Yeah, right, Eve thought. She would go through the motions of turning in her application, and had no doubt she could get an interview. But based on her interview and work experiences of the past year, she didn't hold out much hope of getting the job.

When Eve called Monday morning, the interviewer asked for a general rundown of her qualifications. "We already have nearly sixty applications. I need to screen the applicants before setting up the interviews."

Discouraged by the fact that the ad had just come out, and sixty people had already applied for the position, Eve mustered as much enthusiasm as she could manage and listed her qualifications—which to her own ears sounded pretty impressive. "I'm a mother, and I did home daycare for a year. I've also had four years of teaching experience—three in elementary, one in preschool..."

Apparently the interviewer agreed with Eve in her assessment of her own qualifications. "I already have six interviews scheduled for this afternoon, but if I cut my lunch short, I can squeeze you in first. Can you be here at 12:30 this afternoon?"

Eve arranged her hair carefully and put on light makeup and a conservative gray suit for the interview. To avoid the chance of anything's happening to make her be late, she arrived forty-five minutes early and parked the Shadow under a tree.

At precisely 12:30, Eve walked in through the door. The interviewer's office was thickly carpeted, with paneled walls. The interviewer herself was a heavy-set woman with a pretty face, pale blue eyes, and short black hair. "I'm Dr. Peterson's accountant," she said by way of introduction. "I do her books and payroll, and she's asked me to do the preliminary interviews for the nanny position. Have a seat."

Eve was surprised to hear that the doctor was a woman. Eve's experiences working for women in the past were not among her fondest memories. But woman boss or no, she needed this job.

The interview went well. The fact that the interviewer was already predisposed in Eve's favor eliminated any nervousness Eve might have felt. "You're definitely the first on our list to be considered. I don't think it will be necessary to take a week to make a decision. I'll do today's interviews, and call you tomorrow."

Eve had been down this road before. How many times had she been the top candidate, only to have the job go to someone else?

By the time Eve arrived home, the phone was ringing. "This is Sharon, Dr. Peterson's accountant. I've decided it would be a waste of time to interview anyone else for the nanny position, and Dr. Peterson agrees. If you could come back in, Dr. Peterson and her husband would like to meet you…"

When Carla arrived home, Eve was waiting to tell her the news. "I got the job! I have an appointment New Year's Day to meet the kids. The job starts the day after New Years."

"Of course," Carla said irritably. "That's what the Energy of the East promised."

Eve had expected Carla to be pleased—possibly even excited for her. After all, now that she had a job, Carla could stop worrying about where Eve's share of the rent and utilities was going to come from.

"Is something wrong, Carla?"

"What could be wrong?" Carla sneered. "You wanted the job. You asked the Energy, and you got it. Whatever sweet little Evie wants, sweet little Evie gets."

The uncalled for comment cut to the core, bringing tears to Eve's eyes. "I would hardly say I get everything I want," she countered. "Do you think I *wanted* to be out of work all these weeks? Do you think I *wanted* to move to Placerville to live in a hotel full of old people?—To be groped by old men, and spend my days *wiping butts* and washing poop-stained sheets? Do you really think I *want* to work as a *nanny* when I have a degree in English and enough office experience that I should be able to get a job bringing in *a thousand a month more than this job is going to pay*?"

"Those things may not be good," Carla argued, "but how do you think it makes *me* feel, always hearing that precious little Eve has been 'chosen' by Jesus to be a natural healer? What makes you so much better than me, that He would choose *you* and not me to work through? How do you think it makes me feel when *you can talk to my guardian angel, and I can't?* When I can't even communicate with my own sub-conscious except through you? And why should *I* have one *old* man in my life, and you get *three younger* men to choose from?"

Eve didn't know how to respond to this outpouring of pain. She felt very bad for Carla, but she wasn't going to let Carla lay a guilt trip on her for something that wasn't her fault. "You know Jesus chose me to be a healer because I've never abused my body," Eve said quietly. "I have no idea why the spirits can talk through me, and not through you. And I don't know why I'm supposed to have *three* men to choose from when your guardian angel says *you* should go for Walter. But I need this job, Carla. *We* need me to have this job. So instead of resenting the fact that I got it, I think you should be glad."

Tears started in Carla's eyes, but were quickly wiped away. "I *am* glad," she said grudgingly. "Sometimes this whole thing just gets to me that's all. Sometimes I wish that for just a little while *I* could be the one that's special."

Chapter 36

With Christmas just around the corner, Eve had used her single credit card to do her shopping, other than Carla's gift. The finished statue was beautiful, and had even won The Magician's stamp of approval.

Eve's weekly Country Western dance lessons were going well. She enjoyed taking lessons with Bernie, but had no interest whatsoever in Bernie beyond that of a friend. Unfortunately, Bernie had different ideas. When leaving the community college after one particular lesson, Bernie had tried to kiss her. When Eve had turned her face away, he had smacked her on top of the head. Though Bernie had made light of it, and made it sound like he'd been teasing, the smack had given Eve a headache that had lasted the entire evening.

Gary had taken Eve to dinner a couple of times, and they often talked on the phone when Carla wasn't home.

Eve had wanted to have a Christmas tree, but since she and Carla were both going to be out of town for Christmas, they decided to simply decorate the living room and the picture window. Carla had a number of Christmas knickknacks she'd collected over the years, and Eve had some Christmas candles and garlands of tinsel. "Shall we put the tinsel around the window?" Eve asked. "What do you think about putting it around the center section and putting the candles on the windowsill?"

"That would be good," Carla said. "I have a holiday centerpiece we can put on the stereo, and a basket of bulbs we could set on the coffee table."

As their gift to her, Eve's mother and sister had split the cost of plane fare and sent Eve a ticket to come to Southern California for the holiday. Carla, as usual, would be spending Christmas with her son and his family in San Jose.

Eve had had her Christmas with Kevin last night. This evening, she, Carla, Gideon, Saul, and Joan were having an early Christmas together. As a gift from Joan to Carla, Eve had purchased a hydro cal reindeer being hugged by a child bundled up in a snowsuit. Joan had picked it out when Eve went shopping, and Eve had painted it according to Joan's specifications. The finished piece was adorable.

Carla's face glowed with pleasure when she opened Joan's gift, and the statue of Merlin. "I love them! How did you paint them without my knowing?"

"I have my ways," Eve said mysteriously.

Carla's gift to Eve was a box containing three tiny bottles of scented bath oil.

After gifts had been opened, Gideon suggested a group hug. Unsure as to how to do this, Eve and Carla hugged one another, only to be engulfed in a field of energy so loving it brought tears to their eyes.

On The Magician's advice, Carla and Eve had each purchased a Lottery ticket with the agreement that if either of them won, they would split the jackpot fifty-fifty. Now, in the aftermath of the hug, Joan suggested they do some creative visualization, envisioning what it would be like if they won. "If you picture it in your mind, and believe strongly enough, you can win the lotto jackpot. All you have to do is believe."

"I know something that might help," Carla said excitedly. "I'll be right back."

When Carla returned to the living room, she was carrying a jug of pennies. "We can pour these out and close our eyes, and run them through our fingers, pretending they're made of gold."

"That's perfect," Joan said. "But first turn off the light, and light the candle on the coffee table."

When the candle had been lit, Joan instructed Carla and Eve to close their eyes and play with the coins. "While you're doing it, I'll tell you what to say. And when we get to the final line, I want you to imagine your words are a boomerang. Fling them out into the Universe and—like a boomerang—they'll return, bringing with them a fortune, if you truly believe."

Seated on the floor on opposite sides of the coffee table, Eve and Carla divided the coins and closed their eyes.

"I am a daughter of God's Universe," Joan said.

"I am a daughter of God's Universe," Eve echoed. Then Eve and Carla repeated it together.

Eve felt a little foolish dribbling pennies through her fingers, pretending they were gold. From across the table, she could hear that Carla was really getting into this.

"Blessed be the sacred laws of God's Universe," Joan continued.

"Blessed be the sacred laws of God's Universe," Eve repeated.

"Blessed be the sacred laws of God's Universe," Carla and Eve said in unison.

"Blessed be the bountiful plenty of His Universe," Joan intoned.

"Blessed be the bountiful plenty..." Eve echoed.

"Blessed be the bountiful plenty..." Carla joined in.

"As a daughter of God's Universe, I am entitled to share in the riches of its bounty," Joan continued...

As Eve raised her hands near her face, she could smell the metallic odor of coins on her skin. Scooping another handful of pennies, she repeated after Joan: "I am a magnet for wealth and riches. Come to me, oh treasures of the Universe. Come to me now..."

In her mind's eye, Eve could see a boomerang being flung into outer space and returning. But she couldn't see the money.

They had repeated this ritual six times or more when Carla suddenly smelled something and opened her eyes. "The candle!"

The candle had dripped wax onto the plate it was standing on, then somehow tipped over and burned the table. Jumping up, Carla dived forward to extinguish the flame.

"A dark spirit somehow got into the apartment," Joan shouted. "It tipped over the candle, and now it's in the Merlin statue!"

Eve's heart lurched, and her mouth went dry. "How did it get in? What should we do?"

"You have to show them your stronger than they are," Joan said urgently. "Tell Carla she has to crush the statue. Put a paper bag over it, and smash it with a hammer. Don't stop until it's been pulverized."

Eve repeated the instructions, and Carla raced to the kitchen for a paper bag and the hammer she kept in the bottom drawer. It had taken Eve a week to paint the statue. In less than a minute, it had been destroyed...

As they were gathering up the pennies, Carla commented that she had loved the statue, and the sons of bitches had destroyed it—just like when she had to throw the heart-shaped rock away. Not only that: they had burned her table in the process. "Do you think the creative visualization will work?" she asked morosely. "Do you really think we have a chance of winning the lottery?"

"Tell her that *her* belief was strong enough," Gideon said. "But in order for the visualization to have worked, you would *both* have to have seen the money."

What had started out to be a perfect evening had deteriorated into a fiasco of disappointment.

Both Eve and Carla were in gloomy moods the next morning when they said their good-byes for the holidays. But when the plane lifted off from Sacramento, Eve's spirits were lifted with it. By the time she arrived in Southern California, she was actually feeling festive.

Christmas with her family was a pleasant time. Eve stayed for five days, and was sorry to see the vacation end. When she returned to Sacramento, her car was waiting in the airport parking lot. She wondered if Carla would be home when she got there. She hoped Carla had enjoyed her visit with her son.

On the drive home from the airport, Eve chatted with Gideon. They hadn't had much chance to talk during her vacation. There had always been other people around. Though Eve's sister knew about Eve's spirit guides, and had expressed some interest in getting in touch with her own, Eve had never mentioned them to her mother, and never intended to. There were some things one told one's mother, and some things one *didn't*. This was definitely one of those things.

When Eve unlocked the door to the apartment and set her suitcase inside, she looked around for Carla. "Carla?" she called. "Are you home?"

"I'm on the phone," Carla called back.

Eve closed and locked the door, and carried her suitcase to her room. As she passed Carla's door, she could hear Carla talking. "I was thinking about it the whole time I was gone...I can't have any privacy. When I go out, she asks where I'm going. When I come home, she wants to know who I've been with..."

Eve couldn't believe what she was hearing. Apparently Carla was talking about *her* and the questions she often asked as a part of everyday conversation. She didn't ask them to be nosey, and had never realized Carla looked at them as prying. If Carla was bothered by the fact that Eve expressed an interest in her life, she should have *said* so instead of allowing resentments to fester.

In her room, Eve quietly closed the door and lay down on the bed. Tears filled her eyes, but she blinked them away. There had been a time when she and Carla had willingly shared their most intimate secrets: a time when there hadn't been anything they couldn't or wouldn't talk about. When had their relationship changed to the point that she couldn't even ask if Carla was going out dancing without worrying that the question would be viewed as prying?

Eve sometimes wished her hearing were less acute. Even with both doors closed, she could hear that Carla was still on the phone. When she heard Carla's door open, she got out of bed and went into the hallway. "Hi," she said, making an attempt to smile. "Did you enjoy your visit with your son and his family?" Damn. There she went again, asking about Carla's private life.

"The visit was fine," Carla said curtly. "We need to talk."

"I agree," Eve said. "Do you want to go into the living room?"

Carla had sat down on the edge of her bed in the darkened bedroom, and was toying with the fringe on a throw pillow. "I want my money."

Eve didn't know what she had expected, but this certainly wasn't it. "I haven't missed a payment," she said uneasily. "If you need me to increase the size of the payments now that I'll be working, I could increase them by maybe twenty-five a month until I get on my feet. Maybe fifty a month after that."

"He told me the money would be there," Carla said coldly. "I shouldn't have agreed to accept payments. I want my money now."

Eve felt as if Carla had pulled the rug from beneath her feet. "I don't understand," she said uncertainly. "Has something happened? Do you have some sort of an emergency?"

"I want my money," Carla repeated.

"But I don't *have* it." Eve was standing in the doorway slumped against the doorjamb. Her head was spinning with the effort to make sense of what was happening. "We agreed I could make payments, and that's what I've been doing. Carla, I don't *have* your money."

When Carla spoke again, her voice was the temperature of ice. "You can get it. You have your car."

Eve couldn't believe this was her best friend speaking. "You're asking me to *sell my car*? But how would I get to work? How would I—"

"You could take out a loan and use the car as collateral."

"I don't understand," Eve said weakly. "Why are you doing this?"

"Because I'm not going to fall for anymore of their damned lies," Carla spat.

"Anymore of whose lies?" Eve asked in confusion. "Are you talking about Gideon? Are you talking about Joan? How can you even say these things?"

"While I was gone, I did a lot of thinking about these so-called spirits of light," Carla said quietly.

"What are you *saying*?" Eve whispered.

192

"What I'm saying is, hasn't it ever occurred to you that they might all be bad? That instead of being spirits of God they may all be spirits of Satan?"

The tears that had formed in Eve's eyes now spilled onto her cheeks. How could Carla say such a thing? A sob escaped Eve's throat as she ran into her room and closed the door behind her. Tearful spasms racked her body, making it difficult to breathe. Aware that she was on the verge of hyperventilating, Eve covered her mouth and nose with her hands. "Why is Carla doing this, Gideon?"

"Sweetheart," Gideon said softly, "Carla's jealous of you. The jealousy is like a knife in her side. Every time a man calls you, it's like a twist of that knife. She doesn't want to be roommates anymore. She's planning to ask you to move out."

Move out? Eve couldn't believe what she was hearing. Where could she find an apartment on her own when she hadn't even started her new job? Eve could understand Carla's feelings, but that didn't lessen the sense of betrayal. If *she* was feeling betrayed, she could only imagine how *Joan* must be feeling.

The next day was Saturday. Eve waited until she was sure Carla had gone out before opening the door and coming out of her room. She had cried into the wee hours of the night, leaving her eyes puffed, and her sinuses swollen. It hurt to know what Carla was planning. But now that she knew, she had to act fast.

The first thing Eve did was place a call to her mother to ask if her mom would be willing to co-sign for a loan against the Shadow. "Carla's calling in the balance of the two thousand dollars she lent me when I was out of work and had to move to Placerville."

"Why would she do a thing like that?" Eve's mom asked. "Did something happen? Has she had some kind of emergency?"

"Not that I know of," Eve replied. "She just said she doesn't think she should have to wait. She wants her money now."

Eve hadn't wanted to ask her mother. She had said from the beginning when Carla first made the loan offer that she didn't want the loan if she was going to end up having to ask for her mother's help to pay it back. Both God and the guides had promised this wouldn't happen. Yet here it was. She had asked Gideon last night why this was happening—why the money wasn't available from another source as promised. Gideon had offered no explanation, other than the fact that God had promised the money would be available from another source if and when Carla *needed* it. "Carla doesn't *need* the money," Gideon had said. "She wants it now because she doesn't trust you anymore."

Eve couldn't imagine why Carla had suddenly decided she was untrustworthy. She'd never been accused of being untrustworthy in her life.

Rather than co-sign for a loan against the Shadow, Eve's mother insisted on sending the balance due on the loan. "You'd never be able to afford the payments the bank would charge," her mom said. "And if you couldn't make a payment, you could lose the car. Then where would you be? I'm going to send a cashier's check tomorrow, and you can worry about paying me back later. Tell Carla she'll have her money. But between you and me, I'm disappointed in Carla. I think making an agreement to take payments then backing out on the agreement was a shitty thing to do. Apparently she's not as good a friend as you thought she was."

After hanging up the phone, Eve went out to get a newspaper.

When Carla came home that evening, Eve started for her room, but Carla called her back. "Look, I'm sorry about what I said about the spirit guides all being bad. But it's something I think you should think about."

Ignoring the apology, Eve looked at Carla coldly. "I've made arrangements to borrow the money. You'll have it by the end of the week. And I know you don't want to live with me anymore, so I've put in an application for an apartment."

The look of guilt on Carla's face was genuine. "How did you—It's not that I don't want to live with you anymore. It's just that I want to find something cheaper. I'm on a waiting list for an apartment in a complex downtown. I was going to wait and tell you when I'm ready to give my notice."

Eve was glad Carla at least had the good grace to feel guilty. "I'll know in a couple of weeks whether or not I can get the apartment I applied for. In the meantime, I'll keep looking, just in case."

"But you don't have to move out till after I've given my notice," Carla protested. "And that probably won't be for another three months. How did you know I was planning to move?"

"I didn't know you were planning to move," Eve replied coldly. "I just knew you didn't want to be roommates anymore. Gideon told me."

Carla's cheeks flushed a deep shade of red. "I wouldn't have just dropped it on you like this. I would have told you in plenty of time…"

As it turned out, Eve didn't get the apartment. When her application was turned down a week after she submitted it, Carla said she was welcome to stay on until she could find something else. It was amazing how much nicer Carla was acting, now that she had her money. One might almost say she was being sticky sweet—overly anxious to please.

She and Eve had baked a grocery store pizza and made a tossed salad to go with it. While Carla sliced the pizza, Eve poured the drinks. "I really feel bad about what I was thinking," Carla said. "It was just that I'd told Laura about the loan, and how you'd been out of work so long and were making such small payments… And we thought maybe you were some sort of con artist. I feel really stupid now."

A *con artist*? Carla and her friend had thought she was a *con artist*? Talk about adding insult to injury!

"Could a con artist have pulled a migraine out of your head, or made a bruise disappear? Unless *you* were *faking* the migraine, how could that have been a con? Would a con artist have borrowed money, then used it to move to Placerville and do *grunt labor in a convalescent hospital*? Besides that, if you'll recall, I didn't ask for the money. It was your idea to lend it. You talked me into it!"

"You're right," Carla said wearily. "You were just paying the loan back so slowly that I started feeling panicky. I mean that two thousand dollars was part of my retirement."

Eve was in no mood to empathize. She'd been hurt and insulted. She was glad she'd be starting her new job in a few days. She could hardly wait to move out.

Chapter 37

On New Years Day, Eve dressed in a pair of black slacks with a red turtleneck sweater and drove to the house on Elm Street where she would be working as of tomorrow. The sprawling ranch style house was redwood, located on a dead end street on two acres of land.

When Eve stepped onto the front stoop, a shaggy haired dog poked its head under the beige drapes and barked. "Quiet, Ralston," a masculine voice said. "Go lie down."

The door opened, and Frank Peterson stepped aside. "Come in. Carol and the girls are in the living room."

Frank was a man of medium height with dark hair and a long nose. Though Eve smiled a greeting, the smile was not returned. Frank's stiff demeanor reminded Eve of the butlers in Hollywood movies.

Stepping into the house, Eve glanced at the room to the right of the entryway—the one with the beige drapes, where the dog had barked through the window. The room was beige, with dirty handprints on the walls. On one wall were crayon scribbles and a hole in the sheetrock the size of a baseball. Toys were strewn about the hardwood floor. The room was devoid of furniture.

"That's the girls' playroom," Frank said. "This is the living room in here."

The living room to the left of the entryway was dim. Carol Peterson was seated on the sofa, flanked by her two daughters, dressed in their Sunday finery. "Hello. Did you have any trouble finding us?"

"Not at all," Eve said. "You gave very good directions."

Dr. Peterson was a tall, large-boned, blonde woman with shoulder length blonde hair and an attractive face. "Girls," Carol said, "this is Eve Tarlton. Starting tomorrow, Eve will be your new nanny."

Looking at the older of the two, Eve remarked "Hi. You must be Cindy." And looking at the younger sister, "You must be Jessica."

The older girl, Cindy, looked a lot like a smaller version of her mother, except that her hair was shorter and her features were thinner. The younger sister, Jessica, strongly resembled her father. Eve hoped she would outgrow the resemblance before she reached adulthood. If not, she was going to grow up to be a very homely woman. Not that her father was homely. But his features on a woman would definitely not be attractive.

"Girls," Frank said, "Why don't you tell Eve about yourselves. Cindy, you can start."

"I'm seven years old," Cindy said. "I'm in second grade. I take tap and ballet lessons, and I'm in gymnastics."

"It sounds like you're a very busy little girl," Eve replied. "What about you, Jessica? Do you take lessons too?"

Either Jessica was very shy, or she didn't feel like talking.

"Jessica takes lessons too," Cindy said. "And she goes to preschool."

In an effort to draw the little girl out, Eve commented that her pink dress was very pretty, and that she wished that *she'd* had a dress like that when she was a little girl.

"Do you like to play games?" Cindy asked.

"Yes," Eve said. "I like games. Sometimes when my son was a little boy, we used to make up games to play together."

"What's your son's name?" Cindy asked. "How old is he?"

"His name's Kevin, and he's in high school."

"Guy, that means you must be *old*," Jessica said.

If that was the best Jessica could do, Eve wished she had kept her mouth shut…

The first week on the job was sheer hell. Eve arrived each morning at seven, woke the girls, and fixed their breakfast before their father left for work. It didn't take long to realize that as long as Frank was home, Eve had no authority. It was obvious from the outset that any instructions she gave the girls while their dad was in the house would be undermined. To make matters worse, the girls knew it as well as she.

Each day, once their father left for work, the battle of wills began. For starters, both girls viewed Eve as a servant who was there to cook their meals, clean their rooms, chauffeur them wherever they needed to go, and put up with whatever *crap* they wanted to dish out. When they spoke to her, their voices were not only insolent, but also dripping with condescension. Some- thing was definitely going to have to give, and it wasn't going to be *Eve*.

On Monday afternoon between school and Gymnastics, the first day of her second week on the job, Eve took the girls into the living room and told them to sit down. "I want to have a talk with you about why you think I'm here."

Seated on the sofa across the room from Eve, the girls looked at each other uncertainly.

"You first, Jessica," Eve said. "Why do *you* think I'm here?"

"To baby-sit us and be our maid," Jessica replied.

"And what about you, Cindy?"

"To cook for us and clean our house," Katy said. "And to take us where we need to go."

At least Eve now understood where she ranked, as far as the girls were concerned. "It's time we understood each other," she said. "And it's time you understood what my job is all about."

At that point, Jessica called Ralston to "Come," and Cindy stood up as if she were ready to leave.

"Sit down," Eve said. "And leave Ralston right where he is. I'm not through talking."

Uncertain of how far they should push their luck, Cindy sat back down. Jessica picked up a throw pillow and covered her face.

"Put the pillow down, Jessica." When the three-and-a- half-year-old had complied, Eve went on. "It's true that I'm here to cook your meals, and to drive you to school and wherever else you need to go. But I am *not* your servant, and I am *not* your maid."

"What are you, then?" Jessica sneered.

"I'm your *nanny*," Eve said firmly. "I'm here to take care of you, but I'm also here to teach you."

"We don't need *you* to teach us," Cindy said. "We already have a teacher."

"That's your teacher at school," Eve replied. I'm your teacher at home. I'll be teaching you manners and respect: how to be polite, and treat other people the way they should be treated. I'll also be teaching you a sense of responsibility—starting with taking responsibility for your rooms. Starting today, I've folded your laundry and put it on your beds. It's your responsibility from here on out to put it in your drawers where it belongs."

"We don't do that," Jessica snickered. "That's your job.'

"Starting today," Eve said through clenched teeth, "It's *yours*. It is also your responsibility, starting today, to pick up your own toys and put them away when they're not being played with."

"I'm going to tell my daddy you're trying to make us do your work," Jessica said. "He'll fire you." Exchanging smirks with her older sister, Jessica folded her arms across her chest in a gesture of finality.

"We know how to get rid of nannies," Cindy said smugly. "We've got three fired before you. We can get you fired too."

"Tomorrow you may get me fired," Eve said brusquely. "But today you're putting your laundry away."

Eve never knew whether the girls told Frank about the new rules or not. But if they did, Frank didn't mention it. Thus the new routine began, and for the first time in their lives the girls were assigned daily chores. Rather than lightening Eve's workload, enforcing the new rules made her workdays seem longer. But she knew the time would come when her consistency would pay off.

Working eleven-hour days had not been what she'd had in mind when she applied for this job. Granted, with the girls in school, it wasn't eleven hours of solid work. But it was eleven hours away from home: an extra two hours each day for no extra pay that she wasn't free to visit, or shop, or clean her own home, or do whatever she wanted to do.

Her typical workday began at seven, when she would arrive at the redwood house and let herself in to pack the girls' lunches and cook breakfast before waking Frank and the girls. It wasn't all that hard to rouse Frank. But the girls were a different story. It generally took fifteen to twenty minutes to get them out of bed and in to the breakfast counter where their now cold breakfast was waiting. Once

Frank was gone, she would help the girls get ready for school—not an easy task where Jessica was concerned.

By the time the girls had had their usual morning squabble, and Jessica had fussed and argued over what she was to wear, dawdled over brushing her teeth, run screeching through the house at the sight of a hairbrush, locked herself in the bathroom, and somehow managed to lose her shoes, it would normally be 8:25 by the time Eve hustled them out of the house and into the car. This meant that Cindy would arrive at school when her classmates were already saying the Pledge of Allegiance, and Jessica would arrive at preschool twenty minutes late.

From the preschool, if it wasn't grocery day or Eve didn't have Frank's dry cleaning to take to the cleaners, she would return to the redwood house where she would make the beds, vacuum the dog hair in every room, mop the kitchen floor, take Ralston for a walk, and do the dishes. After lunch, it would be time to pick Jessica up from preschool and face the daily struggle of getting the little brat's seatbelt fastened when she didn't want to wear it. Except for Cindy's imperious attitude—which was improving—*she* was basically a nice little girl. But Jessica set Eve's teeth on edge. The child knew every button to push, and didn't hesitate to push them. "You can't make me," were her four favorite words.

Back home, it was time to put Jessica down for a nap—also not an easy task— and do three loads of laundry. At one forty-five, Eve would wake Jessica and half-drag, half-carry her to the car to pick Cindy up from school. From there, they would return home just long enough for a snack and for the girls to change into their tights and leotards, then it was off to tap or gymnastics. Eve would have preferred to leave the girls there and take a break to go somewhere on her own, but she was expected to stay and watch the lessons.

At four, Eve would drive the girls home where she would put dinner on the stove and supervise their homework while it was cooking. When homework was done, it was time to coach them on the Bible verses they were expected to have memorized in time for their weekly church activity. By six when either Frank or Carol arrived home, the girls would be through with dinner, and Eve and the girls would be seated in the living room reading stories together or watching T.V. Eve knew that Frank got off work early enough that he could easily be home by five o'clock. Instead, he rarely came home before six, and would often push it to six:fifteen.

If Eve hadn't had a social life to look forward to after hours, she wouldn't have been able to take it.

She had seen Gary several times and spent many hours talking to him by phone. Still, she was surprised when he called Wednesday night and asked her to spend the weekend with him at a cabin in Tahoe. She hadn't been to Tahoe since she was married to Kevin's father. It would be fun to get away for a weekend and play in the snow.

Friday evening, Eve was packing her bags when the phone rang. It was Gary saying they were going to have to take a raincheck on the weekend in Tahoe. He was going to go to a classic car show in Reno instead. Eve was welcome to go to the car show with him if she wanted to. It ticked Eve off that Gary had waited till the last minute to tell her he was changing their plans, then invited her as an after thought to go along. She wouldn't have gone with him at this point even if old cars had been the focal point of her life.

With Carla no longer available to go dancing, Eve had formed a friendship with a lady named Felicia. Shortly into their friendship, Felicia had told Eve about her frequent headaches. As soon as Eve had felt comfortable about mentioning it, she had told her new friend about the healing energy, and Felicia had allowed her to put the energy into the opal ring she always wore. Since that time, whenever Felicia had a headache, she would hold the opal ring to her forehead, and the headache would go away.

Eve was debating about asking her to go to tonight's dance at Sacramento Singles, but leaning strongly toward staying home with a good book. Though he rarely called her anymore since the night she refused to kiss him, Eve was uncomfortable with the knowledge that Bernie would be at the dance. Besides, the way she was feeling tonight, she'd be better off staying home.

"I think you should go," Saul said. "You've been working hard all week, and you deserve a break."

"I know," Eve said, "But Felicia doesn't really care for Sacramento Singles. She thinks the men there are too old."

"Call her anyway," Saul urged. "What do you have to lose?"

When Eve placed the call, Felicia said she had a splitting headache, and was planning to just go to bed.

"Have you tried the opal?" Eve asked.

"I don't use the opal for my headaches anymore," Felicia groaned. "It used to make the headaches go away at first. But now it only seems to make them worse."

When Eve had hung up the phone, she asked Saul why the ring would make Felicia's headaches more intense.

"There's the possibility she's touched hands with someone who's in touch with the dark ones," Saul said. "If someone from the occult touched the ring, it would have undone the energy—possibly even replaced the positive with negative."

Eve made a mental note to ask Felicia next time she saw her if she'd want the ring refreshed. But she was hesitant to do that because Felicia didn't know about Eve's contact with spirit guides. To tell her might freak her out.

"You don't need Felicia," Gideon said. "You know enough people at Sacramento Singles that you'd be comfortable going there by yourself."

"No," Eve said. "I'm just going to stay home and watch a movie on HBO."

"If you stay home, you know you'll be sorry," Saul said. "You know you always have a good time, once you're there. And they won't be having another dance this month. I think you ought to put on your miniskirt and go."

"I agree," Gideon put in. "You're always easier to get along with when you've gone dancing the night before."

If Eve had known how to do a raspberry, she would have done it. She knew Gideon was only teasing. But there was probably a grain of truth in what he'd said.

The more she thought about it, the more sense it made that if she went to the dance she'd be able to get her mind off Gary and the lost trip to Tahoe...

The dance was held in a large room with tables and chairs at one end, the dance floor in the middle, and a bar and disk jockey at the other end. By the time Eve arrived, most of the tables were taken and the dance floor was already crowded. Eve had found a seat, and was looking over the crowd when Bernie spotted her and came off the floor to ask her to dance.

Several songs later, Eve was taking a break when she saw the blonde man walk in. Apparently no one had told him the unofficial dress code for Sacramento Singles. Instead of a suit, or slacks and a sports coat, he was wearing boots and jeans and a blue flannel shirt with a navy blue turtleneck underneath. Eve guessed him to be five to ten years older than she. In contrast to the pale color of his hair, his skin was deeply tanned, hinting of long hours spent working or playing in the sun. Oddly enough, it wasn't his blonde hair or large nose that stood out as his most noticeable feature. It was his eyes—blue, like Eve's: the color of a cloudless sky on a sunny day. Eve wondered if he would ask her to dance.

Before going back out onto the dance floor, Eve decided to get a Coke. She hadn't noticed that the blonde man was at the bar getting a beer, till he turned around as she was approaching. Startled by the eye contact, Eve had already passed him before she realized he had smiled and spoken. Turning back to look over her shoulder, she caught him looking back at her. This time she smiled and spoke in return. Yes. He definitely would ask her to dance.

Three songs later, the blonde approached and introduced himself as Chet McCrellis. He said he was a construction worker, and didn't normally come to these dances, but tonight he had come to see his friend Walt. The friend he had come to see was the older man Joan had said was interested in Carla.

When Chet took Eve's hand to lead her onto the dance floor, Eve was aware of the calluses on his fingers and palm. When he pulled her close and buried his nose in her hair, she became aware of the faint lime scent of his cologne. Since re-joining the singles circuit, Eve had become very aware of masculine scents. Considering that whatever scent her dance partner was wearing would be rubbed off on her and mingled with all the others, it could turn out to be quite a scent concoction by the end of the evening. This was one of the reasons she rarely wore cologne of her own.

As Eve and Chet danced first one slow dance, then another, when Chet wasn't busy nuzzling her neck or smelling her hair, or telling her how great she felt in his arms, they talked.

Caught off guard by Chet's offbeat sense of humor, Eve found herself laughing till her sides actually hurt. She'd had too many hard times in recent months. It felt good to laugh, and let herself go. Judging from the gleam in Chet's eyes, he was enjoying her company as much as she was enjoying his.

When Eve told Chet she was a nanny, she was pleasantly surprised by his reaction. She didn't know what she'd expected. Disdain? Condescension? Perhaps the typical question: *Isn't a nanny just a glorified baby-sitter?* She should have given him more credit than that. When Chet heard the word "nanny" his eyes lit up. "I've always wanted to *date* a nanny—to have my own personal Mary Poppins." It was definitely beginning to sound as if Chet could turn out to be romantic interest number three.

But when the second dance ended, Chet excused himself, saying he needed to go talk to Walter, and making no mention of seeing Eve later. If he was going to become a romantic interest, he would have to do better than that.

Eve had danced with a couple other partners when the music suddenly stopped, and the disc jockey asked that the dance floor be cleared. A corner of one of the wooden squares in the floor had come loose and was posing a hazard. Eve was standing on one side of the dance floor with her partner and a crowd of perhaps fifteen other couples. Across the floor was a second crowd of perhaps twelve or fifteen more. It seemed to take forever for a repairman to come out on the dance floor and repair the damaged square. Eve didn't know what had become of Chet. When she'd glanced toward the tables a moment ago, she had seen Walter talking to a small group of women. Chet had been nowhere in sight. Was it possible he'd left without saying "Goodnight," or asking for her phone number? Eve hoped not.

When the floor had been repaired and dancing had resumed, Eve danced a couple more with the same partner before being escorted back to her table. She was sitting at the table sipping her Coke when the disc jockey announced there would be a short intermission. Intermission from what? They'd already taken a twenty-minute break to fix the blasted floor!

During intermission, the disc jockey put on a stack of oldies but goodies, and headed for the bar. Glancing up, Eve saw Chet bearing down on her from across the room. Considering that there was an empty chair at her table, Eve assumed that he intended to sit down. Instead he dropped to one knee at her feet and reached for her hand. What in the—

"Earth angel, earth angel," he sang with the record, "will you be mine?" At the table next to hers, Eve saw two women smiling behind their hands. From across the room, Bernie was giving her a look that asked if this guy was for real. Eve was wondering the same thing herself.

"...I'm just a fool. A fool in love with you. Oo hoo hoo hoo hoo..."

Wishing she were invisible, Eve squirmed in her seat. "Would you please get up?" she whispered. Actually, his voice didn't sound that bad; but he was drawing attention. When at last the song ended, there was a smattering of applause.

Eve was relieved when Chet got up off his knee and sat down in the chair beside her. When he scooted his chair closer and put an arm around her shoulders, it felt so natural she didn't resist. She couldn't believe how comfortable she felt with this man she hardly knew. He wasn't at all the type she normally dated. His rugged features brought to mind actors such as Charles Bronson and Nick Nolte— men who, rather than being handsome, had a raw sex appeal.

The first song, when the dance resumed, was a mixer. Chet took Eve's hand and led her onto the dance floor.

"You're supposed to stand in line with the other men," Eve said. "I stand with the other women, and everyone takes turns dancing with everyone else."

"I couldn't care less what we're supposed to do," Chet said. "I want us to dance every dance *together*."

Eve wasn't normally one who broke established rules. Still, she guessed it wouldn't be the end of the world if they didn't take part in the mixer. "Okay," she said. "But the others aren't going to like it."

"Who cares what anyone else thinks?" Chet said, leading her into the aisle between the facing rows of men and women. "It's just you and me, and we can do whatever we want."

Toward the end of the evening, when they sat down to take a break, Chet asked for Eve's number. After she'd given it to him, he debated whether to memorize it or write it on his hand. In the end, he suggested giving Eve *his* number instead. "That way if you want to see me again, you can call. If I don't hear from you, I'll know you weren't interested."

This was the first time a man had ever offered Eve his phone number without taking hers as well. But she liked it this way. This way, the ball was in her court. "I have a pen," she said, "but you'll have to write your number on a napkin. I don't have any paper."

As she slipped the napkin into her purse, Eve told Chet she'd give him a call in two or three days. Later, walking her out to her car, Chet made a wrong turn and they ended up on the patio under the stars. "I'm going to kiss you," Chet said with a crooked grin.

This was certainly a different approach from what Eve was used to—having a man stand there and announce he was going to kiss her. "Is that right?"

"Yes," he said as he gathered her into his arms. "I've always wondered what it would be like to kiss Mary Poppins..."

When they got to Eve's car, Chet got inside to keep warm. They talked a while longer and kissed some more, each kiss deeper than the one before. It definitely wasn't like Eve to act like this with a man she'd just met—or with any man, for that matter—necking in the car like a couple of teen-agers... When Chet got out to leave, he walked around and tapped on the driver's side window. "Just one more kiss, then I'll say goodnight..."

Eve waited three days, then called Chet Tuesday evening. Chet answered the phone on the first ring. "Hello?"

"Chet? This is Eve."

"I was just trying to call you," Chet said. "But I couldn't remember your number. I remembered part of it, and I was combining that with every number combination I could think of. I've called doctors, lawyers, and Indian chiefs..."

"I told you I'd call you in two or three days," Eve said with a smile. "Today's the third day."

"I know you said two or three days," Chet said. "But after we had so much fun together, I expected you to call the next day. When you didn't, I thought sure you'd call the next. But when two days went by and you still didn't call, I was afraid I'd blown it by not writing down your number. I was afraid I'd never see you again."

Finally, a man understood what it was like to be in a position of waiting for the phone to ring. "I said two or three days," Eve reminded him. "This is the third day."

"I'm just glad you called," Chet said. "I was running out of number combinations. Would you like to go out to dinner tonight? If you like Mexican food, we could go to El Torrito's."

Next to meat and potatoes, Mexican food was Eve's favorite.

"Do you have jeans and boots you could wear?"

"Sure," Eve said. "I take it that means you don't want me to dress up."

"What I wore to the dance the other night was the most dressed up I ever get," Chet said. "As cute as you looked in that little miniskirt with those little black shoes, I can hardly wait to see you in jeans and boots."

Eve was glad Chet liked boots and jeans, because that's the way she preferred to dress: that, or jeans and tennis shoes.

When Chet picked her up that evening to take her to El Torrito's, he was wearing his usual jeans and boots with a flannel shirt, open at the throat and rolled up at the sleeves. His chest was tanned, but hairless. "I knew you were gonna look sexy in jeans and boots," he said with a lopsided grin. "And that sweater's not half bad either." The pink and white bulky sweater had been a Christmas gift from Eve's brother-in-law. It was the first time she'd worn it. She was glad now she had.

Later, in his S10, Chet told Eve he hadn't intended to go to the Sacramento Singles dance the night they met, but a little voice kept prodding him to go. Now he was glad he'd listened.

It was the first time Eve had ever gone on a date in a pickup truck. The gray S-10 was immaculate, except for the fact that it smelled of cigarettes. Eve hadn't realized Chet was a smoker. His kisses had tasted of mint.

Over dinner, they talked about their lives—previous marriages, reasons for divorce, children... Eve told about the fire that had burned the restaurant she'd traded her house for, and how the fire and its aftermath had caused her to lose everything she'd owned. The topics of conversation were heavy, but neither seemed to mind.

Eve liked Chet. She wanted to spend more time with him. But if he wasn't going to be accepting of her guides, it was pointless to pursue a relationship. The time had come to tell him about *them*...

"I've lived in a house that had spirits," Chet said. "They scared the shit out of my kids. There was one that used to stand at the foot of my daughter's bed at night. It had a black cloak with a hood, and she couldn't see its face."

Eve recognized the description as the same spirit as the one who used to torment Kevin when he was a little boy: the one who had cast the energy net over him and stung him when he tried to get out of bed to run to her. "Those aren't the kind of spirits I'm talking about," Eve said. "The ones *I'm* talking about are guides. Everyone has them. They're not scary at all. One of them is my guardian angel. The other is my healing guide. My healing guide taught me the art of natural healing."

Chet had listened in silence until now, but Eve could tell he was dying to speak. When he did, it was to say there was no such thing as a good spirit.

"That's where you're wrong," Eve argued. "My guides are very loving and wise—sometimes even funny."

By the end of the evening, despite the fact Eve had pulled a headache out of his head, Chet remained unconvinced, but still said he would call her tomorrow. When Eve got home, Saul asked how she liked Chet.

"I like him a lot," Eve said. "But he says there's no such thing as a good spirit. My relationship with you and Gideon would just cause trouble if I got involved with him."

"Don't be so quick to make a decision," Saul said. "I know what he said tonight. But my advice is to give him another chance."

Gideon was quick to second the motion. It seemed to Eve they were pushing awfully hard. She had thought *she* was the one who was supposed to be making this decision. Given the fact she wasn't attracted to Bernie, and Gary had proven to be selfish and inconsiderate, if Chet was the third man and she didn't choose him, she'd be out of luck. She knew better than to *ask* if he was the third man. They'd never tell her and take the chance the dark ones were listening.

"What's it going to hurt to go out with this guy again?" Saul asked. "You said yourself he's fun to be with. And I know you're physically attracted to him. Humor me on this, Sweetheart. Just give him another chance."

When Chet called the next evening and asked if Eve would like to go to Denny's for dinner, she told him since Denny's was just down the street, she'd meet him there. Over patty melts and fries, Eve mentioned to Chet that she had a lot of things in storage that she needed to sort through this weekend so she could bring her belongings to the apartment. That way, she'd be able to save on a month's storage rent, and wouldn't have to move things from two separate locations when she managed to find an affordable apartment.

"Let me go with you," Chet said. "We'll use my pick-up. We can start early Saturday morning and have breakfast at Denny's. Then we'll go to your storage shed, and I'll help you sort. It'll be fun."

Eve couldn't imagine why any man would want to help a woman sort through boxes of junk and memorabilia. But it would be nice to have the company. "Okay," she said. "If that's what you want to do. But it's *not* going to be fun."

When Chet came Saturday morning to pick Eve up, Carla answered the door.

"You must be Carla," Chet said. "How are you doing, Honey?"

"And you must be Chet," Carla replied. "Come in. I'll tell Eve you're here."

Eve could hear them from the bedroom. When she came out to the living room and saw Chet for the first time in a short-sleeved flannel shirt with the sleeves rolled up, her eyes widened at the size of his biceps. At the dance, in the long-sleeved shirt he'd been wearing, she'd had no idea he was into weight lifting. She didn't have long to ponder. Chet closed the distance between them in two long strides and pulled her into his arms. The kiss lasted so long that Carla came to her rescue: "Will you please let the poor girl come up for air?"

Breakfast at Denny's was lighthearted. On the way to the storage shed they made an agreement that anything in the memorabilia that stirred memories of pain or anger would be discarded to throw in the dumpster.

The knickknacks in the first box were hydro cal figures Eve had painted for the restaurant she and Nick had owned when they were married. The restaurant had been burned by an arsonist, and they'd been forced into bankruptcy as a result. When Eve opened the box, her eyes welled with tears.

"Dumpster?" Chet said.

"Dumpster," Eve agreed.

Chet emptied the box into the trash bin, then returned to take Eve into his muscular arms and stroke her hair till her tears had subsided. The next box contained memorabilia having to do with Eve's first Christmas with Nick and his son, and the next after that contained items from when Eve was a teacher. She kept the school related items and dumped the box having to do with Nick.

When Eve came to the box containing the manuscript of a novel she'd written while married to Nick, she dissolved in tears. They'd had such high hopes that this book would be the key to getting back on the board after their restaurant had burned. They'd acted out the romantic scenes together so Eve could hone in on precisely what her heroine would experience when the hero kissed her and caressed her body. They'd even acted out a physical struggle so Eve could test her description of how to break free of a chokehold. Dabbing at the tears with her arm, Eve lovingly laid the dog-eared manuscript aside and turned to another carton.

It wasn't until she and Chet were in the pick-up headed back to the valley that Eve realized her manuscript was not in the truck. "Where's my manuscript?" she asked frantically. "We must have left it. We have to go back."

"It made you cry, so I threw it in the dumpster," Chet said. "I'm sorry. I didn't realize you wanted to keep it."

"But that manuscript took me a year to write! I was planning to expand it when I get a computer, and try again to find a publisher!" Eve knew it wasn't Chet's fault. They'd agreed to throw away anything that upset her. She should have told him the manuscript was an exception.

That night, when Chet took her to Denny's, their waitress escorted them to their favorite booth. After dinner, they came back to the apartment and sat in the S10 in the parking lot talking for nearly three hours—kissing, talking, then kissing some more. At the end of a long kiss, Chet cupped Eve's chin in his hand and looked into her eyes. "I adore you."

This was a first for Eve, having a man say he adored her. If Chet was to be the third romantic interest, this was definitely a good sign.

When Eve went to answer an ad on an affordable apartment where the fact that she was new on the job wouldn't pose a problem, Chet went with her. Since the tenants hadn't moved out yet, the only apartment available to show was the manager's. "The apartment is almost identical to mine," the manager said. "The only difference is my carpet's beige, and yours will be brown."

Eve didn't particularly care for the location of the apartment complex, and the stairs leading to the second story apartment were badly in need of a coat of paint. But the manager's one-bedroom apartment was neat and attractively decorated. The only real problem appeared to be the lack of storage space.

"There are storage units available on the second floor," the manager said. "Twenty-five a month will get you a four by six room."

Over-riding Eve's hesitation, Chet told the manager she would take the storage unit. He would pay the storage fee until she was on her feet. "I'll store some of my stuff in there too, if that will make you feel better," he said. "That way you won't have to feel guilty."

With the storage problem solved, the only problem remaining was coming up with the four hundred dollar security deposit. Eve didn't mention the deposit to Chet. She didn't want him volunteering to pay it himself.

Though Eve and Chet were meeting every evening at Denny's now for dinner or coffee and hot chocolate, Eve still had an obligation to continue her dance lessons with Bernie. When she confided to Bernie that she'd found an apartment, but didn't know yet how she was going to come up with the deposit, Bernie offered to lend her the money. Though Eve appreciated the offer, she thanked him and said she couldn't accept it. Instead, the following day, she went to the manager's apartment after work and told him her predicament. The manager agreed to allow her to make the deposit in three monthly installments.

The following week when Eve drove to the community college to meet Bernie for their lesson, Bernie asked her about Chet. "Are you really dating that guy you were with that night at the Sacramento Singles? He had his nose in your ear half the night. He didn't even know how to dress."

"We have a lot in common," Eve said. "We even both used to be into freelance writing. I enjoy his company. He's fun to be with."

Bernie had taken Eve's arm, and they were walking toward the gym where the Country Western dance lesson was to be held. "What did you do about the security deposit on your apartment?" Bernie asked.

"That's taken care of," Eve said. "I'll be moving in next week."

Bernie's mouth and moustache twisted in a derisive sneer. "You sold out, didn't you. You slept with that guy so he'd pay your deposit."

If Eve could have reached Bernie's face, she would have slapped it. Instead, she stopped dead in her tracks. "Not that that question deserves an answer," she grated, "but, for your information, the manager agreed to let me make the deposit in payments."

Realizing he had gone too far, Bernie apologized, but the damage had been done.

"You know what, Bernie? I don't really feel like dancing. You'll have to dance with the teacher tonight. I'm going home."

"Aw come on, Eve," Bernie said. "I didn't mean it."

Ignoring his pleas to forget he'd ever said it, Eve turned and stalked back in the direction of her car. He had the same as called her a whore, then asked her to forget it. *Bastard.* If she never saw him again, it would be too soon.

Chapter 38

When moving day arrived, Chet showed up early dressed in jeans, a rolled sleeve flannel shirt and cowboy boots, to load Eve's belongings into the gray S10. As always, his smile and enthusiasm were infectious. Eve felt a surge as she watched the bulge of his muscles when he lifted her end tables into the truck bed. She didn't know what she'd have done without him. She couldn't have afforded to hire a moving van. And she didn't know anyone else she could have asked to help.

When they arrived at the apartment house, Eve went to the manager's to get the keys to her apartment and storage while Chet parked the truck as close to the stairs as he could manage and began to unload.

Rather than climb the stairs empty handed, Eve stacked a couple of medium weight boxes and carried them up. The white paint on the steps and stair rail was peeling. When Eve got to the top of the stairs, she glanced down and saw that someone had spilled a cup of coffee on the battleship gray porch and hadn't even bothered to clean it up. She hoped this wasn't typical of tenant pride in this apartment house. If it was, she might as well be living in a slum.

The gray building was wicket shaped, with a pool and a small patch of lawn in the center, edged in pink and white azaleas. Eve's apartment was halfway down the long section of building that formed the cross piece of the wicket. Chet was waiting outside her apartment, smoking a cigarette.

When Eve got to the apartment, Chet extinguished the cigarette on the sole of his boot and took the boxes so she could unlock the door. Eve had yet to see any of the apartments other than the manager's. When she swung open the door, her heart sank into her tennis shoes. *This* apartment wasn't like the *manager's*! His had been light and airy. This one had dark brown paneling on the walls. It looked like a tomb!

Stepping inside, Eve looked toward the kitchen straight ahead. The wooden half bar serving as a partial divider was scratched and deeply gouged. The kitchen floor, from what Eve could see from this vantage point, was the color of chewed gum. The manager's lino had been white, to match his white appliances.

As if in a trance, Eve walked to the kitchen. Several of the brown counter tiles were cracked. Apparently the grout between them had deteriorated. That, or someone had dug it out. The gas stove was pea green; the refrigerator pastel pink. This wasn't a kitchen. It was a nightmare!

Afraid of what she was about to find, Eve walked down the dark hallway to the small bathroom at the end. The cheap bathroom lino was a hideous pattern of gray and bubble gum pink, stained purple along the length of the tub from water seeping underneath. The shower/tub alcove had no plastic curtain or glass door enclosure—only a huge rust stain around the drain. By the sink, the ivory counter tiles were pitted. A shudder of revulsion coursed through Eve's body when her gaze dropped to the base of the toilet, streaked with yellow stains. Tears of anger and disappointment coursed down her cheeks.

Behind her, Chet hadn't said a word.

"I can't live here," Eve said brokenly. "This place is a dump."

Now that the shocked silence had been broken, Chet gathered Eve into his arms. "It doesn't look like the manager's place. But it can be fixed up. You'll see."

His strong arms felt warm and comforting, but not comforting enough to dispel the feeling of gloom that had settled over her. "The living room looks like a cave," Eve moaned. "The kitchen looks like something from tenement housing. The only decent room in the entire apartment is the bedroom, and *it* doesn't even have curtains."

"I'll help you," Chet said. "We'll fix it up together. It'll be fine. You'll see."

The thought of coming home to this at the end of an eleven-hour day at work was almost more than Eve could take.

Her first three evenings in the apartment were spent unpacking boxes, lining cupboard shelves, and arranging and re-arranging her meager stock of furnishings. Now that Eve was no longer competition, and Carla was no longer thinking of her as a con artist, Carla called nightly to chat—just as she had done when Eve lived in Placerville.

Each afternoon when he got off work, Chet would take a nap at his own apartment before coming to Eve's where dinner would be waiting. The fourth day, when Eve arrived home from work, she was surprised to see Chet's S10 already in the parking lot. She hadn't given him a key to the apartment—only a key to the storage. He must have brought a load of things over. Trying not to look at the chipped paint and dirty porch, Eve climbed the stairs and walked the distance to her apartment. When she opened the door, she gaped.

Leaning against the partial divider, grinning from ear to ear, Chet was having a beer. "Surprise."

Surprise wasn't the word for it. The dark paneling was gone from the living room walls. The walls had been textured and painted white. Gouges in the divider bar had been filled and stained. In the kitchen and dining area, the gray chewing gum linoleum had been scrubbed till it gleamed, and partially hidden beneath two mauve throw rugs Chet had bought to match Eve's kitchen utensils. Two silk plants in white macramé hangers had been hung in the kitchen window.

"How did you get in to do all this?" Eve gasped. "Does the manager know you took down the paneling?"

"The manager let me in," Chet said with a grin. "I told him this apartment looked like shit. When he found out I was in construction and it wouldn't cost him a cent, he gave me the go ahead to fix this place up. I figured I'd re-grout the tile in the kitchen, and spray paint the stove and refrigerator with almond appliance paint."

On a roll, Chet laid out the rest of his plan. "I have a piece of white lino with a pale ivory design that I can put in the bathroom. Maybe in a few weeks, I can replace the lino in the kitchen. Once you get some pictures on the walls and set your little knickknacks out, this place is going to look cozy."

Turning to face him with tears in her eyes, Eve smiled a tremulous smile. "I can't believe you're doing all this for me."

"I can't let my little honey live in a dump," Chet said. "Besides, I plan to spend a lot of time here. So I had an ulterior motive."

It seemed to Eve that lately she was always crying. "You are so sweet," she said through her tears. "Thank you."

While Chet was out on the porch having another cigarette, Eve called Carla to tell her what he'd done. "Are you sure Chet's not really Chad?" Carla asked.

"What you mean, am I sure he's not Chad? Chad's out of the picture."

"Maybe not," Carla said. "I've been thinking a lot about this. I think maybe Gideon and Saul lied about what Chad looked like so nothing would happen to keep you two apart, but *Myra* almost screwed it up when she told you he was clean shaven and blonde! Remember? She said he had blonde hair and dark skin. *Chet* has blonde hair and a dark *tan*. Myra told you Chad loves to travel. *Chet* loves to travel, and they both love to dance! Think about it, Eve. What did you tell me Chet said to you that night in his truck? He said he *adores* you—exactly what Myra said Chad would do. She also said Chad likes to read, and has a horse ranch. *Chet* lives in an *apartment* now, but I think you should at least check that one out."

How could Eve not have seen these things herself? If Gideon and Saul had lied to protect her relationship with Chet, she couldn't very well ask *them* to blow his cover. But she could darned sure get some more information from Chet!

After she was off the phone, Eve brewed a pot of coffee for Chet and sat down at the table with a Pepsi to wait for him to come back inside. His smoking habit was the one thing that bothered her. She didn't have an ashtray to her name, and didn't intend to buy one. Maybe if he got tired enough of having to go outside to smoke, he'd give it up. Eve could hear him outside joking with her next-door neighbor.

When Chet came back inside, Eve asked him to sit down. "There's something I was wondering about. You always wear jeans and flannel shirts. Have you ever lived on a ranch, or owned a horse?"

"Yeah," Chet said. "When I was married, I used to board ten Arab mares and I owned an Arab stallion. His name was Zodi. He was the grandson of Raffles."

Eve had never heard of Raffles, but assumed he must be famous. Otherwise Chet wouldn't have mentioned it. "What about books?" she asked, rising to pour Chet a cup of coffee. "We talked about a lot of things the night we met, but you didn't mention whether you like to read."

Chet had pulled out a chair and sat down with his legs stretched out under the table in front of him, and his arms crossed in front of his chest. "I used to have a library of books, mostly about world religions. That was also when I had long hair and a beard. My hair was darker then. I'd sit in my bed with books all around me, and study about ancient history and world religions. When we split up, my ex-wife sold all my books at a garage sale."

This was unreal. Everything the spirits and Myra had said about Chet was true, except that the most of the things were from the past—not current, as they'd been presented to be. The only thing missing was the hairy chest. Was this all part of the camouflage?

"Before we met," Eve asked in a tiny voice, "did you ever have dreams about me? Did you ever wake up smelling of a strange cologne that hadn't been there when you went to sleep?" There. It was out. If he didn't know what she was talking about, he would probably think she was a blooming idiot.

"I never remember my dreams," Chet said. "What man *hasn't* woke up smelling of a strange cologne at one time or other? But I prayed about you."

"You *prayed* about me? What did you pray?"

Chet took a sip from his coffee and winced. "Man, that sucker's *hot*. I told God exactly what I wanted in a woman. She had to be small—five foot two just like you—and I wanted her to have blue eyes just like yours. She had to like dancing as much as I do, and not get jealous when I talk to other women. And she had to be willing to let me be myself. You fit the bill all the way down the line."

So Carla was right. Chet *was* Chad. Eve knew now for certain which of the three men she'd been meant to choose. "I think I could love you," she said softly.

"Well I'm glad of that," Chet answered. "Because I think I could love you too. And there's nothing I'd like more than to be the man who gives you back everything you've lost in your lifetime."

Those were without a doubt the sweetest words any man had ever said to Eve.

Chapter 39

For the next three months, Eve and Chet were together every evening and every weekend. Since Chet loved to travel and Eve didn't, they compromised by choosing a different site each weekend to go for a one-day jaunt. Everywhere they went, Eve took her camera.

At Marine World, Eve unwittingly pleased Chet to no end by waiting in line for hamburgers then serving him at the outdoor table, and later laying her head on his shoulder as they watched the whale and dolphin show. At Calaveras County, where Chet bought a frog to take part in the jumping frog contest, Eve took notes on logging events for use in the novel she intended to rewrite. When they went to see the giant redwoods, they marveled at God's creations, and cringed at the desecration men had caused by carving their initials in the magnificent trunks, and cutting down the tallest tree of all just to show it off at the New York World Fair.

One particular Sunday, Chet said he'd like to go to Placerville to see where Eve used to work and live. Eve took him on a tour of the hospital, and introduced him to Mrs. Stillwell. While she was there, she took the time to raise Mrs. Stilwell's bed and hold the old lady's hands in hers. At first Mrs. Stillwell didn't recognize Eve in ordinary clothes, but the instant she felt the energy, she knew. "You look so pretty in that blue sweater. I should have recognized your eyes right off, but I didn't until you touched me."

"What about that Aspercreme?" Eve asked with a smile. "Is it doing the job for you?"

The shriveled little woman seemed to have grown even smaller since Eve left. "It works pretty well," she said with a conspiratorial smile. "But you'd better beef it up while you're here."

In the bed next to hers, Mrs. Japetto suddenly cried out, "I'm blind! I can't see!"

Mrs. Japetto had been asleep when Eve came in. Now as Eve glanced her way, she smiled. "You need to open your eyes, Mrs. Japetto. If you open your eyes, everything will be fine."

"Oh," Mrs. Japetto said in a reedy voice. "That's better. Is that you, Eve? Could you re-adjust my pillows and change my sheets? I'm wet. Maybe before you go, you can give *me* some of that healing energy like you gave Irene."

"I'll call your aide to change your sheet," Eve replied. "If we're still here when they serve your lunch, I'll feed you. Okay?"

Chet had wanted to meet the patients he'd heard so much about. Now was his chance to experience them firsthand. From the room down the hall, he heard Thelma's voice crying for her Mama to take her home. He met Florence, and was treated to a string of obscenities. And everywhere he walked, Norma followed in her wheelchair. "What's my name? Do you like my ear rings?"

At lunchtime, Eve fed Mrs. Japetto, and Chet helped Mrs. Stillwell. When they were ready to leave, Mrs. Stillwell squeezed Eve's hand and nodded toward Chet with a smile. "He's a keeper, Dear."

Before starting back down the hill, Eve and Chet stopped at Bob's Big Boy for a late lunch. "I used to eat here all the time," Chet commented. "Sometimes I'd eat brunch at the country restaurant across the street."

Eve didn't tell Chet that she'd actually gone to the country restaurant looking for him. Some things were best left untold.

On the way back to the valley, they stopped at a roadside display of Indian beadworks and dream catchers. One in particular caught Chet's eye. "Look at this, Angel. It would be perfect with that Indian picture you have."

The dream catcher was a large circle of colorful beadwork with white eagle feathers. Eve agreed it was beautiful. She'd never seen one quite like it.

"How much?" Chet asked the Indian behind the table.

"Fifty dollars."

"We'll take it," Chet said. "My little Angel has the perfect spot for it."

Eve wouldn't have spent the fifty dollars herself. But the dream catcher *would* look great in her living room. "I love it. Thank you."

"Before you put it in your car," Saul said in her head, "you need to clear it. There's an evil spirit that comes with it."

"In the name of Jesus," Eve said under her breath, "I command you to leave."

When Eve got into the S10 to go home, a gust of wind picked up her hair just as she slammed the door. "Ow!" she cried. "The door closed on my hair!"

The truck door had slammed shut on her hair, pulling several strands out by the roots. "That'll teach you to try to keep us out, bitch."

"We can't take this home," Eve said irritably. "There's a dark spirit attached to it. It just talked to me in my head."

"There's nothing wrong with the dream catcher," Chet snarled. "I bought it, and we're taking it home! In the name of Jesus, leave this dream catcher and get *out of this truck*. Leave us the fuck alone!"

By the time they got the dream catcher home, they had said enough prayers that they were convinced whatever evil spirit had been "attached" to it was gone. Eve hung it next to the Indian portrait, in the living room above the loveseat.

Actually the apartment was starting to look good: looking better all the time.

Couched between weekend outings and other leisure activities, Chet replaced the bathroom lino, spray painted the kitchen appliances, and re-grouted the kitchen tile, as promised. Eve made curtains for her bedroom, and hung pictures and silk plants in every room. When they weren't talking about everything under the stars, Chet was singing—making up his own lyrics to familiar tunes. The words to his songs were always about Eve. "Once in love with Evie, always in love with Evie. Ever and ever, she's my turtle dover. I will always love her, you see? Cause Evie is in love—with—me."

When Chet came down with a virus and was unable to work, Eve endeared herself to him forever by getting up an hour early each morning to drive to his apartment and serve him his breakfast before going to work herself. She wasn't skilled enough yet in healing to be able to cure a virus, but at least she could do everything in her power to keep him comfortable.

After Chet was well, together, he and Eve wallpapered the lower third of her dining room walls with a whimsical pattern of baby ducks, and covered the top edge with chair rail molding. Except for the chewing gum color of the linoleum, the kitchen and dining room had been transformed.

When the renovation was finished, Chet took Eve and Kevin to dinner to celebrate, and brought Kevin back to Eve's to get acquainted. It was the first time Chet and Kevin had met, and the first time Kevin had seen his mom's apartment.

"What do you think?" Chet asked Kevin after they'd been there for awhile. "Don't you think your mom's apartment is cozy?"

"It's nice," Kevin replied, glancing around, and grinning at the duck pattern on the dining room wall. "It looks like my mom."

All in all, life was good now that Eve had met Chet at last. But she missed Gideon.

Gideon had told her long ago that when a permanent mate came into her life he would be fading into the background so as not to interfere; but more recently he'd explained that as she progressed toward her goal as a powerful healer, his job as her protector would become more and more demanding. Eve missed her daily talks with him, but understood that if he was involved in psychological warfare he couldn't afford to be distracted.

Eve was glad Chet had come to know Saul, and no longer believed all spirits were bad. She was concerned about a patch on Chet's neck below his ear. The skin on this patch had grown red and scaly, and it wasn't responding to her healing touch. When Eve asked Saul about it, he said it was a pre-cancerous condition. The reason it wasn't responding was that her healing powers weren't developed enough yet to deal with this kind of problem. A visit to a dermatologist confirmed Saul's diagnosis.

They had spent the day shooting pictures of old barns, and were sitting in Eve's living room snuggled on the loveseat Eve had purchased at a garage sale when she was going with Whit. "This is Kevin at his freshman prom," Eve said, pointing to a snapshot in her album. "He's really changed since then. And this was me three years ago when I had short hair."

"My teeny tiny Angel," Chet said affectionately. "This album goes back fifteen years, and you're the same size now as you were back then. You haven't gained an ounce. My ex-wife had a *great* figure when I married her. But then she let herself go. It's good to know I don't ever have to worry about *you* gaining weight."

Within three days after Chet made the comment about never having to worry about Eve's gaining weight, she began to bloat from everything she ate or drank. Maintaining her weight became a constant struggle.

Chapter 40

The sound of a gunshot startled Eve awake. Loud voices from the apartment next door sounded as if they were coming from her own living room. "You son of a bitch!" a woman's voice screamed. "Get your fucking ass out of here before you hurt the baby!"

Frightened, Eve shrank beneath the covers. She knew the young couple next door were having marital problems. The husband had told Chet he was out of work, and Eve knew he was a heavy drinker. Often he would stand outside leaning on the porch rail, drinking one beer after another, and muttering beneath his breath.

Eve shrank even deeper into the covers when she heard the sound of the police pounding on the neighbor's door. "Police!" a deep voice shouted. "Open up!"

Eve heard the door open, then the sound of muffled voices followed by the retreating sound of footsteps. Then silence.

She was tempted to call Chet, but it was three in the morning. They'd been up till midnight talking on the board, and Chet needed his sleep. Eve's guides preferred to talk through the board when Chet was around so he could see with his own eyes that Eve wasn't swinging the pendulum, rather than speaking telepathically to Eve and having her relay their words to Chet. Lately it seemed that their time together was being dominated by conversations on the board.

"Sweetheart," Gideon said, "This is Gideon, and I'm of the light. I don't want you having anything to do with your next-door neighbors. His drinking is getting worse, and he's dangerous when he drinks. And while we're on the topic of dangerous, I hadn't mentioned this before, but there's a man who lives in a downstairs apartment that's been watching you when you come and go from the parking lot."

Eve had seen a homeless man several times hanging around by the dumpster, but the man Gideon was talking about lived in a downstairs apartment. Eve wondered if he could be the gray-haired man she'd seen in the laundry room. She had sensed that he was watching her, but when she'd glanced in his direction, he'd been looking the other way.

"That's the one," Gideon said. "You need to stay clear of him. He's basically harmless, but he has fantasies."

The next day, Eve took her dirty laundry with her to work. No point in tempting fate. That evening after work, she went to Chet's apartment in Carmichael. Since his refrigerator and cupboards were empty and they didn't really feel like going out, they sent out for pizza. They were seated at the dining room table eating sausage and pepperoni pizza when there was a tap at the door.

When Chet answered, Eve could see from where she was sitting that the person at the door appeared to be an old lady. Her hair was gray, and her cheeks heavily rouged. "Can you spare an old woman five dollars?" the old lady asked. Her voice was slurred, as if she'd been on a binge.

Apparently Chet recognized the woman. At any rate, he invited her in, and dug in his pocket for a five dollar bill. Why would Chet encourage an obvious alcoholic? He should have offered to brew a cup of coffee!

"My name's Martha O'Hannalan," the visitor slurred in a thick Irish brogue, approaching Eve, and extending her hand. "Who might you be?"

The smell of cheap whiskey was overwhelming.

Now that Chet wasn't standing between them, Eve could see that the drunken visitor was wearing a beige floral print dress with thick nylons and clunky black shoes. Her arms were covered by the sleeves of a black sweater. Accepting the hand that was offered, Eve inwardly cringed. "I'm Eve."

The handshake was strong, and the hand heavily callused. Seen at close rage, the pores on the woman's broad nose and sagging cheeks were huge. Above her lip was the faint trace of a shadow. This wasn't a woman! It was a *man*, and not a very attractive one at that! What was wrong with Chet that he couldn't see that?

"So where are you off to tonight?" Chet asked.

"I thought I'd stop off at the Boot," the visitor slurred. "There's a smalltime dealer there I've had me eye on. If luck is with me, I'll collar him tonight."

Collar him? Was this guy talking about a citizen's arrest? In his condition, he'd be lucky to "collar" a skunk!

Up to this point, Chet had played along with the game, watching Eve's reaction through the corner of his eye. Now he introduced his friend as being Tom Barstow, a retired officer from the F.B.I. who lived in a neighboring apartment. "Tom likes to go out in drag to catch small time drug dealers and pimps."

Relieved to know that Chet wasn't as naïve as she'd feared, Eve listened to the explanation with an uncomfortable smile. "I was wondering," she said weakly.

"Do you happen to have any lipstick in your purse?" Tom asked.

Eve always carried a tube of lipstick, but she had no desire to share it with a man! Both Tom and Chet were looking at her expectantly. If she said she didn't have any, Chet would know she was lying. With obvious reluctance, Eve dug through her purse and produced a tube of mauve frost.

"I don't have a mirror," Tom said. The drunken slur and accent were gone. "Could you put it on for me?"

This couldn't be for real. In another moment, Eve would wake up and realize it had all been a dream. But there he was standing in front of her with his mouth partially open, waiting expectantly. "I've never put lipstick on anyone else," Eve said uneasily.

"I'm sure you'll do just fine," Tom said with a wink. The moment was surreal. With a trembling hand, Eve raised the tube to Tom's mouth and tried to shut out the sight of his rouged cheeks as she traced his lips. It gave her the creeps. When she'd finished, she retracted the lipstick and shakily put the cap back on the tube.

When Tom had gone, Eve couldn't resist asking Chet if he had any other weird friends he hadn't told her about. Before Chet could answer, there was another tap at the door. "Martha" must have forgotten something.

But when Chet opened the door, it wasn't Tom. It was a young man who was obviously strung out on something, asking for a cigarette. "I was down in the parking lot, and this dude asked me for a smoke," he said in a rush. "When I took out a pack, he grabbed them and took off. He stole my fucking cigarettes, man. He took my fucking life!"

"Hold on," Chet said. Leaving the door open, Chet went into the bedroom and returned a moment later with a pack of Camels. "Here. You can take the whole pack."

"Thanks, man. You saved my life. I'll pay you back man. You saved my life…"

After he'd closed the door and locked it, Chet turned back toward Eve. "That was—"

"Don't even bother to explain," Eve said. "I thought *my* neighbors were weird. But even with what happened last night after you left, they're nothing, compared to yours."

Chet put the pizza in the oven to re-heat, and popped the top on another beer and Pepsi. "What happened last night?"

Before answering, Eve took a drag from her Pepsi. "The couple next door had a fight. There was a lot of screaming, and there was a gunshot."

"A gunshot! Was anyone hurt?"

"Not that I know of," Eve replied. "The police came and took the guy away."

After hearing about the gunshot, Chet didn't want Eve to go home that night, but Eve insisted. Overriding Chet's objections, she assured him the neighbor had no beef with her. "Besides, he's in jail for the night. I'll be fine."

When Eve pulled into the parking lot of her apartment complex, she looked in all directions before getting out of the car, then quickly climbed the stairs and all but ran to her apartment. Once inside, she locked the door, sank onto the loveseat and picked up the remote control.

She was watching a romance on cable T.V. when she heard running footsteps on the porch, followed by thunderous pounding on her door. "Angel!" Chet's voice shouted. "Angel! Open the door!"

Chet? She'd just left him half an hour ago. What was he doing here?

When Eve opened the door, Chet burst in. His feet were bare, his shirt was hanging open, and his eyes were wild. "Are you alright?" he asked breathlessly. "After you left, I got this awful feeling that something was going to happen to you. The feeling was so strong that I jumped into the truck and sped all the way here. I didn't even take time to put on my shoes."

217

It took nearly fifteen minutes to calm Chet down. "I don't like you living here," he said. "This is not a good area. These clowns that live in these apartments are low lifes and dopers, and I know you're not careful enough. You take too many chances, going out alone."

"I *live* alone," Eve argued. "How else do you expect me to go out when I leave?"

That night after Chet had gone home, Saul had a talk with Eve. "Chet's right about the dangerous characters who live in these apartments. But until you're more secure financially, you can't afford to move anywhere else. I've been thinking: You and Chet are together every minute that you're not at work or sleeping. *You're* paying rent. *He's* paying rent. And you're no safer at his apartment than you are here."

"What's your point?" Eve asked. "If you're trying to scare me, you're doing a good job."

"My point is that maybe you and Chet should look for a house together. If you found a house in a nice neighborhood, you could share the rent. And you wouldn't have to worry about your neighbors."

The next night, when Chet came by after work, Eve told him what Saul had suggested.

"We wouldn't have to look for a house," Chet said. "You could move into my apartment with me."

There was no way in hell Eve would move into Chet's apartment complex with the derelicts who were living there, but she didn't want to say so and hurt Chet's feelings. "Saul said it's no safer there than it is here," she said instead.

Chet's reaction to Saul's suggestion was not immediately positive. Chet liked his Carmichael apartment. It had been his bachelor pad since his divorce. He'd made some good friends and had some good times there. It had been there that he'd said the prayer that brought Eve into his life.

"Unless we could find a nice house we could afford with a yard and a big garage, I don't particularly want to move again either," Eve said. "But it *would* be nicer to live in a house where you didn't have neighbors next door shouting through the wall, or neighbors downstairs that play their T.V. half the night.'

The more Eve thought about it, the more Saul's suggestion made sense. It seemed pretty obvious she and Chet were in this thing for the long haul. Why should they keep the road hot between Roseville and Carmichael when they could live in one house halfway in between? By the time she saw Chet the next evening, Eve had an argument prepared. As it turned out, the argument wasn't necessary.

"If we're going to look for a house, we're going to need some more furniture," Chet said. "What do you say we go to Levitz this weekend to see what we can find?"

Though Eve checked the local papers and called three property management companies, there were no houses to be had right now in their price range. Not that there was a rush. If it took them awhile to find a house, that would just give them more time to shop for a good deal on furniture.

Excited at the prospect of moving in with Chet, Eve breezed through the week at work, oblivious to Frank's miserly ways and Jessica's efforts to goad her. When

Jessica told a lie about Eve to Carol and Frank, even *that* didn't phase her. She simply told her side of the story, and left them to believe what they would. It was on the way home Friday evening that the drunk driver banged into the back of her car. Fortunately, they were at a stoplight and the car was going less than ten miles an hour. But the jolt was still sufficient to give Eve's back and neck a jolt.

By the time the police had been called and she'd exchanged insurance information with the other driver, Eve's head was throbbing and her lower back was killing her. By the time she arrived home and paged Chet, she was in tears.

"Where are you now?" Chet asked urgently. "Did they take you to the emergency room?"

"No," Eve said. "I'm okay. I just need to lie down."

But Chet wouldn't take "No" for an answer. Within an hour, he was knocking on Eve's door, insisting on taking her to the hospital for x-rays. After a two-hour wait, Eve was taken into the emergency room where a doctor asked how she was feeling. "You're looking pretty peaked. I'm going to send you down to x-ray." That was the extent of the examination. The bill for the doctor's services was three hundred dollars.

X-rays were another six hundred. "Don't worry about it," Chet said. "I'll put it on my credit card and we'll send the bill to your insurance."

The x-rays revealed that no bones had been broken. Eve hadn't thought they had. The medical report told her what she already knew: that she had a probable whiplash and trauma to her lower back.

"What you need is some T.L.C.," Chet said. "I'm taking you home with me."

Too tired to argue, Eve allowed Chet to take her back to his apartment where he installed her in his bed, then went into the bathroom and turned on the water. While she lay on his bed massaging her temples, through the sound of running water, Eve could hear Chet in the kitchen opening the refrigerator. When he returned, he was carrying a bowl of Cool Whip.

"This is for you," he said. "I put some lemon dish soap in the bath water and a candle on the side of the tub because I know you like bubble baths by candlelight. This is for you to eat."

Eve had told Chet she sometimes liked to pamper herself by running a fragrant bubble bath and eating whipped cream from a champagne goblet. But that was in a *sparkling clean tub in a clean bathroom*—not in a bathroom where the sink and tub were blackened by grime and suntan oil, and the countertop was cluttered with a comb full of hair, a razor, and globs of dried toothpaste! Making an effort to conceal her dismay, Eve allowed Chet to help her to her feet and lead her to the bathroom.

The flickering light of the votive candle illuminated the blackened tub, brimming with lemon-scented suds. "Thank you," Eve said in a choked voice. "This was really—sweet of you."

"I'll just set the whipped cream here on the side of the tub," Chet said. "I'll be in the other room. You can call me if you need me."

When Chet had gone out and closed the door behind him, Eve looked at the tub and shuddered with revulsion. She couldn't take a bath in that! But if she didn't, it would hurt Chet's feelings. For a moment, Eve considered sponge bathing so she would have the lemon scent on her skin without having to sit down in the water. But then what if Chet walked in, expecting to find her immersed in the bath suds and found her sitting on the side of the tub? There was no hope for it. She would have to take the bath and pretend like she'd enjoyed it...

A tap at the door fifteen minutes later gave Eve the excuse she was waiting for to pull the plug and climb out of the water. "I'm just finishing up," she called. "I'll be out in a minute..."

When she came out five minutes later wrapped in a thin orange beach towel, Chet asked if she'd enjoyed her bath.

Eve didn't want to lie to Chet and say she'd enjoyed it. But she didn't want to tell him the truth and say it had made her skin crawl. So she compromised. "It was definitely an experience."

"Did you like the candle and whipped cream?" Chet asked eagerly. "I didn't have a champagne goblet, so I had to use a cereal bowl."

Eve was reminded of the time Kevin picked her a bouquet of weeds for the table and put them in a Coke bottle full of muddy water. "Yes," she said, "It was very sweet."

Thinking back over her experiences with Chet—helping her sort her things in storage and making it *fun* when the task had seemed overwhelming, moving her into her apartment when there'd been no one else to help, fixing up her apartment to make it livable, racing to her rescue in his bare feet when he imagined she was in danger, forcing her to go to the emergency room then footing the bill when she had no cash to pay it, now fixing her a candle lit bubble bath in a grease blackened tub, and serving whipped cream in a cereal bowl—Eve smiled. He didn't exactly qualify as a knight in shining armor. But so what if his armor was a little rusty? He was *her* knight in rusty armor, and she was glad she'd found him.

The next weekend, despite the ongoing pain in her back, Eve went to the hydro cal store where she'd bought the wizard statue for Carla. The day she'd bought the wizard, she'd seen a statue of a knight on a horse, charging into battle with his sword raised above his head. If they still had it, it would make a perfect gift for Chet. She could paint the horse black, and the armor silver. And around the hinges in the armor, she could paint faint traces of rust. On the base, she could use her engraver to inscribe "To my Knight in Rusty Armor..."

The finished statue was a sight to behold. Eve could hardly wait to give it to Chet. She had set it in a box for safekeeping. She didn't want a replay of what had happened to the Indian statue when she'd lived in the haunted house.

The night she was to give it to him, Eve waited till after dinner, then made a grand production of presenting it.

"I love it!" Chet exclaimed, reaching into the box to lift the statue out. But as he lifted it out, he accidentally bumped the sword against the side of the box and snapped it off. Fortunately, the sword blade broke off in one piece.

"Don't worry," Eve said. "I can glue it back on and no one will ever know it's been broken."

Chet had set the statue on the dining room table and was examining it closely. "I can't believe how you painted all the tiny details," he marveled. "If it weren't for the size, this thing actually looks real!" The sword had broken off at the shaft, leaving the knight holding what looked like a crude hammer. "I don't want you to glue the blade back on," Chet said. "It's perfect the way it is. This is me—your rusty night—charging into battle with his framing hammer! Thank you, little Angel."

The next few weeks were a sea of pain for Eve. Chet managed to keep her vertebrae in place with deep nightly massage and chiropractic adjustments he'd learned from his grandfather, who'd been a chiropractor. But pain kept shifting from one side of her back to the other. The doctor Eve worked for made appointments with her physical therapist for treatments with an ultrasound machine. But Eve had suffered both a whiplash and a lower back injury. Healing was slow and painful...

Given the fact that they were planning to move in together, once Eve was on the mend, Chet decided it would be a good time for Eve to meet his mom and sister. Eve had a few days' vacation time coming. They could stop off in L.A. and spend a couple of days with *her* sister before going on to San Diego to see his family. Eve's mom normally spent six months out of the year in California. It was too bad she'd already left to go back to West Virginia.

The trip to Southern California would be a welcome break from the normal routine. It would have to be short—two days in L.A., and one in San Diego—but it would give enough time for everyone to get acquainted. They could make another trip later on when they could stay longer.

The night before the trip, Eve and Chet were talking through the board when the Energy of the East expressed a wish to speak. It always amused Eve when the Energy of the East spoke, considering that he claimed not to like humans. "Car trouble is planned for you on the way to Southern California. I'm not suggesting that you cancel your trip. I'm merely warning you to be careful."

An image of the wreckage in the outskirts of Placerville flashed into Eve's mind. "Maybe we shouldn't go," she said worriedly. "If there's something wrong with the Shadow—"

"There's nothing wrong with the Shadow," Chet said. "I just took it in for a tune up last week, and they checked it out from bumper to bumper."

"But if the dark ones have planned to cause trouble—"

"The dark ones are *always* causing trouble," Chet said. "I want you to meet my mom and sister, and I want to meet your sister and niece. I've got my credit cards in my wallet. If the car breaks down, we'll just have to use them to get it fixed." Chet didn't realize when he spoke them that his words were prophetic.

The first third of the trip was uneventful, with Chet singing along with every song, making up his own words when he didn't know the lyrics. Eve had never known anyone who sang as much as Chet. It was as if he couldn't stand the silence. They were halfway to L.A. when the red light came on, warning that there was a problem.

"It figures that they'd wait till we were in the middle of nowhere," Chet grated.

Miles from the nearest town, they had no choice but to get the Shadow fixed at a gas station. Using his credit card, Chet paid through the nose for the repair. But that had been expected.

When they arrived at Chet's sister's, Chet introduced Eve as his little woman before introducing his sister. "Angel, this is my little sister, Annaleegooga."

It didn't surprise Eve that Chet had assigned an unusual nickname to his sister. He had nicknames for all five of his own kids. His nickname for Kevin was The Flea.

Jane was shorter than Eve, with close-cropped brown hair and a worried face. Her house was dark, filled with antiques and cozy knickknacks. "Come in and sit down," she said. "Are you hungry? Can I get you something to drink?"

"No thanks," Eve said. "We stopped for lunch on the way."

Eve hadn't really known what to expect. But one thing she hadn't anticipated was feeling immediately at home with Chet's sister. In no time at all, they were chatting as if they'd known one another all their lives.

"We want to go visit Sam," Chet said. "I want to see for myself how she's doing."

'Sam' was the nickname Chet had assigned to his mother when he was a teenager. More specifically, Samuel P. P Morrison of Lucky Logger Beer. Sam, for short. No one else called her Sam. To everyone else, she was Beth.

"She's not doing very well," Jane said. "The doctor has her on medicine for depression, and it causes her not to be able to think straight. I can't get her to come to my house because we're Mormon, and a neighbor told her Mormons are evil. She doesn't even want me to come to visit."

"I'll talk to her," Chet said. "I'll tell her what the neighbor said is just bullshit. Sam will listen to me."

"Mom *always* listens to *him*," Jane told Eve. "She always has, ever since we were kids."

Rather than run the risk of having her mother reject her, Jane elected to stay home when Chet took Eve to the assisted living facility. Beth wasn't in her room when they arrived. "She's in the dining hall feeding the parakeet," a nurse said. "If you want to wait, I'll tell her you're here…"

When the nurse returned, she was accompanied by a woman barely four feet ten with short brown hair and glasses, wearing a brown flowered dress and flat-heeled shoes. "Hey, Sam!" Chet said loudly. "I brought someone to meet you." Gathering his mother into his arms, Chet nearly lifted her off the floor. "You feel like you've gained a little weight. They must be feeding you right."

"Oh yes," Beth said in a frail voice. "They feed me right. They let me feed the parakeet. It's a pretty bird. It's my job to take care of it."

"That's good, Sam," Chet said. He had released her from the hug and was standing with his arm around her shoulders. "I want you to meet Eve. Eve's my little woman."

"Hello," Eve said, taking Beth's frail hand in hers. "It's nice to meet you. Chet's told me a lot about you."

"Has he?" Beth asked. "That's nice." Her eyes had the blank expression of a person who's been sedated.

Later, seated across from Eve in a window booth at Denny's, Chet wiped the tears from his eyes. "My poor little mom. They've got her so drugged up she hardly knows her name. If it wasn't for that bird they let her take care of, she wouldn't even have a reason to live."

Eve knew from stories Chet and Jane had told her that their mother had always been a very strong woman. Well versed in natural healing, she'd been somewhat of a physical fitness nut—insisting that the entire family eat a healthy diet, and doing her exercises every morning with Jack LaLane. But she'd also been dependent on their dad, to the point that she didn't know how to balance a checkbook, and had never even learned how to drive.

On the drive home the next day, Chet voiced the wish that he could bring his mom to live in Sacramento. "If Sam was near us, we could take her off that medication, and things would be different. She looks to me as the man in the family. Sam's never really felt secure unless she had a man to take care of her."

Eve agreed that it would be good if Chet's mother could be moved to Sacramento where he could visit her on a regular basis, but it would never work for Beth to live with them. With both of them working, she couldn't take care of herself during the day. Besides, having a dependent parent living with them right off the bat would be lethal for their relationship.

"Maybe I could check with some assisted living communities near us," Eve said thoughtfully. "I could find out what their requirements are: how independent their residents have to be…"

Chapter 41

The house Eve and Chet found was a three-bedroom bungalow in Citrus Heights with two baths, a two-car garage, and a quarter acre of land. As with Eve's former apartment, dark paneling in the family room gave the feeling of living in a cave. The one wall that wasn't paneled was papered with yellow flowers. Apparently whoever had papered the wall hadn't known much about wallpapering. The paper was hanging loose in one top corner, and had started to lift at the seams. The same was true of the paper in the kitchen and master bath. The dishwasher space in the kitchen was empty, and the dark brown lino was scarred. The cove-based lino in the master bath had come loose from the wall, and the seats on both toilets were chipped. The house's one saving grace, other than the large backyard, was that the price was right. With Chet's construction experience and Eve's decorative talents, they'd have it fixed up in no time. But first things first: Before even unpacking the boxes, Eve made a trip to the metaphysical bookstore to buy amethysts to establish a pyramid.

"Now that you and Chet have found one another, you're more of target than ever," Saul said. "The dark ones know how powerful you're destined to become, Sweetheart. They'll do anything they can to stop it."

When Eve had positioned the amethysts out of sight in each end of the house and Chet had put one in the hall smoke detector, Eve began the ritual of calling the energies into the stones: the Energy of the South into an amethyst on the windowsill in the office, the Energy of the East into a stone on the family room mantel, West into a stone on the living room windowsill, and North into a stone in her bedroom that she had placed in a clay pot containing a silk Pothos.

The evening of the first day in their new home, Saul told Eve to get the board out. The Energy of the North had a gripe to air. The Energy of the *North*! He *never* talked. Curious as to what he would have to say, Eve took out the board and the pendulum.

The pendulum immediately began to swing. "This is the Energy of the North, and I'm of the light," he began. Eve sensed from the feel of the pendulum that the Energy of the North was angry. "The Energy of the East got the mantel," he continued. "The Energies of the South and West got the windowsills. So why did *I* get stuck a in dark room in the *flower pot*?"

"I'm sorry," Eve said. "I didn't realize you'd have a preference."

"Of course I have a preference," the Energy said. "If my stone must be relegated to the darkest room in the house, it at least deserves to be in the jewelry box!"

Suitably contrite, Eve moved the tingling amethyst from the flowerpot to the wooden jewelry box in the center of her dresser. When all the stones were settled, Eve called the power of the energies together to fill the pyramid with their power of protection. On a roll, she asked that the Energies permeate the entire house—the roof, the foundation, the walls, the plumbing…

When Eve picked the pendulum up again, it began to swing in a forceful manner: an indication that someone was displeased. "This is the Energy of the North again, and I'm of the light," the pendulum spelled out. "How dare you treat me with such disrespect?"

Eve had no idea what he was talking about.

"First you stick my stone in the dirt in a clay flowerpot, then you try to call me into the toilet!"

"I didn't ask you to come into the toilet," Eve protested.

"Permeate the entire house: the roof, the foundation, the walls, *the plumbing…*"

Whoops.

Prior to asking the energies to permeate the plumbing, Eve hadn't thought through the ramifications. "I'm sorry," she said. "I didn't mean any disrespect. If I worded it differently, and asked you to guard the plumbing, would that be acceptable?"

Much to Eve's relief, the Energy of the North gave his grudging assent.

Now that their house was protected, Eve was free to think of other things such as getting their telephone hooked up and calling her mother and sister to give them the new number.

Her sister Cheryl was supportive of her moving in with Chet, but her mother had definite reservations.

"Think of it from a practical point of view," Eve reasoned. "With two of us to share the bills, we can live in a decent neighborhood. The house we're renting is just five minutes from Kevin. And you won't have to worry about my going out dancing, now that I'm with Chet."

When Eve had hung up from talking with her family, she suggested that Chet call his sister to give her the new phone number and address, and ask how his mother was doing. When Chet placed the call, he turned the phone on speaker so Eve could hear what was being said.

The news about his mother was not good. The doctors had increased her medication and wanted to transfer her to a psych ward.

"But how can they put her in the psych ward when she's not crazy?" Chet argued.

"That's just it," Jane replied. "The medication she's on causes her to be in a fog all the time. I looked up what they're giving her, and found out three months is the limit for how long anyone should be on it, and two of the drugs she's taking aren't even supposed to be mixed! They've had Mom on them for over a year."

"Assholes," Chet said. "What if I were to drive down there and talk to them?"

"Yelling and swearing at them isn't going to do any good," Jane said worriedly. "They already hate *me*, and think all I do is complain. I'm going to go through all my records of past prescriptions and get the information together to show to another doctor. Maybe if I can get another doctor to say the medication they're giving her is wrong, I can get them to take her off of it."

"We need to get her out of that place and bring her to Sacramento," Chet muttered.

"The condition she's in, she'd have to be put in a nursing home," Jane replied. "Even if you could find one that had room for her, you don't have the money to pay for it, and neither do we."

With the problem of Chet's mom a real concern, but not yet a top priority, Eve and Chet fell into a routine. Two evenings a week, they would go out to dinner. One evening, they'd go Country Western dancing. Other evenings, they'd work together on the house, go to Kevin's ballgames, or Eve would work on craft projects while she and Chet talked. Sometimes, Kevin would come to visit or introduce his latest girlfriend.

On weekends, Eve and Chet would drive to the country or to historic towns for Eve to take black and white pictures for the walls. And always, there was Chet's singing. At first Eve had thought it was cute. But hearing it constantly was beginning to grate on her nerves. It wasn't that he had a bad voice. Actually, he did a fair rendition of Elvis and Dean Martin. But he couldn't hit the high notes, and he didn't know half the words. There were times when Eve just wanted to hear the *real* artists singing the *real* songs.

While Eve closeted herself in the converted office/darkroom to develop and print the black and white pictures they'd taken, Chet would work on the lawn, or wash and wax the car and S10. Later, they'd sepia tone the pictures together. At day's end, they would take out the board...

The problem with talking on the board was the constant interruptions. Things had been so simple when Eve had first gotten in touch with her spirit guides. She hadn't had to worry then about interruptions from the dark ones every time she talked to her guides or picked up the pendulum. Now it seemed that for each hour spent on the board, at least half the time was spent dealing with interruptions and having to clear the house.

Eve didn't understand why God wouldn't control the interruptions Himself, if He wanted her to be a natural healer in touch with spirits of light. She was getting sick of the worn out explanation that the earth was Satan's realm, and God and Jesus wouldn't use excessive force *or* allow their *angels* to use their full power to deal with the problem. It was like putting an arsenal of bombs at their disposal, but issuing an edict that they had to fight with slingshots.

Eve would have been tempted to cut off communication entirely if it weren't for the fact it had been drummed into her head that she was destined to become a great healer. In one session of uninterrupted communication, Saul had told her the plan was for her to specialize in healing burns. According to Saul, the time would eventually come when she and Chet would have to move to the country. Word would spread of her healing abilities, and burn victims—particularly children— would be brought from throughout the country for her to lay hands on them and heal them. It was a wonderful dream. But for now it was the pits, being the target of dark spirits and having to waste the majority of her free time talking on the board— taking five minutes or more to complete a sentence.

It might not have been so bad if only Eve's time was involved. But now Chet's time was being dominated as well. Board sessions now included first clearing the house of negative energy room by room, strengthening the energy pyramid, playing environmental music on the boom box, and holding a piece of Tourmaline in Eve's hand. It wasn't that tourmaline had any particular significance other than its beauty. But this particular chunk had been imbued with energy specifically for protection of the board and pendulum. It was Chet's responsibility to be vigilant and make sure all the rules were followed. Beyond this, both Eve and Chet had to be aware that when one was the target of darkness, dark spirits often melded with ordinary items being brought into the house—particularly items made of metal—in order to gain entry into their home. In Chet's case, the culprit was his stainless steel thermos, otherwise known as his coffee pot. Chet couldn't seem to remember to bless it, and Eve often paid the price:

It had been a bad day at work. Jessica had tried to feed an electric cord to the cat, Frank had gotten on Eve's case about using Arm & Hammer laundry detergent instead of Amway, Eve had started an unexpected period, and Ralston had thrown up on the carpet in every room. By the time Eve arrived home at six thirty, she was in no mood to be messed with.

Chet's truck wasn't in the driveway or garage. Apparently he was working late. When Eve walked into the house, she heard a rustling noise coming from the direction of the kitchen. A chill crept down her spine as she tiptoed to the fireplace in the family room and picked up a poker. The sound was getting louder! Silent as a cat, Eve crept to the archway and peered into the kitchen. The kitchen was empty. The rustling sound was coming from the cabinet side of the refrigerator. A cold clammy feeling seemed to emanate from the room. *Shit.*

Fed up with the harassment, Eve stalked into the kitchen. The sound was coming from the breadbasket. Eve didn't know what was in there, but whatever it was, it didn't belong in her house. "Alright, Asshole," she said through clenched teeth. "Come out and show yourself."

She had no idea what good the poker would do in the event she was faced by a demon.

At the sound of her voice, the rustling of bread wrappers stopped, and there was an instant of dead silence before the mouse climbed out of the basket and walked to the edge of the counter where Eve was standing.

Startled by the rodent's brashness, Eve gaped. The mouse stood there staring Eve boldly in the eye, then turned and scampered toward the stove where it dipped its head into the metal at the stove's edge and disappeared.

It occurred to Eve *now* that she should have asked Gideon or Saul what was going on *before* she armed herself with a poker and crept into the kitchen. But the thought hadn't occurred to her. "Saul?" she asked. "What the heck just happened?"

"This is Saul, and I'm of the light. It was a dark spirit in the form of a mouse. Dark spirits often choose to appear in the form of small animals so no one will suspect what they really are. And you're right. You should have asked before charging in there on your own."

Ignoring the chastisement, Eve asked how the dark spirit got in. "I strengthened the pyramid before I left for work this morning."

There was a moment of silence as if Saul didn't want to tattle. "Chet came home this afternoon," he said reluctantly. "He forgot to bless the coffee pot."

Two weeks later:

When the first Thanksgiving in their new home arrived, Eve and Chet chose to stay home and cook a full course dinner, then drive to Placerville to see Mrs. Stillwell. It had been one year ago today that Eve had eaten Thanksgiving dinner with Mrs. Stillwell in her room, and given her half a day of use from her crippled arthritic hands. Eve had received a letter from the old lady last week, dictated to a volunteer. The letter had told Eve how much Mrs. Stillwell missed her, and asked her to come as soon as possible. "I have a feeling I don't have much time left."

Eve hoped her friend was wrong about her impending death. But she knew quality of life had been factor for quite sometime. With her hands and feet crippled by Rheumatoid Arthritis, the poor woman could barely raise a glass of water to her lips. With no one to talk to beyond comments about the food or weather, there was really little she could do other than watch T.V.

When Eve and Chet arrived at the hospital, Mrs. Stillwell was sleeping. "She's had a bad day," Mrs. Japetto said from the next bed. "She's been in a lot of pain. She told me the other day she wished you'd come."

Eve was standing next to the hospital bed holding Mrs. Stillwell's hand and stroking her cheek when Mrs. Stillwell woke up. "Eve! I'd been praying that you would come…"

That night, to get her mind off Mrs. Stillwell and her problems, Eve gathered all her silk plants together and brought them into the kitchen for a bath. She'd never been good with real plants. That's why she had only silk. The one live plant in the house was Chet's: a Dieffenbachia, and it was dying. Little wonder. Chet hadn't watered it in nearly three weeks.

Glancing now at the drooping plant on the counter, Eve took pity and gave it a drink of water. When the next day, it was even droopier than before, she decided to see if her healing touch would perk it up.

Standing in front of the counter a foot from the Dieffenbachia, Eve closed her eyes to see the green and call the healing energy into her hands. In the background, she could hear Chet singing in the bathroom: a senseless ditty he'd composed about her, sung to the tune of the Mexican Hat Dance. "Oh there's no one as sweet as my sweetie that I love from her head to her feetie…"

When her hands were tingling, Eve opened her eyes and placed her hands on either side of the plant. "Okay, little plant. Here it comes." Moving her hands in an upward motion, she concentrated on infusing the wilted plant with energy.

Again and again, cupping her tingling hands around the plant, she lifted them in a sweeping upward motion.

"What are you doing?" Chet had come into the kitchen and was looking at Eve curiously.

"I'm trying to see if my healing energy will revive your plant," Eve replied. "I think it's looking better already."

Apparently she was right. By morning, the plant was standing tall and strong. If only the healing energy worked as well on Mrs. Stillwell...

Two weeks later, Eve received a letter informing her that Mrs. Stillwell had passed away.

Chapter 42

It was amazing to Eve how many forms it was possible for demonic harassment to take. Yesterday alone, she'd put half a ham down the garbage disposal, only to learn later that the ham had been fine. It was her taste buds that had been temporarily affected. Then there'd been the smell of poop in the car. Thinking a stray animal had somehow gotten into the car and left his calling card, Eve and Chet had searched the Shadow from bumper to bumper before Saul finally got through to tell them they were simply being harassed.

With harassment and interruptions becoming more and more frequent, the time had come to take stronger measures. "You need to make a decent board," Saul said. "Not a board made of paper or cardboard. There may be times when Jesus himself wants to talk to you. A makeshift board is disrespectful and does nothing to discourage interruptions."

"What kind of board are you talking about?" Eve asked. "I suppose I *could* make one out of wood."

"Chet needs to be the one to make it," Saul replied. "He's a carpenter, like Jesus. And he's studied the Bible…"

When Chet got home from work, Eve greeted him at the door with a hug, a kiss, and a reminder to bless the coffee pot. Over a dinner of steak, salad, and mashed potatoes, she told him about Saul's request. "He wants you to make a board using hand tools only. No power tools—no electric saw or electric sander. And since dark spirits don't like being around gold, he wants you to incorporate gold nuggets into the design."

That evening Chet read the story of Noah's ark. "The best thing would be if I could make the board out of gopher wood like Noah used, but there's no gopher wood in this country that I know of. The closest thing I can think of would be redwood."

And so it was decided. Chet would make the board of redwood. He and Eve would take a drive to Grass Valley to take pictures and visit the old mine shaft and mineral shop. If they didn't find the nuggets they needed there, they would stop in Auburn on the way home and get them at a mineral shop there.

With Chet working on the board for a total of five evenings plus Saturday, which equaled a spiritual number of six, that left the seventh day to get the gold nuggets. Chet sawed the wood by hand, to a precise measurement of nine inches by twelve—both dimensions being multiples of three. Years ago, he had done a study of numerology as it pertained to Biblical events. Aside from the obvious significance of the number three as it pertained to the Father, Son, and Holy Spirit, Jesus started his ministry when he was thirty years old. His ministry lasted three years. He died at age thirty-three. After being crucified, he lay in the tomb two days and arose on the third. There were twelve tribes of Israel. God created the universe in six days. On the seventh day, he rested... Since he'd been involved with spirits, he'd noticed that spirits also did things in multiples of three.

The making of the board became a labor of love for Chet. Sanding it with fine-grained sandpaper, he rounded the edges to a perfect match. When the board had been sanded to the texture of satin, he painstakingly carved the arc of letters with a chisel, then oiled the board with olive oil. The first three coats of oil enhanced the grain and stained the wood a beautiful shade of reddish brown. But Chet didn't stop with three. By the time he was finished, he'd applied seven coats in all.

The day they chose for their excursion to the mountains was intended to be a fun day, starting with breakfast at Denny's, then driving to Grass Valley where they planned to visit the North Star mining museum. When they arrived in Grass Valley, Chet followed the signs to the Powerhouse. and museum. Set in the side of a hill, next to a stream, and approachable by a narrow cement staircase or a long cement ramp, the Powerhouse museum building was surrounded by a graveyard of hydraulic gold mining equipment. Even when they read the names, Eve had no idea what the equipment had been used for, except for the sluice box that was at least twenty feet long. There were metal "Pelton" wheels as tall as Eve, and as wide across, painted brick red, and a huge red pipe with a nozzle on the end that was over a foot in diameter.

"You'd think they'd arrange these things in some sort of order," Eve commented. It seemed to her that what had been done here was like scattering the parts of a car engine, and expecting a person with no experience as a mechanic to know how they fit together.

When they entered the crowded dimly lit building, Eve was assailed by a feeling of claustrophobia. She barely heard what the guide was saying as he explained what typically took place in an assay office. When they proceeded into the dim museum where picks, shovels, mining hats, mineral samples, and other mining paraphernalia were displayed, Eve's throat and chest contracted. Clutching her throat, she gasped. "I—can't breathe," she wheezed. "I don't know what's happening."

To her left, at shoulder height, was a gigantic quartz crystal. The jagged crystal must have weighed five hundred pounds! Eve had the odd feeling she and the quartz crystal were *connected* by an energy field that no one else in the room could feel. Her head was spinning, and she felt like she was going to faint.

"Get away from the crystal," Saul said urgently. "It's absorbing your energy!"

"It's the—quartz," Eve said, clutching Chet's arm. "I have to—get out of here."

Alarmed, Chet put an arm around Eve's waist and half supported her weight as he guided her out of the museum, past the assay office, and out into the sunlight.

When Eve was clear of the building and had climbed the cement stairs to the parking lot, Saul spoke in her head. "You're sensitive to even the smallest of crystals," he explained. "To a person who's not sensitive, the giant quartz is no problem. To a person of your psychic powers, it's overwhelming."

Before driving to Auburn to look for gold nuggets, Chet took Eve to a small café where he ordered a coffee for himself and a Coke for her. "I thought you were going to pass out on me back there."

The Coke made Eve's heartbeat even more erratic.

"Take some deep breaths," Chet suggested. "Close your eyes, and try to relax."

If this was what being "sensitive" was all about, Eve wished to high Heaven she'd never been chosen. Before being put in contact with spirit guides, she had never had problems like this. She'd visited mineral shops plenty of times before with no ill effects. She'd gone into *caverns* deep in the earth, for pity's sake. "I think I'm okay now," she said weakly.

On the drive from Grass Valley to Auburn, Eve leaned against the back of the S10's bench seat and closed her eyes. She was glad she had Chet to do the driving. She didn't enjoy outings nearly as much since she'd become sensitive to crystals and negative energy. She couldn't even go into a crowded theater or store anymore without becoming nauseous from the negative energy around her.

She was glad Chet didn't expect her to talk. He had turned the radio on to a "shit kicking station," and was singing along, tapping the steering wheel to the beat. His vocal rendition was punctuated by comments about Auburn—his old stomping grounds.

When they got to old Auburn, they parked the S10 and got out to walk. In one shop along the way, Chet spotted a display of hair bows in the window. Eve had been searching for large clip hair bows for weeks to wear when she pulled her hair back in a banana clip. Here were bows in every color imaginable. "Let's go in and try one," Chet suggested.

Once inside the crowded boutique, Eve took a banana clip from her purse and pinned her brown hair back and up. Chet held a pink bow to the top of the clip and grinned. "Perfect. You look like my little doll." By the time they left the shop, Chet had bought ten clip bows—one in every color of the rainbow, plus black, white, floral, and polka dot! Eve thought it was cute that a grown man with muscles the size of melons could get excited over hair bows to put in his lady's hair.

Hand in hand, Chet and Eve walked the short distance to the Gold Panning Supply store while he regaled her with more anecdotes about his old stomping grounds. The shop with its brown board and batt front was old, and reminded Eve of something out of a John Wayne film. The clerk behind the glass display case was bald, about five and a half feet tall, with suspenders and coke bottle glasses. "What can I do you folks for?"

"We want to buy some gold nuggets," Chet replied. "About the size of my little fingernail. We'll need seven."

"What are you folks planning on doing with the nuggets?" the clerk asked curiously. "Gonna make some jewelry?"

Caught off guard by the question, Chet hesitated for only a moment. "Not jewelry," he said. "I'm making something *else* for the little woman." If the clerk saw the grin, he didn't comment. Only Chet and Eve understood the significance.

Late that afternoon when they got home, Chet used a nail set to drive three impressions near the right edge of the satin smooth board, then placed a nugget in one of the impressions. In order to make the gold flush with the board, he laid a piece of wood over top the nugget and hit the wood several times with a hammer. When he took the wood away, the gold was flat—flush with the surface of the board. One down. Six to go...

Chet had imbedded two more nuggets for a total of three, when he decided to break for dinner. To avoid misplacing the remaining nuggets, he laid them next to the board for safekeeping.

Eve was standing at the sink peeling carrots. Approaching from behind, Chet growled and dipped his head to nuzzle the side of her neck. "It's almost done, Angel. Just four more nuggets to go."

"I sure hope the nuggets will make a difference." Eve didn't really expect to see much improvement. Moving to Placerville where there was gold under the ground was supposed to have rendered her immune to harassment. But she hadn't really noticed much difference between Placerville and the valley. If gold under the ground hadn't helped, how did Saul expect a few little nuggets to stop interruptions?

"How much longer till dinner?" Chet asked into the side of her neck.

"At least fifteen minutes," Eve replied. "I'll put the ribs under the broiler while the carrots are cooking."

At odds with what to do with himself while he was waiting for dinner to be ready, Chet decided to drive the remaining nuggets into the board.

From the kitchen, Eve could hear him moving things around on the dining room table. "Did you come in here and do something with the nuggets? I left them right here. Now they're gone."

"You know I haven't left the kitchen," Eve called back. "Maybe you accidentally knocked them off the table."

Despite the fact that Chet was certain he'd left the nuggets next to the board, he got down on his hands and knees and searched the brown shag carpet under and around the dining room table and chairs. "Damned spirits," he muttered. When the search of the floor proved futile, as he'd known it would, Chet began systematically moving everything on the table: the redwood board, the salt and peppershakers, Eve's purse... But the nuggets were nowhere to be found. "Ask Saul if he knows what happened to the fucking nuggets," Chet said irritably.

"Saul?" Eve said. "Do you know where they are?"

"First off, Saul chastised, nuggets intended for use on the board are not *fucking* nuggets. The board was being made in case *Jesus* ever wanted to talk to you. It shouldn't be surprising that the dark ones would want to interfere. The four nuggets are gone, but the board already has three imbedded in it. Three's a good spiritual number. Tell Chet Jesus is pleased with the board, but he needs to learn to control his language."

That night, Chet received a call from his sister saying that their mother was getting worse. "Now she won't even let them give her a bath."

"What do you mean she won't let them give her a bath? Chet said. "Sam's one of the cleanest people I know."

"They scalded her last week," Jane said tightly. "They have this chair that they strapped her into, then dipped her into a tub of water. The temperature was too hot, and they scalded her. I cried when I saw her, Chet. It was so pathetic. Now, she screams every time they try to give her a bath."

"Assholes," Chet grated. "We've gotta get her out of there, Annaleegooga. I want to bring her to Sacramento. I don't care what it costs."

"Her insurance is used up," Jane said. "At least here, she has a guaranteed bed. If we move her there, there's no telling what it will cost each month. All she has is her social security. We don't have the money to pay for the rest, and neither do you."

Tears had welled in Chet's eyes, and his fists were clenched in fury. "We've gotta at least get her off that medication so she can stand up for herself and let us know what's going on."

"I'm working on it," Jane said. "But I'm fighting the system. It's going to take time…"

Chapter 43

"Crimson silk?"

Now that the new board had been made and Eve had made a new pendulum from a gold chain and gold drop earring, Saul had told her the board and pendulum needed to be wrapped in pure silk when not in use. Not just any silk; the silk had to be crimson to represent royalty and Jesus' blood. It seemed that in addition to having an aversion to gold, the dark ones had an aversion to pure silk—particularly crimson; something to do with deflection of negative energy.

In addition to the new board and pure silk wrapper, Saul instructed Eve to make a Protection Box. The box was to be divided into multiple compartments—a separate compartment for each person or thing that was important to her and Chet. She was to buy enough amethysts to put one in each compartment. And she and Chet were to each design a personal icon. The icon had to be made from a continuous line without lifting the pen or pencil, and must be symbolic of what they wanted most in their lives. The icons were to be private and secret. They weren't even to share the icons with one another. These icons were to be placed in the protection box in separate sealed envelopes, and Eve was to select the six strongest amethysts she could find: three to be put in the envelope with her icon; three to be placed with Chet's. The Protection Box housing the icons and amethysts had to be made of natural materials, not including metal.

Choosing the people and things Eve wanted to protect was easy. Constructing the box and designing the icon was the hard part. Eve's finished icon was a heart with a wavy line running through the center. The heart represented love. The wavy line represented the river of life, good health, and continuous spiritual and healing energy. In order to make the icon with one continuous line, Eve had to make the heart first, then retrace the upper left quadrant and draw a wavy line to the left of the heart from the stopping point, then *retrace* the wavy line and continue it to the right through the center of the heart and beyond.

Though Eve didn't see what Chet drew for his icon, she suspected he'd taken the easy way out and drawn something the equivalent of one-size-fits-all. It took only moments for him to complete it.

The first several times the spirits of light spoke through the new board and pendulum, there were no interruptions. But with the temporary improvement in communication came a new line of attack from the dark side. Chet was working on a roof when the pain first struck his ankle, the force of the blow nearly knocking him off balance. The intermittent pains continued throughout the day to the point that Chet was forced to work on his knees to avoid falling off the roof.

When he arrived home at the end of the day, Eve greeted him at the door. "Don't forget to bless the coffee pot. How was your day?"

Chet put his arms around Eve and spoke into her hair. "Not good, Angel. I kept getting these shooting pains in my ankle. When the first one hit, it caught me by surprise and I almost fell. The only thing I could figure is the dark ones were trying to knock me off the roof."

"Do you really think that's what was happening?" Eve asked worriedly.

"Judge for yourself," Chet replied. "One shot missed my ankle and hit me in the foot." I said 'You missed, mother fucker.' So it shot me again. This time it hit the mark—twice as hard."

"This is Saul, and I'm of the light. The dark ones were shooting Chet's ankle with negative energy. They chose that ankle because they could see from the heat it was giving off that it's his weak spot. He needs to protect it by wrapping it in pure silk." At that moment, Chet's ankle was shot with another bolt of negative energy. "Tell him to take off his sock and wrap his ankle in one of your silk scarves before he puts it on again."

Eve wasn't even certain that she owned a silk scarf. As far as she knew, most of her scarves were polyester blends. When she went to her bedroom to search her scarf drawer, the only pure silk she could find was a multi-colored floral scarf that had belonged to her grandmother.

"I can't wear that thing to work tomorrow," Chet protested. "What if someone saw it? They'd laugh me off the crew."

"Who's going to see it if it's inside your sock?" Eve asked reasonably. "Which would you rather do? Get shot in the ankle with negative energy, or wrap your ankle in Grandmother's scarf?"

That evening, the next day, and the next after that, Chet wore the silk scarf beneath his sock and was mercifully free from attacks. Then came the day when he was up on a roof and the scarf worked its way loose and out of his sock. Engrossed in his work, Chet didn't notice the scarf sticking out from under his pant leg until a member of the roofing crew saw it and asked what the hell it was.

It wasn't funny to Chet, but when he told the story to Eve, she laughed till she had tears in her eyes: "Benny saw this flowered thing hanging out from under my pant leg, and asked me 'What the hell is *that*?' At first I didn't know what he was talking about. But then he grabbed it and pulled it out, and held it up for the whole crew to see. 'Hey, guys! Look at what Pop was wearing under his pants!' The others knew better than to tease me about it, but they were looking at me like I'd lost my fucking marbles."

Dabbing at her eyes, Eve tried to speak, but the image of Benny pulling the flowered scarf from Chet's pant leg brought on another spasm of laughter. "What—What did you say?" she wheezed.

"I couldn't very well tell them what it was for, so I didn't say anything," Chet grumbled. "I just stuffed it back in my sock and went back to work."

Later that evening, Even had a second reason to laugh—also at Chet's expense. The wooden toilet seat in Chet's bathroom had been cracked for quite some time. Recently, the crack had gotten worse.

Chet had taken a Field & Stream and gone into the bathroom. Five minutes later, Eve was in the kitchen putting away the dishes when she heard the shout: "Fu—ck!" He didn't say it like a one syllable word. He drew it out, pronouncing each letter of the word with precision.

Tossing the dishtowel aside, Eve raced down the hallway. "What's wrong?" she called through the bathroom door.

Apparently when Chet had sat down on the toilet seat, the crack in the wood had spread. When he'd leaned forward to rest his elbows on his knees, the weight shift had caused the crack to close, pinching his "dick" in the process. Though Eve tried not to laugh, she couldn't control it. Chet failed to see the humor.

Eve had already done most of her Christmas shopping for Chet. Now she knew what her final gift would be. She would get it when she took Kevin shopping. Kevin was fifteen years old now—thin, but muscular—almost a man. She wouldn't have many more opportunities to take him shopping during the holidays. Tomorrow, she'd be taking him to pick out a shirt for Chet, which she would pay for but would have Kevin sign the tag.

But when Eve told Kevin the story of the toilet seat and that she planned to get Chet a new one for Christmas, Kevin begged her to let the toilet seat be from him. "Mom, you've gotta let *me* give it to him. You can get something else for you to give him. But please let me get him the seat. *Please...*"

Eve had never been able to resist Kevin when he begged. Given the relationship he had developed with Chet, the toilet seat *would* be the ideal gift for him to give...

On Christmas Eve when they celebrated Christmas with Kevin, Kevin handed Chet his gift with a solemn expression. "I want you to know that a lot of care went into the choice of this gift. I wrote you a poem for the occasion." Attached by a Santa Claus sticker to the outside of the gift was a handwritten poem:

"Summer, winter, fall and spring, hours of comfort this gift will bring. I heard the old one put you in a pinch, but fixing the problem will be a cinch. No more will your precious manhood get stuck, and force out the bellow of the word 'F—k!' So grab your newspaper and have a seat. Sit back, relax, and find some relief. Merry Christmas.—The Flea. Arms draped across one another's shoulders, holding the oak toilet seat at arm's length in front of them, Eve's two favorite guys posed for the camera. Chet, in turn, snapped a picture of Eve sitting at the clavinova he'd bought her to replace the piano she lost in the aftermath of the fire. All in all, it was a wonderful Christmas.

But when Eve and Chet drove to San Diego in January, things definitely did not go well.

While Eve stayed with Jane working on Christmas ornaments for next year, Chet went by himself to take his mom to lunch. He was gone for nearly three hours—long enough that Eve and Jane became concerned. When Chet finally returned, his face was drawn.

"How did it go?" Jane asked. "Is Mom alright?"

"No, she's not alright," Chet grated. "When I got there to pick her up, she looked like some kind of urchin. She wasn't even wearing her own clothes! They had her dressed in a stinking blouse that was too tight, and pants that hit her above her ankles. Even the shoes they had on her were too small!"

"You didn't cause a scene did you?" Jane asked apprehensively.

"You're damn right I did!" Chet sputtered. "I yelled 'Who the fuck is in charge around here?' and when the nurse came, I yelled at her to get my mom dressed in her *own* damned clothes. I wasn't going to take her to lunch looking like a fucking street person."

Eve hated when Chet used that sort of language. She could understand his being upset, but swearing wasn't going to solve anything.

"What did the nurse say?" Jane asked weakly.

"There was nothing she *could* say," Chet ranted. "I told her if I ever came here and found my mom looking like that again, I was going to turn their asses in."

Later, after Chet's brother-in-law and nephews came home, Chet visited with them for a little while, then motioned Eve to follow him into the bedroom. "The spirits are messing with my mom," he whispered.

"What do you mean?" Eve whispered back. "She's never done anything to get involved with spirits." Eve knew that Beth had once received a visit from the ghost of her dead grandfather. But she'd always been a staunch Christian. She'd never had anything to do with the occult.

"When we were at lunch, she pointed out the window, up in a tree," Chet said. She said "A boy named Danny is sitting up there. *You* can't *see* him. But I can."

Eve could imagine the shock on Chet's face at hearing his mother say an invisible boy was sitting in the tree outside the Fish & Chips.

"She said Danny knows what's going on, and that he comes into her room and helps her when they hurt her."

Eve's muscles tensed, and her heart began to race. "When *who* hurts her?"

"The C.N.A.'s," Chet grated.

Eve couldn't imagine a C.N.A. doing anything to hurt a sweet little woman like Beth. "It must be the medication. It's causing her to hallucinate."

Chet flopped crossways onto the bed and slugged the mattress with his fist. "It's not the medication, Angel. I'm telling you it's the fucking spirits!"

Eve couldn't help wondering if Chet was getting paranoid.

"This is Saul, and I'm of the light. Chet's right, Sweetheart. Dark spirits often prey on people who are lonely, or highly sedated. That's when they're most vulnerable. Danny's not the only spirit who's attached itself to Chet's mother. There's also one that appears to her as a little girl."

"*Damn*," Eve whispered.

Poor Beth. She was such a sweet lady. She didn't deserve any of what was happening to her, but she had no way of protecting herself. Jane apparently couldn't do it. Chet and Eve were going to have to step in. They might not be able to stop spirits from harassing her, but they could darned sure take steps to get her away from that hospital.

Chapter 44

When Eve and Chet returned to Sacramento, Eve began a search in earnest for a facility to move Chet's mother to. It would have to be one that would accept Medicare and Social Security as full payment. Despite the fact they were both working, Eve and Chet couldn't afford to supplement the payment, and neither could Chet's sister and her husband.

It took three months to find a hospital that would take Beth. In the meantime, life continued. Eve and Chet attended Cindy and Jessica's school plays and open houses, and all of Kevin's football games, and Eve took lots of pictures: old fashioned pictures of the girls in costume, portrait style pictures of Kevin and his girlfriends, action pictures of his football games... Chet bought Eve a new enlarger for her darkroom, and built her a feminine workbench in the garage where she could use her band saw for woodworking projects. Eve began work on rewriting the manuscript Chet had thrown away.

When word finally came that there was a semi-private room available at a hospital in Davis, Chet called his sister and told her he would buy two airline tickets—one for her, and one for their mother—so Jane could accompany their mom to Sacramento and see the facility where they'd be putting her. "Bring some of her ceramic chickens so we can put them in her room," Chet suggested. "We're going to buy her a bright colored comforter for her bed and a big picture for the wall, and Eve's going to make her a silk flower arrangement. We'll get her fixed up nice and cozy."

The flight to Sacramento was a nightmare for Jane. Jane had no knowledge or understanding of spirits. As far as she knew, her mother was hallucinating. Eve sympathized with Jane as Jane told her in private after they got home from the airport about how embarrassed she'd been when the stewardess had stopped to ask if she could get them anything, and her mother had been holding a napkin in her cupped hands, talking to an imaginary little girl cradled in the napkin! Eve suspected, and Saul corroborated her suspicion, that the little girl in the napkin was the dark spirit Saul had told her about, but she couldn't very well say that to Jane.

Eve liked Chet's sister, but was glad when Chet took her to the airport the following morning to return to San Diego. With Jane gone, perhaps they'd be able to explain to Chet's mother that the little girl was not really her friend, and that she needed to tell the little girl to leave.

That evening, Kevin came over to visit, and was there when Chet's mother peed her pants in the living room chair and insisted that *Chet* give her a bath. Damn it. Why did this have to happen while Kevin was here? Eve could tell by Kevin's body language how uncomfortable he was feeling, but she hadn't seen him in over a week, and she hated to suggest that he leave. As it turned out, Beth took the matter out of her hands. Chet had asked Eve to run the bath water and get his mother undressed, believing she was capable of bathing herself. But Beth peeled off only two thirds of her clothes, and refused to take off her panty hose and bra. When Eve allowed Beth to test the temperature of the bath water, Beth agreed that the temperature was right. But when Eve tried to persuade her to take off the rest of her clothes, the older woman pushed past her and walked uncertainly out into the hall. "I want Chet. Where's Chet?"

"Chet! Kevin!" Eve called. "She's coming down the hall, and she's not dressed!"

From the living room, Eve heard Kevin's voice. "That's it. I'm out of here. Later, Mom!"

Damn. "Okay, Sweetheart! I'll call you tomorrow!"

Stripped to her bra and panty hose, the elderly woman didn't have a wrinkle on her body. Her breasts were sagging, and her waist had thickened. But she had the skin of a much younger woman. In the hallway, Chet was averting his eyes as he tried to steer his mom back toward the bathroom. "Mom, you're going to have to let *Eve* help you. Angel, *I* can't give her a bath. I don't want to see my mom in the nude!"

Eve knew exactly how Chet was feeling. The mother he loved was already deteriorating before his eyes. To see her in the nude would be the final degradation.

"It's okay," Eve said, taking Beth's arm. "Beth, I'm just going to help you wash off the pee so you'll smell nice. The water's fine, and nobody's going to hurt you."

Soothed by Eve's voice, Beth went along peacefully till Eve closed the bathroom door. Then her eyes began to dart, and her hands began to flutter. Sensing the older woman's panic, Eve re-opened the door and left it ajar. "We need to take off your panty hose and underwear," she said softly. "After we get your clothes off, I'll help you get into the bathtub. You can wash *yourself* if you like."

"I want to leave them on," Beth said in a shaky voice. "I don't want to take my underwear off. Don't try to make me take it off."

What had those C.N.A.'s *done* to her?

"It's okay," Eve crooned. "You can leave it on." One way or the other, the urine smell needed to be washed off Chet's mother *and* her clothing. If she got into the tub with her underwear and panty hose, it would kill two birds with a single stone.

When the bath was finally finished, Eve helped Chet's mother out of the tub and dried her off, then helped her into her bathrobe and slippers. While they'd been in the bathroom, Chet had built a roaring fire in the fireplace. Eve had brought Beth out to the family room to sit with Chet by the fire while she made a snack and a pot of hot chocolate. From the kitchen, she could hear Chet trying to make conversation.

"Why are you bouncing your foot like that, Sam?"

"Because the little girl likes it," his mom replied. "You can't see her. She's sitting on the toe of my slipper."

"That's not a little girl, Sam," Chet argued. "That's a spirit, and you need to tell her to go away."

"She's my friend!" Sam said loudly. "Don't talk about her like that. You'll hurt her feelings." Smiling at the invisible child, Beth continued to bounce her foot.

"Think about it, Mom," Chet reasoned. "If she's little enough to fit on the toe of your shoe, she can't be a real kid. And she's not your friend. She's an evil spirit, and you need to tell her she can't stay."

"Don't listen to him," Beth said to the spirit child. "You can stay with me. You don't have to go."

Cringing at what she was hearing from the family room, Eve turned the fire off under the hot chocolate and set the pot on a hot pad to cool. She didn't really want to go out there, but it sounded like Chet needed her.

Eve had come into the family room and sat down on the floor at an angle from the brown loveseat where Beth was sitting. Suddenly, Beth turned on her with a look of sheer hatred. "Why don't you just leave? You don't belong here. This is *my* house."

Shocked by the outburst and unsure of how to respond, Eve didn't reply.

"You're not my mom talking," Chet shouted. "Who are you?"

For a tense moment, Beth looked at her son in confusion. "I'm—It," she said in a crackling voice. "My name is It."

Blood drained from Chet's frightened face, and his hands began to shake. "In the name of Jesus, get out of here, It! Leave our house, and leave my mom alone!"

Beth released a sigh and like a deflated balloon, slumped forward. Chet's strong arms shot out to catch her. "Mom?" he asked in a quivery voice. "Mom? Are you okay?"

"Yes," Beth answered. "I'm okay. Don't squeeze me so hard. You're hurting me."

Weak with relief, Chet held her a moment longer, then released his mom and apologized for holding her so tight. "You had me worried, Sam. For a minute, I thought...But it's all over now. What do you say we—"

But Beth was no longer paying attention. As if in a trance, she stood and crossed the carpet to stand gazing into the fireplace. For a long moment she stood looking into the fire, all four feet ten and a half of her in her little pink bathrobe and corduroy slippers. And then she spoke. "Alright," she said in a tiny voice. "I'm coming."

"Chet," Eve said shakily, "She's talking to something in the fire. You'd better—"

Before Chet realized what was happening, his mother had bent down, intent on going into the fire. "Mom!" he shouted. "Stop!" Leaping from the loveseat, he grabbed her, just as she would have stepped into the fire.

Struggling in his arms, Beth tried to break free. "The little *girl's* in there," she said pitifully. "She's calling to me to come to her."

Clutching his mother to him, Chet rolled his eyes heavenward and prayed for God to help him. "She's not a little girl, Sam. She's an evil spirit. She's trying to hurt you. But I'm not going to let her...I'm not going to let her..."

Eve's mind flashed back to a night long ago when she'd gone out of body in an effort to protect Kevin, then back to the present. *Dear God in Heaven*, she thought weakly. *They were trying to kill her.*

That night, for everyone's protection, Chet put his mom to bed in his room and locked the door. Neither he nor Eve even tried to sleep...

The next day they took Beth to the doctor for a preliminary check-up before admitting her to the convalescent hospital. How they managed to get through it, Eve would never know.

The doctor was a soft-spoken man in his mid-forties with pale skin, prominent cheekbones, and light brown hair. It occurred to Eve that the white medical smock made him look anemic.

The doctor agreed with Chet that the medications his mother had been on should not have been combined, and should have been discontinued after three months. Much to Chet's relief, he agreed to take Beth off all medication until further notice. But when the doctor asked Beth her age and she said she was twenty-seven, Chet's heart sank. Eve could see it in his eyes.

After calling a nurse to take Beth into another room, the doctor faced Chet with a solemn expression. "There's no easy way to say this," he said kindly. "Your mother has advanced symptoms of Alzheimer's. I know you had hoped that without the medication she'd get better. But I'm afraid it's only going to get worse."

Alzheimer's! When Beth had originally gone into the assisted living facility, she'd been in *excellent* health with the exception of being depressed. Her husband of fifty years had just died, for cripes sake. When he'd been alive, he'd kept her totally dependent on him. When he died, she'd suddenly been thrust on her own, with no experience or knowledge of how to survive. Who wouldn't have been depressed in her situation?

"If they'd given her counseling instead of putting her on the stupid drugs, she'd be fine now," Chet said bitterly. "The damned doctors gave her twice the dose she was supposed to have for her size, and combined two that weren't even supposed to be mixed! If my mom has Alzheimer's, the fucking doctors gave it to her!"

"Please control your language," Dr. Martin said. "The walls here are thin, and there's a patient in the next room."

When Chet continued to rant, the doctor turned to Eve and addressed the rest of his remarks to her. The prognosis was not good. Beth would rapidly lose the remainder of her memory. Eventually, she would be unable to feed or dress herself. Toward the end she would forget how to swallow, and enter a semi-catatonic state.

Chet's white hot anger kept a lid on his grief till he put his mom into the passenger seat of the Shadow. When he opened the driver's door and stepped aside for Eve to climb into the back seat, Eve held out her arms. That's when Chet lost it. Collapsing into Eve's embrace, he allowed the grief to pour out of his body. His breath came in huge racking sobs—the tears of a man whose heart had been broken. "My little mom," he sobbed. "My little Sam. She never hurt anyone in her life. The stinking doctors destroyed her mind, and now she's going to die."

When they arrived at the convalescent hospital, Chet couldn't bring himself to be the one who took his mom through the door. "I'll do it," Eve said quietly. "You can wait outside till we take her to her room. Then you can come in to sign the papers."

Putting an arm around Beth's waist, Eve guided her gently toward the double glass doors. Apparently Beth thought this hospital in Davis was the same one where she'd lived in San Diego. "This is my house," she said in a dull voice. "Take me inside. I want to go to bed."

Chapter 45

It wasn't long after admitting his mother to the hospital that Chet was told that, due to the fact that he was always swearing at them, the dark spirits had put a series of nine curses on him—one for each time he had called them "fucking spirits" in the past week. These curses included aspects of work, health, and his relationship with Eve. It was important that he take steps to render them powerless. "He needs to go on a purification diet for six days," Saul said. "Raw vegetables and pure water only. No salt. No cooked foods. No fruit or juices. No alcohol or caffeine. Every night while he's on the diet, the two of you are to light candles and recite the words I'm going to dictate to you."

The words Saul dictated filled an entire page for each type of curse that had been placed on Chet. Each evening, they were to light three candles prior to beginning the ritual. Before and after each rejection, they were to say the words, "I am a child of God. I reject the curse that has been placed upon me by sons of Satan, and/or by their master..." All told, the nightly ritual took more than an hour to complete.

For the next six days, Chet hated the very sight of food. To him, raw vegetables without salt were like water without wet. He preferred to go hungry and not eat at all.

By the end of the week, Chet has lost ten pounds, and hopefully counteracted the curses that had been cast upon him. But with the curses lifted from Chet, the dark spirits turned their attention to Eve. Eve was seated on the loveseat, cradled in Chet's arm, when a sudden pain caused her to cry out. Though she'd never been in a fight in her life, it had felt like she *imagined* it would feel to be slugged in the eye.

"What's wrong?" Chet asked.

"I don't know. Something just *hit* me. I want to go take a look in the mirror." Gingerly touching the area beneath her eye, Eve got up and went into the dining room to look in the mirror above the table. "I don't believe this. I have a black eye!" A punch to her upper arm caused her to squeal. "I just got hit again. What the hell's going on?"

"Father," Chet said, "Eve's being attacked. "I pray that you'll make them stop and leave her alone."

When another blow hit her, and another, and another, Chet stood up and shook his fists toward the ceiling. "Leave her alone, you mother fuckers!" he shouted. "If you want to fight with someone, give *me* your best shot. But leave my little angel alone!"

Suddenly Chet clutched his head and doubled over.

"What is it?" Eve asked in alarm.

"My head," Chet gasped. "It feels like it's caught in a vice!" His face had gone pale as paste, and his lips had lost their color.

"Let's go in the bedroom where you can lie down," Eve said worriedly. "I'll see what I can do to get rid of the pain."

In the bedroom, Chet lay down on the bed in the darkness, but the pain in his head only got worse. "Now they've hit my sinuses," he moaned. "They're completely blocked. I can't breathe through my nose."

Though Eve tried to pull the negative energy from his head, it was too strong for her. As the pain grew steadily worse, she began to panic. "Saul, I need your help!"

But Saul didn't answer. Apparently the dark ones were blocking communication.

"Hang on," Eve said worriedly. "I'll try to clear the house and strengthen the pyramid. Maybe then Saul will be able to get through."

While Chet lay moaning on the bed, Eve ran to the kitchen and struck a match to a candle. "This is Saul, and I'm of the light. Run a bowl of water, and ask God to bless it. Then sprinkle the Holy Water in each room before you call the energies to bolster the pyramid." Eve knew that priests in the Catholic Church believed they had authority to bless water and make it Holy because of the fact they were of the church. But she didn't recall reading about Holy Water in the Bible, or that God would bless water only if called upon by a priest. In desperation, she held a bowl beneath the faucet and ran it full of water. "Please, God," she prayed. "Please bless this water and make it holy. Through your blessing, please give it the power to drive the dark ones out of our home. Chet shouldn't have challenged them. But he did, and now they're hurting him. Please…"

Hands shaking, Eve carried the candle and water bowl through the hallway and into each room. With each sprinkle, she said the words, "In the name of Jesus, I command you to leave our house and our property." When she reached the dark bedroom where Chet lay on the bed writhing and clutching his head, Eve set the candle on the dresser. "Just hang on," she said in a quivery voice. "I think I have the house cleared. I'm going to call on the energies now."

Eve's entire body was trembling as she made the rounds to call the energies into the amethysts on the windowsills, the fireplace, in the jewelry box, and in the smoke alarm. From the bedroom, she could hear Chet's voice praying for God to just let him die.

"He doesn't mean it," Eve prayed frantically. "The house is clear now. Please help me to help him."

"You should be able to pull the negative energy out now," Saul said in her head. "But you and Chet need to show that you're one. As things stand now, you're each too vulnerable to attack. United you stand, divided you fall. I want to perform a marriage ceremony. It won't be legal in the eyes of the law, but in the eyes of the dark ones the marriage will be binding."

Eve didn't know what being married or single had to do with what had just happened. But if Saul wanted to perform a marriage ceremony, she was willing to go along with it. Anything to be able to get rid of Chet's pain...

Chapter 46

The cluster headache and sinus blockage had been a lesson to Chet. He no longer thought of himself as invincible.

Eve didn't understand how last night's fiasco could have happened. Granted, Chet had been a fool to issue a challenge. But how were the dark ones able to get in in the first place to start shooting Eve with negative energy? What was the point in having a guardian angel if he wasn't going to guard? What was the point of having a pyramid of protection if it wasn't going to protect? In her estimation, being "chosen" was definitely not what it was cracked up to be.

Chet had been gone for nearly three hours. Allowing forty minutes each way, that was still over an hour and a half at the hospital. Eve hoped nothing had happened to his mother.

Kevin had come by unexpectedly, and he and Eve were having a nice visit. Eve had just finished telling him about the fantasy pictures she was making for Cindy and Jessica. When Kevin was younger, Eve had made an album of fantasy pictures for his stepbrother as a special homecoming gift when he was released after three months in the hospital. She hadn't made a fantasy picture for Kevin at that time because that would have taken away from the special meaning of his stepbrother's gift.

"Do you remember the fantasy pictures I made for Michael when you guys were younger?"

"I always wondered why you never made *me* one," Kevin replied. "I always wished you would—either that, or write a kids' book with me as one of the characters."

Letting the book fantasy slide for the moment, Eve zeroed in on the picture. "You never said you wanted a picture."

"You never asked."

This simple statement tore at Eve's heart. Kevin had never been into pictures when he was growing up. He'd made an effort, whenever possible, to be somewhere else when Eve took out her camera. She'd had no idea that all these years he had wished she'd made a fantasy picture for him. "Is it too late?" she asked quietly. "Now that you're in high school, are you too old for fantasy pictures?"

Tears started in Kevin's blue eyes, but were quickly blinked away. "No, I'm not too old. I'd like to have one, if you'd want to make it."

Eve had made the fantasy pictures for Michael in 1987 by cutting parts from one snapshot to combine with another, then taking a picture of the montage in black and white and tinting the finished product. One picture had shown Michael riding a stegosaurus across the plains in the dead of night. Another had shown him sitting underwater, playing with his toys on the floor of a lake, a stream of bubbles going up from his mouth. Standing next to him with its head above water was a long necked brontosaurus. Now it was 1991, and Eve was making fantasy photos again. The picture she had made of Cindy showed her the size of Thumbelina in the pot of silk flowers sitting on her dresser.

"Do you have anything special in mind?" Eve asked Kevin. "Or do you want me to just use my imagination?"

"I'd like to have a picture of me with Jesus that looks real," Kevin said. "One that looks like He's really there."

Looking at her son with his sideburns and five o'clock shadow, blue eyes glowing with childish excitement, Eve had an irresistible urge to hug him. At the same time, she wanted to ask if he'd lost his mind. "You want a picture with *Jesus?* Where am I supposed to find a realistic picture of Jesus?"

"You asked me what I wanted," Kevin said with a shrug. "I'm sure you'll come up with something." The mischievous grin that tugged at the corners of his mouth was typical of Kevin when dealing with his mom.

"I think I hear Chet's truck in the driveway," Eve said, glad to have the opportunity to change the subject.

It was obvious when Chet came in that he was agitated. But he kept the cause of his agitation to himself and took the time to visit with Kevin and ask him how things were going with him and Cheri. Cheri was the girl Kevin had been going with off and on ever since the eighth grade.

"As a matter of fact, she has a birthday coming up," Kevin said, looking toward Eve and giving her a wink. "I was just about to ask my mom to do a fantasy picture of *her* for me to give her as a birthday gift."

After Kevin had left, Eve asked Chet what was wrong. "Is your mom alright?"

Chet's fists clenched and his arm muscles flexed with the strength of his emotion. "Mom and I had been visiting and talking. I'd been bringing up things from when I was growing up, asking if she remembered—and she did. She remembered when I used to have my Union paper route, and she used to get up at four in the morning to help me roll my papers. At least she said she did, but I couldn't be sure. Then I went to get her a cup of coffee, and—" Tears of helpless fury welled in Chet's blue eyes. His blonde hair was disheveled, and his face was filled with torment.

"And?" Eve said. "What happened?"

"When I came back with the coffee, it wasn't my mom." Chet's words ended on a tattered sob. "It was my mom's body, but the eyes weren't hers," he said pitifully. "She looked at me like she hated me. And when she talked, the voice wasn't hers. It was a fucking spirit talking."

"What did it say?" Eve breathed.

"It told me to leave, and not to come back. It said 'We don't want you here. You're not one of us.'"

So now, to use Saul's terminology, the spirits that had "attached themselves to Beth" were once more speaking through her mouth. "You left without saying anything to upset it?" Eve asked anxiously.

"Of *course* I left. I may be stupid, but not *that* stupid," Chet said through clenched teeth. "I wasn't about to challenge it. Not after what happened the last time."

Chapter 47

"The protection box, and pyramid of energy are about as useless as teats on a rooster," Chet ranted. "We have to do something more."

"We've been waiting for you to come to that realization," Saul said through Eve. "There is something more that can be done. But you're going to have to read your Bible to discover what it is. Tonight God wants you and Eve to read the book of Ezekiel, thinking in terms of how it could apply to your current situation. Chet, you have to be the one to do the reading aloud. It can't be Eve reading to you. God will cooperate, but only if you'll do your part. You have until midnight to come up with a plan."

In Chet's new collection of books, there were several versions and editions of the Bible. Together, seated on the bed, leaning against pillows propped against the wall, he and Eve pored over each chapter of Ezekiel in the new international version, trying to make sense of what God wanted them to do. The going was slow. Chet had never been a fast silent reader, even as a kid. His oral reading was even slower, and infinitely more laborious. By the end of the first hour, Eve's eyelids were growing heavy. By the end of the second, *Chet* was barely awake.

By eleven o'clock, they were no closer to having a plan than they'd been when they started three hours ago. "Let's go back to that part at the beginning," Eve said through a yawn.

"We can't," Chet replied through a yawn of his own. "Saul said I had to read the entire book of Ezekiel. For all we know, what we're looking for could be in the last chapter."

At eleven forty-five, Chet read the final verse. And still they had no idea what they were supposed to do.

"Start over," Eve persisted. "We need to read that part near the beginning—something about destroying Jerusalem."

Holding his eyes open with an effort, Chet turned back to chapter one. When he reached chapter four, he snapped awake. "This is it!" Basically, what they were reading was a description of an effigy. God was telling the prophet to make an effigy of Jerusalem and destroy it. When this effigy was complete and had been destroyed, God would actually cause the same to happen in real life. "We'll make something to stand for the dark ones, then we'll burn it!"

"What could we burn?" Eve asked. "And where could we burn it? There's a law against burning things in the yard."

"We could get something to burn on the barbecue," Chet said excitedly.

"You mean like charcoal briquettes?"

"Why not?" Chet asked. "We could make each briquette stand for a thousand dark ones. Make that ten thousand. For every briquette we burn, we could ask the Father to kill that many dark ones."

"In order to do that," Saul put in, "you would have to mark each briquette with a symbol."

"What kind of symbol would be bad enough to represent the dark ones?" Eve muttered. "Maybe a goat's head..."

"What about an upside down cross?" The excitement in Chet's voice was contagious. "We could scratch an upside down cross on each briquette. The upside down cross is a symbol of Satanism."

For the next several weeks, the first thing Chet did each evening when he got home from work was to light up the barbecue to begin roasting "dark ones." At first he was content to burn ten briquettes each evening. Then it was twelve, then eighteen. By the end of the sixth week, he was up to half a bag each night. Eve could barely keep up, scratching the symbols into the surface of the briquettes.

At first Chet burned the briquettes at dusk, so as not to draw attention from the neighbors. The backyard was surrounded by a redwood fence, but he always made certain he was dressed, just in case. As time went on, Chet cared less and less what the neighbors would think even if they saw him.

In the meantime, Eve had been assigned the task of *concentrating* on killing demons through the *power of her mind*. It wasn't enough to concentrate while Chet was burning briquettes. She was supposed to be concentrating every spare moment—even at work, when the girls were at school.

One particular Friday night, Chet was angry over the fact that he'd spent the day at work being attacked. As was their habit, he and Eve intended to go out to dinner at their favorite Mexican restaurant. But Chet was itching to start the barbecue. "Start scratching the symbols, Angel. A hundred thousand spirits are gonna burn tonight!"

No longer concerned about listening ears or prying eyes, Chet went out on the patio and started the barbecue before changing out of his paint splattered work jeans and flannel shirt. While the barbecue was heating up, he stripped down to his Jockey shorts. The night air was cold—too cold to be barbecuing spirits in his underwear, but Chet didn't seem to mind.

Hugging her arms to her chest and shivering, Eve stayed with him for the first fifty or so briquettes. When she could no longer take the cold, she went inside to watch through the glass patio door. From inside where she could view the scene more objectively, the ludicrousness of the scene suddenly struck her, and she had to cover her mouth to keep Chet from hearing her laughter.

Either the cement beneath his bare feet was freezing, or Chet was doing a war dance! Hopping from one foot to the other, he was tossing coals onto the fire.

Between each batch of coals and the next, he was shaking his fists at the sky. "Burn, you mother fuckers! Burn!"

Thankfully, no one called the police. If they had, Chet would probably have been carted away.

Eve spent the majority of the following week searching for a realistic picture of Jesus—one that looked like an actual person, rather than like a painting. The picture she finally found was on the cover of an Adventist Review magazine. The next step was to provide a background. For this, she purchased a scenic print of a distant mountain and field of wildflowers, with a stream cascading over a bed of rocks in the foreground. It was a simple matter to add wispy cotton clouds over the mountain, and to cut out the picture of Jesus—head and shoulders—to position amidst the clouds.

The next step was to take a picture of Kevin to position by the stream. Kevin preferred to have an open Bible in his hands, and be looking off into the distance. In order to have him looking toward the vision of Jesus in the clouds, Eve shot the picture from a profile view.

When she had developed the film and printed the picture of Kevin in the appropriate size, Eve placed it on the print, standing beside the stream. The montage looked good except for the area around his feet. His shoes simply didn't blend with the ground he was "standing" on. Eve would have to create a rock to put in the foreground and camouflage his feet. A search of all the magazines in Eve's closet failed to produce a picture of a rock. But she did succeed in finding a photo of a breakfast with a *biscuit* that could pass for a boulder. Cut to size, it would make a perfect rock…

Eve was pleased with the finished montage, but couldn't help wondering if Kevin would prefer a familiar setting, as opposed to the country scene by the stream. For this, Chet suggested that they drive to Eve and Kevin's old "stomping grounds" in the outskirts of Reno, and take a desert picture with Mount Rose in the background.

It was a relaxing day, taking pictures of scenery and stopping in Truckee to eat. When they arrived in Reno, there was a light snow on the ground. Perfect…

It took a couple more days for Eve to take black and white pictures of the montages she'd created, develop the film, print the pictures, and tint them to her satisfaction. The wildflowers in the original print had been white and yellow, but because Eve knew purple and blue were two of Kevin's favorite colors, she tinted the flowers in shades of violet, lavender, blue, and deep purple. The sky in this picture was tinted pale blue with white clouds. For the picture with Mt. Rose, Eve decided to make it at sunset. For this, she tinted the sky in shades of pink and orange. When the pictures were finished, she framed them in white frames. Now, the only fantasy she had yet to fulfill was to write a book using Kevin as a character.

Chapter 48

With Beth's health going downhill, and her memory failing more and more, Chet's sister made a trip from San Diego to visit. Eve dreaded the possibility of a confrontation. It had been a long time since Jane had seen her mother, and it was very important to her that her mother recognize her and know she'd come to visit. Eve was hoping against hope Beth would recognize Jane, and that the spirits who had attached themselves to her wouldn't choose to speak.

The drive to Davis was basically silent. Judging from the set of his jaw, Chet had the same reservations as Eve. Eve knew Jane had legitimate concerns of her own.

When they arrived at the convalescent hospital, Chet chose a parking space near the main doors. The most noticeable factor when entering the hospital was that there was no urine smell. That was one of the things Eve and Chet had liked about this hospital from the beginning. Beyond the cleanliness issue, the staff members here were kind and understanding, and everyone loved Beth—or Sam, as Chet called her. Chet had made sure everyone knew his mom was Irish, and that her favorite color was green. As a result, the staff often dressed her in green and talked to her about Ireland.

When a check of the living and dining rooms failed to locate his mother, Chet asked the main nurse if Sam was in her room. "She rarely comes out anymore," the nurse said kindly. "We told her you were coming. She's sitting up in her room waiting."

The semiprivate room was located midway down the hall on the left side. Beth's bed was the one by the door, positioned beneath a large framed print of two young girls sitting in a field of flowers. When she'd first seen the print, Beth had thought she recognized herself and her twin sister when they were children. The comforter on her bed was not the blue floral print Eve had bought her. That had disappeared soon after she'd bought it, and been replaced by the peach quilt that was on the bed now. Eve suspected the floral print had made its way to a room somewhere down the hall, and that some other family was wondering what had happened to the *peach* quilt they'd bought for their own mother. On the wall to the right of his mom's bed, Chet had mounted a wooden shelf and glued Sam's collection of ceramic chickens to the wood so patients wandering from room to room wouldn't be tempted to steal them. Apparently someone had tried to take one anyway. When she couldn't pick it up, she had broken it off at the ankles. Only the orange colored feet remained. Across the room, Beth's roommate's bed was positioned beneath a window—something Eve had never been able to understand, considering that Beth's roommate was blind.

Pathetic in her pants that were too large, huddled in her wheelchair beside her bed, with a shawl clutched beneath her chin, Beth looked up through rheumy eyes as Chet came through the door. "Hey Sam," Chet said. "Where are your glasses? Eve and I brought Annaleegooga to see you. She flew all the way from San Diego just to visit you."

Crossing to the wheelchair where her mother was seated, Jane blinked back her tears. "Mom? It's Jane. Do you recognize me?"

The old lady looked up through a haze of confusion. She had aged twenty years in the short time Eve had known her. "Daughter," she said in a pitiful voice, reaching out to clutch the sleeve of Jane's coat.

That single word brought tears to Jane's eyes. "That's right, Mom," she said brokenly. "I'm you're daughter. I'm here, and I love you."

Later, on the drive home, Jane cried when she told Chet and Eve how much it had meant to her when Beth called her *Daughter*. "It's probably the last time I'll see her alive," Jane said, dabbing at her nose with a tissue. "I don't want to come again, and risk having her not recognize me. I want this to be the last memory."

"Thank you, God," Eve mouthed in the back seat. She'd been so afraid something bad would happen—that Beth would tell Jane to leave, or that the spirit would talk through Beth's mouth and tell Jane she wasn't one of them. When Beth had grasped Jane's sleeve and called her "Daughter," tears had spilled from Eve's eyes, and she'd felt almost faint with relief.

The next evening, Chet's daughter came to dinner to visit with her Aunt Jane. It had been months since Chet had even heard from his daughter. Of his five grown children, only two bothered to keep in touch on a regular basis, and Lucy wasn't one of them. In honor of the occasion, Eve and Chet decided to fondue.

While Chet visited with his sister and daughter in the family room, Eve set the table then returned to the kitchen to cut the sirloin steak into bite-sized pieces and put them on a platter with the mushrooms and water chestnuts. When she'd finished with the platter and made a tossed salad, Eve called to everyone to come to the table, and asked Chet to light the fire under the fondue. "The fondue forks are color coded," she cautioned. "So be sure to remember your color. As soon as the oil's hot, we'll be ready to roll."

Jane and Lucy were both barely five feet tall. Seated across from one another at the oblong oak table, except for the fact that Lucy's closely cropped hair was blonde, they looked like mother and daughter.

Chet set the iron rack with the ceramic pot in the center of the table on a place mat, and filled the pot with peanut oil before lighting the Sterno in the holder beneath it. By the time Eve had poured and served the drinks, the peanut oil had reached a rolling boil.

"I've never fondued meat before," Jane said. "You'll have to show me how to do it."

"It's easy," Chet said, shoving a mushroom and a chunk of meat onto a blue handled fondue fork. "You just stick the fork through whatever you want to cook—kind of like a shish kabob—then put it in the oil like this..." Here, he placed the fondue fork in the bubbling oil and rested the handle on the side of the pot. "Then leave it in, and let it cook till it's done. If you want to, you can use more than one fork at a time. When one's done, you take it out and let the others keep cooking while you're eating."

The women followed suit, and placed their loaded forks in the pot across from Chet's.

Normally, the mere act of dropping a piece of meat into the oil would have caused the oil to sputter, and surround it with bubbles. But, for some reason, this wasn't happening tonight. The mini shish kabobs were merely sitting in the oil, as if the oil were straight out of the bottle. "What's going on?" Chet said, adjusting the Sterno holder. "This thing's not even cooking."

Prior to putting the skewered meat and mushrooms into the pot, the oil had been boiling. Now, despite the flame beneath it, the oil was barely hot to the touch. "Maybe the meat and mushrooms are too cold," Eve said hopefully. She didn't believe that for a minute, but she felt the need to offer *some* explanation. "Let's heat the oil on the stove, then try again."

Everyone at the table took their fondue forks out of the pot and laid them across their plates.

"You should get an electric fondue pot," Lucy commented. "I have one myself, and *it* heats the oil every time."

"So does the Sterno," Eve muttered. In her mind, she completed the thought: *Unless it's being messed with.*

Avoiding Jane's questioning glance, Eve carried the pot to the stove and turned on the burner. She knew Jane suspected what was going on. Chet had told her about spirit harassment. In less than thirty seconds, the oil had returned to a rolling boil. Carrying the pot carefully to the table, Eve warned everyone the oil was hot. "Be careful, and watch out for splatters."

Once again, everyone put a fondue fork of meat and mushrooms into the oil. And again, the food lay in the pot as if the oil were nothing more than cold water.

When Chet had heated the oil on the stove a second time and still the skewered food refused to cook, Jane suggested baking some potatoes in the microwave. "I'm not really all that hungry," she said unconvincingly. "A baked potato and a salad will be fine for me."

"You're not going to just have a baked potato and salad," Chet said irritably. "This thing has never done this before. It's going to work!"

Fifteen minutes later, the oil was still barely hot to the touch—not even hot enough to burn a finger, let alone cook a steak. The situation was so ridiculous there was nothing left to do but laugh. Anyone outside who had heard the laughter would have thought there was a stand-up comedian on the scene. Everyone at the table was holding his stomach. "Will someone *please* just give me a baked potato?" Jane wheezed.

Eve knew Jane knew what was going on, but she wasn't about to tell Lucy.

Chapter 49

As time passed, Eve wondered what had happened to the plans that she become a great healer. Since joining forces with Chet, it seemed the only person she'd had a chance to use the healing power on was *him*. It was hard to believe she'd been working as a nanny for nearly three years, and that Kevin was now a senior in high school—*or* that Chet had lost half his muscles when he went on a protein diet to curtail his spreading waistline.

Eve couldn't help wondering why things had changed so much after she became involved with Chet. What had happened to the *fun* times with her spirit guides? Gideon rarely spoke to her anymore. She and Chet were constantly being harassed. And Saul's explanation of the current state of affairs was unsatisfactory. She wasn't even *using* her healing powers, for Pete's sake. Why would the life she was currently living draw the attention of the dark side?

It had been a long day, and Eve was exhausted. With Chet's snoring a worse harassment than the dark ones, Eve had long since moved to the bedroom across the hall. Ghostly visitors had become an almost nightly occurrence. One night it was her sister who wasn't even dead, coming into her room and sitting down on the edge of the bed. "Sister," she whispered. "Sister." That had freaked Eve out to the point that she'd called her sister to be sure she was alright.

Another night, it was a chorus line of six male can can dancers, each about an inch and a half tall. They were dressed in tails with top hats and canes, and they were performing in a *spotlight* on the pillow next to Eve's head! In Chet's room across the hall, there was a laughing green skeleton "projected" on his wall with blood dripping from its bony hands.

The touch lamp in the family room had become a constant problem, but it was a playful spirit of light who was doing that. Chet would turn it off each night before going to bed, but the instant he reached the end of the hallway the lamp would come back on.

This particular night, it was *Chet* who came into Eve's room, in the form of an apparition only three feet tall!

Eve rolled out of bed and crossed the hall to Chet's room. "This is getting ridiculous," she said irritably. "I just had another visitor. He looked just like you, but was only a head taller than my bed. This place is getting to be like Grand Central Station."

"I don't know how you can be so nonchalant," Chet said. "This kind of stuff totally freaks me out. But you just seem to take it in stride."

"What am I supposed to do?" Eve asked. "Run screaming down the hallway? What good would that do?"

Irritating as the visitations were, what got to Eve most was that they'd started messing with her camera. She'd always enjoyed photography and been confident of her picture taking abilities. She especially enjoyed taking action pictures of Kevin at his football games. Usually the harassment took the form of causing the shutter to stick or the flash to misfire—but *only* when taking pictures of Kevin. Eve had prayed many times for God to stop the harassment, but either he didn't hear her prayers, or else he refused to act on them.

A few days after the miniature Chet visitor, Eve was working on a craft project that she had spread out on the dining room floor. The overhead light had a seventy-five watt bulb, but the light was too dim to read the instructions. "We really need to put a brighter bulb in that light fixture," Eve commented. "It's too dark in here."

The seventy-five watt bulb in the overhead fixture instantly began to glow brighter. Eve and Chet gaped at one another, then began to laugh. "It must be the same guy that does the touch lamp," Chet commented. "What do you say, Bruce? Can't you do better than that?"

The light immediately clicked to a brighter setting—this time, the equivalent of two hundred watts! "Thank you, Bruce," Eve said with a smile.

Over the next several weeks, Bruce continued to play with the lights in the family and dining rooms. On one occasion when Chet's son came to visit, as Steve was leaving, Chet decided to freak him out. "Come here, Mooler." ('Mooler' was the nickname Chet had assigned to Steve.) "I want to show you something."

Steve was a tall handsome man in his mid-thirties, with wavy brown hair and a thick moustache. Curious as to what his dad wanted to show him, he followed Chet into the office area of the dining room and watched as Chet switched off the overhead light.

"Okay, Bruce," Chet said. "Do your stuff."

When the light clicked on in response to Chet's request, the blood drained from Steve's face, and Eve thought he was going to faint. "I'm out of here, Dad. Maybe I'll call you later."

Eve could only imagine what was going through Steve's mind. He'd been the object of spirit harassment as a child when he and his family had lived in a house inhabited by spirits. Chet and his wife had been members of the Adventist Church at that time, and had often been involved in discussions of hauntings and harassment by demonic forces. In his study of the early writings of the Adventist prophet, Ellen White, Chet had read about the Fox sisters—two sisters from the 1800's who had claimed to be able to communicate with the dead through knocking on the wall. The sisters claimed to have devised a code—one knock for this, two knocks for that... They claimed spirits of the dead returned the knocks, speaking in code to answer their questions. Ellen White had identified the sounds to be the knockings of a Satanic force.

After reading about the knockings, but prior to any other known spirit activities in his house, Chet had heard a knocking sound one night on the wall at the head of his bed. It had been too dark outside to check the sound that night, but the next morning he'd gone out to investigate. The area of the house adjacent to the bedroom had been clear of bushes and branches, or anything else that could have accounted for the knocking sound the night before.

Reasoning that an animal must have come into the yard during the night, but unable to imagine what an animal could have done to produce the knocking sound, Chet had felt a chill course through his body.

That night and the next, though he had lain awake listening, there'd been no reoccurrence of the knockings. The third night, the sound had returned: Knock knock. Heart in his throat, Chet had crept out of bed and put his ear to the wall. There it was again! Chet's arm and hand had trembled as he lifted his fist to knock in response—not twice, but *three* times to test whether the two knocks had been a natural phenomenon or the knockings of a spirit: Knock knock knock.

The sound of Chet's heart had thudded in his ears as he'd waited with baited breath for a response. He hadn't had long to wait: knock knock knock. Three knocks! Something or someone had answered by knocking three times instead of two! There could be no question now. He was dealing with a spirit.

It had been after that that the harassment had begun: pans banging in the kitchen cupboards, paint cans being flung about the garage, a cloaked figure appearing at the foot of the children's beds…On one occasion, Steve's brother Paul had been picked up out of his bed and transported to the living room couch in the middle of the night. With memories like those, no wonder Steve freaked out!

Several nights later, Eve and Chet were talking to Saul on the board when Saul said that *Jesus* Himself wanted to talk to Eve about resuming her training as a natural healer! A year ago, the idea of Jesus speaking to her would have seemed preposterous. But when she'd been in Placerville, He had, after all, said He was disappointed that she didn't talk to Him as often as she used to when she was a child. If she was to be a natural healer and the power was to come from Him, it seemed reasonable that He'd want to speak to her.

Eve's heart skipped a beat when the pendulum told her the time had come for her to prepare to work directly with Jesus instead of through Saul. Saul had trained her well. Now the time had come to move on to the next step. The speaker got as far as insisting that she cut out fast foods and soft drinks and drink eight glasses of water a day, when He was interrupted by a dark one. If this truly was Jesus speaking, Eve couldn't understand why He would stand for the dark ones interfering. It didn't make sense that He wouldn't use his power to squelch them. Dropping the pendulum in irritation and disgust, Eve gave voice to her feelings. "Why doesn't He *do* something about the interference?"

Eve was seated in her usual spot in the brown chair kitty corner from the matching loveseat, still holding the board and pendulum in her lap and the tourmaline in her hand. The environmental tape was playing on the stereo boom box. Chet was in his customary spot, lying on the loveseat across from the fireplace. "It doesn't fit with my idea of Jesus either," Chet said. "He's the creator of the world! All He'd have to do is say one word, and the dark ones would be history! Letting them interrupt Him like this makes Him look like a wimp."

It seemed to both Eve and Chet that something was wrong with this picture. But their thoughts were not God's. They couldn't hope to understand Him.

The board session took nearly two hours—two hours of saying ten or twelve words, then being interrupted and having to start over. The gist of the communication appeared to be that Eve's body was impure. If Jesus was really going to work with her, she would have to improve her diet. Eve had never been a water drinker, even as a child. He wanted her to start with eight glasses a day— eventually to progress to ten or twelve!

Eve refrained from comment, but she was certain He read her thoughts. There was no way she could drink that much water. She didn't even *want* to. If having Saul as her healing guide brought the constant attention of the dark ones, what would it be like if she was working with *Jesus*? Granted, she was honored to have been chosen. But judging from past experience, He wouldn't use His power to stop the dark ones from harassing her. Eve had no desire to become a martyr.

She was discussing her feelings with Chet when a fleeting movement caught her eye. The movement had been in her upper field of vision. Rolling her eyes upward, Eve gaped. An apparition that looked like a propeller was spinning above her head! When she tipped her head back for a better look, the apparition disappeared. When she returned her head to its normal position, the apparition returned. "The pyramid must be down," Eve said uneasily. "There's a propeller of some sort spinning over my head. I can see it when I roll my eyes up, but when I tip my head it disappears. We need to clear the house!"

"Get out of that chair and come over here!" Chet shouted. "Get away from it!"

Eve did as Chet had suggested, but the apparition continued to haunt her. This was the first time, other than the mouse and the penis-shaped plume of smoke, that she'd witnessed an apparition that hadn't come under cover of darkness. The dark ones were getting bolder.

Chapter 50

It was the culmination of what Kevin had worked so hard to achieve, other than grades. Since elementary school, it had been his dream to be on a high school football team. When he'd reached high school age and made the team in spite of his slender stature, he had made it a personal challenge to play as well as any jock on the team. Now the final season was over. Tonight, awards would be handed out.

Eve had reserved a page in Kevin's photo album for a picture of Kevin accepting his award. Memories of football games when she had stood on the sidelines in fair weather and foul snapping pictures of Kevin for his album nagged at the back of Eve's mind. Even when she'd managed to *get the shots* without harassment, invariably something had gone wrong in the darkroom. Finally she'd given up on developing the film herself and begun taking it to a B&W lab for processing. But even there, things had gone wrong. Pictures of scenic barns came out perfect. Still lifes of flowers and fruit: no problem. Portraits of the girls Eve nannied for: beautiful. But when it came to pictures of Kevin—special occasion pictures that mattered—invariably something went wrong. Why should she expect tonight to be any different?

Eve hated when negative thoughts came to mind. She was perfectly capable of snapping a picture. She'd tested her camera this afternoon to make sure everything was in working order. The film was new, and the batteries in the flash were fresh. When Eve and Chet arrived at the school cafeteria, parents in casual dress were already seated at the cafeteria tables. At the left end of the room, a separate table had been set up for handing out the certificates and awards. A few team members were chatting in the back corner, but Eve couldn't see Kevin.

At the center table, Tom and Lorraine were waving to indicate they had saved Eve and Chet a seat. Eve wondered if there were any other families here like Kevin's: families where parents and stepparents sat together and chatted like casual friends. Eve noted that Lorraine had brought *her* camera. Good. That would at least provide backup. But Lorraine wasn't one to get into the center of things. Whatever pictures she took would be taken from her seat. There was no way she'd go up front to snap a picture.

When the coach began calling the players' names and the players began filing into the cafeteria, Eve left her seat at the table to position herself at the front of the cafeteria where she could see the players' faces as they received their awards.

"This first player weighs one hundred ninety-five pounds, and that's one hundred ninety-five pounds of pure muscle on the offensive line," the coach said into the microphone. "When he first tried out for the team three years ago, he couldn't catch a ball. By the end of his second year, he was our most valuable offensive player. I'm talking about Mark Swanson, number 39. Come on out here, Mark, and get your award."

To test her camera and flash and make certain they were working, Eve snapped a picture of Mark and each of the other team members as the coach said his piece for each, and handed out the awards. Focus; snap, flash. Focus; snap, flash. Both the camera and flash were working perfectly.

"This next player really kept me on my toes," the coach said with a grin. "Sometimes it was a little hard to take, because if I ever misspoke or made a mistake he was right there to question me and force me back on track." Kevin! The coach had to be talking about Kevin. "He wasn't one of the bigger players on the team. He weighs in at only a hundred thirty-eight pounds. But if they were giving an award for heart, it would go to him. Pound for pound, he played as well as anyone on the team. I'm talking about number 49—Kevin MacDuff."

When Kevin approached the table, pointedly ignoring the fact that his mom was crouched right in front of him with her camera, Eve focused in and pressed the shutter release. The button refused to click, and the flash unit refused to flash. *Damn.* In a panic, Eve muttered a prayer and tried again. Still no click; still no flash. No click, no flash. No click, no flash. As he passed by where his mom was kneeling, Kevin mouthed the question, "Why didn't you take a picture of *me*?" And then he was gone and the next award was being presented.

Focus: Click, Flash. The camera and flash worked perfectly.

White hot anger coursed through Eve's veins. Her muscles tensed, and her teeth clenched of their own accord, in mute expression of pent up fury the likes of which Eve had never known. Avoiding Chet's eyes, she returned to her seat.

"What happened?" Chet whispered.

"What do you *think*?" Eve grated. "I don't even want to talk about it."

Later, after the awards ceremony was over, they walked away from the cafeteria in the darkness. Eve was glad Chet didn't try to comfort her. There could be no words of comfort. *God how she hated them—hated the dark ones.* Hatred wasn't a strong enough word to express the loathing she felt for them. "Asshole sons of bitches," she said through clenched teeth, "I *hate* them! *I hate this frigging camera.* I just feel like throwing it as far as I can!"

"No angel," Chet said. "It's the dark ones trying to get you to do it. Don't—"

Before Chet could stop her, Eve drew back her arm and threw the case containing her Minolta across the schoolyard fifteen feet or more. The camera and case crashed into the side of a metal garbage can.

Shocked into silence, Chet hesitated for a moment, then started across the grass, intent on retrieving the camera.

"Leave it," Eve snarled.

"I'm not leaving the camera here," Chet argued. "You'll feel better tomorrow, and be glad I got it."

"I don't need a camera," Eve said in a barely audible voice. "I used to love photography. Now I hate it. I'm not going to be taking pictures anymore."

Chet returned to Eve's side, holding the camera case in the hand that was away from her so she couldn't grab it even if she wanted to. "You can't let them upset you like this," he said. "You're just playing into their hands. You can't give up on photography. That's just what they want you to do."

"Let's don't even talk," Eve snapped. "I don't give a damn if I play into their hands. I've *had* it. I can't take anymore."

The drive home from the high school was silent. Chet knew better than to try to reason.

When they arrived home and Chet put the car in Park, Eve didn't wait for him to turn off the ignition. She opened the passenger side door and stepped out, slamming the door behind her. Chet followed at a safe distance as Eve stalked to the front door and fumbled with her key at the lock. "Damn it to Hell and back," Eve grated. "I *hate* them. I *hate* them. *I hate them!*"

When the door finally opened and Eve stepped inside, she let out a scream that echoed through the house. Tearing at her hair like a madwoman, she stalked into the family room.

"Angel," Chet said quietly, "The camera's not broken. Look. The case protected it."

Taking the camera case from Chet's hands, Eve examined it with icy detachment. "If the camera's not already broken, I'm going to smash it."

This time Chet didn't try to stop her. "Alright Angel," he said in a tone of resignation. "Do what you have to do."

As if in slow motion, Eve took the camera out of the case, raised it above her head, and flung it across the room. "There. Are you satisfied? Now you don't have a camera to *mess* with, Assholes."

It didn't occur to Eve at the time that she had just cut off her nose to spite her face.

Chapter 51

Following the fiasco surrounding the football awards ceremony, Eve didn't snap a picture for more than a month. Eventually, she took the Minolta in to see if it could be repaired. She knew the lens wasn't broken. It was the camera body that concerned her.

The man behind the camera counter was wearing a red toupee. Eve knew it was a toupee because it was lopsided on his head. "How can I help you?"

"My camera's broken," Eve replied. Laying the dented camera on the counter, she waited for him to comment.

"What happened?" the man asked with a frown. "It looks like somebody threw it against a brick wall."

"Close," Eve muttered. "Can it be fixed?"

The red-wigged man removed the lens and held it to the light to examine it. "The lens looks like it's still in good shape. But I'm sure you must realize the body's shot."

"So what's the bottom line?" Eve asked impatiently. "Do I have to get a new camera, or can you fix the old one?" She really didn't mean to snap. It wasn't this man's fault her camera was broken. It was just that throwing the camera across the room had been such a stupid move.

"You can buy a used Minolta body to fit this lens, but it'll cost you a hundred dollars."

"You're saying that once I have the new camera body, it'll be as good as new?"

"It won't be the equivalent of a newer camera," the man said. "It won't have the features the newer cameras have. But it will have the same features you had before, and the camera will be in excellent shape. Any lens that fit the old one will fit this one too."

The camera Eve took home that day was identical to the one she'd broken. As an afterthought, she'd bought a new flash unit, and new batteries for both the camera and flash. Kevin would be graduating next week. His Grandma and Aunt Cheryl would be coming for the occasion. She couldn't let their visit go by without taking pictures, and she couldn't count on *Lorraine* to get pictures of graduation.

Lorraine's camera was a point and shoot. In dim light, the flash was automatically activated. Considering that the light from her flash would only reach fifteen feet, the only way to get a decent shot of Kevin on stage would be for Lorraine to use at least 1000 ASA Film, and Eve was certain Lorraine wouldn't do that.

Eve's mom and sister came the day before Graduation. It was good to see them. Normally, if Eve wanted to see them she had to fly to Southern California to visit *them* since her niece's family lived there too. But an event such as high school graduation was important enough to make an exception.

Eve was so proud of Kevin she could burst. He had come so close to being valedictorian, only missing by three thousandths of a point. The A- that had cost him the honor of being valedictorian had been given in his freshman year because he and his classmates had talked in class. Frustrated and angered by students talking when they should be studying, his teacher had made a "statement" by refusing to give an A for the term, regardless of whether it had been earned or not. She'd had no way of knowing that this impulsive act would one day cost one of her students so dearly.

As salutatorian, Kevin had been given the honor of calling the names of graduates during the second half of the ceremony to come forward and receive their diplomas. This meant he would also be calling his own name. He had told Eve he had something special planned. When he called his own name, he wanted his mom to be ready to capture the moment on film…

"Do you think we'll be warm enough without a wrap of some sort?" Eve's mother asked.

"It's going to be at least 80 degrees," Chet replied. "That suit you're wearing will be more than enough."

Eve's mother and sister had flown in yesterday afternoon. Both were wearing suits. Eve, too, was wearing a suit—forest green, with a white silk blouse. In honor of the occasion, Eve had bought Chet a corduroy sport jacket to go with his jeans and western boots.

"I can't believe Kevin's old enough to graduate," Eve's sister said. "He's such a good looking guy, but he sure doesn't look eighteen."

It was true Kevin didn't look his age. Looking younger than one's years ran in the family. Based purely on appearance, it was hard to believe that Kevin would soon be a freshman at the University.

There was no lack of conversation on the drive to the Convention Center. Chet told the story of how his father had grown up on a farm in North Dakota, and had graduated from sixth grade at age 21. Eve's sister brought up the story of when Kevin was a month-old baby and his eight-year-old cousin had freaked Eve out by taking him for a ride on her skateboard. Eve was glad Kevin's grandma and Aunt Cheryl had been able to come. Having them here to represent her side of the family made his graduation even more special.

When they arrived in the vicinity of the Convention Center, Chet parked approximately a block away. Eve was glad she'd chosen to wear only one-inch heels. Her shoe heels beat a tattoo along with her mother's and sister's as they walked at a brisk pace from the car to the building where the graduation ceremony would be held.

On the sidewalk in front of the Convention Center, several girls in burgundy caps and gowns had come outside and were chatting with a group of adults who were having one last cigarette before going in for the ceremony. One girl with glasses and a long brown French braid reminded Eve of a wobbly crane. Eve was certain she'd never worn high heels before.

At the double doors, Chet stepped to one side and let the ladies walk in first. In the lobby, a student handed each of them a program.

"I hope Tom and Lorraine are already here," Eve said. "Tom said they'd save us a seat if they got here before we did."

Inside the auditorium the seats had already begun to fill up. "There's Lorraine up front in the third row, waving," Chet said. "You should be able to get some good pictures from that distance."

Remembering what had happened at the football awards ceremony, Eve muttered a silent prayer that Chet was right.

As they approached the row where they'd be sitting, Tom and Lorraine stood to stay "Hello" to Eve's mother and sister. Though Cheryl had remained in touch with Tom, exchanging cards at Christmas time, it was the first time she and Eve's mother had seen him since his and Eve's divorce. It was also the first time either Cheryl or her mother had met Lorraine. Greetings and exchanges were cordial, but a bit guarded on the part of Eve's mother. She respected Tom for living up to his responsibilities, but had yet to forgive him for what he'd done to Eve.

Though Chet had intended to sit next to Eve, he found himself relegated to a seat between her sister and mother. Eve took the seat next to Tom. If Kevin was able to look down from the stage at his family, she wanted him to see his parents together.

"Thanks for saving us these seats," Eve said with a warm smile. "Chet had to work late, and we couldn't get here any sooner."

"No problem," Tom replied. "We were one of the first ones here."

It was typical of Tom to be among the first to arrive at any function, just as it was typical of Chet to get there at the last minute.

Eve had loaded her camera with high speed film for dim lighting, set the switch on her camera to On, and attached the automatic film advance. To test that all was operating correctly, she aimed the camera at the floor and clicked the shutter release. Perfect.

A moment later, the lights in the auditorium dimmed and the stirring strains of Pomp and Circumstance issued from the corner speakers. Regal in their burgundy caps and gowns, the class of '94 proceeded down the aisle past rows of proud parents and grandparents and climbed the steps to the stage where they took their seats on the rows of folding chairs awaiting them.

"I see Kevin," Cheryl whispered in Eve's ear. "He's on the end on the second row."

It was the first time Eve had ever seen her son wearing glasses. The gold wire frames on the small-lensed glasses actually looked rather distinguished. Eve didn't know why Kevin had elected to wear them tonight—probably because he'd be reading names of his classmates during the second half of the ceremony.

Prior to the presentation of diplomas was the presentation of special awards. Kevin's name was called five times. Five times he came forward to accept his award, to the accompaniment of applause from the audience. Tears of pride filled Eve's eyes.

When three students had shared the honor of being tied for Valedictorian and the announcement was made that Kevin had missed being Valedictorian by only 1/3000 of a point, a collective "Aaaaaaawwwww" of sympathy drifted through the audience. Eve knew how Kevin was feeling at this moment. He had shared with her how angry he was with the teacher who had given him the minus in his freshman year—the minus that had nothing to do with his performance in that particular subject; the minus that had cost him the well-deserved honor of tying for first place for valedictorian.

As one by one the names were called and the diplomas handed out, each was greeted by a burst of applause from both the audience and the seniors on stage. A few times, the applause was punctuated by whistles and shouts—not at all the decorum Eve had expected.

During the second half of the program, Kevin stepped forward and took the microphone. Eve snapped a picture. She didn't know what he had planned for his own name, but whatever it was, she was ready...

"And last, but not least, myself: Kevin MacDuff." When he said his name, Kevin raised his arms above his head in a gesture of victory. Eve snapped a picture. Then Kevin took her and everyone else by surprise when he bent double, lifted one knee, and jerked back one elbow with a cry of "Yessssssss!" The shutter release refused to click. Eve tried again, but again, the shutter release was blocked. Kevin had done the surprising thing he'd asked Eve to take a picture of, and it had happened again: The dark ones had kept her from getting the picture.

Later, when Kevin joined his family outside the Convention Center, he whispered in Eve's ear that at the moment he made his move, a voice had sounded inside his head: "We're messing with your mom's camera."

Eve was glad that at least the spirit had told him. He knew that she'd tried. It wasn't her fault. Damn the son of a bitching spirit to Hell.

267

Chapter 52

It had been a good weekend. Eve and Chet had driven to the mountains to take pictures of old barns without fear of harassment, since these pictures didn't count. Of course Saul had gone with them. On the way home, Saul was in a jovial mood, poking fun at Chet's driving, and teasing him about his unruly hair.

There was one interruption, but this time the dark spirit talked inside *Chet's* head. "Thought you could get away from us today, didn't you, Bonehead?"

"Bite me," Chet grated.

"I can't," the dark spirit replied. "We don't have teeth!"

Despite his irritation, Chet couldn't help laughing. "In the name of Jesus," he chuckled, "Get out of this car."

When they got home, Eve performed the usual ritual of turning on the environmental tape and making the rounds of each room to clear them. When she had called the energies into the amethysts and felt that the pyramid was strong, she sat down on the loveseat next to Chet to enjoy the fire he had built in the grate.

Eve had never cared for environmental tapes in the past, with the exception of a tape she'd once had of a bubbling stream. Environmental tapes reminded her of health food stores and the odors that went with them. The New Age tape that was playing now wasn't bad: It was just that she was tired of it. Cradled in Chet's arm, Eve told him of her plan to hang the group of sepia toned barns in the office.

"That'd be good," Chet agreed. "Maybe next weekend we could drive to Nevada City to get a picture of the covered bridge to add to the group."

Eve had opened her mouth to reply when something on the tape brought her up short. What was that sound in the background?

Chet was staring at the boom box with a strange look on his face. "Did you hear it too? It sounded like voices. But I didn't understand what they were saying."

"Rewind it," Eve said nervously. "Let's listen to it again."

Chet crossed the room and rewound the tape, then returned to the loveseat and sat down next to Eve. The eerie voices in the background of the New Age music were a chorus of both male and female. Upon close attention, they appeared to be chanting.

"Those weren't on there before," Eve whispered. "What are they saying? It sounds like they're saying to give up!"

"That's what it sounded like to me too," Chet said softly. "Let's rewind it and listen again."

This time the voices and message were clear: "Give up. Give up. Give up up up. Give up. Give up. Give up up up. Give up Chet."

An iron fist gripped Eve's chest, and for a moment she couldn't breathe. "They said your name! Are they telling *you* to give up? Or are they telling *me* to *give* you up?"

Chet rewound the tape and listened a final time, then ripped the tape from the cassette. As he did, an electrical surge ran the length of his arm. "We've got to get rid of this thing. I'm going to take it out and put it in the garbage right now."

Eve's heart was doing a drum roll. She felt as if she were going to faint. When Chet returned, Eve went to the closet to take out the tourmaline and board before sitting down on the loveseat to surround herself with light. "Saul?" she asked hesitantly. "What's going on?"

"This is Saul, and I'm of the light. It's just another form of harassment. They haven't succeeded in scaring you for awhile. So now they've tried another approach. It looks like it worked."

It had worked, alright. Eve felt a little better, now that she knew Saul wasn't upset by what had happened. But the memory of the voices set her nerves on edge. When Chet returned, his face was lined with concern. "This isn't the first time I've heard their voices on a recording."

Not the first time? What was he saying?

"Several years ago, when I was married to Marilyn and we were members of the Adventist Church—It was just like this. We had a record of the Heritage Singers. One day the record was fine; the next day there were other voices on it. They sounded almost like they were computerized. I knew they weren't human."

Eve had known Chet's step-daughters had been the target of demonic harassment, but this was the first she'd heard about voices. When she asked the next question, her mouth was dry. "Why didn't you tell me this before?"

Chet didn't know why he hadn't mentioned it before. It just hadn't come to mind till now. He had thought at the time he was being targeted for harassment because he was on the true path. He knew now that wasn't so.

In an attempt to get their minds off what had just happened, Chet suggested they go to Denny's for fries and a Coke. Of course Saul and the gang went with them.

When they arrived home a couple of hours later, Saul asked Eve to take out the board in case anyone else wanted to talk. Once on the board, he requested that Eve get a tablet and pen. "We want you to make a list," he said. "We want you to write down everything you believe about your guides and the spirit world beyond a shadow of a doubt. Beliefs that can't be shaken no matter what happens."

"I'll get the paper and pen," Chet volunteered.

Saul continued to talk through the board while Eve was waiting for Chet to return. It seemed strange that *Saul* could often talk without interruption when the creator of the world could not. When Chet returned and sat down in the brown recliner, Eve laid the board aside and began to write:

1. I believe in God, and that Jesus is His son who died on the cross and was resurrected.
2. I believe that Gideon is my guardian angel, and that he was my husband in a prior life.
3. I believe that Saul is my healing guide, and that the healing power comes from Jesus.
4. I believe—

"You fucking little cunt," a voice said in her head. "This is Gideon, your so-called guardian angel, and I'm of the fucking light."

Horrified, Eve dropped the pen.

"What is it?" Chet asked. "What's wrong?"

Eve's face was ashen, and her hands were trembling uncontrollably. "There's a dark spirit talking to me in my mind. He's claiming to be Gideon, and he's saying horrible things."

"It's not really Gideon," Chet said. "*Ask* if he's of the light."

A sob rose to Eve's throat, nearly choking off her words. "He already said he is."

"I thought spirits of darkness couldn't claim to be of the light," Chet said. "I thought—"

"Tell him to shut his fucking mouth, bitch. I'm not just *claiming* to be Gideon. I *am* him. If you only knew how I've laughed at you—believing all that bullshit I fed you about reincarnation, and getting turned on when I told you about how we made love. I'd *like* to fuck your slippery little—"

"We have to fix the pyramid," Eve said urgently. "We have to clear the house!" She was trembling so badly it frightened Chet.

On his feet now, Chet raised his voice. "I don't know who you are that's talking to Eve. But in the name of Jesus Christ and the blood He shed for us, I command you to leave this house!"

This time the voice spoke inside *his* head and the blood drained from his face. "*Fuck* Jesus Christ. And fuck his blood."

"It won't leave," Chet rasped. "Talk to Saul."

Eve picked up the pendulum with a trembling hand, and the pendulum began to swing: "This is Chet's 'buddy,' the Holy Spirit talking, and I'm of the light. I want to speak to Chet."

"This one has to be real," Chet whispered, sitting down on the loveseat to listen. "No one else knows I used to call the Holy Spirit my buddy."

Chet had once told Eve the Holy Spirit was his buddy. But apparently, he'd forgotten about that. Eve wanted to believe this was the Holy Spirit. But if this was the Holy Spirit talking, why did it feel so wrong?

"Chet," the pendulum continued. "I'm surprised at you. With all your Bible studies, you still fell for the doctrines the demons were handing out. *Eve*, I could understand. She's never studied the Bible in depth. But *you*…"

Tears welled in Chet's eyes and spilled over onto his cheeks. "I'm sorry," he whispered. "I should have known better. I'm sorry…"

"You *should* be sorry," the pendulum spelled out. "You're not talking to the fucking Holy Spirit, you stupid bastard. This is *Satan*."

Eve dropped the pendulum as if it were a hot coal. *Why?* Why was this happening? If the dark ones were cutting off communication with her true guides, why weren't her guides doing anything to stop it? "We need to call the energies into the amethysts and strengthen the pyramid again. After we've done that, we can fill ourselves with white light, and…"

"This is the Spirit of the East," a voice said in her mind. "Don't bother calling me into a fucking stone, because that's not going to protect you."

A chill of fear coursed through Eve's veins. "In the name of Jesus," she whimpered, "I command you to leave."

"Shut up, bitch. And pick up the pendulum. I want Chet to hear what I'm saying."

Moving like a zombie, Eve picked up the pendulum. Immediately, the pendulum began to swing, coming to an abrupt halt at the end of each sentence. "For an educated woman, you are incredibly stupid—believing that a fucking crystal, or icon, or imaginary light could protect you. That's as stupid as hanging a *dream catcher* on the wall to keep us out."

Tears were streaming down Eve's cheeks. The lump in her throat made it impossible to speak.

"You were so easy," the Energy sneered. "A touch of little boy charm, and you were caught—hook, line, and sinker."

The feel of the pendulum suddenly changed. This time, it was Caruso. "This is Caruso, and I'm of the light, just like Gideon. Gideon told me how they suckered you in by making you think your kid was in danger. He also told me you're a pushover for schmaltz. I guess I proved that. I actually had you *feeling sorry for me* when you thought I couldn't do anything right!"

Throughout all that had been said, Chet hadn't said a word. Not since being chastised by Satan. He looked as if his life's blood had been drained.

In a state of shock, Eve mouthed Saul's name, dreading to hear his answer. "Saul?" she said in a quivery voice, "Are *you* a dark one too?"

"I'm afraid so," Saul murmured. His voice in Eve's mind was soft—not loud and insulting as Gideon's had been. Through her mind's eye, Eve could see his face with its brown skin and soulful brown eyes. In her mind, he looked the same as before—distinguished yet playful; wise; handsome, with his closely cropped crown of white hair; and oh so very loving. Yet he had just admitted to being a demon! "I wish I could say I weren't. But I am."

"But I *loved* you," Eve sobbed.

There was a moment of silence before Saul spoke. "I know you did, Sweetheart. That was part of the plan. What wasn't part of the plan is that *I* would love *you*." In her mind, Eve could see the pain in his face. His voice broke momentarily, and then it was strong. "We're not supposed to love anyone," he went on. "But the fact is, I *do*. That's gotten me in trouble, more than you know."

Blinded by tears, Eve buried her face in her hands, pressing her palms to her eyes to shut out the mental image. She couldn't believe this was happening. She was sitting on the loveseat in front of the fire, and her world was falling apart around her.

"I want you to listen closely to what I'm going to say," Saul went on. And then the image was back. Why did he have to look so loving? *How* could he look so loving when his words cut like a knife?

Chet reached out to take Eve in his arms. His embrace, meant to comfort and reassure, merely served to deepen the pain she was feeling.

"I'm going to be in trouble for telling you this," Saul said softly, "but I'm going to say it anyway. You've been on the wrong path with your fascination with psychic things. Your parents started you out on the right track, but you got off track when you were in high school and college."

As Saul spoke, Eve repeated his words aloud so Chet would know what he was saying. Even through the haze of pain in her mind, she knew Saul was speaking of Ouija Boards and Automatic Writing, and of the college course in Folklore and Mythology that had caused her to lose faith in the stories of the Bible. She was crying so hard now she couldn't breathe through her nose. But her tears didn't blur the image of Saul in her mind. His face now was stern: his brow creased in a frown. "Don't ever go to a psychic again. Stay completely away from the psychic realm. Don't ever speak to a spirit again—*not even me*, unless you want to end up in hell with the rest of us. Promise me, Sweetheart..."

A muffled sob was Eve's only reply. She felt as if there were a gaping hole in her chest. Her heart had been ripped out and trampled on, and she didn't know how she would ever survive.

A searing pain suddenly gripped Chet's thigh. In an automatic response, Eve placed her hands over the pain, then slowly pulled them away to draw out the negative energy. But she couldn't even *feel* the energy now. "The healing power's—gone," she said brokenly. "They've taken it away."

Eve felt like a rag doll that had been cast aside and thrown into the garbage. For a year before Chet, and almost three years since then, her spirit guides had been her constant companions. She'd loved them like she loved her own family. Now it was as if her family had died, and taken with them the healing power—the one thing that had made her special.

"My whole personality was wrapped up in the healing," she said dully. "Without *it*, I'm nothing."

Chet instinctively held her tighter, but that only added to her pain. "Don't ever say that," he said tearfully. "You're my little angel. You're Kevin's mother. You're a creative lady. And you're one hell of a writer. You still have all those things. *They* haven't been taken away."

Eve heard the sound of Chet's voice, but his words fell on deaf ears. Lies. That's all it had been. Just four and a half years of lies. And now this.

"You still have *me*," Chet said into her hair. "I'm still here with you, and I'm not going anywhere."

Eve loved Chet. It was important to know that he was still with her. That, at least, wasn't a lie. But why couldn't he see that the floor had just fallen from beneath her feet, and she had nothing left to stand on?

For the next three weeks, Eve went through the motions of living and working. But inside, she was little more than a zombie. She didn't really miss Gideon that much. He had said he was going to back off once she was with Chet, and that's exactly what he had done. But she missed Saul terribly. And she missed the ability to heal with her touch, even if it hadn't been the real thing.

Eve knew Chet was worried about her. She could see it in his eyes and the way he hovered over her. It was as if he viewed her as a blown glass figurine that would shatter the instant it wasn't protected. Eve knew Chet was feeling these things. But at this point, she was powerless to reassure him.

Could it be that Saul had been telling the truth when he'd said that he'd grown to love her, or was he the greatest deceiver of all? What had prompted the spirit guides to reveal themselves for what they really were? Was it the fact that she'd been baptized as a child? Had God made them do it? Had they been setting her up for four long years, just waiting for the right moment to devastate her? Or had the longstanding joke simply grown tiresome? Eve supposed she would never know.

Chapter 53

The fact that Eve no longer communicated with spirits did not mean they were out of her life—or out of Chet's, for that matter. There were still the shooting pains; still lights going on and off by themselves. (They knew now that Bruce was not of the light; no pun intended.) And still, there were the nighttime visitors. It never failed to amaze Eve how creative the spirits could be in the ways they chose to appear. From a mouse in the breadbasket, to a dismembered head, to a 4 x 6 wooden beam propped against the bedroom door.

The lines in Chet's face had grown noticeably deeper since the night the spirits revealed themselves. Eve knew it was because he was worried about *her*, but she didn't know what to do about it.

Finally, in desperation, Chet paid a visit to a Christian bookstore where he bought a book on spiritual warfare. He and Eve agreed to read the book from beginning to end before attempting to follow its advice. Every evening after work, they would build a fire in the family room fireplace and Chet would lie on the loveseat while Eve read to him.

They had read several chapters, and were beginning to have doubts. "It says you're supposed to call them out," Chet said uneasily. "But if a person's not possessed, what good's that going to do?"

"You're probably not actually calling them *out* of a person," Eve said. "You're probably just talking to spirits that are sticking close to that person, hanging around to harass him."

"I don't know about this stuff," Chet said. "Calling on a demon of sloth, a demon of greed... If you ask me, this author's a fanatic. To hear him tell it, every health problem and bad personality trait anybody has is caused by a demon."

"It sounds crazy to me too," Eve said nervously. "Let's re-read some of the anecdotes before we try it."

While Chet continued to lie on the loveseat, Eve sat in the brown recliner and read each anecdote aloud. "I don't know that I believe the dark ones are that involved in most people's daily lives," she said doubtfully.

"You'll never know unless you try what he says," Chet replied. "Next time something negative happens, try saying a prayer, and see if it goes away."

It seemed to Eve that the author was paranoid, and that automatically assuming every negative thing that happened was the result of demonic harassment would simply invite more of the real thing.

It took three evenings of reading and discussion before Eve and Chet were finished with the book. On the fourth evening, although they were a little nervous, both felt they were ready. But first, they went out to dinner. Chet always felt he could talk more openly in a restaurant than he could in their home.

Looking across the table now at her "knight in rusty armor," Eve said a mental prayer of thanks that Chet had come into her life. In the nearly three years they'd been together, they'd shared more mind-boggling experiences than most people experienced in a lifetime. These shared experiences had brought them close on a level that most couples only dreamed of.

"You're doing it again," Chet said.

Eve had been voicing her opinion about some of the more controversial aspects of what they'd read in the book on spiritual warfare. Stopping mid-sentence, she looked at her hands. Her right elbow was bent, and her hand was lifted to shoulder height, fingers splayed in a gesture of tension. If she didn't have her hands to talk with, she might as well be mute. "You got the message," she said with a grin.

When they arrived home and walked in through the garage, their first impulse was to call the energies into the amethysts and strengthen the pyramid. The routine had been drilled into their heads for so long that it had become second nature. Even now that they knew the spirits were evil, it was hard to break the habit.

"How about if you lie down on the loveseat, and we'll do you first?" Eve suggested. She didn't really expect anything to happen, and she knew Chet didn't either. But they might as well go through the motions.

Before beginning, Eve closed her eyes, and together she and Chet said a prayer for protection. God had not answered her prayers for protection in the past, but Eve suspected this was because of what she'd been involved in. Now that she was out of it, she hoped he would listen.

She began by calling on any of the demons suggested in the book who might be present. Lying on the loveseat with his arm across his eyes, Chet was breathing deeply.

"If Chet has a demon of greed, in the name of Jesus, I command it to reveal itself."

The deep breathing continued, but nothing more.

"If Chet has a demon of envy, in the name of Jesus, I command it to reveal itself."

Still no reaction.

"If Chet has a demon of sloth…"

No reaction.

When Eve had finished with the list of demons named in the book, she began thinking of possible demons on her own. "If there's a demon of headaches…" Chet's stomach began to lurch. "In the name of Jesus, I command you to come out!"

Except for the lurching of his stomach, Chet didn't move. He appeared to be in some sort of trance. His stomach heaved two or three more times, then the spasms stopped.

Speaking to the demon of headaches, Eve shakily ordered it in the name of Jesus to leave their house and property and never come near them or their loved ones again. The book hadn't given the specifics that Eve included. But she figured while she was at it, she'd better cover the bases.

"If there's a demon of fatigue…" Chet's stomach began to lurch again, and tears dribbled from the outer corners of his eyes.

"In the name of Jesus, I command you to leave our house and property and never come near us or our loved ones again."

Searching her mind for anything else that might be associated with Chet, Eve remembered that he'd once had a pre-cancerous skin condition. "If there's a demon of cancer—"

Chet's stomach and chest began to lurch violently. Tears streamed freely from his eyes. Frightened, Eve stared at his heaving chest. What she saw caused her eyes to widen with shock. A mist—or more accurately, a wisp of fog—rose from Chet's chest and hung in the air. "In the name of Jesus," Eve said loudly. "In the name of Jesus, I command you to leave our house and our property, and never to come near us, our property, or our loved ones again!"

The wisp of fog left the vicinity of Chet's chest and floated across the room, then changed direction and headed toward Eve! Shrinking back against the chair, Eve shouted. "In the name of Jesus, get out of our house! Stay away from me!"

The fog appeared to dissipate. Shaken, and at a loss to think of any other potential demons to call from Chet, Eve issued a general command. "If there's any demon present that I haven't thought of, I command you in the name of Jesus—"

Revived from the trance, Chet opened his eyes and gave his breathing a chance to return to normal before attempting to speak. "What happened?"

"You had a demon of cancer," Eve rasped. "It came out of your chest, like a cloud of fog." Her words came in a rush. "It started to come toward *me*."

"You actually *saw* something come out of my *chest*?"

Eve wasn't actually certain the mist had come *out of* his chest. It had risen from his chest, and it had *looked* like it came out of him. "I saw a faint mist, kind of like a wisp of smoke," she said in a trembling voice. "It rose straight up from your chest, then floated across the room. I hollered at it, in the name of Jesus, to leave. But instead of leaving, it started toward *me*. When I yelled again, it just sort of faded away."

"Thank God the cancer demon didn't touch *you*." Chet's eyes had grown bloodshot, and his whole body was trembling. "Before we do anything else, I need a break. Do you want a Pepsi?"

The thought of a soft drink sounded good to Eve. Given what had just happened, she knew she should be frightened. It was obvious Chet was. Eve supposed her past experiences had prepared her, in a way, for what she'd just experienced. Having witnessed a giant penis rising out of a candle, and a mouse that could disappear into metal, she doubted there was much of anything that could really surprise her.

When Chet returned with the Pepsi, Eve accepted it with a nervous smile.

"I guess we'd better do *you* now," Chet said uneasily.

Eve was reasonably certain nothing more was going to happen. But she couldn't quit before going through the entire ritual. "Okay," she said with an explosive sigh. "I guess I'm as ready as I'll ever be."

"Okay," Chet began. "Here goes. If there's a demon of sloth…"

Eve felt a little ridiculous, sitting here in the brown recliner sipping her Pepsi and listening to Chet trying to banish demons she was certain didn't exist.

"If there's a demon of envy…"

A faint smile touched Eve's lips. Chet had often told her she didn't have a jealous bone in her body, and he was right.

"If there's a demon of gluttony…"

Considering that Eve had been extremely slender all her life—up until Chet's smug comment—and was often accused of eating like a bird, she doubted that gluttony would ever become a problem.

On to the next question it was obvious that Chet was no longer concerned, and was just going through the motions. "If there's a demon of cancer…"

No reaction.

"If there's any demon that hasn't been mentioned, any—"

An unseen force caused Eve to grip the aluminum can of her soft drink tighter. The force seemed to be trying to lift her arm—trying to make her throw the can at Chet! Confused, but strangely not overly alarmed, Eve leaned forward and set the can on the floor. She didn't know what was going on. She would never knowingly try to injure Chet. A muscle tightened at the corner of her mouth, and she felt as if her lips were drawing downward.

Chet's face blanched, and the fright that Eve saw there made her blood run cold. He looked as if he'd come face to face with a monster.

"In the name of Jesus—" Leaping off the loveseat, Chet lunged toward the sofa and grabbed Eve's hands in his. "Saul, in the name of Jesus—"

Eve felt as if she were watching a movie. She could see the fear in Chet's eyes as he knelt before her; feel the strength of his grip on her hands. But she had no control over her facial muscles. She felt her lips twist in a derisive sneer. Despite her love for Chet, a feeling of loathing threatened to overwhelm her. Her lips moved, and she heard her voice. But it wasn't her speaking. It was someone else. "I'm not Saul, mother fucker."

Chet was crying now, and his eyes were wild, but he refused to release Eve's hands from his grip. "Gideon!" he shouted. "In the name of Jesus, I order—"

Eve could feel the cool breeze coming in through the open sliding glass door. If the breeze could come in, Chet's voice could certainly go out. What if the neighbors heard? How could she even be thinking of *that* at a time like *this*? The feeling of loathing overwhelmed her again, and Eve felt her lips moving as the spirit spoke. "I'm not Gideon."

Eve heard the sound coming from her mouth; felt the sneer that twisted her lips. But it was as if she were an on-looker, not a participant.

"If you're not Saul, and you're not Gideon, in the name of Jesus, tell me who you are!"

Suddenly Eve was in charge of her body. Only moments ago, she'd been totally calm. Now she was terrified. "Oh God," she shrieked. "Oh God, Chet, I know who it is! It's Paladin, the spirit from Saffron! The one that used to stand by the fireplace. The one I hugged and said he could stay!"

Chet tightened his already painful grip on Eve's hands. Even to Eve's agitated state, he looked like a wild man. "Paladin? If it's you, I order you to leave our house! *Leave my angel the fuck alone!"*

"She's not yours," Paladin sneered. "She's *mine.*"

Chet's eyes looked beseechingly toward the ceiling, and the volume of his voice filled the house and beyond: "Father!" he cried, "In the name of your son whose blood was shed for my angel and me, make this dark spirit leave my Eve alone! Make him leave our house and never come back!"

Powerless to stop the demon from using her mouth and voice, Eve listened to its words and saw the horror in Chet's eyes. "She's been mine ever since that night at Saffron. I won't let her go. She's *mine!*"

Never releasing his grip for an instant, Chet clutched Eve's hands as if he were fighting for her life. "I won't let you have her, you mother fucker! In the name of *Jesus*, get out of our house! *Go back to Hell where you belong!"*

An unseen force caused Eve to writhe in the chair, and a keening scream to issue from her throat. Eve heard the screams, and knew that they were hers. But she was powerless to stop them. What must the neighbors think if they could hear?

"In the name of Jesus, I command you!" Chet shouted. *"Go back to Hell where you belong!"*

The spirit used Eve's voice one final time. As it spoke, the voice faded into the distance. "I already am." Then, more faintly, "I already am." Then it faded into nothingness, and at last it was gone.

In control again, Eve was certain the spirit was headed for Kevin, just as the demon had when they'd lived in the house on Saffron. "He's going for Kevin!" she shrieked. "God in Heaven, don't let him hurt Kevin!" Tears of panic coursed down her cheeks. "In Jesus' name, don't let him hurt Kevin! Don't let him hurt my son!"

Folding Eve into his arms, consumed by fright of his own, Chet tried to quiet her fears. "God won't let him hurt Kevin, Angel. He's gone back to Hell where he belongs. Kevin will be alright."

Eve heard Chet's words, but she wasn't at all convinced. Why hadn't God made the spirit leave the *first* time Chet called on Him? What if Chet had given up? What would have happened to her *then?*

Eve didn't believe for a moment that the spirit she called Paladin had possessed her. The bad things that had happened since she first met him had come from external forces, not from within her. She did believe he'd either cursed her life or been with her for years, causing bad things to happen. If the spirits hadn't revealed themselves—If Chet hadn't bought the book, and they hadn't discovered Paladin's presence—he could have dogged her footsteps forever!

After what had just happened here, there was no way Eve and Chet could spend the night in this house. "Get your clothes and your notes," Chet said. "We're spending the night in a motel."

Eve didn't bother asking why Chet wanted her to take the notes she'd amassed over the years. She just gathered her things and went out the door.

"I'll be there in a minute," Chet called after her. "I'm just going to grab a tablet and pen, and a big envelope."

Once in the truck, Chet told Eve his plan. "Let's not go to the motel right away. I think we should go to a restaurant. We can make some notes there of what's just happened, and put them with what you already have. I think we need to send this to the Christian Research Institute. They need to know what the dark ones can do, even to someone who was raised as a Christian."

Eve wasn't familiar with the Christian Research Institute. But if they could get the word out, she wanted to help. If even one person who was thinking of getting involved with spirit guides could be dissuaded, it would be worth it.

Since Denny's was near the Motel 6, that's where they decided to stop. There, in a private booth, Eve laid out her notes.

"We'll make sure the pages are in order, and mail them as is," Chet said. "But we need to make notes on what happened tonight, and put them in, too."

The drive two hours later to the Motel 6 was tense, with Chet saying over and over again, "I was afraid I'd lost you, Angel. But there was no way in hell I was going to let him have you."

Once in the room at their motel, both Eve and Chet were too agitated to sleep. "After we've mailed your notes and they're out of our hands, we can let God take care of it," Chet said. "But I think it's important to get rid of everything else we have, that had to do with the spirits."

"We can't just send the Institute the notes," Eve argued. "What if we send a dark spirit along with them? Who knows what might happen when they open the packet?"

Up to this point, Chet had been pacing the floor. Now he paused and ran a nervous hand through his disheveled blonde hair. "We'll call them first and let them know what we're sending. We'll tell them they need to say a prayer before they open it."

Now that they had a plan of action, Eve felt a little better. For the rest of the night, they discussed the list of things that needed to be disposed of: the board, the pendulum, the tourmaline, the amethysts and peridot, the protection box, the plant that had returned to health when Eve infused it with energy, the dream catcher, the New Age tapes…

"We'll take most of the stuff to the dump," Chet said. "But I don't think it would be good to dump everything in one spot."

"I agree," Eve said. "We don't want to dump the crystals where there's a chance that anyone would find them and take them home."

The next morning, Eve called Information for the number of CRI. When she placed the call to the Institute, a secretary with a friendly voice answered. "The director isn't in. Maybe I could help you, if you'll just tell me what you're calling about."

"I'm sending you a package," Eve said urgently. "But before it gets there, I wanted to warn you what's in it so you can say a prayer for protection before you open it."

"What is it?" the woman asked warily. "What are you sending?"

Eve debated how much she should tell the secretary. She didn't want the woman to open the package when it arrived. She wanted it to go straight to the director. "It's several pages of notes about my experiences with 'spirit guides' who claimed to be of the light, but they were really spirits of darkness."

"You're sending us notes on *spiritism*?" the woman asked uncertainly.

"It's more than that," Eve answered. "It's information that goes against what most Christians believe about the spirit world." When the woman didn't reply, Eve rushed on. "My husband and I got a book that supposedly told us how to get the spirits out of our lives. When we did what it said, all Hell broke loose. We took our notes, and left our house. We couldn't spend the night there. I'm calling you from a motel."

For a moment, Eve thought the woman had hung up. When she finally spoke, her voice had lost its friendly tone. "Are you talking about spiritual warfare? If you are, that's not something a Christian should get involved with. Maybe what you need is an exorcist."

"I don't need an exorcist," Eve grated. "I'm not possessed. I just wanted to warn you before you open the package—"

"You don't have to worry about us," the woman said smugly. "The Devil can't touch a true Christian. He flees at the sound of Jesus' name."

"My husband is also a Christian," Eve grated. "But when he told a dark spirit to leave in Jesus' name, the spirit told him to fuck Jesus, and fuck the blood that was shed for us!"

"That can't be," the woman argued. "According to—"

"I'm mailing the package today," Eve interrupted. "Do whatever you want with it."

The return home was uneventful, despite trepidation on the part of both Eve and Chet. They spent the weekend amassing everything they could think of that could be remotely linked to their contacts with the spirits. "We have to dump the boom box," Eve said firmly.

"There's nothing wrong with the boom box," Chet argued. "Why do we need to dump it?"

"Because the spirits' voices came through the speaker. Because we played our tapes on it every evening when we talked to the spirits on the board."

"I guess you're right," Chet said reluctantly. "We need to get rid of the family room furniture too."

The brown chair was where Eve had sat every evening to converse with the spirits. It was also where she'd been sitting when she saw the propeller over her head, and when Paladin used her voice to claim she belonged to *him*. The loveseat was where Chet and his mom had been sitting when the little girl spirit called her into the fire, and where he and Eve had been seated when the spirit guides revealed themselves. But they also needed to trash the Indian picture and the birch coffee table with the imprint of Gideon's image. These things, they hauled in Chet's truck to the County Dump. The rest, they saved for Ha!loween.

On Halloween night, all that was left to dispose of was the protection box with the amethysts it contained, the containers they'd used to camouflage the pyramid stones, and the stones that had been used to *construct* the pyramid.

They would dispose of the amethysts as secretly agreed. The camouflage containers, they would burn in the barbecue that had been used to roast dark ones in effigy. They had agreed to wait till this particular night in order to make a statement to Satan that they wanted him out of their lives.

Now, as Eve got a chair to climb on to take the protection box down from the closet shelf, Chet proceeded to each corner of the house gathering the pyramid amethysts and the containers they'd been concealed in. "Man, Angel," he called from the bedroom. "I can feel the energy all through my hand."

Chet had never felt the energy in stones before. Once, Saul had given him permission and power to pull negative energy from Eve's lower back, but crystals had been totally Eve's domain. Until now, although Chet had tried, he'd been unable to feel the energy of crystallized minerals—even the giant quartz that had nearly caused Eve to faint. When he got to the apex of the energy pyramid and reached for the amethyst in the hallway smoke alarm, Chet's heart was in his throat. "Here goes nothing."

Concerned by the fear she heard in his voice, Eve carried the protection box into the hallway just as Chet touched the alarm casing.

"Shit!" Chet shouted. "I can feel the vibration all the way through my arm! We've got to get this thing out of the house!"

As Chet disconnected the smoke alarm, Eve could sense the tension building inside him. "I've never felt anything like this," Chet told her. "My arm's going numb all the way to my shoulder!"

"It's probably a good thing you saved that one for last," Eve said worriedly. "If it has this much energy when the other stones are gone, who knows what it would have been like if they were still in place!"

Holding the smoke alarm at arm's length, Chet headed for the door. "You stay in here, Angel. I'll dump this thing in the garbage can for now. If I'm not back in a minute or two, come out to get me."

Eve watched from the doorway as Chet walked across the yard to approach the plastic garbage can at the end of the asphalt driveway. In the dim light from the neighbor's window, she could barely make out his shadowy figure as he dropped the smoke alarm into the trash then jumped back from the can, frantically brushing the negative energy off his hands and forearms. Eve could imagine what he must be feeling right now. She'd felt the cobweb sensation a thousand or more times coating her own hands and arms, sometimes more intensely than others. On a scale of one to twelve, she'd experienced as high as a ten. Judging from Chet's frenzied reaction, he must be experiencing a twelve!

When he returned to the house, Chet's face was ashen. "I don't like the thought of having that thing on our property, but I don't think it would be a good idea to take it with us when get rid of the amethysts. At least this way it's out of the house. The garbage truck comes tomorrow." Two dots of color had returned to Chet's cheeks, but his eyes beneath his heavy brows were haunted.

"I can feel the vibration of the amethysts through the cardboard of this box," Eve said nervously. The Protection box she was holding contained twelve small stones, each in its own compartment. The cardboard box seemed to hum in her hands with a vibration equivalent to what could be felt by turning up the volume and placing her hands on a radio. The vibration was weak, but appeared to be growing stronger.

Though they hadn't discussed it at home, for fear that revealing their plans would cause problems, they had secretly agreed in advance to take all the purple stones to Orangevale and dump them over the Hazel Avenue Bridge into the rocks below. They didn't want to run the risk of anyone's finding the amethysts and inheriting a spirit that might have come with them. Under cover of darkness, they drove to the bridge.

"This box is getting warm in my lap," Eve said uneasily. "The amethysts must be heating up!"

Chet had pulled off on the side of the road. The bridge lay dead ahead. "Give me the box."

Eve handed the box of amethysts to Chet and watched with trepidation as he disappeared into the darkness. Seated in the truck with the window rolled down so she could hear if Chet should cry out for her, Eve muttered a frantic prayer for his safety. Her eyes ached with the effort to peer into the darkness.

When a minute turned into two, and two into three, Eve began to wonder if she should get out of the truck. What could be taking Chet so long? All he had to do was open the box lid and dump the stones over the bridge railing. But there was no question that the dark ones hated Chet. The night he'd challenged them had been evidence of that. They'd hurt him so badly he'd prayed to die. And how many times had they attacked his weak ankle, hoping to make him fall off a roof? Oh God. *What if they've pushed him over the railing?* The drop to the rocks below the bridge had to be at least fifty feet. A fall like that would have killed him!

Get a grip, Eve told herself. *If they'd pushed him over the railing you'd know it, because Chet would have screamed.* Why was he being so quiet? And why wasn't there any traffic? Only one car had passed since they got here, illuminating the bridge with its eerie light.

Another minute passed, then two... Eve's hand was on the door handle and her heart was thudding in her throat when she saw Chet in the headlight beams, coming out of the darkness.

Eve hadn't realized she'd stopped breathing until she saw Chet coming, and released the breath she'd been holding.

"Here," Chet said, handing the empty box to Eve through the driver's side window. "I didn't want to throw this over. We'll tear it up and burn it on the barbecue when we get home."

They had turned back and headed home when Eve became aware that the bottom of the box in her lap was still warm enough to feel the heat through the legs of her jeans. "This box is still warm. Are you sure you dumped all the Amethysts?"

"Look in it yourself," Chet said. "I turned it upside down and shook it."

Eve opened the white box and peered inside. In the dim light of the truck cab, the twelve compartments appeared to be empty, but she felt in the corners just in case. Sure enough, a single stone had managed to get lodged in a crack. "We have to turn back," she said. "There's still one stone in the box…"

Eve felt as if a load had been lifted as they drove to Denny's in Citrus Heights after dumping the last of the amethysts.

Reaching across the seat of his S10 to take Eve's hand, Chet heaved a sigh of relief. "Well, Angel, we did it. And we don't have to worry about anyone getting hold of the amethysts. As soon as it rains, they'll settle between the rocks, and no one will ever find them."

They had gathered the amethysts and taken off for Orangevale as soon as they both got home from work, before any trick-or-treaters could come to the door. After what they'd been through, there was no way in Hell they were going to hand out candy for Halloween. Their days of celebrating Satan's holiday were a thing of the past.

As they turned into the Denny's parking lot, Eve spotted a young child dressed in a devil's costume. She had never understood why history and costume makers always depicted Satan with horns. Apparently they didn't know he had once been the handsomest of God's angels before being cast out of Heaven. It occurred to Eve that the dark spirits themselves had probably perpetuated the horned image. No one would be frightened by a Prince of Darkness who looked like Rock Hudson or Cary Grant.

Over a tuna melt for Chet and a patty melt for Eve, they reviewed the list of items that had been tossed, to make certain nothing had been forgotten. "We need to check all of the closets," Chet said. "We've made so many notes, there's no telling where we might have put them."

"I agree," Eve said. "And I think we should throw away your Adventist magazines too. Ellen White had out of body experiences, and got her doctrine from a spirit, so I don't think we should have the magazines in our house."

Chet agreed.

By the time they arrived home, the last of the trick-or-treaters were off the street. "I'm going to take this box and the containers from the pyramid out to the barbecue to burn them," Chet said. We don't want to take a chance on anyone taking them out of the trash."

Eve watched from the family room as Chet opened the sliding glass door and went out onto the patio. The night air was cold, but Chet didn't seem to mind. Eve figured he must be running on adrenaline. There was no need to go out for charcoal. They still had half a bag that had been slated to burn in effigy.

The burning tonight was less dramatic than when Chet had shaken his fists at the sky and shouted "Burn, you mother fuckers! Burn!" He was obviously enjoying burning the containers, but he'd apparently learned a lesson.

When the fire had died down, Chet came inside and enfolded Eve in his arms. "Well Angel, we did it. The only thing left is the barbecue."

That night, a crash awoke them with a start. The noise sounded like it had come from the patio! Though their hearts were thudding, they weren't about to investigate. Burrowing deeper beneath her covers, Eve could hear Chet praying in the bedroom across the hall. "Father, protect my angel and me tonight. We showed them we don't want them in our lives anymore. Be with us tonight, and every day and night, and help us to be strong. In Jesus' name, amen."

In the morning before leaving for work, Chet went outside to investigate.

"Angel!" he shouted. "Come out here! You have to see this!"

Alarmed, Eve rushed to the patio door and looked out. The barbecue they'd used for burning dark ones in effigy, and that Chet had used last night to burn the last of their ties to the spirit realm, had collapsed in a heap amidst a pile of ashes.

The barbecue had been fine last night. The legs had been sturdy; no missing screws or traces of rust. There could be no logical explanation for its collapse, other than that it had served its purpose.

"Well Angel," Chet said with lift of his eyebrows. "It looks like the end of an era."

Chapter 54

Despite the fact that Eve and Chet had made a supreme effort to break free of spirit involvement in their lives, demonic harassment not only continued—In many ways, it seemed to grow worse. There was no way of proving that their problems were caused by harassment, and not just a run of bad luck. But they hadn't had these problems before, and no one seemed able to come up with a plausible explanation.

Eve's car was a prime example. In the course of six weeks, it had been in the shop not once but *five times*—each time for a different problem. Each time it was taken in, they were told there was nothing wrong. The bill for rental cars alone ran into the hundreds. And that didn't include the cost of the two times the car had to be towed. The car was only four years old. Yet for what they were paying for maintenance and rentals, Eve might as well not be working.

The lights were pretty much being left alone, but now the heater switch on the thermostat was being messed with. At bedtime, Eve would turn off the switch, making a point of telling Chet that's what she was doing. As regular as clockwork, the switch would be turned back on at six o'clock in the morning. A couple of mornings, for variety's sake, the heater had been left alone and the stereo turned on.

And then there were the medical bills. Mysterious chronic pains were still undiagnosed despite thousands of dollars spent on laboratory tests that either proved inconclusive or showed nothing wrong. Sometimes Eve wondered what was the use even bothering to go to the doctor.

Through it all, Eve was glad that at least for her son, things seemed to be going well. She rarely mentioned the spirits to Kevin. It took her by surprise when Kevin called one Saturday morning to tell her about a book he'd read about how to get spirits out of one's life. Eve's first reaction was to say "No Way!" She wasn't about to fall prey to that again, stirring up problems by following the advice of *another* author who didn't know what he was talking about.

But the more they talked, and the more Kevin heard about the kind of things that were going on in his mom's life, the more convinced Kevin became that she needed to go through the steps outlined in the book. "Let me bring the book over, and we can talk about it," he urged. "I did the steps in the book myself, and things are going better already in my life. I think if you and Chet were to try it, you'd find that things would improve for you too."

That afternoon while Chet was at work, Kevin brought the book over and shared with Eve the premise behind it. "It doesn't work to just say you don't want spirits in your life," he said earnestly. "You have to denounce each and every one of them to let them know you mean what you're saying. But before you can even do that, you have to denounce everything you've ever done that would encourage them to come into your life in the first place."

Eve was very proud of the young man Kevin had become. During his high school years she had worried a lot, praying he would reach college age without being killed or maimed. Now, midway through his freshman year at the University, he was maintaining an A average in his lower division classes, and was active in a Christian group on campus. It was ironic that the son Eve had tried so hard to protect as a child was now here in her dining room wanting to protect his mom. Eve could see in his eyes that Kevin believed what he was saying, and that he was desperate to help her. But the memory was strong of the night she and Chet had tried what *they'd* read about getting rid of spirits. Chet had been afraid he would lose her that night. Suppose it happened again with Kevin? No. She couldn't risk that.

"Think about it, Mom. You've told me yourself you used a Ouija Board in high school, and that in college you did automatic writing. Those two things alone set you up. I know you've been to psychics. And I'm sure there've been other things."

"Sweetheart," Eve said, "You don't know everything that happened that night when Chet and I demanded that the spirits identify themselves. I'm telling you, all Hell broke loose!"

"That's because you were challenging them," Kevin argued. "That should *never* be done except in a group—and only then with a lot of prayers for protection. With this method, you're not challenging. You're just denouncing them."

"Yeah, well," Eve said with a notable lack of enthusiasm, "It's been my experience that spirits like to show off. If we start stirring things up, who knows what might happen?"

"I'm not talking about stirring things up," Kevin said. "I'm talking about denouncing them. This isn't something you do by yourself. You have to have someone who understands it to help you, and for obvious reasons I don't think it should be Chet. I've taken part in several sessions with my friends. I think I should be the one to do it with you."

Eve didn't like the idea that Kevin was doing this with his friends. She certainly didn't want him to do it with *her*. "No," she said. "I don't want you to. I love you too much to take the chance of your being hurt."

"I'm not going to be hurt," Kevin argued. "*I've* already denounced them— including the one in the black cloak that used to come into my room when I was a kid, and the ones that were in my room that night a couple years ago telling me Jesus didn't love me. God protected me when I denounced them, and he protected the friend who was helping me. I've also done this for friends who had spirit problems related to drugs—but God protected us then too."

When Eve still continued to resist, Kevin brought out the *big* guns. "I've prayed about this for you, Mom, and I feel impressed that since the reason you accepted the guides in the first place is because you wanted to protect *me*, I need to be the one to do this with you." What Kevin appeared to be saying was that the time had come to complete the circle. "You can't do it for yourself, Mom. But I think it should be done when Chet's not here. Please let me do it with you."

That night Eve didn't tell Chet what she and Kevin intended to do. She knew if she told him, Chet would try to talk her out of it.

The following day Kevin waited till early afternoon to make sure Chet was gone before coming over. Though Eve offered him a soft drink, Kevin demurred, saying he'd prefer to just get started in case Chet decided to come home early.

Seated at the walnut dining room table with one hand on his Bible, Kevin began by reading aloud a series of items relating to the occult or psychic realm. To each item, Eve was to respond by saying whether she'd ever been involved with or had experience with that item; if she had, she was to denounce and reject it. The first on the list was Astral Projection. "I know you've done this one," Kevin said. "The night you went out of body at Saffron to try to protect *me*."

The incident was as fresh in Eve's mind as if it had happened yesterday. "I didn't do it intentionally," she said with a shudder. "*I didn't even know about out of body experiences till I said a prayer and it happened.*"

"I know," Kevin said. "That's what you told me. But I don't understand it. I don't think *God* would make you go out of body when that's involved with the occult. Maybe it was a dark one who did it to you. "

"You may be right about that," Eve said uneasily. "But I guess we'll never know."

"Even though you didn't go out of body on purpose, it won't do any harm to denounce astral projection," Kevin said. "Just say 'In the name of Jesus, I denounce and reject it.'"

"Okay," Eve agreed. "I guess you're right. In the name of Jesus, I denounce and reject astral projection."

"What about Astrology?" Kevin said next. "Have you ever been involved in Astrology?"

"I used to read the horoscopes in the newspaper, and I had my chart done once," Eve replied. "In the name of Jesus, I denounce and reject Astrology."

By the time Kevin reached the end of the list, Eve had denounced and rejected nearly two dozen things—all of which she had done over the years without realizing they were of the occult.

"Now comes the hard part," Kevin said. "You need to say the name of every spirit who ever contacted you, and denounce it by name." Kevin's voice was steady, but a muscle twitched at the corner of his eye. He was trying to be brave, but Eve knew he was as nervous as she.

"I can't do that," Eve said. "If I say their names, I'll be calling them back."

"They're probably already here," Kevin argued. "You said yourself you're still being harassed. A spirit can only be one place at a time. If they're gone, as you say, they won't even hear when you say their names. If they're here, you need to make it clear that you're rejecting them once and for all."

"I *made* it clear Halloween night when Chet and I dumped the amethysts over the bridge!" Eve protested.

"Maybe you made your intentions clear, but I don't think they're all gone, Mom. You tell me you threw them out of your life, and in the very next sentence you tell me you're being harassed. How can that be if they're really gone?"

Eve hated when Kevin was so logical. She had raised him to think that way, but sometimes it could be hard to take.

"Let's take an analogy," Kevin said calmly. "A person has a heart attack on the street, and a crowd gathers round. One good Samaritan starts giving him CPR and hollers 'Call 9-1-1' All of the people in the crowd hear him, but no one makes the call. They don't make the call because he wasn't talking to *them*. It's the same with the spirits. If you don't reject them individually, they don't feel they have to go."

Eve *had* told some spirits by name to leave, but Kevin was right: she hadn't told them all.

"If you don't want to say their names yourself, let me say them for you," Kevin suggested. "I think I know the names of most of them."

Eve didn't want to say the names herself, but she wasn't about to let her son say them. "I'll say them," she said nervously. "But if it looks like there's going to be any trouble—"

"I already had a group of Christian friends pray with me before I came here," Kevin interrupted. "They're probably still praying for us, even now. What do you say we get started?"

Eve knew that if Chet were here he would step in at this point and try to stop her. But Chet wasn't here, and the words Kevin was saying made sense. "Alright," she said quietly.

"Good," Kevin said. "First, I think you need to denounce the one who claimed to be your guardian angel."

Before saying Gideon's name, Eve drew a calming breath. Her hands in her lap were as cold as frost. "In the name of Jesus, I denounce—"

Even before she said the name, an unseen force took hold of her hands and began to shake them violently. Eve tried to hold them still, but the force was too strong. "Oh God," she thought frantically, "Not again…"

"Say the name!" Kevin shouted. "Say the name and denounce him!"

Eve's hands were being shaken so violently it was impossible to form the words. It was as if an invisible force were interfering with her speech. "In the n-name of—In the name of J-Jesus, I denounce you, G-" The name was on the tip of her tongue but she couldn't get it out! "I denounce you, G- Gid- I denounce you, Gideon! I reject you and cast you out of my life!"

The shaking stopped as suddenly as it had begun. Eve had been shocked when the spirit grabbed hold of her hands. How could this be when only months ago she and Chet had thrown everything away that linked them to the spirit realm? Had their statement on Halloween night meant nothing?

"What about the guy you said looked like an organ grinder?" Kevin said shakily. "The one that couldn't tell time?"

"Caruso," Eve said. Though she waited for a sign, there was no reaction. "In the name of Jesus, I denounce and reject Caruso."

One by one, Eve ticked through the names. When she started to denounce the Energy of the East, the shaking returned—more fiercely than before—and her teeth began to chatter uncontrollably. Clutching his Bible in white knuckled hands, Kevin cried out in a trembling voice. "Father, in the name of Jesus, protect my mom! Don't let them hurt her!"

Eve's hands were being shaken so violently that her knuckles were banging against the under side of the table. Even in her frantic state, Eve knew her hands would be swollen and bruised—if she lived to see tomorrow. "Say the name!" Kevin shouted. "Say the name, and denounce it!"

"In the n-name of J-Jesus," Eve stuttered. "I denounce the Sp—" Just as before, the name stuck in her throat. "I denounce the Sp- Spirit of—" Why couldn't she say the words? It was as if the message from her brain to her vocal chords had somehow been short-circuited. "Sp—Spirit of the—East! I denounce and reject the Spirit of the East, in Jesus' name!" At the sound of its name, the spirit released her forearms and the frenzied shaking stopped, leaving Eve exhausted.

Obviously shaken by what he'd just witnessed, Kevin took Eve's hand in his. "I think we should say a prayer before you denounce the healing guide."

Somehow even though she knew he was evil, Eve didn't really believe Saul would deliberately hurt her. Still, panting for breath, she clutched her son's hand and listened in silence as he prayed for protection. When the prayer was finished, she drew a deep breath.

"In the name of Jesus," she said in a quiet voice, "I denounce and reject Saul, and cast him out of my life." Tears streamed down her cheeks, and a lump formed in her throat. Though her hands shook in a parting tremor, Saul departed without a scene.

"I was afraid that was going to be a bad one," Kevin said.

Eve could see that Kevin had been physically and emotionally drained by what he'd witnessed thus far. But at least he hadn't been emotionally scarred. Her own hands were aching from being banged against the table. From outside she could hear the voices of neighbors returning from their trip to the mountains, blissfully unaware of the drama unfolding within these walls.

"Are we finished?" Kevin asked. "Are you sure you haven't forgotten any? Think hard, Mom. You need to reject them all."

"There's one more," Eve said quietly. "It's a nasty one. I know it's here. I can sense its presence."

"Do I know about this one?" Kevin asked warily. His hand on the Bible was trembling, but he wasn't about to stop—not till he knew his mom was safe.

"It's the one from Saffron," Eve murmured. "The one that used to appear by the fireplace, leaning against the mantle."

Kevin had never seen Paladin himself when they lived in the house on Saffron. He hadn't seen the couple that appeared in Eve's doorway either—only the faceless demon dressed in a long black cloak. But he knew the story of Paladin. Eve had told him when he he'd revealed his own experiences when he was in junior high.

"You *have* to say its name," Kevin pressed. "If you don't—" At that point, Kevin's thin body stiffened in his chair and his head was thrown back as if he were suffering a seizure. The words he was trying to speak froze in his throat.

"Oh God," Eve whimpered frantically. "Kevin? *Kevin?*"

The invisible force took hold of Eve's body and began shaking it as a mad dog might shake a rag doll. Powerless to fight it, Eve prayed frantically in her mind to make it stop. *Dear God don't let it use my vocal chords. Don't let it show its face.* Her heart was racing so fast she feared it would burst. "In the n-name of J-Jesus—" The shaking became even more violent, nearly knocking her off the chair. Eve felt as if she were having a convulsion; yet, the bulk of her fear was for her son. Oh God. What was happening to him? "P—P—Pal—God, help me say the name. *P— Paladin!* I denounce you! I reject you!" The vicious shaking grew less intense, but showed no sign of stopping.

Suddenly Kevin's voice returned. No longer paralyzed, he leaned forward across the table. His pupils were dilated, and tears were streaming down his chalk-white face. But his voice was strong. "Paladin! My mom and I *both* denounce and reject you! In the name of Jesus, we command you to *leave!*"

And then the spirit released Eve. The shaking stopped, and the dining room was quiet—so quiet the sound of their breath was amplified as Eve and her son looked at one another from across the table. It was over.

"Thank you," Eve said softly. "I love you more than you'll ever know." What her son had done for her had taken more courage than any man twice his age would have shown. "I am so proud of you, Sweetheart."

Kevin wiped away the tears still drying on his cheeks and rose to circle the table. Bending to give his mom a hug, he released a tremulous sigh. "I'll admit it now: I've never been so scared. When they took away my voice and paralyzed my body—I've never prayed so hard in my life."

Standing abruptly, Eve dabbed at her own tears and changed the subject. "How about if I fix us a BLT and some soup? I think we could both use a hot lunch."

Over lunch, they talked about Kevin's classes, Chet's and Eve's work, and Eve's on-going novel: anything to avoid talking about what they'd just been through.

The following day, Kevin returned to go through the list of denouncements with Chet. The experience was, thankfully, uneventful. Things were definitely looking up.

But still the harassment continued. Not as much as before, but the spirits were still a part of their lives. When Eve told Kevin this, Kevin was convinced that something of significance had to have been overlooked. "Think about it, Mom. What are you and Chet doing, or what might you have forgotten about that could give the spirits an 'in'?"

"Nothing!" Eve said. "We've dumped the boom box and replaced the family room furniture and living room coffee table with new. The board and crystals are gone. We even dumped what was left of the barbecue."

"There has to be *something*," Kevin insisted.

"Well, there *isn't*," Eve said, raising her voice in frustration. "Unless you want to count my job, there's nothing that—"

Her job! That was it! When she first returned to the Valley, desperate for a job, the Spirit of the East had promised the nanny position would be hers if she wanted it. Considering her qualifications, she could probably have gotten the job on her own, even if the spirit hadn't influenced the interviewer. But the fact was the interviewer had canceled over 50 scheduled interviews in Eve's favor.

"What *about* your job?" Kevin asked.

Eve gave Kevin a brief rundown of how she had gotten the job, but Kevin was of the opinion that it had been her qualifications that had swayed the interviewer in her favor. "Think about it, Mom. You're a *mom*; kids love you; you've had your own daycare; you've been a teacher... Anyone would be crazy not to hire you to take care of their kids."

Still, it bothered Eve that the job had been promised by the Spirit of the East. That had been almost three years ago. Three years!

A feeling of dread swept over Eve. Three and multiples of three were spirit numbers on both sides of the coin. Satan was well acquainted with spirit numbers. So were the angels that had fallen with him. It had been Eve's experience that multiples of three were just as important to the dark ones as they were to the Holy Trinity. Saul had once said that dark spirits often *speak* in threes: Of three sentences spoken, either two will be the truth and the third will be a lie, or two will be lies and the third will be a truth. Half the bad things that had happened to Eve and Chet had come in groups of three. As a matter of fact, it had been just after meeting Paladin and giving him permission to stay in her home that Eve was rear-ended three times in three months!

The more she thought about it, the more apprehensive Eve became. Jessica, the youngest child in her care, had been more or less under control since Eve had put her and her sister on the discipline system she'd developed for use with Kevin and his former stepbrother. But Jessica was a chronic liar. She had lied about Eve in the past, and would have gotten Eve in trouble if Eve hadn't had proof she was lying. Eve already knew spirits were capable of putting thoughts in people's minds. Since putting the girls on the system, Eve hadn't exactly been Jessica's favorite person. What was to stop the spirits, in honor of her *third* anniversary, from planting something in *Jessica's* mind?

"I think you should give your notice at the end of the month," Chet said. "You can be thinking between now and then what you want to do. If you want, you can take some time off before you look for another job."

Three weeks later, the night before the day Eve was to turn in her notice, Gideon's voice spoke to her in a dream. "Don't quit the job before the three years are up, bitch. If you quit the job early, bad things are going to happen."

Eve awoke from the dream in a cold sweat. The air in the bedroom was heavy with the negative energy she'd been made to feel so many times when she was a healer. Her first thought was to wake Chet, but she decided against it. It was enough that one of them would be awake for the rest of the night. Better to let Chet sleep, then tell him in the morning.

For the rest of the night, all Eve could think of was Gideon's threat that something bad was going to happen if she quit the nanny job before the three years had run their course. What bad things could he have been talking about? Were they going to happen to *her*? To *Chet*? To her *car*? To their *belongings*? A dozen or more possibilities flitted through Eve's mind. None of them were pleasant.

In the morning, over breakfast, Chet listened in silence as Eve described the dream and the fears it had instilled. "I don't know what to do," Eve said. "If I quit early, he said something bad is going to happen. But if I finish out the third year, I'm afraid it will be even worse."

"I agree," Chet said tensely. "We can't let them scare us into staying with that job. We have to break the chain."

"Then I guess it's been decided," Eve said shakily. "I'll turn in my notice today."

Later that morning, while the girls were still in school, Eve drove to Carol's office to submit her resignation. Because of her status, Eve wasn't required to wait in the waiting room. She was told she could go on back to Dr. Peterson's office. When Carol came in wearing her doctor's smock, with her hair pulled back in an attractive French braid, Eve thought for a fleeting moment she would miss Carol and the bonding times they'd shared. She wouldn't miss Jessica or Frank. But she *would* miss Carol and Cindy.

"Has something happened?" Carol asked. "Does this have anything to do with Jessica?"

"No," Eve said quickly. "Nothing's happened. I just can't take the eleven-hour days anymore. I need to spend more time at home."

There was a moment of silence as Carol Peterson peered into Eve's eyes for signs that something more was wrong than what Eve was telling her. "We'll miss you," Carol said at last. "At least Cindy and I will. I don't know about Jessica. You've done a lot for the girls—and you've been a big help to Frank and me. It will be hard to find a replacement."

"I'll stay two weeks," Eve said. "Hopefully you'll be able to find someone by the time I leave."

"You're sure there's nothing I can say to make you stay?"

Eve had considered making an offer to care for the girls in her own home. But even if Carol agreed, that wouldn't be breaking the chain. "I'm afraid not," Eve said. "I really like *you*; and Cindy and I have gotten very close. But eleven hours a day is just too long to be away from home."

Eve had feared the negative energy would overwhelm her when she quit, or that Gideon would influence Carol to fly into some sort of rage. Instead, things had gone smoothly. She felt as if a lead weight had been lifted. That night, she and Chet went to Black Angus for dinner to celebrate.

"So what now?" Chet asked, reaching across the table to take Eve's hand in his. Her hand looked so feminine with its soft skin and perfectly shaped nails. His, in contrast, were callused and stained. His fingernails and cuticles were hopeless. "Do you want to take a vacation? Or do you want to start looking for another job?"

What Eve wanted to do was write. But she knew she couldn't make enough money at writing to pay her share of the bills. "I don't know what I want to do," she said morosely. "I can't go back to office work. The spirits caused me to lose one secretarial job—possibly two. I can't take the chance of that happening again. And I can't go back to teaching. My teaching credential has lapsed."

"What about putting your application in with the state?" Chet suggested. "You certainly have the skills for a state office job. Once you're in with the state, it takes an act of congress to get you out!"

The thought of driving to Sacramento in freeway traffic everyday to be cooped up in an office cubicle all day long till it was time to face the traffic again sounded like sheer Hell to Eve.

She knew she was being a defeatist. She also knew that nothing Chet was likely to suggest would appeal to her at this moment.

That evening they watched a movie on pay per view before going to bed. Tomorrow and for the next two weeks, Eve would return to work as a nanny. Once that job was over, she hadn't a clue what she was going to do.

Now that the decision had been made to quit and she'd turned in her notice, Eve wished the two weeks were over. She hoped Carol wouldn't tell the girls. She'd had trouble enough getting control of them in the first place. Now if they knew she was leaving, they would feel they could do as they pleased. Jessica, at least, would feel that she'd won.

The night of the day Eve had given her notice, she slept better than she'd slept in years. The next morning, stifling a yawn, she reached out to shut off the alarm clock. Just two more weeks. Then she could sleep in.

The shag carpet felt soft to her feet as Eve shuffled to the laundry room to get a towel from the dryer. Chet was already up and dressed, digging through the laundry for a pair of clean socks. "Good morning," Eve said. "Could you use a hug?"

"I can always use a—" Turning toward Eve, Chet froze. His eyes took on the same look of fright Eve had seen the night Paladin showed himself. "*Why are you doing that?*" he asked.

"Doing what?" Eve asked in confusion.

"Why are you doing that with your face? Come on, Angel. Stop fooling around."

Eve truly didn't know what Chet was talking about, but he was beginning to scare her. "I'm not fooling around, Chet. I don't know what you're talking about."

"Go look in the mirror," Chet said quietly.

Terrified at what she was about to see, Eve approached the bathroom with trepidation. Her face didn't *feel* that much different—maybe a little tightness in the left cheek—"

Afraid to look, Eve closed her eyes as she stepped into the bathroom and stopped in front of the mirror. When she forced her eyes open a moment later, the blood drained from her cheeks.

The face in the mirror was hers. But it was horribly distorted! The left side of her mouth was twisted upward and the left corner of her eye was pulled down like some hideous Halloween mask. A feeling of numbness spread through Eve's body. Raising a cold hand to her face, she brushed her cheek and lips with the tips of her trembling fingers. What in the world was happening? A person didn't just go to bed at night looking normal and wake up looking like some kind of a monster! *Gideon* had done this to her!

He had told her if she quit the job something bad was going to happen. And now he'd maimed her! A lump rose in Eve's throat as she covered her face with her trembling hands. "Why, God?" she sobbed. "Why did you let him do this to me? I quit the job to prove I was on *your* side. *Why didn't you stop him?*"

And then Chet was at her side, taking her in his arms. "Try not to worry, Angel. I'll call your work and tell them you're sick. Then you need to call Carol's office and make an appointment to find out what's going on. Maybe she'll be able to help."

When Eve called and told Carol what had happened to her face, Carol told her to come in this afternoon. Her schedule was full, but she would make time to see Eve.

When Eve walked into the waiting room that afternoon, she ducked her head to avoid making eye contact with the patient across the room who was openly staring. Every seat in the waiting room was filled.

Behind the reception desk to the left, the receptionist smiled an overly bright smile and nodded. Normally, she would have asked Eve how the girls were doing. Today she simply showed her teeth in that forced smile that was no doubt intended to hide her shock at the sight of Eve's face. "You can go on back to the first examining room on the right. I'll let Dr. Peterson know you're here."

Eve was thankful she qualified for preferential treatment. Glancing neither right nor left, she walked through the waiting room to the corridor, and down the hall to the examining room.

The wait couldn't have been longer than five minutes, but it seemed like an hour to Eve. She'd always hated sitting on examining tables with nothing to support her back. At least this time, though, she had all her clothes on, and her feet weren't in the stirrups. A feeling of pure and utter hatred coursed through her body at the thought of her so-called guardian angel and what he had done to her face. What *it* had done, she corrected herself. How could she have ever loved such a monster? She'd been on the verge of *falling in love* with him before Chet came into her life. How could she have been so fooled? To think she had once asked him to *hug* her. The thought of his—*its*—touching her now, made her skin crawl.

Suppose there was nothing Carol could do for her face? Suppose she was doomed to look like this forever! It happened to other people: burn victims; victims of strokes. Was it possible it could happen as a result of a spirit attack?

There was a light tap before the door to the examining room opened and Carol came in. She was wearing her white doctor's smock with a stethoscope around her neck. She looked unusually sweet today with her French braid pulled forward over her shoulder. Though she smiled a greeting, the smile was short lived. "How long has your face been like this, Eve?"

"It was like this when I woke up this morning," Eve said.

"Can you pull your lip down? Can you straighten it out?"

"No," Eve said. "It's like I have no control over it."

Fifteen minutes later, after doing a thorough test of Eve's facial muscles and asking Eve a hundred or more questions, Carol pulled a chair over by the examining table and sat down to face Eve. "What you have appears to be a form of Bells Palsy. It's the reverse of how Bell's Palsy usually looks. Your mouth is twisted upward. With Bells Palsy, it normally twists downward. The good news is that it isn't permanent. It will eventually go away."

A wave of relief, tempered by caution, coursed through Eve's body. "Eventually? What do you mean by 'eventually'?"

"There's no way to tell," Carol replied. "It could be two weeks. It could be six months. Or it could be more or less."

Six months? She couldn't be expected to hide in the house for six months! And if this was the way she was going to look, what would it do to her relationship with Chet? "I don't want the girls to see me like this," Eve said quietly. "I know I told you I'd stay two more weeks. But I can't come to work looking like I'm wearing a mask."

"I understand," Carol said softly. "I'll make other arrangements."

When Eve got home, she called her mother and told her what had happened, minus any reference to Gideon or his threats. Her mother was sympathetic, and urged her not to be discouraged. "At least you know it's going to pass eventually. It's just something you're going to have to get through."

From Eve's point of view that was easier said than done. In the space of twenty-four hours, she had gone from a pretty woman to a twisted hag, all because she'd refused to give in and stay with her job till her third anniversary.

By the time Chet arrived home, not only was Eve's mouth twisted up and her eye pulled down; her nose and eyes were red from crying, and her sinuses felt like they were going to explode.

Avoiding eye contact, Chet asked if Eve had called Kevin yet.

"I called him," Eve answered. "He said he's coming here this evening, but I don't want him to see me like this. When he gets here, I want you to just tell him I'm asleep."

When Kevin arrived at seven-thirty, Chet explained that his mom was feeling really down and didn't feel up to seeing him right now.

"See if you can get her to come into the living room," Kevin suggested. "Tell her we don't have to have the lights on."

From the bedroom, Eve could hear what was being said. She didn't want to face Kevin tonight and have him see her with her face like this. But she really needed to have his acceptance. She needed to hug him, and be hugged in return. This was her son who understood what she was up against! He'd seen what they did to her when she rejected them. If she didn't go out there and talk to him now, he wouldn't understand…

"Hi, Sweetheart," Eve said from the shadows.

"Hi Mom," Kevin said. "How are you doin'?"

Kevin was looking very handsome in his 49ers jacket. To his credit, his facial expression didn't change when he saw Eve. Crossing the entryway to give his mom a hug, he murmured a suggestion that they go into the living room to talk.

Eve took the living room easy chair, kitty corner to the loveseat where Kevin was sitting.

Reaching out to take her hand in his, Kevin looked into Eve's eyes. "It really doesn't look all that bad, Mom. I'm not saying it looks good. You'd know I was lying if I said *that*. But I don't think it looks as bad to other people as it looks to you."

"Is that why the other patients in the waiting room were staring at me?" Eve asked. "Because it *doesn't look that bad*?"

"You said the doctor said it isn't permanent," Kevin said. "How long did she say it was going to last?"

"She said a few weeks to six months or longer," Eve said morosely.

"Then it's not the end of the world," Kevin said. "It's going to be hard. But you can get through it. In a few months, you'll be as good as new."

Eve didn't return to work. Instead, at Chet's suggestion, she stayed home and continued working on the novel that Chet had tossed the day he went with her to her storage. It had been a tough transition for Eve to make. But Chet had finally convinced her that if she wanted to write he would work to support them as long as it took till she was published and had made a name for herself.

During the next several weeks, Eve barely stayed afloat in the sea of depression that had overwhelmed her. During the day, she wrote, and refused to look in the mirror except on spirit days: three days, six days, three weeks... The palsy lasted six weeks to the day.

Chet had just returned home from work and given Eve a bear hug. He had opened his mouth to ask what was for dinner when suddenly his face lit up. "Angel! The Palsy's gone! Go look in the mirror!"

Afraid to look, lest she be disappointed, Eve didn't immediately race to the bathroom.

"I'm telling you it's gone!" Grasping her arm, Chet half-dragged Eve down the hallway. "Look in the mirror," he said. "Look!"

The face gazing back from the mirror was Eve's, exactly as it had looked before she quit the job. Once more, Eve found herself engulfed in a bear hug. "I can't believe it's over," she whispered. "The curse, or whatever it was, is gone."

Chapter 55

After the Bells Palsy was gone, both Eve and Chet noticed a sharp dip in harassment level. They were actually beginning to live a normal life. Chet bought Eve a computer for her writing, and they even signed up for a class in Country Western dancing. Although Eve wrote and sold a few articles, her main interest focused on rewriting the novel Chet had mistakenly thrown away. In the meantime, Chet's ankle was doing fine; and the lights, furnace, and stereo no longer appeared to have minds of their own.

It wasn't long after the disappearance of the palsy that Eve and Chet's landlord put their house on the market. They had hoped to be able to stay in this house till they could afford to buy either this one or something else. Except for the fact that it had spirit activity—and that was something that was likely to be a fact of life *wherever* they went—this house, with the home improvements they'd made, was well suited to their needs. If the landlord had offered to let them take over the payments, they would have bought it. But the down payment he was asking was more than they could afford.

What galled Eve most was that their notice had been presented in writing. The notice had arrived in today's mail.

"The least they could have done was give us a warning," Chet fumed. Chet had just arrived home from work. He was dirty. He was smelly. And his hair looked like he'd just come through a wind tunnel. The last thing he'd expected to be hit with was that their landlord was planning to sell the house out from under them. "Just last month his wife told me we could rent this house as long as we wanted it!"

It had come as just as much of a shock to Eve as it had to Chet. Their landlord, Larry Parsons, was an odd sort of person, but they'd always maintained a good rapport with his wife Martha. It seemed strange that Martha would be a party to sending what amounted to an eviction notice without first talking with them to see what could be worked out.

"Maybe this will turn out to be a blessing," Eve said. She had finished cooking a dinner of pinto beans and cornbread, and was carrying the serving dishes to the table. "When you think about it, an awful lot of spirit stuff has gone on here. If we move somewhere else, it will be like the final chapter."

"We're never going to find this much house anywhere else for the amount of rent we've been paying," Chet said. "Mmmmm. Those beans and cornbread sure smell good. I love when you fix this kind of meal, Angel. It reminds me of my mom's cooking."

"Yeah," Eve said distractedly. "My mom used to cook meals like this too. It says in the notice that Larry wants us to let him show the house to potential tenants. I don't know about you, but I'm not willing to do that. What do you want to drink?—Milk? Or coffee?"

"I'll have a glass of milk," Chet replied. "We can make a pot of coffee later. Just give me a minute to go wash up."

By the time Chet returned from the bathroom, Eve had poured his milk and sliced a tomato and avocado to put on a serving plate. Taking a seat at the table now, she reached for the butter. "We have a month before we have to move. We can look in the classifieds. If there's nothing there, we can check with some rental agencies. I just hope we don't have to move to an apartment."

"We're not moving to an apartment," Chet said, smearing a steaming piece of cornbread with butter. "I don't care if we have to settle for a two-bedroom house with one bath, as long as it has a big yard with trees. What would really be nice is if it had a couple of pine trees and a three-car garage."

Eve had just taken a bite and was in the process of chewing. She waited till she'd swallowed before replying to Chet's comment. "How many houses do you know of in a neighborhood we can afford that have a three-car garage and pine trees, let alone a big yard?" She knew from when they'd been looking for a house to rent before they'd found *this* one that most of the rental houses available were either in bad areas or else they were the eyesores of decent neighborhoods. Anything as nice as the one they currently had would rent for a thousand dollars or more. They had lucked out when they rented this one. Thanks to their flawless rental history, they'd gotten it for seven-twenty-five.

"I'll ask some of the real estate ladies I do business with," Chet said through a mouthful of cornbread. "Maybe they can find something for us." Chet had a growing list of realtors he worked with that was almost as long as his arm. He was always there for them, bailing them out when they were in a bind. It wasn't unreasonable to expect that one of them might be able to help.

But the realtors Chet checked with over the next several days told him he was dreaming. A house like he wanted, for the amount he could afford to pay, just didn't exist unless he wanted to move to Rio Linda. The houses listed in the classifieds were either out of their price range, or houses they wouldn't want to live in.

After two weeks of looking with no results, Eve decided a prayer was in order. The last time she'd said a prayer for a house, it had been to her so-called guardian angel. A demon had answered that prayer. This time she'd broken ties with the psychic and spirit realm. Hopefully *God* would hear her prayer and answer.

"Father in Heaven," she prayed, "You know our landlord has put our house on the market and we can't afford to buy it. We're going to have to keep renting, but we can't afford to pay much more than we're paying now. We want to find a nice place on a quiet street with lots of trees. The size of the front yard isn't all that important, but we'd like to have a big backyard—hopefully with a pine tree or two for Chet. I'm hoping for three bedrooms, two baths, a fireplace; and it has to have a bright, airy kitchen. Chet would like to have a three-car garage." Eve realized this was a tall order. But it couldn't hurt to ask. "I don't know whether a house like this exists in our price range," she went on. "But if it or something close does exist, would you please help us find it? In Jesus' name, amen."

There. She'd done it. She had prayed for a house without fear that the other side would answer her prayer.

That afternoon, Eve called a property management company from the yellow pages. The voice on the other end of the line was cordial, but discouraging. "You're not going to find a big yard for what you can afford. And I'm afraid you might as well forget the trees and three-car-garage. People who own houses in *that* kind of neighborhood just don't put them up for rent. We do have a couple of duplexes for a little more than you're currently paying, but I'm afraid that's all we have."

What she was saying was no surprise to Eve. Eve hated the thought of paying additional rent for a house that wasn't even as nice as the one they'd be leaving; but that appeared to be what it was going to be. She was about to hang up when the rental agent told her to hold on for a minute.

When the woman returned, she told Eve she and Chet must be in luck. "My secretary heard what I was saying, and she said a property just became available fifteen minutes ago that might fit what you're looking for. The only thing is that it's a hundred dollars a month more than you're currently paying."

"When can we see it?" Eve asked excitedly. She didn't know how she'd convince Chet of the extra hundred dollars a month. It might mean not going out to dinner for awhile...

"If you want to drive by now," the woman said, "I'll give you the address. Then if you like it, you can call and I'll meet you there to show you the inside."

Eve's heart was skipping beats when she hung up the phone.

Before leaving to look at the house, Eve looked the short street up in the Thomas Guide. Apparently this house was on the border of where three communities came together. You couldn't be much more centrally located than that. The block-long street ended at a park. That meant there was a good possibility of trees.

Eve had no problem finding Shady Lane. When she gave the signal to turn right off the main street, she smiled. The neighborhood looked to be around thirty years old, with custom houses, each different from the rest. Half the street didn't even have sidewalks. Maples, oaks, and Ponderosa pines lined the street, giving it the feel of a rural neighborhood right in the midst of the city. *Chet would love this*, Eve thought excitedly. Checking the address on the note in her hand, she slowed the car to a crawl. Seventy-five-ten: That should be on the right side of the street. Seventy-five-o-six...Seventy-five-o-eight...Seventy-five—"

Next door to seventy-five-o-eight was what had to be the longest house Eve had ever seen. In the large front yard, two huge trees provided shade for the entire yard and house. Lining the driveway were half a dozen towering Italian Cypress.

Growing more excited with each passing moment, Eve signaled to turn into the driveway.

The house was white with blue trim. Pink azaleas and varied colored camellias bordered the front of the house, beneath the bedroom windows. Eve parked in the driveway and got out to peer through the bay window, straight through the house to the fairy tale backyard, with its cement retaining wall and raised woods-like flowerbed of wildflowers and azaleas beneath towering redwoods, and fruit trees of various kinds.

Stepping behind the Chinese Maple in the flowerbed beneath the kitchen window, Eve peered into the kitchen. Off-white cabinets, white counter tiles, white wallpaper with mauve and blue flowers… The kitchen seemed to *glow* with light. It was as if the house had been built to order.

And the garage! The attached garage was divided into two distinct sections— one singlewide, and one double. Just what Chet had wished for.

Eve could hardly wait to get home and call the property management company to ask them not to show the property to anyone else until she and Chet had had a chance to see the inside…

Chet made out the deposit check that very evening, and Eve called to give their notice on the house on Rocky Glen.

"But *why are you moving*?" Martha asked in her Hungarian accent. "I thought you were happy there."

Puzzled by the landlady's question, Eve told her they were moving because she and her husband had put the house on the market, and they couldn't afford to buy it."

"There must be some sort of mistake," Martha said. "Larry put our other properties on the market, but not the house you're renting on Rocky Glen! The other properties have caused us nothing but problems. But you and Chet have been perfect tenants! When Larry gets home I'm going to tell him he made a mistake. I'll have Larry call you when he gets in."

Eve was shaking her head as she hung up the kitchen phone. "*Now* Martha says this house is not *for sale*. She's going to have Larry call us to straighten out the mistake."

"They're a little late," Chet said wryly. "We've already given a deposit. Besides that, I want that other house!"

One week later:

Since they were packing to move anyway, Eve and Chet decided to let the house on Rocky Glen be shown by appointment only. Half their belongings were packed in boxes, so the landlord couldn't expect the place to be immaculate.

The first couple to look at the house appeared to be very interested. The wife asked Eve several questions about the neighborhood, and the husband went wild over the garage workbench Chet had built for Eve. When the couple followed the landlord down the unlit hallway, the overhead light suddenly switched on. Neither Eve nor Chet had gone near the switch.

Startled, both the landlord and the prospective tenants gaped at the light. But the landlord quickly recovered. "Oh. I guess they've installed a sensor."

Right, Eve thought. *If you call Bruce a sensor*. When Eve looked across the room at Chet, she could tell by the grin on his face that he was thinking the same thing...

For once in Eve's life, packing to move was a pleasure rather than a chore. Since the house on Shady Lane was empty, she was able to transport boxes in her car and store them in the three-car garage. Chet had arranged for a friend to help with the heavy stuff on moving day.

But when moving day arrived, the friend didn't show up, and didn't bother to call to say he couldn't make it. With friends like that, Eve didn't figure Chet needed any enemies.

They had resigned themselves to renting a large dolly and trying to move the furniture and refrigerator alone, when Ken Felcher—a friend of Chet's who hadn't been included in the moving plans—showed up on their doorstep with his son Robert. Ken was a thin man in his mid-thirties with a conservative haircut and laughing brown eyes. His son was a chunky boy of ten, with thick red hair and a mass of freckles. "I was going to take Robert fishing today," Ken said. "But when we were ready to leave, I asked which he'd rather do: go fishing, or help Chet and Eve move. He said, "Let's help, and I agreed. So here we are. Where do we start?"

With the help of Ken and his son, moving time was cut in half.

Exhausted but happy, Chet clapped Ken on the shoulder. "You were a lifesaver today, Little Buddy. And you too, Robert." Though Ken was very slim, Chet's habit of calling male friends "Little Buddy" had nothing whatever to do with size.

Later that evening after Ken and his son had left, Chet and Eve decided to drive to the house on Rocky Glen and check to make sure they hadn't forgotten anything. In the passenger seat on the drive over, Eve reached across to touch Chet's hand. "We've thought we made the break before, but this is definitely the end of an era."

Except for a light across the street, the neighborhood was dark when they pulled into the driveway of the house on Rocky Glen. As Chet turned off the ignition, an unexplained feeling of heaviness settled into the car, setting Eve's teeth on edge. "Do you feel it?" she asked.

"Feel what?"

"I don't know how to explain it," Eve said uneasily. "It's just a weird feeling. Kind of like the air's thick and kind of damp."

"I wasn't going to say anything," Chet said. "But I feel it too. I started feeling it the minute we turned onto the street. I don't want to stay here any longer than we have to. You stay in the car while I go inside and take a quick look around. It'll only take a minute."

When the "minute" Chet planned to stay turned into five, Eve began to become concerned. Reaching across to the S10's steering wheel, she gave the horn a beep. Two minutes later, the front door opened and Chet staggered out, clutching his stomach, and doubled over as if in pain.

"What's wrong?" Eve asked in alarm. "What happened?"

"The fucking spirits beat me up," Chet's voice, normally strong, sounded as if it were coming from inside a barrel. "There was no way to fight back, Angel. It was like somebody slugged me in the stomach, then gave a kidney punch to my back. They hit my arms, my legs... I feel like I got run over by a semi."

"You didn't see or hear anything?"

"I didn't have to see or hear them," Chet groaned. "I could feel them, and that was enough."

Chapter 56

There wasn't an immediate turn around when Eve and Chet moved into their new home. It took time for Chet to get control of his paranoia and stop thinking that every accident or pain was somehow related to demonic harassment; time for Eve to get over her grief and come to terms with the deception.

Both she and Chet loved their new home. It was light and airy, with plenty of room. It had a three-car garage and a beautiful yard with flowers of every color, and pine trees that scraped the sky. It was everything Eve had prayed for: this time, handpicked by God. Eve couldn't help contrasting it to the house her so-called "guardian angel" had picked for her: the house that had turned out to be inhabited by spirits. Then there was the restaurant she'd later *bought* with that house.

Her prayers about the restaurant had been very specific. "Please God," she'd prayed, "I want to make the trade: but *only if it's best for everyone concerned.* Only if there's *no possible way anyone could be hurt by this,* please make it happen. In Jesus' name, amen."

It had been a deal made in Heaven; or so it had appeared. But it had turned out to be a deal from Hell, and Eve had ended up losing everything she owned. The thought had occurred to her more than once that Satan, not God, had answered yet another prayer.

Since falling in love with Eve, Chet had made it his mission to try to replace everything she had lost. The going had been slow, but he was making progress. It had definitely helped that since breaking away from the spirits and moving to the new house, his business had more than doubled. Eve was making good progress on her novel, and things were going well. But there were still the occasional nighttime visitors. Now when it happened, a prayer in Jesus' name made them instantly disappear—at least for Eve. *Chet* had had a couple of run-ins where the spirits in his room had refused to leave.

Why were the dark spirits allowed to harass them now that they'd cut all ties? After all, they were Christians. Weren't Christians supposed to be immune?

Based on the extent of the spirits' powers—the ability to see into people's bodies, change a Sprite into a strawberry daiquiri, beat a person up without even showing their faces—Eve and Chet now both firmly believed that the spirit guides were actually dark angels who had sided with Satan and been kicked out of Heaven. They had learned from experience that saying "I'm of the light" means absolutely nothing, and surrounding oneself with a protective white light makes about as much sense as holding an umbrella over your head and expecting it to protect you from an avalanche.

It was Friday night, and they'd just gotten home from having dinner at their favorite Mexican Restaurant. Eve was brewing a pot of coffee, and Chet had built a roaring fire in the grate. Continuing the discussion that had begun at the restaurant, Chet lay down on the carpet and propped himself up with his elbows. "Everybody thinks if a spirit does something good, that means it's a good spirit. Nobody thinks a bad one could do anything good."

From the kitchen, Eve called back that if the dark ones didn't do *some* good things, no one would want to get involved with them. Carefully carrying a brimming mug into the living room, Eve warned Chet the coffee was very hot. "I didn't put any sugar in it, but if you want sugar I'll get you some."

"Black is fine," Chet said. "Sit down here and talk to me."

Rather than taking a seat on the sofa, Eve sat on the floor and leaned against it. "I have no idea what made them do it, but I'm really thankful the guides finally revealed themselves to us. I still have a lot of questions, though: a lot of things I don't understand."

"Like what?" Chet asked.

"Like why God would let an evil spirit claim to be Him or the Holy Spirit. And why the dark ones can still read my mind; or why they're still allowed to listen to my prayers."

Chet's eyes widened in surprise. "What makes you think they can still read your mind?"

"Because one night when I was praying, I asked God in my head if I could speak to the Holy Spirit. When I did, the 'Holy Spirit' answered back. I asked him a lot of questions, and he gave very wise answers. But all of a sudden it struck me that it might not be the Holy Spirit talking at all. So I said, 'Father, in the name of Jesus, if this isn't the Holy Spirit talking to me, when I ask him another question, please don't let him answer.' Then I asked another one, and when I did, the answer came back garbled."

Silence fell as Chet processed this information. "If that's the case, and they're still reading your mind," he said thoughtfully, "that explains a whole lot of things."

Eve was aware of the things Chet was referring to, but she didn't want to go there. Instead, she broached another topic that had been bothering her. "We know that when we lived at the other house and were still involved with spirits, that's why telling the dark ones to leave in the name of Jesus didn't work. But why is it that *even now when we've broken away*, there are times that it doesn't work for you?"

"What do you mean?" Chet asked in confusion. "When hasn't it worked?"

"Just last week when there was one in your room," Eve replied. "The night you felt a presence and when you opened your eyes, there was a dark form standing beside your bed."

"Oh yeah," Chet said. "I had to tell it several times before I could get it to leave."

It seemed to Eve that, now that they'd cut all ties with the spirit and psychic realm, there was no reason why telling a dark one in the name of Jesus to leave shouldn't work. Shouldn't work for *Chet*, that is. It always worked for *her*.

"When I suspect I'm being harassed, I always say the same prayer," Eve said. "Father, I think I'm being harassed by the dark ones. If I am, in the name of Jesus, please make them stop. When a dark one comes into my room, I say 'Father, in the name of Jesus, please make it leave,' and He always does. There has to be something different about what *you* say that somehow gives them the right to stay."

"I'm not giving them any right to stay," Chet said defensively. "I say 'In Jesus' name, get the fuck out of my room!'"

"That's it!" Eve cried.

"*What's* it?"

"You're trying to do it on your own! You have to ask *God* to do it. You have to say, Father, in the name of Jesus, please make it go away."

Mulling over what Eve had just said, Chet put another log on the grate and poked at the coals to stir life into the fire. "*That's* why they wouldn't leave at the other house. We were telling them *ourselves*, in Jesus' name. But there were times when we asked God to make them leave too, and He didn't do it. Why wouldn't He have answered our prayers at the other house?"

Eve couldn't believe Chet had said that. "You seem to forget what we read just last week: God says He'll set His face against people who are involved with spirits. We were involved with spirit guides. *So of course He wasn't going to answer our prayers about that or anything else!*"

The passage hadn't made a distinction between spirits of light and spirits of darkness. God had said flat out that He'll set his face against any man or woman who turns to spirits or mediums. Period.

"I remember now," Chet said. "It talked about divination, too."

Eve knew from her own reading that divination covered the gamut from Tarot cards to pendulums, and everything in between that was used as a supernatural means of getting information—including psychic readings! If she'd known these things years ago, she never would have used a Ouija board, or done Automatic Writing in college. And she certainly wouldn't have gone for psychic readings or gotten involved with spirit guides!

She had no doubt that Saul had told the truth the night the spirits had revealed themselves. If she'd continued in the direction she'd been going, despite the fact that she was basically a good person, her soul would have ended up in Hell.

It was six months after moving into their new home that Chet received a call from the hospital in Davis saying that his mom had stopped eating, and they saw no point in putting her on life support. It was just a matter of time.

The last time Chet and Eve saw her alive, Beth was in a catatonic state doing *sit-ups* in bed.

"My sweet little mom," Chet said with a tearful grin. "She used to do sit ups with Jack LaLane. Now, here she is doing them when she can't even eat." Bending to kiss her cheek, he said on a broken sob, "You've fought a good fight, Sam. But I know you want to be with Dad. It's ok to let go now. Jane and I will be alright."

Chapter 57

Over the next five years, Chet's business continued to grow. Eve continued to hone her skills as a writer. And God's hand could be seen in every aspect of their lives.

But when Eve began thinking the time had come to buy a house, they were faced with a dilemma. Their income was high enough to make bigger payments, but they didn't have enough for a typical *down* payment. When they had moved into this house, Eve had told the landlord if he would ever consider selling this house with no money down, they would be first in line to buy it. Considering that that hadn't happened, Eve's first thought now was to contact a realtor. But Chet didn't want to do that. He felt that God had given them this house, and he didn't want to even *think* about moving.

Time for another prayer. "Father," Eve prayed, "We need to stop pouring money down the drain as rent. This house has been great, and we're thankful for it. But it's time to *buy* a house now. I don't know where we can find another house as nice as this one that we could afford to buy. But Chet doesn't want to move anyway. He figures you gave us *this* house, so this is where he wants to stay. That would be fine if we could afford to *buy* this one, but we can't. Our landlord told us a long time ago, if we ever want to buy it he'll sell it to us; but his wife said if they sold it, they'd have to get the going rate, which right now is out of our price range. We don't have the down payment needed to qualify for a house of this value. But so far I haven't been able to talk Chet into considering anything else. Something needs to give. I'm putting it in your hands, Father. In Jesus' name, amen."

Unbeknownst to Eve, Chet had also said a prayer. "Father, my angel wants to move, and I don't want to. I know she's right that we need to buy a house, but if we're going to buy one, I want it to be this one. So please bless my situation. In the name of Jesus, amen."

As often happens with God, the answer to their prayers did not come immediately.

Six months later, their landlord called to ask if they'd like to take over payments on their house. "My wife and I would like for you guys to have it, because we know you love it as much as we do. You can keep on renting as long as you want, but if you're interested in buying it, you can take over the payments with no money down. We'll give back your security deposit, and we'll pay half of the closing costs." In one fell swoop, God had answered both prayers, even beyond their hopes or expectations.

One year later:

The aroma of roast turkey and pumpkin pie wafted down the hallway to the bedroom where Eve was sitting at the computer. She had over an hour before guests were due to arrive: plenty of time to check her e-mail. Of the fifteen incoming messages, thirteen were spamming. One was from her mother. And one was from her friend Katy in Mobile, Alabama.

It had been two weeks since she'd heard from Katy, and Eve had been worried about her. The Thanksgiving note was evidence that at least she was still alive and kicking.

"Dear Eve,

"I almost sent you an e-mail last night, but decided to wait till this morning to write. Usually if I try to write to you when I'm scared, my computer crashes."

Eve knew that what Katy said was true. Her computer sometimes did the same thing—especially when she was trying to write to Katy to offer her support or advice.

"Now that I know how to recognize them and what to do about it," Katy went on, "the times I get harassed are happening less and less. Last night I was sitting in the living room chair reading a book when I felt something lifting my hair. It was like a bad case of static electricity. My hair was standing up on my head! When I said the prayer you taught me, it stopped. Isn't it great how God hears our prayers even if we can't say the words out loud? I just said in my mind, 'Father, I'm being harassed by the dark ones. In the name of Jesus, please make them stop."

Eve knew from experience how frightening it could be, living alone with spirit problems to contend with. Katy could have gone her entire life not knowing what was happening to her, and being powerless to stop it, if a friend hadn't introduced her to Eve.

Katy was the daughter of Katherine Foster, a woman who had been born with a caul over her face. As a result, as Katy had told it, her mom had been tormented all her life by the ability to see "spirits of the dead." Eve didn't believe for a minute that the spirits Katy's mom had seen were ghosts. Spirits of the dead didn't hang around on earth—not according to the Bible. Eve knew from personal experience that the dark ones could appear in any guise they chose. In the case of Katy's mother, they had chosen to appear as ghosts.

Katherine had believed her ability to see "ghosts" was a gift, but had often thought it seemed more like a curse. She'd been glad Katy hadn't inherited the "gift."

But Katy *had* supposedly inherited a gift of a different sort. She had inherited the ability to know when evil spirits were near. The problem was they seemed to be everywhere. Sometimes she could tell by the fact that the tiny hairs on her neck and arms stood at attention. Other times she could tell by the sound of bird's wings fluttering close to her ear. Eve knew from personal experience that dark spirits could choose whether or not to make their presence felt. It was possible for a dark spirit to be present with no warning signs at all. Gideon and Saul had been dark spirits, and they'd been with *her* on a daily basis for years. Yet she'd never had any negative feelings when they were near—until the end. On the other hand, the spirits in her house on Saffron had chosen to make their presence known by goosebumps, or raising the hairs on her skin, or causing the air in the room to feel cold and heavy.

The spirit or spirits Katy was dealing with seemed to be particularly drawn to her bedroom. At night, as she lay frozen with fear, they would often play with her hair as they had in the living room chair—lifting it into the air as if by static electricity. Once, lying in bed, she'd felt a presence in her bedroom and the invisible being had *jumped* on her. The mattress had actually bounced with the jolt! Terrified from that night on of sleeping alone, Katy had signed on to work the night shift so she could sleep during the day.

Until she was introduced to Eve, Katy had never told anyone about her "gift." When she told Eve, Eve's reply had caused her to cringe:

"Based on what I know from my own experiences with the spirit realm, what your mother had was not a gift," Eve had told her. "The ghosts she was seeing weren't ghosts at all. They were evil spirits pretending to be ghosts. That's all it was: just a masquerade. And the 'gift' you think you have for knowing when evil spirits are near isn't a gift at all. I believe it's demonic harassment."

At first, Katy had been hesitant to believe what Eve told her. Why would evil spirits single *her* out for harassment? She'd done nothing to attract their attention. She'd never even used a Ouija Board!

"You're forgetting about your mother," Eve had told her. "Since *she* was involved in the spirit realm, you were automatically vulnerable. And what about psychic readings? Have you ever visited a psychic?"

Without even trying, Eve had hit the nail on the head. Katy had often visited psychics in the past, and had planned to visit one that very afternoon. "Then you've mentioned two links already," Eve had told her: your mother's experiences with so-called *ghosts*, and your own involvement with psychics."

What you need to do is cut all ties to the psychic and occult: books, records, tapes, fortune telling tools, amulets, crystals that are associated with powers, automatic writing...*anything* you have or do that's linked to the psychic/spirit realm. Don't give the things away or throw them in a dumpster where someone else might get hold of them. *You need to destroy them.* Once you've done this," Eve had continued, "don't make a big production of trying to find out if there are still spirits around. Don't call them names or try to get them to show or identify themselves. (This will just give them a chance to show off.) God can take care of any confrontations. All *you* have to do is let God know you don't want to be tied to the realm these things represent anymore."

"Speaking from my own experience, once you've done these things, if you tell God you want Him and His son to be part of your life, He'll be there for you and start answering your prayers. I'm not saying He'll give you everything you ask for, or that you'll never be harassed again. But now you'll have God on you side. When you're being harassed by a dark one, you can say a prayer in Jesus' name, and God will make it stop and leave you alone."

Eve might have gone on to add that even if a person's never been involved with spirits, psychic things, or the occult—even if he's a kind and loving person who's never hurt a fly in his life—if he hasn't declared himself to be on God's side, God sees him as choosing to be aligned with the dark side; and that's definitely not a good place to be. That was a pretty rough paraphrase of what Eve had learned from the Bible, but no matter. She'd already said what Katy needed to hear. Katy had been raised a Christian. To say anything more to her would be preaching.

Over the course of the next several weeks under Eve's guidance, Katy had dug deeper, and found additional links: among other things, there was her preference for movies and documentaries that dealt with the occult. She had even once ordered a white witchcraft kit to put a love spell on the man she'd hoped to marry! The kit had never arrived, and she had never actually cast the spell, but the desire to cast it had been there.

"The spirits once told me that when a person buys or borrows a book or anything else having to do with the occult or psychic realm, a spirit often comes with it," Eve had told her. "If you'd received the kit, I'm sure a spirit would have come attached." Though she hadn't mentioned it, it had occurred to Eve that even the act of *ordering* the kit would have drawn attention.

When Katy had followed Eve's advice and cut all ties to the psychic and occult, Eve had given her the prayer to say to stop the harassment. It would have been pointless to give her the prayer sooner.

The way Eve figured it, before *she'd* cut ties, *she'd* had at least three strikes against her: first the Ouija board, then her association with psychics, and finally her relationship with spirits. Katy'd had just as many ties to break as she, if not more.

"The next time something strange happens and you suspect you're being harassed," Eve had told Katy, "like maybe when you hear the fluttering, or feel something lifting your hair, say 'Father, I think I'm being harassed by dark spirits. In the name of Jesus, if that's what it is, please make them leave me alone.' If it stops when you say the prayer, you'll know it was harassment. If it doesn't, you'll know it wasn't."

The prayer had set Katy free.

Now Katy had joined the ranks, trying to convince Eve to write a book about her experiences. Chet and Kevin had been dripping for years on that very topic. But so far Eve had refused. She wasn't ready to face the demonic harassment that would be sure to come with writing it. The fun times and humor would be easy to write. But there were too many frightening and painful memories that would have to be dredged up: too many traumatic scenes that would have to be recreated; too many experiences she'd be hesitant to share, because they made her look like a fool.

"I know you must get tired of hearing this," the e-mail message continued, "but there are thousands of people out there just like me who could be helped if you'd write the book. You know in your heart God wants you to write it. Girl, the things you told me changed my life. If Mr. B. hadn't put me in touch with you, I don't know what I'd have done."

"Have a happy Thanksgiving, and say Hi to Chet. Love you guys." signed, Katy

"P.S.: I wish you guys could be here tomorrow to keep me from eating all the leftovers and pumpkin pie (smile)."

"P.P. S. I really mean it. When are you going to write the book?"

"Are you going to stay in there all day?" Chet called from the kitchen. "Billy Bill and the Beau will be here any minute, and you're not gonna be ready."

Billy Bill was Chet's name for his close friend and unofficial business partner. The Beau had been his best friend for thirty years.

"I'm coming," Eve called back. "I was just checking my e-mail. We got one from Katy. She said to say 'Hi.'"

"Oh," Chet replied. "How's she doing?"

Eve closed out her e-mail and signed off before answering. When she came into the sunlit kitchen, Chet was sneaking a dinner roll from the basket. "Katy's doing ok," Eve said. "She had a scare last night, but she said the prayer and it went away. She's still on my case about writing that book. She thinks God wants me to write it. I don't know about *that*. But she also believes thousands of people could be helped by reading about my experiences. Maybe she's right."

"That's exactly what The Flea and I have been trying to tell you," Chet said through a mouthful of bread. "But you never listen to *us*."

It wasn't that Eve didn't listen. She'd actually given it a lot of thought. Katy's case was unusual, tied as it was to Southern superstitions. But psychic and spiritual readings were gaining in popularity. Psychic readers were advertising on T.V.! Toy stores were selling Ouija Boards and eight balls *as if they were games*! How many people had innocently become involved, and were now wondering why they had so many problems?

"Maybe I will write the book," Eve said thoughtfully. "I could call it Pure Light since that's what I was destined to become."

"Nah," Chet said. "Pure Light wouldn't catch anyone's attention unless they're into New Age. It needs to be something about guardian angels."

Guardian angels... Maybe Chet was right. "How about 'Deceived'?" Eve mused. "No...*Betrayed*. 'Betrayed by Her Guardian Angel.'"

One month later:

Seated at her computer with a Michael Bolton c.d. in the E drive and a steaming mug of hot chocolate on the bookshelf beside her, Eve began to type:

Prologue: 1966

"I need a show of hands. How many in this lecture hall believe in Superman?"

The End

About the Author

From the time Stacie Spielman was old enough to hold a pen, she has loved to write. For almost as long, she's had a fascination with the paranormal—particularly with guardian angels.

Stacie Spielman's qualification for writing *Betrayed by Her Guardian Angel* is that she lived it. She *is* the Eve Tarlton in the book. For years, Spielman's husband and son tried to convince her to write her story. But it took a friend's putting her in touch with a woman whose life was a nightmare of demonic harassment, to convince her how badly this book is needed. It took this woman's saying Spielman's story has changed her life, to convince the author to put her story in writing.